THE CALLINGS

The Callings

HENRY CHAPPELL

TEXAS TECH UNIVERSITY PRESS

This book is typeset in ITC Berkeley. The paper used in this book meets the minimum requirements of ANSI/NISO Z39.48-1992 (R1997). ∞

Designed by Barbara Werden
Calligraphy by Brandi Price
Map by Brad Carter

Printed in the United States of America

Library of Congress Cataloging-in-Publication Data

Chappell, Henry C.
   The callings / Henry Chappell.
       p.   cm.
   ISBN 0-89672-494-8 (cloth : alk. paper)
   1. Panhandle (Tex.) — Fiction. 2. Comanche Indians — Fiction. 3. Ethnic relations — Fiction. 4. Young men — Fiction. 5. Aged men — Fiction. 6. Healers — Fiction. I. Title.

PS3603.H376 C35 2002
813'.6—dc21

                                                                        2002010537

        00 01 02 03 04 05 06 07 08 / 9 8 7 6 5 4 3 2 1

Texas Tech University Press
Box 41037
Lubbock, Texas 79409-1037 USA
1.800.832.4042
ttup@ttu.edu
www.ttup.ttu.edu

For my mother,
Cordie Mae Chappell,
who taught me to love a good tale.

ACKNOWLEDGMENTS

Like most literary projects, this one is a collaboration. Without the help of my family, friends and colleagues, *The Callings* never would have been completed.

First and foremost, I want to thank my wife Jane, who tirelessly supported my work and gently nudged me whenever I stalled, and my daughters, Jamie and Sarah, who cheerfully endured their moody, preoccupied father. I am eternally grateful to Judith Keeling for her patience, vision and persistence. Her advice and sensitive editorial touch significantly improved this book. I would also like to thank Dr. Fred Rathjen for suggesting a number of improvements to the original manuscript; Dr. Lou Rodenberger, who helped me find my way to the end of the story; Wyman Meinzer for introducing me to several excellent books on the buffalo hunters; Dr. Paul Carlson and the members of the Texas Tech University Press Editorial Committee for directing me to the latest scholarship and wisely advising moderation in certain areas; my aunt Jane Maglia for sharing her knowledge of Appalachian faith healing; and my friends in the DFW Writers' Workshop for their humor, encouragement, and honest criticism. Any errors or misinterpretations are mine alone.

I must also acknowledge the help and support of my old friend Brad Carter with whom I have shared so many windy West Texas camps. This novel grew out of our hours of campfire talk and imagining.

Several books were indispensable in helping me develop the cultural, historical and ecological background of the novel: Ernest Wallace and E. Adam-son Hoebel, *The Comanches: Lords of the South Plains* (1986); T.R. Fehrenbach, *Comanches: the Destruction of a People* (1974); W.W. Newcomb, Jr., *The Indians of Texas* (1995); Paul Carlson, *The Plains Indians* (1998); John R. Cook, *The Border and the Buffalo* (1989); Walter Prescott Webb, *The Great Plains* (1981); Frances Haines, *The Buffalo* (1970); and William H. Leckie, *The Buffalo Soldiers: A Narrative of the Negro Cavalry in the West* (1967).

Although the events in this novel have a basis in history, the Tenth Cavalry's capture and interrogation of the Comanchero Ybarra, the Army attack on the Comanche encampment on the Pease River, and the Wanderers' raid on the farm on Big Keechi Creek are fictional. For these and other liberties, I ask for the reader's indulgence.

F O R E W O R D

Komantcia: *Ute word meaning, "anyone who wants to fight me all the time."*

In the sixteenth century A.D., a Native American people that would later come to be known by European Americans as Shoshone (from the Cheyenne name Shishin-ohts-hit-ahn-ah-oh, meaning "Snake People") lived in the eastern Rocky Mountains above the headwaters of the Arkansas River in present day Wyoming. They called themselves Nermernuh or "People" from the root word of their Uto-Aztekan dialect, Nerm or "Human Being."

Late in the seventeenth century, about forty years after the People came into possession of Spanish horses, a split occurred among the Nermernuh, and a large band drifted out of the mountains and onto the southern Great Plains into present day eastern Colorado, western Kansas, western Oklahoma and northwestern Texas. Theory and legend abound, but the reasons for the split and subsequent migration are lost in antiquity. The result, however, was that in three decades a short, stocky mountain people, poorly adapted for pedestrian travel on the plains but anatomically perfect horsemen, ascended from a subsistence level culture to the Southern Plains' dominant horse culture. The Utes called them Komantcia, which by the early 1700s had mutated into the Spanish name *Comanche*.

Once established south of the Arkansas, the People waged war for control of the Southern Plains. Skirmishing and long distance raiding against the Utes to the northwest, the Pawnee to the northeast and the Tonkawas and Jumano to the south were nearly constant for two centuries save for occasional treaties formed for the purpose of waging more effective war against other enemies. The People saved their bitterest and bloodiest warfare, however, for the Apaches who controlled most of the Southern Plains prior to the Nermernuh migration.

By 1725, the People had all but destroyed the Eastern Apache culture; the remnant bands had been driven into the Chihuahuan Desert mountains of northern Mexico, southwestern Texas and eastern New Mexico. Comanchería now extended from the Arkansas River southward to the Balcones Escarpment just north of San Antonio and from just west of present day Fort Worth to the eastern foothills of the Rocky Mountains.

The People were secure as few other Native Americans had ever been. Innumerable bison supplied a never ending source of food, clothing and shelter, while the province of New Mexico held a ready supply of Spanish horses for the taking. The Comanche horse herds swelled to tens of thousands, and traders out of New Mexico — Comancheros — were eager to trade guns, ammunition, knives, needles and blankets for Comanche buffalo hides. Comanche warriors swaggered in the streets of San Antonio while soldiers along the Spanish frontier huddled in their presidios in fear of horsemen who could ride full speed into the midst of clumsy infantry, shooting arrows and lifting scalps, then vanish on the open plains.

By the early nineteenth century, as many as fourteen thousand of the People lived on the Southern Plains. Long distance raids deep into Mexico provided a steady supply of horses, loot and captives. Broad war trails beaten bare by thousands of unshod hooves ran out of Comanchería and converged at the Rio Grande. As the Texas frontier encroached on Comanche territory the People struck the remote settlements with impunity, and both the Mexican and Texan frontiers retreated. Lightly armed Mexican settlements attempted appeasement with gifts while the Texans asked for treaties they had no intention of honoring. The People rode in broad daylight along their war trails, horses, booty and captives in tow.

But Mexican captives and encroaching whites brought contagions to which the Comanches had no resistance. Epidemics of smallpox in 1816 and 1839 and a cholera epidemic in 1849 decimated the bands. By the 1840s, Texas Rangers, more like the People than their white employers, were raiding deep into Comanchería and exacting a huge toll with lightning massacres of entire camps. After Texas statehood, the Second U.S. Cavalry, following the Rangers' precedent, pursued the Comanches relentlessly.

Comanche raiding subsided and the settlement line moved further into Comancheria, yet the Texans demanded complete expulsion of the People. Treaties were signed and broken by both sides — the U.S. Government could not control westward expansion and the Comanche chiefs had little control over the many autonomous bands of warriors spread about the plains.

In 1859, the State of Texas formally expelled all Comanches into Indian Territory north of the Red River. Texas retained all of its unsettled lands when it joined the United States, and since Comanches were not Texas citizens, the reasoning went, they were trespassers. Comanche raiding continued albeit on a drastically reduced scale. Bands returning to their old hunting or wintering grounds were considered invaders and were pursued relentlessly.

With secession, the Civil War and the subsequent removal of federal troops, the People resumed raiding in both Mexico and Texas with renewed vigor. Depredation reached new levels as organized Ranger companies were called away to serve in the Civil War. Settlers flocked to forts, and the frontier in Texas receded. Federal Indian agents had little motivation to try to halt Comanche raiding in Confederate Texas.

The People's return to glory was short-lived, however. The end of the Civil War brought the return of Federal Troops, most notably light cavalry capable of long range patrols and deadly punitive expeditions. Again harried unmercifully, most of the prominent Comanche chiefs agreed to sit in council with representatives of the U.S. Government. A treaty was offered the People in October 1867 at Medicine Lodge Creek in present Barbour County, Kansas.

The terms were simple: the People were to withdraw into three million acres of reservation land in the Indian Territories (land formerly owned by the Chickasaws and Choctaws) and cease all hostilities against whites. Furthermore, they would not interfere with the construction of railroads, roads and forts constructed on reservation land. The People would be furnished seed, agricultural training, clothing, food and other annuity goods as deemed appropriate for their well being by the "The Great Father," the President of the United States, and they would be allowed to hunt buffalo in the Texas Panhandle. If the People refused the terms of the treaty, they could expect a harsh military reprisal.

The Yampareekuh Comanche civil chief Ten Bears presented the People's position. His eloquence stunned the white attendees:

If the Texans had kept out of my country, there might have been peace. But that which you now say we must live in is too small. The Texans have taken away the places where the grass grew the thickest and the timber was the best. Had we kept that we might have done the things you ask. But it is too late. The whites have the country which we loved, and we wish only to wander the prairie until we die. Any good thing you say to me shall not be forgotten. I shall carry it as near to my heart as my children, and it shall be as often on my tongue as the name of the Great Spirit. I want no blood upon my land to stain the grass. I want it all clear and pure, and I wish it so that all who go through among my people may find peace when they come in and leave it when they go out.

Despite their distrust and the draconian terms, the chiefs agreed to the treaty. Ten Bears had been taken to Washington, D.C. and had seen what must have seemed like an unbelievable number of whites and incredible wealth and power. The whites signed, knowing full well that nothing could be done to stop the encroachment, even onto reservation lands, and undoubtedly they were aware that the Texas Panhandle held most of the southern bison herd.

The council at Medicine Lodge Creek brought together the largest gathering of Comanche Chiefs ever assembled for negotiations with the United States Government. The Penateka (Honey Eaters), The Detsanawyeka (Wanderers), the Tanima (Liver Eaters) and the Yampareekuh (Yap Eaters) were all represented.

Two bands, however, were notably absent.

And when the Lord thy God hath delivered it into thine hands, thou shalt smite every male thereof with the edge of the sword:

But the women and the little ones and the cattle and all that is in the city, even all of the spoil thereof, shalt thou take unto thyself; and thou shalt eat the spoil of thine enemies, which the Lord thy God hath given thee.

DEUTERONOMY 20:13-14

White hunters assist the advance of civilization by destroying the Indians' commissary. . . . Send them powder and lead, if you will, but for the sake of a lasting peace, let them kill, skin and sell until the buffaloes are exterminated. Then your prairies can be covered with speckled cattle, and the festive cowboy, who follows the hunter as a second forerunner of advanced civilization.

GENERAL PHILIP SHERIDAN
TO THE TEXAS LEGISLATURE, 1875

THE CALLINGS

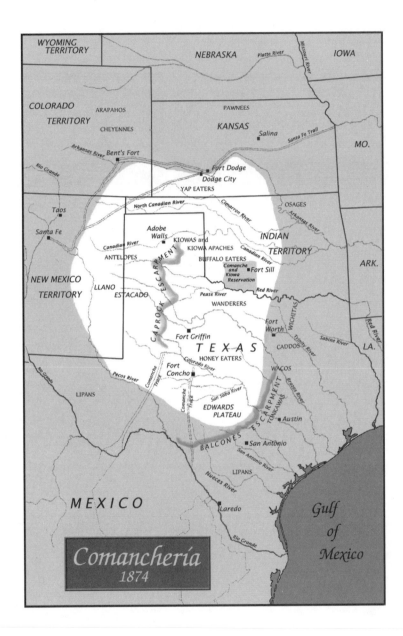

Comancheria
1874

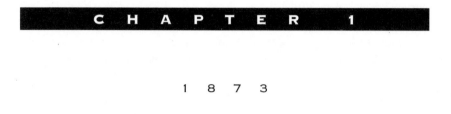

C H A P T E R 1

1 8 7 3

That spring the rains came early to the Staked Plains, heavy and often with hail that laid waste to what remained of the gray shortgrass. The creeks and narrow prongs of the High Plains rivers swelled to red torrents that cut the naked banks and carried the alluvium far out onto the eroded plains to the east. The air warmed, and the buffalo grass and blue grama came up green and lush with Indian blanket and horse nettle, and the bison began to move out of the red canyons and river brakes, working their way westward up the thousands of draws and drainages that lead to the High Plains caprock.

In May the calving began, and the southern herd, with its scattered bands of cows and calves and the distant bulls grazing two and three together, stretched from the south prong of the Little Red northward across the Canadian River to the Cimarron. Packs of gray wolves shadowed the bands and circled warily as cows licked their offspring clean with blue-gray tongues. When the wolves came near, the bulls, with their bare flanks and lion's manes of ratty wool, bellowed and charged, their rope-like tails erect like tails of scorpions, and the wolves loped away.

With summer the rains came less often. The beasts grunted and rolled, snorted and shook like dogs, and the dust rose in the wind, forming high reddish-brown columns and twirling dust devils. They shook against the swarming flies, and kingbirds and swallows flitted about in noisy pursuit. Vultures circled overhead, waiting like the wolves.

The days lengthened, and the bands drifted further out onto the High Plains, further from the edge of the caprock. The wolves followed, waiting, anticipating the difficult birth, the still birth, the isolated cow or the calf trampled in a stampede. At night the shifting wind carried their howls, and the cows herded their calves into the center of the bands. The bulls stamped their hooves and raised their flared nostrils to the wind as if to verify what they already knew.

The days grew hotter. The grass yellowed, and the herd left bare ground in its wake. Weeks passed tinder dry before thunderheads formed again to the west. At dusk the first low rumbles reached the herd. The beasts stood facing the wind, and for a while the calves cavorted in the coolness. By nightfall thick tentacles of lighting were reflected on the wind-wrinkled surface of the playas, and the herd moved to low-lying shelter. The cows lay against the lee sides of swales with their calves lying against their undersides.

At first the rain came in huge, widely separated drops; then in diagonal sheets. The calves moved tight against their mothers, and the cows sheltered them with their great shaggy heads. Blue sheets of lightning spread over the plain, and the calves trembled and lurched at the deafening thunder claps.

Above the swales the old bulls stood in groups, massive and adamantine. Water streamed from their beards and naked flanks and the lightening glinted in the curves of their wet, black horns.

CHAPTER 2

That fall the government beef did not arrive at the Indian agency near Fort Sill. Summer had been wet and mild by plains standards, and though the People — the Comanches — had found few buffalo in Indian Territory, they had lived well on antelope and deer and cattle stolen on swift raids into Texas. Throughout the summer there had been monthly deliveries of beef which sometimes came butchered to be picked over by the women and at other times live on the hoof to be coursed like buffalo and lanced or shot full of arrows while the Quaker agent and soldiers watched and shook their heads in disgust and disbelief.

On delivery days the three reservation Comanche bands — the Yap Eaters, the Wanderers and the Honey Eaters — srode in for provisions. The women rode gelded paints dragging travois; the bristling, bare-chested warriors carried short bows or six foot-lances and rawhide shields decorated with feathers, horse tails and dangling scalps. Soldiers sat their horses and glared at the warriors' vulgar gesticulations while the hapless, sweating Quaker agent tried meekly and in vain to supervise the rationing. The People shared with their Kiowa neighbors, but additional soldiers were required to protect deliveries to the Wichita and Osage.

On the day of the final summer apportionment the Comanche women picked through the piles of fetid, crudely butchered beef, slapping at flies and laughing and jabbering while the men sat their horses and insulted the attendant soldiers in trader Spanish and broken English and tried to coax them into various wagers involving feats of horsemanship. The soldiers laughed and returned the insults. Finally a corporal named Biggs agreed to run his big half thoroughbred against a small scruffy mustang ridden by a warrior named That's It. The two groups were trying in three tongues and pidgin sign language to sort out the terms of the wager when a band of sixteen warriors appeared from the west and rode among them.

They were of the People, but unlike the reservation Comanches, who wore cowhide moccasins and cotton or woolen breechclouts, their garments were made entirely of antelope skin. They rode smirking amongst the group, leering at the women and smiling defiantly at the silent onlookers. The women watched wide-eyed at first then averted their faces. The soldiers drew their rifles and laid them across their saddles. The expressionless reservation Comanches sat their horses.

The leader of the Antelope warriors, a young, tall half-breed with aquiline features, gray eyes and long braids wrapped in beaver skin, turned his horse and pointed his lance at the reservation Indians. For several minutes he screamed at them in Comanche. At times he stood in his stirrups for emphasis and thrust his lance or pounded the ground with its butt. Finally he laughed cruelly and spat then sat his horse and waited for a response.

One of the reservation Comanches, a stocky, middle-aged warrior, naked save for breechclout, moccasins and leggings, rode forward to meet the half-breed. He carried a three foot bow in his left hand. The half-breed watched; his eyes widened for an instant in recognition. The older man stopped his horse inches from the big Indian's. They spoke in Comanche.

"Quanah," the older man said.

"Uncle," the younger said in the quick tongue of the northern Comanche. "I am surprised the Wanderers are being fed by the whites."

"It has been hard here. The Texans are strong. We agreed in council to stay north of the Red. The Antelope and Buffalo Eaters live far to the north, farther than the whites go."

"You never cross the Red?"

The older man smiled with his eyes. "Just for cattle." He looked away and the smile vanished. "If you touch their women or take their children, the Texans come like wolves. They come no matter where we go. The Texans value their women. They come and leave nothing alive. Our women have no hair left to cut."

The half-breed pointed northwest with his lance. "They cannot follow. They will die of thirst."

The older man looked beyond the lance tip. "After the hungry time, perhaps. One of my wives expects a baby. There are so few of us now."

"There are many wives and little ones south of the Del Norte."

"And many soldiers north of it. Next spring, perhaps."

"I am sorry. This saddens me."

Expressionless, the big Indian turned his horse and the warriors of the Antelope band rode away to the northwest. The women watched them go and then quietly turned back to their work. Their men, having lost all interest in wagering, sat their horses and ignored the soldiers.

Cuts Something preferred the mild seasons. This had not always been the case. As a young man he had lived for the summer raiding. He had reveled in the stories his father and uncles told of the old days when the People moved their entire village south of the Del Norte and raided continually from one summer to the next, taking hundreds of horses and mules and captives. In those days, he was told, the Wanderers rode brazenly along their war trails in broad daylight and strode through the Mexican settlements making sport with the terrified women, and no one dared challenge them. It had been a grand time to be Comanche, before the white sicknesses and the mounted soldiers and the relentless, hating Texans who pursued the People deep into Comancheria.

By the time he had come of age as a warrior it was safe only for quick raids into Mexico or the dangerous Texas settlements where captured women clawed and bit and spat; where a white woman chopped off his older brother's thumb with an ax before he could get a lance in her; where the murderous, angry Rangers seemed to appear from nowhere.

Now in middle age he enjoyed autumn. On cool nights after his noisy wives had gone to sleep he could wrap himself in a buffalo robe and sit outside his lodge before a small fire. Often he rested his back against one of the meat poles and fell asleep watching the flames die. In early autumn he could sleep through the night, but as winter neared he would wake shivering and stiff and crawl into his lodge and under his stack of buffalo robes. On bitter cold nights he would tug one of the rawhide strings that ran under the walls of his lodge and into his wives' lodge. Thus summoned by the string tugging at her bedding the chosen wife would appear and crawl under his robes and shove her ample bottom against his belly to warm him.

Cuts Something was the only warrior in his band who slept outside his lodge, and many of his contemporaries and several of the women, including his three wives, considered the practice beneath the dignity of a respected war chief. But Cuts Something, as he aged, fretted less and less about his stature.

He had acquired his odd sleeping habit years earlier after his only son, then a small boy called Quail, became infested with fleas while trying to dig up a litter of swift fox pups. The boy entered his father's teepee to complain about the itching and, finding the lodge empty, sat on the bed of robes and waited for help. That night fleas covered Cuts Something the instant he lay down. Rabid oaths and a cold bath in the Pease River followed.

His oldest wife, She Invites Her Sisters, found the incident amusing until Cuts Something took her bedding for himself and told her that until she could rid his robes of the fleas she could make due with the thin scratchy blankets they had bartered from Comancheros. He then enjoyed her bitter complaining and frantic beating of the robes. His impish younger wife Fast Girl laughed as well until She Invites Her Sisters slapped her smartly on the lips.

After days of beating and washing and horrid infestation of her person, She Invites Her Sisters burned the robes then nagged Cuts Something until he traded a horse to her father in return for acceptable bedding. In the meantime fleas had taken over both his and his wives' lodges. By the time the women had cleaned and moved the lodges he realized that sleeping outside suited him.

Now on reservation land far north of his home river, the Pease, he sat wrapped in a single robe before a small fire of burning buffalo chips. His wives had searched long and hard for the chips and those they found were old and desiccated. He supplemented the chips with foul smelling elm and now regretted it. Quanah's taunts disturbed him. He knew why the Wanderers had agreed to the treaty with the whites, and whenever he talked with the other reservation Indians the reasons seemed valid. But in the presence of the Antelope, the most arrogant and conservative of the People, the reasons seemed pathetic. Yes his second wife was pregnant, but Comanche women had always ridden regardless of their condition. Cuts Something himself had been born as his band moved from their flat shortgrass hunting grounds to the sheltered brakes of the Pease. His mother simply dismounted and gave birth to him. Two of her sisters stayed behind to help, and after she had rested for a few hours the three rode on to the Pease.

Still, the thought of moving his band to the Llano made him tired. Lately everything tired him. Hunting; riding; Fast Girl. Most mornings his legs were sore and unsteady when he crawled out of his buffalo robes. On clear mornings he would hobble out of his teepee and stand in the sun's warmth before taking short steps to limber up. After a few minutes he might amble about camp or visit his cousin and best friend, That's It, before eating a morning meal of reservation beef, corn and unleavened bread. On cold, rainy days he might crawl out of his robes and rebuild the little fire in his teepee or summon She Invites Her Sisters to do it for him. Then he would warm himself before standing and taking the day's first unsteady steps outside to relieve himself.

He had not yet taken to smoking in the lodge with the old men, but he could see the inevitable. All but the youngest warriors still treated him with great respect, but he had not led a raid in three summers and felt little inclined to do so. Most of his life he had been consulted about matters of war and rapine. Now he found himself increasingly called upon to settle disputes, direct hunting activities, plan camp movement and counsel reckless youngsters.

Some of the youngest warriors, adolescents who had recently had their visions and received their medicine, were beginning to show contempt. One in particular, Otter Belt, accused him of holding the young men back, of preventing them from winning their war honors.

Otter Belt would be trouble. Two summers earlier, he led a group of boys on a prank against the old men. While the men smoked and exchanged stories in their lodge, the boys rode their horses at a gallop around the lodge raising a thick cloud of dust. Then Otter Belt pitched a paunch full of water up and into the flue. The paunch burst, drowning the fire and smoking the men out of the lodge and into the dust.

The old men insisted that the boys should be disciplined, but the younger warriors found the incident hilarious. Boys would be boys, they said. Soon they would be warriors. They might die young and should be allowed their fun. A brave man did not live to see old age anyway. Old men had to accept their lot.

Cuts Something saw his future that day. Worse yet his beloved old friend Sees How Far It Is was among the elders smoked out of the lodge. A few days later while Otter Belt was away carousing with his friends, Cuts Something lured several of the camp dogs into the boy's teepee with scraps of meat. He then tied the entrance closed and went back to his own lodge for a nap.

That night howls of laughter came from Otter Belt's part of the camp, and the boy stomped about demanding that the culprit reveal himself. Although several in camp had seen Cuts Something going about his prank, and many more knew about it, the secret held. Several days later Cuts Something caught the boy afoot and rode him into a big prickly pear flat. While Otter Belt stumbled about in the ankle high cactus, Cuts Something said that a warrior should not have to confine his wives to his teepee to keep them. That said, he pointed his lance at the boy and told him that Sees How Far It Is had not enjoyed the smoke and dust.

At first, Otter Belt looked at him in wonder; then realization set in, and his expression became defiant. Before he rode away, Cuts Something suggested that unless Otter Belt enjoyed sleeping in the cactus there had better be no more pranks. The boy's family had since treated Cuts Something coolly but had made no issue.

On mild days after he had ridden for awhile, hunting or traveling to the agency or to the Cheyenne or Kiowa encampments to trade horses, Cuts Something's muscles loosened and sweat ran down his back and sides and he felt as though he could ride into Mexico again. When they encountered small bands of bison he could still inspire awe among the warriors by shooting a dozen arrows into the beasts at full gallop. At times he chose the lance, and no one was better at finding just the right spot behind the last rib where the lance could be driven into the soft organs.

On those days he and the other mature warriors talked again of raiding and fighting the Utes and the Texans and made bold plans to do so. But later, back at camp after they had dismounted and eaten and had sat before their fires, the day's brief return to glory would be enough and they could think only of their wives' warm flesh and the buffalo robes and sleep. The old hate and lust were ebbing and it bothered Cuts Something when he considered it.

Lately he had no choice but to consider it. The young warriors, particularly Otter Belt, badgered him constantly about his reluctance to raid and make war. He appeased them by suggesting raids against the farming Chickasaws, and some of the experienced warriors had taken the boys on such raids. The parties returned with sorry horses, mules and skinny cattle and occasionally scalps and handsome Chickasaw or Cherokee women. Cuts Something worried little about reprisal. The Army would not take action over a few scalped red farmers, and the miserable *tahbay-boh* agent would only make pathetic appeals.

Much to his dismay the sight of the young warriors violating the naked, prostrate women did not arouse him. Instead, he was reminded of a certain night on the Tongue River.

These token raids were wearing thin. The young men talked of more ambitious campaigns against the Texans. Cuts Something's warnings of the soldiers' murderous reprisals were ignored if not scorned. Most of the older warriors still deferred to his judgment, but he could feel his authority fading. The young men would almost certainly be lured into foolishness by the possibility of booty and war honors. For what was a Comanche if not a warrior? Cuts Something had earned his honors, and the others would not rest until they won their own or died trying. The People knew no other way; would consider no other way.

His only son, now called Elk Rub, would soon be seeking his medicine. That's It, Elk Rub's mentor, had filled the boy's mind with the glory of the old days and had taught him to hunt and shoot. The boy had proven his prowess time and again over hundreds of hours of mock battle with the other boys. Yet now they were confined to this pathetic parcel of grassland. The visions and portents no longer came, and all of their medicine seemed useless against the endless columns of soldiers and the ever breeding Texan farmers.

He leaned back against the meat pole and pulled his robe more tightly around his shoulders.

He awoke in the middle of the night and wondered if he could move his legs. Only the faintest orange glow showed beneath the fire's ashes. Slowly, painfully, he crawled across the bare, frosted ground and into his teepee. He wormed into his stack of robes and groped in the darkness for the rawhide strings.

Shortly She Invites Her Sisters, the warmest of his three wives, slid beneath the robes and shoved her scalding belly against his and ground her loins against his thigh. Lost in his thoughts, he did not stir. Perhaps Quanah was right. Perhaps they should join the Antelope on the Llano. In the spring, he thought. After the birthing. After the hungry time.

C H A P T E R 3

In southwestern Kansas along the Arkansas River, the plains lobos were growing fat and sleek on buffalo carrion. They loped from one naked, fly-covered carcass to the next, fighting and yowling, choking down great hunks of flesh. Then, foundered, they lay in the October sun, oblivious to approaching doom. The wolfers were coming, working westward along the Arkansas, lacing the bison carcasses with strychnine crystals and awaiting the writhing deaths, hurrying to peel off lupine hides before sun and bloating made the hair slip.

To the east, in the chert hills along the western edge of the tallgrass prairie, sun-bleached bones were being ricked and carted to railheads for shipment to Eastern sugar refineries and fertilizer plants. But a virgin bone yard was growing on the midgrass plain to the west.

The bison hunters: plainsmen, vagrants, fugitives, unemployed railroad workers. They carried an array of weapons mostly ill-suited for clean killing. Most possessed little knowlege of hunting and skinning. The spoiled, bullet-ridden hides arrived daily at railroad loading points at Dodge, Hays City and Salina.

The better hunters came with large bore rifles, four or five skinners and six span of mules pulling Studebaker wagons loaded with thousands of pounds of lead and brass cartridges and powder. Days or weeks later, the same wagons would leave the killing fields with eight thousand pounds of bundled hides and kegs of tongues preserved in brine.

Blood in their beards and all manner of tiny vermin on their persons, these men knew nothing of their predecessors, the Cibolero lancers, the Apache dog people, the Pawnee and Osage, the Comanche and Kiowa. Not that they would have cared had they known. For they knew this: dried hides — $3.50 each; tongues — 30¢ each. The killing would not last forever. The Comanches and Kiowa were all but whipped, and the longhorn cattle were pouring in by the tens of thousands. Every man for himself, they said. Next it'll be assholes and elbows for the Texas Panhandle. Most of the southern herd's still there, some said. Somebody's gonna get rich.

On the north bank of the Arkansas, the big .50 caliber Sharps and Remingtons and Ballards boomed. Their reports rolled over the plain, and the ever-attendant wolves loped along with the wagons, staying just out of rifle range. At night, starving Pawnee hunters wearing ratty buffalo robes pushed southward from the Platte by the Sioux, rode quietly among the carcasses and chased away the wolves and coyotes to take the best leavings.

Yet even as the big rifles shook the prairie, tiny bands of Yampareekuh Comanche warriors, refugees returned, brazenly sat their horses just out view of the *tahbay-boh* hunters. They sat watching; waiting.

CHAPTER 4

Logan Fletcher hated the flies most of all. On windless days the constant hum drove him just shy of mad. They covered his face and hands and flew into his mouth making him want to scream, pull his hair and claw his face. Of course flies had often annoyed him when he milked the family cow back in Kentucky, but all annoyances seemed a hundredfold worse on the Kansas plains. Except, perhaps, poison ivy which had covered him with several layers of welts and blisters at least once during each of his nineteen summers. But then he had never seen a Kansas summer; for all he knew, the prairie in June might be a vast, unbroken poison ivy pasture. But on this October day, greenery seemed unlikely in such a sere, dusty grassland. Good Christian people, he was sure, would never have the slightest interest in western Kansas. Once the bison were gone the heathens could keep the God-forsaken country if they cared to.

He watched a man named Krebs drive an iron stake through the skull of a dead buffalo cow, the last skinning of the day. Krebs purportedly had worked on the Santa Fe Railroad and claimed expertise with sledgehammers. Raw-boned and hatless, he swiped his long hair out of his eyes between swings. A gaunt, red headed dullard named Muntz trustingly held the stake. They had saved this cow for last because she had been the first kill of the day, and as such, had been purposely gut-shot. The skinners' employers, Ezra Higginbotham and Bob Durham, insisted on the practice despite the stench put off by punctured intestines. The lead cow in a band, upon being shot in the paunch, would drop her head and sicken and slowly die without bolting and spooking the rest of her band. As she weakened, the surrounding bison would mill about confused, making easy targets. Cows usually were easy to skin, but this one had bloated in the afternoon sun. Logan dreaded working with the drum tight hide. Although the skinners preferred young, sharp-horned bulls over old dull-horned brutes with impossibly tough hides, Bob and Ezra never discriminated.

With the stake in place, Logan and Muntz worked with ripping knives, cutting the hide just below the base of the beast's skull while Krebs brought up a span of black mules. The mules were Bob Durham's pride and joy, the only possessions left over from the freight business he abandoned after his partner and two teamsters were ambushed and scalped by a band of Kiowas.

The initial cutting complete, they tied the severed hide to the mule's harnesses, and Krebs goaded the animals into motion. As the hide peeled away, Muntz worked his skinning knife between the meat and the skin to minimize the amount of fat and flesh torn from the carcass.

"By god that's the only way to skin these sumbitches," Muntz said. He spat then wiped the errant stream of tobacco juice from his beard with his bloody sleeve.

Krebs, who as a matter of course disagreed with everything Muntz had to say, looked up from his work. Flies covered his face. "I want you to look at all the goddamn fat left on this hide. We'll make up for our slackin' by scrapin' hides tonight after supper." He slapped absentmindedly at his face. "You know how Ezra is about his hides. Hell, I told Ezra we oughta make a run up to the Platte and bring us back a wagon load of Pawnee squaws."

Muntz spat on his beard again. "Why a load of squaws would put me and you both outta work if they didn't cut our throats."

"I'd work 'em all right," Krebs said, grinning.

Logan ignored the two. He busied himself extracting the dead buffalo's tongue. Bob Durham held in disdain skinners too lazy to cut out and properly preserve the tongue of every downed bison. Krebs and Muntz continued their conjecture on the carnal appetites of Pawnee women though neither had ever seen an Indian outside the vicinity of a settlement or fort.

Logan gave up trying to grip the slimy tongue and resorted to a small meat hook which he found after an arduous search among the wagon's various gory tools. He shook the tongue off into a wash tub containing thirteen other tongues then wiped his hands on the dry grass.

By this time his partners were wrestling with the fresh hide, folding it for loading. He leaned against the wagon, feeling little inclined to help. He had done his part; they could do theirs.

Logan considered the two men heathens of the lowest water, no better than the savages still at large in the wastes. Neither had the slightest respect for or interest in the good news offered by the Gospel. He had tried for the better part of a week to lead them toward victory but had given up in the face of their drunken mockery. Some men, he reasoned, were beyond reach. *For the Lord knoweth the way of the righteous, but the way of the ungodly shall perish.*

He felt much better about his employers. Although both were ignorant of the Word, they were God-fearing men, or at least claimed to be in his presence. Of the two, Bob Durham seemed the most devout despite a few irksome super-stitions regarding the handling and consumption of fowl.

The sun had nearly disappeared behind the featureless horizon. Logan's sweat dried quickly. He wished for his coat, but he had laid it in the wagon early in the day and had forgotten about it. Now it lay under several hundred pounds of green hides. He tried not to think about the shape it would be in when he finally got to it. Krebs and Muntz, both experienced skinners, owned heavy buffalo skin coats which Logan viewed as fine abodes for vermin. He had no plans to abandon his woolen overcoat.

Heavy rifles still boomed sporadically, and even at that late hour carcasses could be marked by groups of wheeling buzzards. The birds waddled and flapped around the darkening mounds. Wolves gathered just beyond rifle range, pacing or sitting on their haunches, watching, waiting for the skinners to leave.

Krebs and Muntz heaved the folded hide into the wagon, both alternately cussing and fantasizing aloud about Pawnee women. In three days, the crew would be heading southwest for Dodge City. They were less than a day's travel north of the Arkansas River, or so Bob had told them. For the past several days Logan had thought a lot about the river. He looked forward to a bath.

Estimates varied among the three skinners, but all agreed that in the eleven days since they had ridden out of Salina, the cook, Earl Romack, had been fired no less than four times and had quit at least twice. Bob Durham had last fired the volatile cook after a heated argument over the proper way to make bannock. Bob asserted that the fried bread should be flipped in the skillet only once; Romack obstinately flipped it until it was burned on both sides.

Now Logan and Krebs agreed that another dismissal was imminent; Romack had relocated camp eighty yards downwind of a fresh killing field. Muntz agreed with their assessment once the blunder had been pointed out to him. For several days, they had enjoyed a very comfortable camp beneath a stand of cottonwoods next to a small creek, but the area had become intolerably rancid from the hide scraping. The coyotes had grown bolder nightly, coming ever closer, until they pulled a bag of cornmeal from Romack's wagon. Consequently Ezra ordered the cook to move camp a mile or so westward along the creek. Romack, probably fearing another firing, had followed the order precisely.

The old cook hunkered over his huge cast iron skillet. He floured a strip of tongue and laid it in the hot grease. He had sourdough biscuits baking in his Dutch oven. For fuel, he had forgone clean-burning buffalo chips for smelly elm and cottonwood.

"By god somethin' stinks," Krebs said. "Somebody shit in your wagon, Romack."

The cook kept his eyes on the frying tongue. "That's Muntz ye smell."

The skinners built another, much larger fire for light and hurriedly stretched the fourteen hides and pinned them taut with wooden dowels. They were almost finished when Ezra Higginbotham and Bob Durham rode into camp from the southwest. The two hunters silently regarded the day's yield then saw to their mounts.

Logan buttoned his damp, greasy coat. The night was clear and cold; he could see his breath. He finished staking the last hide and moved as close to the fire as he could without setting his britches ablaze.

Krebs and Muntz ate sitting on the back end of the kill wagon and with full mouths continued their talk of Pawnee women. The other four men ate sitting about the fire. Ezra arose and walked into the darkness and then reappeared with a buffalo robe draped over his shoulders. He rubbed his gray beard. "Boys, I think they're about gone. We seen only three little bunches this afternoon. I never thought I'd see 'em killed out, but I believe we've done it."

"Maybe they just moved," Logan said.

Bob shifted a piece of biscuit to one side of his mouth. The firelight shone on his dark face above his beard. "If they've moved, they're just gettin' shot somewheres else. I'd say we're about done in Kansas Territory. Man down at Griffin last summer said most of the southern herd's still in the Panhandle along the Canadian." He swallowed and took a sip of coffee. "'Course there's still Comanches and Kiowas runnin' loose over there and they got all the heathens on the reservation tellin' 'em there ain't supposed to be no white folks huntin' buffaloes in that country." He winked at Logan. "Nobody never said nothin' about black folks though. I don't expect they'll mind me shootin' a few."

Ezra snorted. "Hell there ain't no keepin' hide hunters outta there. I say we go soon as we can if we're goin'. Anyways I don't know how to do nothin' else."

Romack said nothing. He chewed the last of his buffalo tongue.

Logan felt he was being let in on a secret. "Y'all ever been there?" he asked in a conspiratorial half whisper.

"Bob's been there once," Ezra said. "Rode up there from the settlements and bought his wife back from the Kiowas. They'd have roasted me, but they didn't know what to think about a little darkie ridin' up on a mule."

Bob stuffed his pipe. "They knowed better than to fool with me."

After supper the skinners worked until nearly midnight scraping flesh from the green hides. They salted the tongues and dropped them atop dozens of others in a hide-lined brine pit. When they finished Romack poured hot water into a wash pan for Logan. Muntz and Krebs crawled unwashed into their bedrolls and began snoring immediately. Bob and Ezra sat talking softly. Romack kept the coffee warm, occasionally fed the fire and punched the spent primers out of the empty brass casings. Logan melted reclaimed bullets in an iron ladle and periodically poured the molten lead into a bullet mold. The fire pit had been dug in the shape of a key hole and the ladle sat atop coals dragged out of the fire and into the slot.

At last Ezra noticed the hysterical yowling coming from the nearby bison carcasses. He got up and walked to the edge of the firelight, drew his Colt Navy and fired four times in the direction of the coyotes. Krebs and Muntz snored without pause. The yowling stopped, and Ezra returned to the fire. He poured himself a cup of coffee, but before he could take a sip the yowling resumed. He shook his head. "Romack," he said softly.

CHAPTER 5

The Quaker agent Lowery lay in his bed, listening. His wife slept beside him, but he did not notice her snoring. He listened, trying to hear through his open window the two dozen horses in the earthen corral sixty feet from his house which doubled as the agency office for the reservation Comanche, Kiowa and Osage. Moonlight streamed into the room. He could see every detail. He took his pocket watch from the night stand, held it six inches from his face and squinted. Nearly one in the morning. He lay back again and sighed.

The Osage worried him little, but the Kiowa and especially the more numerous Comanche tormented him. Earlier, that afternoon in his bare front yard, Cuts Something told him that there must be reparation for the lack of promised annuity goods; the Wanderers had upheld their end of the bargain, and he expected the same from the *tahbay-boh* — the whites. Cuts Something and That's It sat their horses and waited for a reply.

Lowery explained to the typically reasonable Cuts Something that in the eyes of the Great Father, the People had not kept their promises. Raiding continued south of the Red; the People often brought stolen cattle and horses onto reservation land and worse yet, Looks For Hawks, a Penateka Comanche war chief, had two days before shamelessly brought several captive white children to the agency office and offered them up for ransom, and the Cherokee and Choctaw were begging for protection.

Cuts Something said he had no control over the Honey Eaters or the Yap Eaters, much less the Antelope or Buffalo Eaters who were growing fat on stolen cattle and enjoying the Texans' women immensely. But the Wanderers, he said, had stayed on the reservation and now expected the promised beef, sugar and coffee. Yes, some of the younger warriors had taken a few Cherokee women, but why should the *tahbay-boh* care?

Lowery argued that the Great Father had perforce paid for Comanche depredation in Texas and Kansas and now had no money left for reservation beef. Perhaps Cuts Something could speak to the other bands.

That's It silently watched the commissary horses. At last he spoke in Comanche to Cuts Something who then looked insolently at Lowery and said, "All *tahbay-boh* are liars." Cuts Something glanced at the commissary horses in the earthen corral, and the two Comanches turned and rode toward the Wanderer encampment.

Lowery had believed that God would provide the needed direction, but He had lately been silent. President Grant had assigned oversight of the Comanche, Kiowa and Osage reservation to the Friends, and Lowery took the agent assignment eagerly, though he knew nothing of the Southern Plains tribes. Like all Quakers he vehemently opposed the use of force. He believed the Indian problem could be solved though kindness, agricultural training and conversion to Christianity. After all, had not the Eastern Tribes taken readily to agriculture and the Gospel?

So he came to Fort Sill, strode resolutely among the savages, and much to their amusement, immediately demanded the removal of all military personnel from agency grounds. Over the next five days, the Comanches stole all of the reservation beeves, fed their corn meal to their horses; pronounced the provided blocks of soap unpalatable and therefore worthless and brought three bedraggled, spiritless captive white women, one with her nose burnt completely away, to the agency for ransom. Colonel Grierson demanded a written apology in return for another guard detachment.

Undaunted, Lowery hired a white farmer to plow and plant several demonstration plots, and soldiers erected a number of small shacks as living quarters for the Indians. The Comanches promptly broke the sheds into firewood — buffalo dung had dwindled to short supply — and raided the fields and gorged on green melons. Their resulting violent stomach cramps prompted them to declare all farming bad medicine.

Then the Quaker Commission back East, after learning of the military guard, demanded that Lowery remove it at once or face dismissal. Their peace policy would be followed to the letter. Kindness and instruction would prevail in the end. Fearing for his job, he again dismissed the soldiers.

Meanwhile, the People and their Kiowa allies had learned that the worse the condition of their white prisoners — especially women and children — the more frantic and generous the *tahbay-boh* bargaining. Despair gripped Lowery's wife. Lately she had been given to bouts of uncontrollable sobbing and virtual paralysis. Within him grew the belief that these plains Indians were not God's people at all; that the Gospel was unknowable to them and they could be dealt with only from a position of strength. His attempts at kindness they held in complete contempt — so much so he did not fear for his life. They viewed him as source of amusement unworthy of the slight effort required to kill him. He now understood why his predecessor had deserted the post.

He arose and went to the window. In the light of the gibbous moon he could see the horses and hear their listless movements and at times even their breathing. Surely Cuts Something would not try for the horses on such a quiet night. Still, he regretted the guards' departure.

He eased the cane-bottomed straight backed chair — the one his grandfather had made in Pennsylvania — to the window and with his chin resting on his forearms, sat watching the horses.

Perhaps these people were like the tribes in the Land of Milk and Honey and would have to be crushed before God's word could move forward with the frontier. Had not the Lord at times ordered His chosen people to put their enemies under the sword? He lowered his eyes in prayer and supplication and begged silently for direction. He listened until he heard his pulse. He prayed on.

Lowery's wife stirred. He opened his eyes. The sun had just cleared the eastern horizon and the house cast a long shadow over the corral. The horses were gone.

He sat curiously serene. Perhaps, he thought, the Lord had spoken to him after all. Just then, he noticed the moccasin prints in the sand just outside his window.

Cuts Something and That's It rode southward off the reservation, crossed the Red River and rode to the Pease. They rode west along the sandy river bottom. Each carried a supply of pemmican and a buffalo paunch full of sweet water. Although they had spent much of their lives along the Pease, they could not stomach its salt and gypsum.

The Pease was very low, in places just a broken string of clear pools boiling with bass and bream. The two men stopped to watch a great blue heron hunt one of the pools. The bird stood motionless for nearly an hour before taking a step. Then came the blur of the rapier bill, and the impaled fish struggled weakly. The two men silently watched the kill then rode on.

They rode for two days. Late afternoons they camped in the sand beneath cottonwood trees. They ate pemmican and talked of their old home and what they might do about the coming hungry time and the dearth of government beef. On the third day they left the river bottom to skirt the place where Ross and his Rangers had swept down upon a Wanderer encampment to kill over half of the band and capture Naduah, the wife of Nawkohnee and their daughter Topsannah. Naduah's son, the boy Quanah, and Cuts Something had been upriver hunting and learned of the massacre from a half-dozen warriors who somehow escaped. Now ghosts surely haunted the old encampment and Cuts Something and That's It wanted nothing to do with it.

Sufficiently upriver, they rode back through the brakes and into the river bottom. Mule deer stood motionless, watching them, but the two men let them be. They could take a deer later if the need arose. They saw no bison, but abundant spoor lifted their spirits.

Late afternoon, they camped in a stand of blackjack oak south of the river. They built a small oak fire and ate the last of their pemmican; their appetites had been unexpectedly large in the cool October air. Wolves occasionally howled in the rough brakes on either side of the river.

"We should never have left here," Cuts Something said.

"Why did we leave then?"

"I barely remember the bad times now. The soldiers never let us rest. We had no time to hunt."

"Maybe we should join the Antelope. That is not our country though. But I think it would be better than the reservation. The soldiers do not go out on the Llano. They cannot find water."

"Soon we will know what to do," Cuts something said. He pulled his robe over his shoulders.

Next morning they refilled their water bags at a spring in the hills above the river and set about to find a deer to sustain them for the rest of their journey. They waited motionless, downwind of a clear pool. Coyotes and wolves came to drink, oblivious to the hunters' presence. A column of five does approached along a well-worn trail through the sand bluestem. A horsefly alighted and bit Cuts Something painfully on the back just above his breechclout, yet he did not move. The deer came on. He waited. The deer lowered their heads to drink. He began a smooth draw, but one of the does snorted and the five deer crashed off in all directions through the tallgrass and plum.

Cuts Something stood up straight and relaxed. That's It stepped out of the brush on the opposite side of the game trail and pointed toward the northern brakes. Cuts Something smiled and nodded and each took out a bone pipe which he stuffed with government-issue tobacco and sumac leaves. That's It took out his flint and steel and fired a knot of grass and lit their pipes. They smoked and waited. "I think we will find her dead," That's it said.

Cuts Something laughed. "I think she is still running. Perhaps we should look for your arrow."

That's it laughed and knocked the ashes from his pipe. "I wanted to wait for you to kill her, but I was afraid night would fall before you awoke."

After two pipes they arose and walked into the brush. Very shortly, they found the doe stone dead, her eyes already glazed over and That's It's arrow broken off flush behind her shoulder. They roasted the haunches and hung the rest in a cottonwood well downwind of their camp. That night the wind picked up and blew sand into their meat. Clouds scudded low overhead and frustrated coyotes howled ridiculously from the direction of the hung venison. The men slept poorly, wrapped in robes with their backs to the wind. Each woke periodically to revive the fire and smoke in silence. The fire burned raggedly and hissed and popped and the wind carried the sparks into the darkness.

They awoke at dawn, stiff and sore. They roasted more venison and ate overripe plums gathered along the river. Afterward they cut several thin green limbs and erected a low, crude scaffold, built a cool smoking fire beneath it and retrieved the venison. They cut the venison into strips which they hung on the scaffold. The thick smoke burned their eyes and they held their breath each time they hung a strip of meat. Cuts Something said that they should have brought their women. If they continued doing women's work they would soon be tremendously fat, suckling babies and tanning hides.

That's It did not laugh at his friend's joke. "Soon we will be sitting in the smoking lodge with old men while children laugh at us and pour water into our fires."

Late morning the wind laid, and they roasted the last of their fresh venison and napped upwind of the smoking fire.

Mid afternoon, they awoke. Cuts Something rolled his buffalo robe and fashioned a carrying strap from the green buckskin. He left his weapons arranged carefully at the base of an oak, gathered his tobacco, pipe and flint and steel, shouldered his rolled buffalo robe and headed upriver, That's It watching silently.

Keeping to game trails, Cuts Something walked westward through the bluestem and Indian grass. The summer had been mild and wet, and coveys of bobwhite quail flushed and flew up the brushy draws. He watched warily for rattlesnakes but saw none.

He walked for two miles between the low hills and buttes rising north and south of the river. He carried no water and in the warm afternoon sun, the clear Pease looked inviting, but he knew better than to drink its water. He made that mistake as a child and spent the better part of two days retching.

Four times along the way to his destination, a prominent butte just south of the river, he stopped and prayed to the spirits and lit his pipe, each time offering a puff of smoke to the Sun and to the spirits and to the Earth Mother. With each stop, the bitter tobacco made his thirst more acute. Yet he ignored it. He felt the weight of his people's misery on his shoulders; if the spirits refused his plea for guidance, the People were finished.

The butte loomed close now. He left the river bottom and climbed into the low, sere hills. He climbed easily on all fours to the top of the butte which formed a small mesa barely larger than the floor of the Wanderers' council lodge. Here, when he was fifteen summers, the spirits gave him badger medicine and showed him that beast's tenacity and courage. Delirious after four days of waterless fasting, he saw that morning on the plain beyond the river a badger fighting off two gray wolves for possession of a prairie dog it had dug up. Afterward, he staggered back into camp and told his story and pronounced his manhood. Since then, he had constantly tried to demonstrate the badger's doggedness. The other warriors had often pointed out his thick neck and hard, thick trunk, powerful hands, and legs short and bowed even by Comanche standards, as proof of his kinship with the badger.

He spread his robe on the ground and sat watching the sun, which was still high over the river bottom. Sweat ran down his back and sides and dripped off the end of his nose to form a pool on his breechclout.

He had been to the medicine mounds and to medicine bluff and other places sacred to the People, but it was here that he always felt closest to the spirits. That this place was sacred only to him intensified the feeling and made him all the surer that he had been picked for special instruction. His stature as a warrior had not grown so much from raiding, plunder and thievery, although he had done his share of these things and had done them well. Instead, he gained standing by demonstrating sound leadership in the most desperate situations; engagements with Rangers and battles against overwhelming numbers of Utes or Apaches. In the grimmest times, he had always chosen the right path. When cornered he called on his badger medicine and clawed through his opposition and led others to do the same. But now he was tiring.

That skunk Hays and his Rangers had killed both his father and his grandfather, and in Cuts Something's youth these killings instilled in him an apocalyptic hate of all Texans. But now he no longer believed the People could simply outride and outfight the Texans, although the Rangers had been less in evidence since the whites had stopped fighting among themselves.

Still, he could not forget the way these white men followed the People deep into Comanchería, where for generations no enemy dared go. So many times the raiding parties assumed they had evaded the Texans. They would return to the village and celebrate with scalp dances and resume their daily routines of

ıg, and then one morning the Rangers would materialize at
ıongst them shooting and screaming, eyes ablaze with
..ıd seen it and had survived it twice and had taken scalps
.. had been more dead People than dead Texans.

..ıe queer-looking soldiers with woolly hair and dark brown skin har-
..ı the People unmercifully. These soldiers with their clumsy mounts and
wagons could easily be avoided, but they kept coming; they left the People no
time for rest and preparation for the hungry time.

In their way, the buffalo soldiers were as dogged and ruthless and unmerci-
ful as the Texans. He had often heard that their war chief, Maddox, had suffered in the war between the whites a wound that would not heal. Maddox suffered so that he never slept and in his wakefulness and anger, he constantly
plotted the People's destruction. Many of the elders believed that Maddox's soldiers would stop at nothing; that they would follow him across the dismal
plain to the village of the dead to mete destruction even in the afterlife.

Cuts Something's sweat dried and goose bumps formed on his arms. He lit
his pipe again, and as the sun disappeared behind the red cliffs he prayed again
for the spirits' direction; he prayed that his badger medicine would return and
bring the tenacity and wisdom that had made him the Wanderer's most
respected war chief.

The moon rose above the red cliffs north of the Pease and lighted the river
bottom. Cuts Something wrapped himself in his robe and turned to watch it.
He waited and listened, hoping, but knowing in his heart that the spirits would
not speak so soon. Still he hoped to be spared the pain of an extended vision
quest. Perhaps given the urgency of this quest, the spirits would speak forthwith.

In the moonlight, he could see a line of mesquite and juniper against the
base of the northern hills beyond the river. As boys, he and That's It and their
brothers often hunted small birds there and killed them with their short bows
and crude arrows. Often, they picked a single bird and hunted it to the exclu-
sion of all others. If a sloppy approach flushed their quarry, they would track
its flight and plan another stalk. They communicated through soft whistles and
imitations of bird calls and with subtle hand signals. The game fascinated
them, and they quickly learned which birds, when flushed, would fly a short
distance and alight and which would fly away.

Now, according to *tahbay-boh* laws, the People were not to set foot on their
old hunting grounds.

He nodded then jerked awake. He did not want to fall asleep yet. His vision quests had always been rewarded, but not without pain. Judging from his thirst this first night, the spirits would exact a price for their wisdom. He waited and listened. At length he turned to the east so that the rising sun would be in his face. He lay down and covered his head with the robe and slept.

At sunrise, he sat up and gathered his pipe and tobacco and let the robe fall from his shoulders so as to catch the power and warmth of the sun's rays. Already he dreaded the coming day's heat and the bitter taste of the tobacco in his dry mouth, but the sun and the protective spirits and the Earth Mother demanded offerings of pipe smoke.

By sunset he could barely swallow. Still the spirits kept to themselves. By mid-afternoon on the third day, he could not recall how many days had past since he had left That's It in camp. He slept fitfully. At times he could not differentiate dream from reality. Had he just lighted his pipe or had he dreamt the act? He shivered even in the midday sun. He tried to sing during moments of lucidity but could utter only dry croaks. On the third night delirium set in. Images came to him as he struggled just beneath the surface of his sleep. A raven flapping and wheeling over a labyrinth of red canyons and beyond the labyrinth a great, flat plain and innumerable buffalo spread in small bands to every horizon. Buffalo came off the plain and made their way to the canyon floor where they could graze unmolested by the sleet blowing horizontally out on the plain.

Yet some of the old bulls remained on the unprotected plain. They stood facing the wind and ice hung from their beards and formed beneath their horns and steam came from their mouths and nostrils. They stood after all the other bison had left the plain and the wind and the sleet worsened until the bulls faded into amorphous forms changing shape and shade behind the veil of sleet.

The images came repeatedly. He woke and took in his surroundings. He struggled to sift dream and reality. He dozed again. At last, the badger came to him. Trundling about a prairie dog town it stopped, looked about then sprinted for a burrow entrance. At the entrance, it dug throwing huge plumes of earth into the air behind it. The badger dug frantically then abandoned the hole and started anew at another entrance. Then the raven again and the red labyrinth and the bison pouring into the canyons, and the old bulls fading in the sleet.

At sunrise, he pulled himself up and started for camp. Twenty steps later, he realized he had left his buffalo robe and pipe and flint and steel on the ground behind him. Yet he lacked the strength or resolve to retrieve them. He walked eastward off the butte and into the river bottom. Even walking, he struggled to separate dream from reality. He fell into the tallgrass and sand, pushed himself up and went one. He wondered: was he returning to the Wanderer encampment? Or was he walking over the dismal plain? He fell again. His mind slogged. Was he walking again or still rolling in the grass?

Something restrained him. Somebody. He jerked away and groped for his knife, but found his scabbard empty. Someone yelled at him. He felt and tasted sweet water on his lips. He tried to grab the water with his hands and push it beyond his swollen tongue, but the water seemed trapped in his mouth. At last he swallowed and cried out at the intense pain. The second mouthful went down more easily, and he began to gulp wildly. Someone jerked the bag away. He lunged for the water, dimly aware of the blurred figure before him. He flailed and fell again. The water returned and with it a voice he recognized. He drank again, this time in small sips. Then, satiated, he rolled over on his face and wept softly with relief.

He awoke at dusk. He opened his eyes and saw his horse picketed just beyond the trees and a small fire burning a few feet away. He was ravenous, but too weak to get up. That's It appeared before him, squatted and handed him a strip of smoked venison. He ate it and then another very quickly. Nausea came over him. He lay back again. The nausea subsided and he slept.

He awoke at dawn. A stiff wind carried scattered drops of cold rain. That's It looked at him with concern. Cuts Something took another long drink from the bag and held out his hand. That's It took his hand and began pulling him up, but Cuts Something laughed and shook his hand briskly up and down in imitation of the way the ridiculous white man Lowery always tried to greet them. That's It let go and both men fell on their backs and laughed hysterically.

On their way back to the reservation, they rode through numerous prairie dog towns. But they saw no badgers. Cuts Something would have liked to see a badger.

CHAPTER 7

Logan sat in the skinners wagon and contemplated God's plan while Bob and Ezra worked the edge of a small band of bison six hundred yards to the south. He could see the beasts; dark specks just below the horizon. He heard the reports from heavy rifles, but he could not make out the hunters. Krebs and Muntz, having exhausted the topic of Pawnee women, lay snoring in the back of the wagon. Logan's woolen coat, stiff with blood, provided warmth against the morning chill. He wanted to wash it in the creek next to camp, but thus far he had not been in camp during daylight hours.

Logan considered his pay munificent. Where else could a common laborer earn two dollars a day? He liked and respected his employers if not his fellow skinners. He had grown accustomed to the filthy work. The plains had grown on him; he found prairie twilight and dawn glorious.

Surely God had led him here. Surely He had led him directly to Independence, Missouri; led him to sleep beneath Bob Durham's wagon that first night off the boat so that when Bob arrived the next morning with his team of black mules — magnificent beasts like the ones Marcus Fletcher had employed — Logan could roll from beneath the wagon and compliment and expertly examine them, compelling Bob to offer him a job, advance him two days' pay and put him to work loading lead, powder and brass casings.

That next morning, they found Krebs and Muntz passed out drunk in a hog lot drainage and rode out of Independence, west into tallgrass that at times swished above the mules' heads. Logan saw bison for the first time in the low, flat-topped, rocky hills, the remains of bison and naked wolf carcasses, and bone gatherers pulling their carts. Further west, they descended the low hills and rode onto a midgrass plain that spread featureless to every horizon. The space and distance made him dizzy and he felt insignificant before a distant, unreachable Lord.

In Salina, they rendezvoused with Ezra and Romack. After reprovisioning, they rode southward toward the Arkansas River. For two days, they saw no bison but many antelope which provided a welcome repast. On the third day out of Salina, they encountered bison in numerous bands, although not in the numbers Logan had heard about in the little Missouri River towns and in Independence saloons.

Along the way, Muntz and Krebs dully lectured him on the use of skinning knives and scrapers. He quickly learned what worked and what did not, and Bob left him in charge of the mules. Surely this was providence, he thought. Something would come of it. *In all thy ways acknowledge Him and He shall direct thy paths.*

On this morning he felt he had been a skinner all his life and always would be. Two specks that had been indistinguishable from clumps of sage became riders. At length, Ezra rode up with his Sharps resting across the front of his saddle. Bob rode on eastward. "Thirteen down, boys," he said. "We need to pick it up; get while the gettin's good. Me or Bob'll come back around for you when we're done with the next bunch." He rode away. Krebs and Muntz groggily climbed into the wagons. Logan started the mules toward the killing field.

They rode off the low hill and over a number of grassy undulations before they came to the dead bison, sixteen beasts spread over five acres or so. Logan stopped the wagon, and, as always, walked among the carcasses to see where they had been shot, so that he could recover the 600-grain lead bullets for melting and remolding. He believed he could outshoot both of his employers and had demonstrated his skill several times since they left Salina by shooting prairie chickens with Ezra's Henry repeater. He had also taken a number of the big grouse on the wing with Romack's shotgun. They all enjoyed prairie chicken as a welcome change from bison or antelope, although Bob insisted, without explanation, that the prairie chicken offal should be buried after dark, east of camp.

At times, Logan wished for his old Enfield musket. He had taken hundreds of squirrels with it from the tops of hickory and walnut trees back in the Kentucky highlands. He remembered with pride the turkeys he shot from roosts. But he had sold the gun to a tinker in Paducah for riverboat fare.

Most of the bison had been shot once through the heart or lungs, although a few had initially been hit too far back and had additional holes in their capes. Of course the lead cow had been gut shot. Logan could smell the punctured intestines.

He knew he should just pick a carcass and start the day's skinning, but the glorious morning — clear, bright and cool — invited languor. Muntz and Krebs were already dozing again, sitting on the ground with their backs against a wagon wheel. At the edge of the killing field, a low bank dropped to a dry, sandy wash which nearly hid a dead bison. Logan spied the beast's hump protruding just above the bank. Conveniently, the bison had died upright, its legs folded beneath its body. The bank probably had kept it from falling over. Logan looked back at his fellow skinners. Muntz stood in the back of the wagon, stretching and yawning while Krebs searched for the heavy tools.

Logan knelt and found a bullet wound near the rear of the rib cage — too far back to kill cleanly. He was looking for another hole when he heard a meaty slap and the distant thump and low, rolling swell of a heavy rifle. He looked over the bison's hump and saw Muntz on the ground on his hands and knees, blood gushing from his near shoulder. He wondered if the bumbling skinner had cut himself or had fallen on the skull spike. A half dozen riders appeared at the crest of the low hill he, Muntz and Krebs had topped moments before. They rode down the hill and disappeared among the grassy waves.

Logan heard his pulse. Krebs scrambled over the heavy tools toward the wagon's driver seat. The riders came over a much nearer rise, and Logan knew that he was looking at wild men. His bowels loosened. His imagination had not prepared him for the sight: naked torsos and faces painted vermilion; coal black roaches on shaved pates; morning sunlight glinting on brass earrings and bracelets. Two carried rifles; the others held short bows. Feral screams rose and fell with the prairie contours.

He crouched on rubber legs behind the carcass and peered over the hump. Krebs grabbed the reins and started the mules toward camp. The wagon bounced wildly and Krebs cursed at the top of his lungs and groped with one hand for the Henry beneath the seat. Logan dared not call out to him.

So his time had come, he thought. God willed him to die horribly on the

Kansas plains. In mere seconds he would join the spirit world; would go on to victory. He wondered: should he even struggle? Or should he calmly and resolutely face his killers as his Lord had faced the rabid mob? He heard nothing now. The savages closed like pursuing beasts in a dream. The bison carcass between him and his attackers comforted him like a blanket over the head of child terrified by darkness.

Five of the six riders peeled away in pursuit of Krebs. The sixth rider came on. The sound of nearby hooves jolted Logan from his trance. He pulled off his hat and lowered his head so that he could just see over the bank. The Indian veered slightly and came for Muntz who remained on his hands and knees, stunned and silent. As the savage passed he struck Muntz in the back of the head with a stone ax. Logan heard a sickening *thwack* and dark blood flew from Muntz's head as he fell forward onto his face.

The Indian adroitly stopped and turned his horse, dismounted and drew his knife in a single, graceful motion, bounded to Muntz and yanked the dead man's bloody head up by the hair and slashed off the front third of his scalp and held it aloft, screaming hoarsely in exhilaration.

Logan's mind raced. What if the Indian wanted to torture him? Perhaps he should fight so that the Indian would kill him quickly. He wanted to lie down and curl up, but he could not take his eyes from the carnage. Logan could hear the man's hoarse breathing forty feet away. The Indian was short, bow-legged and powerful. His back muscles swelled as he jerked the corpse about, groping in pockets, painting swaths of ground with blood.

Logan sat down with his back to the bison; the curious serenity returned. He waited. Nineteen years. Who could know why? One simply did his best and then accepted God's will. He would do whatever he felt moved to do when the time came. Perhaps he had been sent west for those few nights on the Missouri River. Who could say what would become of that?

Yet the Indian did not come. Acceptance left him, and his pulse roared in his ears. He waited. He heard the killer talking softly to himself in his own tongue. He held his breath, listening as the man mounted and rode away in the direction the others had gone. Could it be that the savages never saw him? He sent forth a burst of silent thanks. Perhaps, in the excitement of their attack, they had forgotten about him.

The hoof beats faded. He peered over the bank and saw only empty prairie—empty save for Muntz's remains. His stomach rolled. He sat against the dead buffalo, barely able to lift his arms.

His mind slogged. He needed to find Ezra and Bob. He realized suddenly that they might be dead, and Romack too. More terrifying yet, the savages might return. What if the lone Indian rejoined his companions and they reminded him that there was another white man?

He knew that he should flee, but he dreaded leaving his sanctuary. The thought of exposing himself on the open prairie made breathing difficult. He scanned the plains in the direction opposite that the Indians had taken. The prairie looked table-top flat, but held low swales and other contours visible at short range. He stood and willed his legs to work; his stride felt weak and awkward. He stumbled and fell, rolled and got up and continued. His windpipe constricted. He went to his hands and knees and alternately sobbed and gasped for air. He rolled onto his back and prayed. At first he could only plead *please . . . please . . . please . . .* , but he gradually calmed and prayed for peace and strength and God's presence. His prayers calmed him and his windpipe relaxed.

He lay for a while, shading his eyes with his hands. His head cleared and his breathing slowed. He arose, found his hat and continued at a fast walk. After a few hundred feet he came to a bowl shaped swale and hid behind the grass that grew around the edges.

He looked toward the killing field. Black smoke billowed from the low hills a mile to the east. He noticed his thirst and thought of the water barrel on the wagon. He thought again of Bob and Ezra. The two men would certainly return to the kill site if they were still alive. He could die of thirst if they failed to return. Days commonly passed between encounters with other white hunters. More out of fear than reason, he decided to stay hidden.

His stupidity amazed him. If they had been alert and ready with weapons, his companions might still be alive. He knew, however, that he would have fought poorly in his terror. He had never known fear beyond mild apprehension. Nothing in his life had prepared him for that moment when he realized they were being attacked by wild men. He had not known that fear could be so paralyzing. He wondered too about his reactions. When death had seemed imminent, he felt oddly at peace; but in uncertainty, fear held him fast.

By late morning, heat waves shimmered in the distance, and flies and gnats swarmed about his face. He was trying to gather saliva in his mouth when he saw two riders coming over the hill above the killing field. At first he could not discern their race and the terror began anew. His pulse rose again in his ears. He squinted and made out Bob's dark face and the rifle carried across his saddle. He pushed himself up and ran toward them.

They rode out to meet him. Sweat ran down their faces. Bob shook his head grimly and tossed Logan his canteen. "Christ almighty son, I thought sure they had you. Was they Comanches?"

Logan's chest heaved. He wanted to weep with relief. "I reckon." He took a gulp of water. "I don't know. There was six. One got Muntz; the others went after Krebs. He rode off towards camp in the wagon." He took another long pull from the canteen then caught his breath. "I was hid. I can't figure how they didn't see me. I ain't never been so scared. Them painted red and squallin' with them shaved heads."

Ezra had been scanning the horizon. He stopped suddenly and looked wide-eyed at Logan. "Shaved head, you say?"

"Like a Mohawk."

Bob looked at Ezra who nodded in acknowledgment. "Pawnee, I'd say. What the hell is a Pawnee doin' way down here?"

Ezra motioned for Logan to climb onto the rear of Bob's saddle. "Somebody said the Sioux was pushin' 'em hard from the north. Hell they're s'posed to be on the reservation." He spat. "I reckon we better go see what's left of Krebs."

They rode toward the smoke. Logan did not look at Muntz's body, but he could not avoid looking at what lay about the burning wagon. Krebs' scalped, naked emasculated body lay a short distance away. The steel spike they had used to anchor dead bison had been driven into his mouth, through the back of his head and into the ground. Bob said that this was to be expected.

They had not expected the six dead Pawnees, all shot full of arrows and scalped, ragged wounds running down the center of their heads where their roaches had been. One had been stripped and tied spread-eagle using skinning dowels from the wagon. He lay taut, wide-eyed, mouth agape. Logan recognized the face and turned away and vomited. Bob pulled his bandanna over his nose.

Ezra dismounted and pulled an arrow from one of the dead Pawnee. The shaft separated from the barbed head. He counted aloud the three turkey feathers used for fletching.

Bob nodded grimly. "Lord have mercy. Comanche. Yap Eaters prob'ly." He looked at Logan who was still on his knees. "We ain't seen no Indians on these plains in two years. Why the Pawnee has been whipped for twenty years and the Yap Eaters s'posed to be on the reservation." He lowered his bandanna and spat then bit off a chew of tobacco. "I ain't worried about an Indian since I don't know when. I know one damn thing. If I was a Pawnee, I'd face the army and every Sioux in Dakota 'fore I'd set foot in Comancheria."

Logan resumed his retching. He wished Bob and Ezra would conjecture elsewhere. He had not bargained for this. He had hired on to skin buffalo and spread the Word westward. His stomach calmed slightly. He struggled to his feet and looked about, avoiding the faces of the dead. Bob and Ezra, evidently impervious to the carnage, continued their discussion on the improbability of encountering hostile Indians on the Kansas plains in 1873. The mules were gone. Something protruded from beneath a dead horse. Logan walked unsteadily to the carcass and with considerable effort drew a heavy rifle from a parfleche scabbard.

Ezra gave a low whistle. "By god, Bob, that's a Ballard."

Logan studied his find. The gun had exquisite checkering on the Circassian stock and beautiful bluing on the barrel and receiver. On the stock the savage had carved hourglass figures and diamonds and a rude impression of some hoofed creature with outsized spiraled horns. A shriveled scalp dangled at the end of a rawhide string tied to the forend.

Ezra rubbed his beard. "Well sir, I'd say you just moved up a notch." They searched but found no cartridges.

"Don't matter," Bob said. "It shoots 45-70. That's what we're carryin'." Bob rubbed the stock with callused fingers. "This was somebody's baby one time. I bet he don't need it now though." He froze. "Romack! Lawd! We forgot all about him!"

Bob and Ezra mounted their horses. Logan climbed on behind Bob. Ezra shook his head. "We never shoulda left Earl by hisself. I never thought about Indians."

As they rode, Logan looked over the top of Bob's hat. He smelled the sweat in it. The two of them probably weighed barely more than massive Ezra Higginbotham who stood nearly a head taller than Logan. Little wonder, Logan thought, Ezra's tall gelding could not pull away from Bob's scruffy little mare.

They came to the creek and rode east along the bottom. In seconds, the plains had changed forever in Logan's eyes from a desolate but benign place to a malevolent place where death came suddenly and horribly. He had known about slight Indian danger, but had worried little about it. The Kansas plains had been relatively safe for some years; the real danger, he had been told, lay westward in Texas.

Logan had never contemplated such savagery. He had heard the stories but had not taken them to heart. The Pawnee that killed Muntz attacked with an animal fury like mongrel dogs killing a ground hog, or wolves pulling down an antelope or hounds tearing a raccoon to pieces. The man attacked with an abandon Logan had never seen among men. And the dead; he had seen cadavers in caskets back in Kentucky. But they looked serene. Their countenances lacked the horror and pain so evident on the faces of Krebs and the Pawnee.

They rode for half an hour. They topped a low rise and saw Romack in the middle of camp, calmly bundling dry hides.

"Stole my goddamn mules!" Bob Durham yelled to nobody in particular.

CHAPTER 8

In the close air of the council lodge, Cuts Something made his case: the Wanderers should leave at once for the red canyons. There, they could acquire enough meat to take them comfortably through the hungry time. Then they could move back to their beloved Pease River brakes for the winter. The *tahbay-boh* would not pursue them so deeply into Comanchería in the dead of winter. After the hungry time, the People should replenish their supply of meat then join Quanah on the Llano. The Honey Eaters and Yap Eaters, after hearing of the Wanderers' daring, could then be induced to join them. Perhaps even the Buffalo Eaters would move from the sandhills along the Canadian to the high flat plains where the soldiers die of thirst and even the Rangers rarely ventured. There the People could make a stand; they could strike the Utes to the northwest and the mountain settlements to the southwest. Bison blackened the Llano; the People could live there forever. From their new home, they could sweep down upon the settlements, take captives and loot and drive the miserable Texans back into the pine forests as they had done before. The People could strike quickly then ride hard back to the Llano where only they could live in comfort. Once the settlement line had been driven sufficiently eastward, the People could again safely take their old war trails into Mexico.

To understand the alternative, he said, one need only consider the red men who had thus far cooperated with the *tahbay-boh*. The Cherokee, the Choctaw, the Chickasaw. Reduced to breaking the ground and walking behind farting mules. Was this to be the People's fate? He would gladly die first. To survive, the People must fight ferociously and move quickly. They must be prepared to move to remoter country.

The council, six elders in addition to Cuts Something and That's It, sat and listened gravely. Younger, less significant warriors stood silently behind them. That's It occasionally nodded in agreement with his friend's assertions. Cuts Something's vision had been vivid and explicit. That was enough. One by one the other elders agreed; all except Hears the Sunset, always the most cautious of the elders.

"I believe we should send forth scouts before we risk such a move," he said. Only his mouth and gnarled index fingers moved when he spoke in council.

"That would be a waste of four days," Cuts Something answered. "The bison are there. I saw them."

The old man sat in silence. They all sat in silence. Two hours later Cuts Something said, "We can send Otter Belt."

The young man's eyes widened for an instant. He said nothing. Hears the Sunset nodded. "He should go at once. Short Lance should go with him."

One by one the elders rose stiffly and shuffled out. Only Cuts Something remained. At length, That's It returned. "Why are you still here?"

Cuts Something did not look at him. "I cannot feel my legs. Will you help me?"

Cuts Something had recently taken an interest in arrow making. He still relied heavily on his bow despite the availability of good rifles — from Comanchero traders or the white agents who believed the People needed guns for hunting. The *tahbay-boh* agents' stupidity amazed him. The younger Comanche warriors raided with repeating rifles issued by the *tahbay-boh* while the soldiers got by with single-shot carbines.

He did not continue to rely on his bow because he did not approve of firearms. That's It and Otter Belt shot quite well whenever either had a rifle. But his own failing eyesight did not allow him to take advantage of a rifle's superior range and the sight adjustment vexed him endlessly. The rifles seemed to fail at inopportune times. Lay one down in the sand and it would likely be useless thereafter.

His keen interest in a craft normally relegated to old men appalled She Invites Her Sisters. He could not argue with her. The People's arrows had always been made by warriors too elderly to ride and fight. Yet after watching the old men and asking questions — there were few matters pertaining to hunting and fighting that did not interest him — he found himself actually making an arrow under the patient tutelage of his talkative, disheveled old warrior friend Sees How Far It Is. After he worked bison brains and grease into the straight-grained dogwood and ash and hickory shafts and drew them through notched stone plates to straighten them, carefully fitted the iron points and glued on the turkey feather fletching, he wondered how he could have used such graceful weapons for so many years while giving no thought to their origin.

On horseback, hunting or visiting neighboring encampments, he remained watchful for shaft material and lamented the People's meager reservation and the ever dwindling supply of suitable wood. He wondered: how would the People make arrows after all of the good wood had been cut? Where would they get their lodge poles?

Cuts Something took great pleasure in the pile of curing shafts accumulating against the inner wall of his lodge. At times he would pick up a particularly fine specimen and hold it before his true eye, sight down its length and keenly anticipate the finished product. He often took his finished arrows from his quivers and ran his fingers along the smooth shafts, fingered and admired the integrity of the wrappings and ran the fletching across his cheeks and lips. That's It helped him find suitable material and had begun wistfully eyeing the pile of curing shafts.

When he did not carry his weapons — bow, quiver, arrows, lance and battle ax — he kept them arranged just so against his lodge wall. He often found himself sitting on his stack of buffalo robes enjoying the look and symmetry of his weapons. He wanted to prop his shield alongside his weapons, but he kept it hidden in the brush nearly a mile from camp; the touch of a menstruating woman or a single splotch of grease would destroy the shield's power.

As far back as he could remember, the People had used metal arrow heads, either bartered ready-made from Comancheros or pounded from wagon wheels or from copper or cast iron cooking vessels. Sees How Far It Is told him that the People had once used stone tips that cut a more awful wound channel than did the smooth iron points, and that if someone would bring him a suitable piece of chert he would show Cuts Something how to make stone arrowheads. Cuts Something resolved to look into the matter at the first opportunity.

For the time being, however, there were hunting preparations to make. He knew that Otter Belt and Short Lance would return with news of a vast bison herd in the canyon country. He reminded himself that he had better finish a few more arrows before they moved camp.

Although he ate, drank and slept well, his buffalo dreams continued. The wheeling raven. Bison pouring off the caprock. The bulls disappearing on the plain behind the wall of sleet. He knew the bison were there. Still, he watched the sky for ravens. He would have liked to have seen a raven flying in the direction of the red canyons.

Otter Belt and Short Lance returned after four days. They reported bison in number exceeding any the People had ever known. The beasts were congregated on the eastern edge of the high plains and in the red canyons. Acutely aware of the many pairs of eyes upon him, Cuts Something listened to the news, and said nothing.

Late morning, a crier rode through the encampment to announce the news and the impending move. Mothers, small children, desiccated hags and decrepit old warriors, some of them in absurd reservation clothing, emerged from their lodges. Within minutes, the women had collapsed most of the lodges and boys had gathered dozens of mules for loading. Warriors huddled in groups, talking and nodding grimly, while women and older children and gelded Mexican slaves hurried about with stacks of buffalo robes and cooking implements and lodge poles. The camp dogs howled and bustled about excitedly.

An hour later, the Wanderers, four hundred strong, headed southwest toward the Red River. They formed a shifting column a half mile long, horses and mules and mongrel dogs, women riding mules and leading pack animals, mothers laden with infants constrained tightly on pack boards, boys driving the remuda — some eleven hundred horses — and naked children tied to their mounts and warriors ranging miles in advance. Lodge poles now formed heavily-loaded travois or made panniers, carrying baskets loaded with small children and puppies.

On the second day after their departure, the People crossed the Prairie Dog Fork of the Little Red. The horses and the mules struggled mightily in the loose sand and the puppies whimpered pitifully when the water invaded their baskets. The warriors shot their arrows across the river then carefully gathered them upon crossing. They rode on, southwest, for the South Prong of the Little Red. On the fifth day they encamped on a midgrass plain that lay between a deep red gorge to the east and the red scarp canyons immediately below the edge of the caprock.

They saw bison in the distance, grazing in the brakes. Warriors rode away to scout their approach. Boys drove the remuda into a side canyon while the women raised lodge poles and stood one upon the shoulders of another to drape on the bison skin covers. Mexican slaves built meat scaffolds while stolen children, Mexican and white and native, under the watchful eyes and sharp admonitions of the Comanche women, ran about gathering firewood. Adolescent boys rode to canyon springs to fill buffalo paunches with sweet water.

After dark the lodges stretched a quarter mile across the plain, each lighted within by small warming fires. Near the center of the encampment, a large fire burned, and four drummers rhythmically pounded horsehide drums while women chanted a verse so old they did not know its origin; it had been with the People since before the Gift of the Horse.

The People danced not to deities but out of simple joy, secure in their knowledge and in their favored position in the eyes of the spirit protectors. They danced to exhaustion then rested and ate pemmican and drank sweet spring water and then danced again. The singers grew hoarse, and others replaced them. The Wanderers danced into the night. The children imitated their elders and the camp dogs howled and yipped at the commotion. Gradually, dancers drifted to their lodges leaving others humming softly. Each hunter picketed his favorite horse near his lodge. Wolves howled in the distant brakes. The camp dogs bristled and flared their nostrils and whined in response.

At daybreak, thirty Comanche hunters, naked save for breechclouts and fringed moccasins, sat their horses and watched the scattered bands of bison grazing on the plain before them and in the rough brakes beyond. The men rode bareback; some carried short bows; others carried six foot lances. None used a bridle. Each rider slipped his legs beneath a coil of braided rawhide rope wrapped just behind his horse's forelegs.

Cuts Something whooped and the hunters rode off the low rise. They rode low, gripping their horses' manes along with their weapons. They quickly closed to within a hundred yards of their quarry and the nearest bands began to wheel and run; a wave of panic moved forward through the herd toward the edge of the caprock. The hunters rode in among the trailing bison and selected their targets before the beasts could get up to speed. Using only knee pressure, the hunters turned their ponies and drew to within a few feet of their prey. Riding alongside the beasts, screaming, they nocked and shot arrows one after another. Antelope and mule deer flushed before the riders, who squinted and gagged against the billowing dust that covered their greasy braids and sweat-drenched bodies.

The enraged beasts, tails erect, with shreds of hair flying from dusty, ratty early autumn manes, tongues lolling, turned on their attackers, but at each *twang* of the bowstrings, the horses drew away without prompting to avoid the terrible short horns. Most of the arrows found their marks in the bisons' sides; some went clean through and into the ground; others went through one animal and into another. The lancers rode alongside their prey and drove their weapons down and in, behind the rear rib and into the soft organs.

Within minutes, dozens of bison lay dying. The hunters rode back through the dust to survey the killing field and to collect their arrows. Before they could begin the heavy butchering, the ever-attendant wolves moved closer, their nostrils lifted toward the smell of the fresh blood. The women, who had been watching from the hills, jabbered excitedly as they started toward the killing field. By the time the women arrived, the hunters were covered in gore and flies and had already quenched their thirsts with bison blood. The children gathered to beg for slices of warm liver seasoned with salty gall bladder fluid. Already the bison had regrouped and were grazing peacefully again.

Cuts Something sat in the shade of his brush arbor. For the moment, he worried very little about his stature among his people. Otter Belt's sneering had stopped the moment he saw the thousands of bison grazing the shortgrass plains. Even the old men admitted that they had never seen so many buffalo as they had seen earlier that day. Perhaps the spirits had reopened the hole in the ground whence the buffalo originally came and untold numbers poured out to help the People with their war against the *tahbay-boh*. Perhaps the Spirits had seen enough of the white conquest.

He reveled in the camp activity: the smoking and drying of bison meat on the scaffolds; the women feverishly scraping fat and residual flesh from the green hides; children running about with liver stained lips. Better yet, his two older wives had set Fast Girl to scraping hides and were presently scolding her for her sloppiness with the bone adz.

Cuts Something had already gorged on raw liver and a nice fatty chunk of hump meat roasted by She Invites Her Sisters. Later that night at the tongue dance, each hunter would recount his deeds. Cuts Something went over his own exploits and contemplated embellishments. He wondered how he would dance with the severe cramps in his thighs and lower back. He decided that he had grown quite soft riding about the reservation using bridle and stirrups.

He looked toward the distant scarps. Several of the old ones had told him that good chert could be found there. In earlier times, the People came to these canyons to gather flint with which to make their tools and weapon tips. Perhaps he would go there in a few days — after he had laid aside enough meat to see himself and his extended family through the hungry time. Perhaps there would be no hunger this time. The spirits had been benevolent; the badger's tenacity had prevailed once more. He wondered what sort of medicine his son would acquire. Coyote medicine, he hoped. Elk Rub would need that beast's cunning and resilience in the time ahead.

CHAPTER 9

Cuts Something retrieved his arrows from a half dozen dead bison and watched his son Elk Rub in the distance coursing an old bull. The low morning sun lighted the dew-soaked grass, and the breaths of horses and riders and bison hung about their heads. West of the plain, the rust colored scarps shone richly in the new light. The boy had already felled a pair of cows and had put several arrows into the bull, but the stubborn beast, although clearly tiring, continued to charge his antagonist between short rests. Now he stood watching the boy. Elk Rub maneuvered for a broadside shot. He drew his bow, and the bull lowered his head and charged forcing him to wheel his horse and sprint to safety.

That's It, the boy's mentor, shouted good natured barbs at his frustrated pupil who now resorted to circling and feinting to confuse the bull.

The three were out for a short hunt to provide meat for their elderly relatives. She Invites Her Sisters' thrice-widowed mother had visited Cuts Something the night before to ask for help, and That's It's two fathers-in-law were both too decrepit to hunt. Fast Girl's father, still a young and skillful hunter, needed no help. Cuts Something's second wife, Yellow Beads, had no surviving elders and in general was so little trouble compared to his other two wives that he tended to forget about her.

At length the bull began to stagger, and Elk Rub put another half dozen arrows into the beast's heart and lungs. The bull went down for good, and the boy wheeled his horse jauntily and made several passes before his father and uncle, shouting of his prowess and power on each pass. Cuts Something laughed and yelled that the hills would soon be denuded if Elk Rub needed so many arrows to kill a solitary old bull.

The boy reigned his horse to a stop, dusting the two older men thoroughly, then dismounted and drank nearly all of Cuts Something's water. Elk Rub was taller and more aquiline than his father, though not nearly so powerfully built. He returned the nearly empty paunch and wiped his mouth with the back of his hand. Father and uncle grunted their approval, then sent the boy to round up a contingent of women to help with the butchering.

Otter Belt brought news Cuts Something would have preferred to hear another time. The older man, exhausted from the morning hunt and heavy butchering, sat in the shade of his brush arbor. He could barely raise his pipe, and his lower back hurt so that he had ordered Yellow Beads to fashion a back rest of stacked hides.

Otter Belt and Short Lance had been scouting on the flat, high plain just beyond the canyons and had discovered a small band of white buffalo hunters camped in a shallow draw. The white men had good horses and many hides.

Cuts Something tapped the ashes from his pipe. "Why did you not kill them and take the hides and horses?"

"They are well armed. The risk was too great. We could go back with many warriors and take them easily."

Cuts Something nodded. He saw no reason to insult the young warrior, although he and That's It would have stolen the white men's horses and mules under the cover of darkness. Then they would have killed the men at their leisure. Any man afoot on the plains was vulnerable no matter how well armed he might be.

Cuts Something did not feel like riding a half day to kill a few buffalo hunters, yet he knew that if he did not take charge and lead a party against the white men, Otter Belt and others would assume that he was conceding author-ity. "Then you, That's It, Short Lance and I should leave before first light and ride against them tomorrow when the sun is just above the canyons. Do not send a crier to announce the raid. We need not take more warriors against so few white men."

Otter Belt looked disappointed. "Will we wear our paint?"

Cuts Something suppressed a smile. "We always wear our paint when we fight the whites."

Shortly before dawn, in the firelight in his lodge, Cuts Something looked over his weapons. For this task he would need his war arrows — arrows with barbed, loosely attached heads that remained in the enemy after the shafts were pulled away. One did not recover his war arrows as he did his hunting arrows. Cuts Something thought again of Sees How Far It Is' assertion that ragged flint heads cut a more terrible wound than did iron heads. He must not forget about that, he told himself. He set his hunting arrows aside and held up the antelope-skin quiver full of war arrows. He stroked the gleaming, reddish brown antelope hair and delighted in the symmetry of the turkey feather fletching protruding from the open end of the quiver.

She Invites Her Sisters brought in a rawhide sack of pemmican then left without speaking. She placed his buffalo paunch full of water just outside his lodge door. He had eaten very lightly just after he awoke. He would have enjoyed a breakfast of fresh ribs, but he did not want to feel bloated. More importantly, even a single drop of grease on a weapon could destroy its power.

He pulled the quiver strap over his head and arm, picked up his bow and provisions and stepped outside into the darkness. The sky was clear, the moon newly waxing; a light frost coated the lodge skins. Nevertheless he wore only breechclout, leggings, moccasins, and a heavy rawhide wristband to protect the inside of his arm from the bowstring. He secured his provisions on his war horse, picketed just outside his lodge. He then walked southward away from the silent camp, several hundred yards through the frosted grass and low scrub to the place where he had hidden his shield to protect it from grease and the touch of menstruating women. He pulled the shield from a shin oak motte, removed the rawhide cover and ran his fingers over the hardened horsehide and counted the six dangling scalps. He took a different route back to camp, approaching from upwind, which sent the camp dogs into such hysteria that they had to be quieted by gruff shouts and kicks.

That's It was waiting at Cuts Something's lodge. The two led their horses to the edge of camp where Otter Belt and Short Lance sat their horses, waiting. They rode southwest toward the scarp cányons, traversing the midgrass plain and then a cedar-studded badland. A faint, pink glow had formed behind them by the time they made the rough, eroded river brakes.

At dawn, they rode along a wide, sandy streambed bordered by steep red banks lined with hackberry, juniper, prickly pear and cholla interspersed in bunch grass. Turkeys flushed from roosts and deer snorted and crashed away through the scrub. They rode higher, picking their way along tenuous game trails and through narrow defiles and around talus-littered slopes. Cuts Something rode easily now, sweating lightly, his muscles loose. He was glad he had come.

The sun loomed directly overhead by the time they made the high, flat shortgrass plain and turned north riding along the edge of the caprock. Two miles further, they came to a slight drainage then rode west. Shortly, they heard the distant thump and roll of heavy rifles. They rode on. At length, they stopped and dismounted. Short Lance stayed with the horses while the other three climbed the low bank and looked westward. A quarter of a mile away, a thin column of smoke rose from a large swale.

The three slithered on their bellies through the shortgrass, breaking their profiles with low spots and clumps of yucca and sage, yet a pair of teal flushed from the weeds around a small playa. They stopped and waited, afraid to breathe. They heard nothing but the distant guns and birdsong. They crawled on. They came to the edge of the swale and saw below them two white men scraping and bundling hides. The two men worked steadily, never stopping to listen or to look around. Heavy rifles leaned against the wagon and both men had pistols shoved under their belts. The Comanches saw no one else. They hurried back to Short Lance and their horses.

The four warriors remained in hiding until late afternoon. They ate pemmican and sipped water from their water bags. They talked little. The distant gunfire ceased. When the sun was a hand's width above the horizon, they took their war paint from parfleche pouches and blackened their faces in various patterns: streaks, half white, half black; or completely black. Cuts Something diagrammed their approach in the dust. They emptied their bladders and waited.

Cuts Something watched the young warriors. They glanced nervously at one another and swallowed often. He knew what they were thinking and saying with their glances. This was real. All of their training, the hours of mock battle, all of their boasting and fantasizing had led to this moment. Any or all of them could be dead before dark. The time for talk had passed. Very shortly they would meet flesh and blood enemies at close range, enemies who would kill them if they could.

He knew what they were thinking when they glanced nervously, hopefully, at him, for he and That's It had looked the same upon Sees How Far It Is all those summers before in the rocky cedar brakes far to the south, moments before they struck a party of Tonkawas.

Cuts Something felt strong as he always did before a raid. His legs were springy; his arm and back muscles loose. The bow felt good in his hand — solid, substantial. Impending battle always had this effect on him. The mixture of fear and excitement cleared his head and focused his thinking so that his mind worked as easily as his muscles. He pictured the attack, the position of the wagon, the probable position of horses and men. He easily worked through contingencies. He simultaneously took in the sun's position and wind direction and noted the faint stench of distant carrion. He looked at That's It who was squatting, rocking on his heels. That's It met his gaze. There was no need for words. The two had always gone into battle together.

With the sun just touching the horizon they mounted and rode from their hiding place and, keeping low, looped westward around the white hunters' camp. Cuts Something dismounted and crawled away from the sun toward the camp then returned shortly holding up six fingers. They moved quietly to a shallow declivity just beyond the rim of the swale. Cuts Something rode over the rim and shot a skinner who stood next to the wagon; the man hit the ground before anyone in camp looked up. The Comanches rode into the camp, shooting arrows and hacking at men running for rifles. A filthy hunter with a sandy, matted, tobacco-stained beard hanging nearly to his waist ran out of camp and Short Lance put an arrow between his shoulder blades. The man fell forward, and as he regained his feet, the young Comanche rode by and grabbed his hair and cut his scalp away with a single, smooth motion. The man fell screaming and rolling only to be pinned to the ground by three more arrows through his abdomen.

Cuts Something shot two arrows into a man aiming a rifle at him and another into the neck of a hunter trying to mount a horse. Dead and dying white men littered the camp. The young Comanches screamed and slashed while the two older warriors calmly lifted scalps.

CHAPTER 10

"Well, his Daddy was a Methodist preacher," Ezra said in response to the astounded bartender's question. Logan had just spurned the advances of two aggressive whores. Although he considered the women outrageous trash, their explicit suggestion and ferine scent had him squirming in his chair and grinding his teeth. He had been hungry when he sat down; now he had little interest in his meal.

He had long since given up correcting Ezra. He had told him time and again that his father had not been a preacher, but a prominent layman blessed with the gift of healing power. The elder Fletcher had been known in Kentucky's southeastern highlands as Dr. Fletcher, although the title was no more in recognition of his faith healing ability than of his talent for pulling teeth and treating horses, mules and dogs with various medicines formed of honey, ginseng, bloodroot and mutton tallow. The tiny settlement of Fletcher, on the Elk Fork of Greasy Creek, had been named in honor of Dr. Fletcher who often pointed out how seldom places were named after the living.

Logan did not approve of saloons, but in Dodge City, any establishment that passed for an eatery also passed for a saloon. So he sat squirming and grinding his teeth and eating his bacon, fried potatoes and biscuits at a table behind Ezra who sat at the bar. The proprietor had sent a plate out to Bob, who ate sitting in the wagon whenever they visited anyplace populated by more than a half dozen white people. Logan found it odd that a successful business-man and noted plainsman and Indian fighter would bow to filthy, ignorant skinners who would gladly take direction from him in the wilds.

"You know what they say about preachers' daughters," the bartender said, still eyeing Logan with suspicion. Logan thought the comment absurd. What did daughters of preachers have to do with him? He finished his bacon.

Ezra drained his shot glass. "I wish me and Bob had five or six more just like him. A year from now there wouldn't be a buffalo left between the Brazos and the Milk River. Right now though, I'll take any fool that knows one end of a knife from the other."

Bob and Ezra wanted to leave forthwith for the Texas Panhandle. According to rumor, a local hide buyer named Myers was financing a hunting expedition to establish a camp at the adobe-walled ruins just north of the Canadian River. To date, he had nearly fifty men signed on and thirty wagons and adequate numbers of mules and horses at his disposal.

Bob reasoned that the Myers party would not start for the Canadian until early spring; no large party would head for the wilderness on the leading edge of winter. On the other hand, the hides would be in prime condition during the colder months; a small, mobile hunting party could get in and out quickly and make a fortune. But a party of fifty hunters encamped at Adobe Walls was sure to draw the attention and ire of the remaining wild Comanche and Kiowa.

Conventional wisdom held that Indian danger would be minimal during the winter. Ezra had assured Logan that the Antelope would winter well out on the Llano; the Buffalo Eaters might be a problem, but Comanches usually pre-ferred to lay up in one place during the winter. Yet cold weather posed prob-lems. The surgeon at Fort Dodge stayed busy the previous winter amputating the frostbitten hands and feet of underdressed buffalo hunters. When Logan voiced his concern, Bob shrugged and said nonchalantly, "We just have to wrap up."

Logan had harbored no thoughts of buffalo hunting, or, for that matter, a life on the Great Plains, when his dying father urged him to go west to spread the true Gospel. His father, Marcus Lewis Fletcher, had long held that the mes-sage had been corrupted by men and their various denominations and splinter groups. The Church, he asserted, should follow the Word, the Truth as it was written in the Book of Acts and in the Epistles. Anything else was man-made bastardization. The apostle Paul was quite clear and explicit.

Logan had always obeyed his father. Countless times he had watched Marcus Fletcher lay hands upon some wheezing or hemorrhaging person and recite the appropriate scripture and pray ardently to the Lord for mercy and healing. He had seen wounds clot and fevers break and not a few deaths, although according to Logan's own count, his father's successes far outweighed his failures.

Whenever Marcus Fletcher's efforts failed to save someone, Logan questioned, but his father held firm; people must die just as Logan's mother had died at age twenty-eight. She took sick with what everyone assumed was the summer sickness, but she never recovered. The fever and the vomiting worsened and despite all his father's efforts, she died in less than a week.

They buried her in the family cemetery, and Marcus Fletcher, tall, pale and unsteady in his dark coat and boiled shirt, told his son that again God's will had been carried out. The apostle Paul advised against encumbrances of the flesh lest a man become distracted from his Godly mission. His mission was to save souls and to heal the sick.

So they traveled afoot, Logan and his father, through the Kentucky mountains, sometimes alone, sometimes accompanied by the itinerant Methodist preacher Brother Ramsey. They ministered and witnessed, they chased lost souls, and his father healed the sick and comforted the bereaved. They hauled just enough logs to keep food in their bellies and a roof over their heads and devoted the rest of their waking hours to the Lord's work.

At first, Logan followed his father out of obedience; then shortly after his seventeenth birthday he went with his father to a camp meeting. Methodist and Baptist and Presbyterian came together on the mountain. He asked for the Spirit to enter. He prayed and wept beneath the brush arbor, and his neighbors joined and prayed him on to victory. At last he knew.

Two years later, his father sickened and could not heal himself. Lying in bed, unable to bear the weight of a sheet on his abdomen, he urged his only son—his only progeny—to sell the mules and wagon and head west to a clean slate where the Gospel could be taught as the Lord meant for it to be taught. Souls could be properly saved and a foothold gained before corrupting forces from the settled East arrived to fragment the Body and lure men away to blasphemy and idolatry, wicked lives and eternity in damnation and separation from the Father. They both knew that this was the end and the beginning, and his father prayed with him and bestowed upon him his gift and sent him west.

A week after his father's funeral, Logan walked out of the mountains and across the Kentucky farmland, eating and sleeping in the homes of believers and witnessing to unbelievers. He carried his Bible but had no occasion to use his newly acquired gift. He walked along the Kentucky River to its confluence with the Ohio. He walked on to Louisville where he worked at odd jobs until he had riverboat fare to Paducah. He sold his gun for more fare in Paducah, then traveled down the Ohio, then up the Mississippi toward the Missouri. A half day up the Missouri River, several emigrants became ill. Within two hours of the first symptoms, they were spewing vomitus like potato water and their skin shriveled horribly, and their eyes dulled and sank into their skulls. The others spoke of cholera and refused to come near the sick. They talked of abandoning the boat and of throwing the sick overboard.

Only Logan and a Baptist woman from Alabama and a Mormon emigrant named Robert Suggs nursed the sick. Two children died before Logan placed his hands on the forehead of an elderly woman and quoted from the Book of Ezekiel and prayed on the blood of the Lamb. He prayed for His tender mercy, and healing power. At first, Suggs and the Baptist woman stood back and watched him, but as the sickness spread they began calling him to the sickest. They tended the ailing through the first night and all of the next day. During the second night of the sickness, Suggs shook Logan awake and took him to see a small boy with red eye. By the time Logan stepped off the boat in Independence, three had died and eight were recovering.

Thus far on the plains no one had shown the slightest interest in his evangelism or healing gift. Krebs and Muntz, two souls lost forever, had looked at him stupidly and then laughed at his efforts at leading them to salvation. He had been ridiculed by teamsters and hunters in Salina. It had been so different in Kentucky where even the wicked knew of his father and Brother Ramsey. Even the worst men seemed hesitant to laugh in the face of an ordained minister — as if hell had an underbelly awaiting heathens who mocked God's official servants.

Logan saw no way to carry out his mission in the immediate future. The plains were unready for the Message. Some level of civilization seemed necessary. He looked across the room at two skinners each trying to be the first to pull a louse from his person. The two whores watched intently. Perhaps, he thought, his job for now was to help civilization along. According to Ezra, the plains would be wiped clean of bison within five years. The railroad had already come to Dodge City. He could return to the settlements, of course, but, undoubtedly, they were already under corrupting influences. But as soon as the bison were gone, and the Indians were subdued, the emigrant families would stream onto the plains starving for spiritual comfort, and he could be waiting. It appeared that the Lord had provided him with a rifle.

He drank his coffee and thought of the Pawnee attack. For reasons he could not recall, he had left his Bible in camp with Romack that morning. Normally, he carried it under the seat of the kill wagon so that he could read it during the times when they were waiting for Bob and Ezra to finish a killing field. After the massacre, Bob told him that had the Comanches gotten hold of his Bible they would have stuffed a war shield with its pages. Logan shuddered at the thought of meeting a savage who carried a shield lined with the Word of God.

CHAPTER 11

Cuts Something and Sees How Far It Is heaved the large, flat piece of chert into the hot coals, then sat down and smoked their pipes. Cuts Something had found the two-foot by three-foot slab halfway up a sloping canyon wall. With great effort, he had carried, pushed and rolled it down the slope, breaking off fragments all the way. He then dragged it back to camp on a travois.

They watched the heating flint. They were refilling their pipes with Comanchero tobacco when chips began breaking off the edges of the hot slab. Sees How Far It Is retrieved them with a green cottonwood stick. The two men selected the chips that could be most readily fashioned onto arrowheads. When they had a half dozen candidates, they pried the slab out of the fire.

Under Sees How Far It Is's direction, Cuts Something placed one of the chips back on the glowing coals. Sees How Far It Is brought a bowl of cold water from the shade beside his lodge. After the flake heated for a few minutes, Cuts Something quickly retrieved it with two sticks and placed it on the flat side of a split cottonwood limb. Sees How Far It Is wetted a swath of buckskin in the cold water, then rolled it into a palm-sized cylinder. He squeezed a drop of water onto the hot flint. A small flake the size of the water drop broke away with a slight pop.

He misplaced the next drop, and the chip broke in the middle. They heated another and the older man chipped away at this piece until he had fashioned a crude, narrow triangle. They threw another chip into the fire and repeated the process. Cuts Something watched with great interest. At times, Sees How Far It Is tilted the flint with a small thin stick so that the water drops struck at an angle thereby forming a cutting edge. He made several heads in this fashion.

After the points cooled, the older man selected the most promising and held it up for examination. He laughed. "It is a bad point, but you saw how I made it. I never was skilled at flint work."

Cuts Something *had* seen how it was done, and turning the point over in his palm and feeling the jagged yet sharp edge, he saw quite clearly how such a point would make a terrible wound. He would return to the canyon and drag back many slabs of flint which could be hauled to their winter camp on the Pease. What a fine way to spend the winter months, he thought. For now, though, he simply had to try this himself. He squatted and looked closely at the flint fragments, determined to pick just the right one.

Cuts Something had heard the stories, but had never taken them seriously. Yet on the ground before him were leg bones of a beast many times larger than any he had ever seen. Moreover, they appeared to be the front leg bones of a huge buffalo. An Antelope woman told him once of huge, grotesque skulls of unknown beasts found at a blowout on the Llano; perhaps these bones were of the same origin. A boy, Yellow Dog, had found the leg bones among the rubble at the mouth of a dry creek. Cuts Something had been consulted immediately. He found himself at a complete loss. The thought of his country peopled with hunters who could take such huge game shook him.

He carefully examined the brittle bones. The People had used these canyons for generations; he remembered no talk of other hunters — other than the white hunters who seemed to become more numerous daily. Still, he wondered what sort of hunter could kill such a beast. None, perhaps. He decided to look into the matter further. Rumors were flying. Otter Belt and Short Lance, both still swaggering from their first raid against the whites, talked of leading a hunting party in pursuit of giant buffalo. The ever pragmatic women were frightening their children into compliance with tales of Cannibal Owl.

Cuts Something pretended to give the matter little weight. Shortly, after interrogating Yellow Dog as to the exact location of his find, Cuts Something and That's It rode out of camp, purportedly in search of chert. Once out of view, they turned southwest and rode directly to the mouth of the creek where the boy had found the huge bones.

They rode into the canyon and into a riverine woodland. Copses of cottonwood and hackberry, willow and plum were spread about the benches of little bluestem and Indian grass. Above the creek bed, reddish-brown scarps rose hundreds of feet in layers of red mudstone, sandstone and caliche. Further up the creek, toward the head of the canyon, vegetation thinned and isolated junipers clung tenaciously to the slopes.

They dismounted and walked among the rubble that had washed out of the canyon over the eons. Neither man had the slightest idea where to begin or what to look for. They cast about and found nothing. That's It mentioned that there should be deer about.

"We need to see if there are more bones," Cuts Something said. "Perhaps these giant animals come only at certain times. If the spirits were to tell us when they come, we could come and kill them."

"Kill them with what?"

"We have the guns of the white hunters now."

"I do not think any man could kill a beast whose bones are so big. White men could not kill such a big buffalo."

"Perhaps these animals could be driven off the edge of a canyon."

"I do not think they would run from us."

Cuts Something found his friend's pessimism tiresome. If the huge beasts would not run from hunters, then they might run from fire. He walked back to the location described by Yellow Dog. An intermittent creek, now dry, had carved a steep, head-high channel. He walked slowly downstream, keeping his eyes on the ground. He found nothing and walked back to the horses. That's It took a long pull from the water bag and offered the bag to Cuts Something who drank copiously. "There must be more bones," Cuts Something said.

That's It tied the water bag to his saddle. "Maybe wolves carried the bones away. We should look for a deer, I think."

Cuts something did not reply; he mounted his horse. They rode again toward the mouth of the creek. A palm-sized piece of flint caught his eye. He rode back to look at it. It seemed well-shaped for making several arrow heads. He dismounted and picked and dug at it with difficulty as it was partially buried in the sand. He pulled it free then gasped at what he saw. The piece was much longer than he had thought; someone had worked it into a near perfect spear point larger than his hand.

His voice, much higher than normal, quavered when he yelled to That's It. His hands trembled as he turned it over and over and ran his finger over the smooth flutes cut expertly for mounting to a shaft, and the exquisite edge work.

At first, That's It did not realize what he looking at. Then his eyes widened. This was powerful medicine; good or bad, they did not know. "The People used to hunt and fight with stone tipped lances," That's It said. "Perhaps one of our Old Ones made it."

"It is too big. I think it was made by the people who hunt the giant buffalo. I hope they are not still here."

Sees How Far It Is said that he had never seen such exquisite flint work. He did not think such work could be done using the People's method. The medicine man Hears the Sunset said that the People should leave at once. "There are surely bad spirits in the canyons," he said. "Spirits of giant hunters and beasts. What if these hunters return?"

Cuts Something had little regard for the old man's dramatics. He considered their recent good fortune. "Perhaps these spirits guard the buffalo herds. Perhaps these are the spirits that gave me direction and told me to come to this place. Have you ever seen so many buffalo?"

The older men sat in silence. The younger warriors stood behind them, just outside the circle. At length, Sees How Far It Is Spoke. "The hunters who made this spear head will not return. They are gone. An Apache slave who belonged to my grandfather used to tell stories of hunters who came before the buffalo came from the great cavern. These men hunted huge beasts with lances."

"Why would anyone listen to an Apache?" Otter Belt snapped. The older men glared at the young man's rudeness. Otter Belt swallowed and looked at his feet. One did not interrupt a speaker in council, and young men were expected to remain silent so that they could learn from the experienced warriors.

Sees How Far It Is accepted the indirect apology and continued. "Have you forgotten the stories? Who was here before the People came down from the mountains to take the plains and the buffalo for themselves?" He waited. The older warriors looked at the young men to see which of them would respond. None answered. Sees How Far It Is continued. "The Apaches were here. Who can say how long they had been here before the People drove them into the desert?" He glared again at the young warriors.

Cuts Something hefted the spear point then passed it to That's it who did the same. The men passed the spear head around the lodge, and all admired except Hears the Sunset who refused to touch it.

"You should make a lance with it," That's It said. Sees How Far It Is obviously considered the matter settled; he began preparing a pipe. The young men speculated among themselves as to the potential power of the huge spear head. Hears the Sunset left abruptly without partaking of the pipe. After the pipe had been passed, Cuts Something, That's It and Sees How Far It Is conferred quietly. What else, they wondered, waited in the canyons to be used by clever warriors?

Cuts Something sat beneath his brush arbor watching his son approaching through the encampment. He had been expecting this. That's It had warned him the afternoon before. The boy stopped at a respectful distance and sat before his father. Cuts Something nodded pleasantly.

"I am ready to seek my medicine," Elk Rub said. "What do you think of that?"

Cuts Something had already given the matter considerable thought. The boy was only fifteen summers, but he had taken a respectable number of buffalo since they arrived at the canyons. Cuts Something thought his son quite undisciplined in his use of arrows, however. He had spoken to That's It of his concerns, and the boy had recently shown much improvement.

"You are young still. You think you are ready to face Maddox's soldiers? Or the Texans? They will not ride around in circles and wait for you to shoot a quiver of arrows into them. The Texans have already killed many fine warriors — some of them were better with weapons than you are." Elk Rub looked away. Cuts Something knew his comment cut deeply. But the boy's age concerned him.

"I have learned much about the bow. I'm better now. Do you think you would sire a son who is afraid to meet any enemy?"

Cuts Something laughed and slapped his thighs.

"I think I should ride into the canyons today."

Cuts Something looked affectionately at his son. "No. You should hunt more. No one can remember when the hunting was as good as it is now. We will be leaving soon for our winter camp on the Pease. When the air warms again, you can go to the mesa and find your medicine. The spirits have never failed me there. I do not know about these canyons."

The boy started to argue, then stopped.

"Think of this," Cuts Something said. "Now we have enough buffalo to take us through the hungry time. We do not have time to strike the Utes or the Texans. But in the spring! Then you young men will be able to prove yourselves. We will join Quanah on the Llano. The soldiers die of thirst there."

At that, the boy nodded then stood and walked to his lodge. Cuts Something hated deceiving the boy. He did not think they would be riding on the Utes or the Texans in the spring. They would do well to get through the hungry time and join Quanah before the buffalo soldiers started their summer campaigns. But the boy needed something to look forward to.

He stuffed his pipe. He enjoyed his son immensely. He wished he had more sons, but one had been stillborn and then She Invites Her Sisters and Yellow Beads each had born him a daughter. Daughters were fine; when his married, the grooms' gifts of horses had made up somewhat for his lack of respect for the grooms. Fast Girl had yet to bear him a child, and his older wives often encouraged him to take a fourth wife to increase his chances for another son. A warrior of his stature could certainly take a fourth wife, a young one at that.

After considering his current wives' bedevilment he had decided against taking another. The three women quarreled and complained incessantly, and Fast Girl usually instigated the conflict. Life had been so much simpler without her. But she was winsome and much desired by all the other warriors; he took her because he could.

As it turned out, the girl pleased him very little and until recently she had the maddening habit of chattering and laughing during coupling. Cuts Something found the practice outrageous and distracting. He had never heard of such behavior. Worse yet, he found her unresponsive and totally lacking in skills of the flesh. When he complained to She Invites Her Sisters and Yellow Beads, the two women listened knowingly then dashed away to lecture the upstart. He did not know what they said to the girl but her coupling skills improved immediately. Still, he found her much less desirable than his favorite, She Invites Her Sisters. In fact, as long as Fast Girl stayed out of trouble, he could pass several days without thinking about her.

He watched the women and boys riding out of the distant canyons, leading horses pulling travois loaded with green juniper to be used as lodge poles. Already, dozens of poles had been cut, trimmed and peeled and laid in the sun to harden. He thought with satisfaction that the red canyons provided not only meat, but the bones of tall juniper for lodge poles and lances. He needed to cut some poles before they left for their winter camp. His current poles were so worn from being dragged behind horses that his buffalo-skin lodge cover gathered on the ground. Yellow Beads, the most fastidious of his wives, had lately complained that the worn poles were an embarrassment.

He would cut poles soon enough. Or send the women to cut them. First he needed more buffalo meat and hides. The Comancheros always wanted hides, and the women badly needed needles and the warriors wanted guns and ammunition. They had the white buffalo hunters' guns now, but no ammunition. Otter Belt and Short Lance had set fire to the hunters' wagons before they gathered the ammunition; the result had been spectacular though quite unnerving.

The sun was high, and air warm for a late fall day. A light breeze blew through the arbor, cooling him pleasantly. His back and thighs felt much better. The humiliation of reservation life seemed a distant memory or some vague dream. He leaned back against his stack of hides and slept.

Cuts Something was glad they had ridden to the flat shortgrass plain to hunt. He enjoyed the hunting here more than he did on the rolling midgrass prairie near camp. The country was less broken; a hunter could ride flat out with little worry of the nasty falls that were all too common in the brakes. Packing the meat back to camp would take considerable effort, but he, That's It, Short Lance and Otter Belt had brought some of their wives and extra horses and mules to help with the task.

He watched Elk Rub work another bison that bristled with poorly placed arrows. Were it not for the boy's riding ability, some bull would have long since disemboweled his horse. Perhaps two springs from now, Cuts Something thought.

The bison were scattered in small bands of a dozen or so animals. Some of the bands were on the move; others, especially those upwind of the hunters, grazed placidly. Many bison still poured down the canyon trails to the east. Cuts Something knew that all the multitudes could be gone in a few days. As a boy, he often watched herds move by for days at a time. The People would stand atop promontories and swear that the herd stretched to the ends of the world. They would hunt constantly and gorge themselves for they always knew that the beasts would eventually vanish. At night they would listen to the herd splashing across the Pease and then one morning they would rise and there would not be a single bison in sight. Riders would leave camp and search in vain in all directions. Some of the elders believed the bison returned to their hole in the earth. How else could so many animals vanish without leaving a wide, clear trail?

Elk Rub finally killed the bull and started toward another band. Cuts Something rode alongside. "Go back and get some of your arrows. Your quiver is empty."

The boy grabbed his quiver. "Ah!" He peeled off and went back for his arrows.

"Maybe you should hunt with a lance," Cuts Something shouted. The boy either ignored him or did not hear him. Cuts Something assumed the former. The boy could ride though.

That's It caught up with him. "Where is Elk Rub?"

"He is getting his arrows. He was trying to hunt without them."

That's It had been drinking from his water bag. He laughed and gagged and spat out a mouthful of water. "He always shoots deer in the heart. I tell him to shoot every day. The buffalo excite him too much. He is still a boy."

The five hunters had fourteen bison down. "We need to get the women," Cuts Something said. They started for their temporary hunting camp near the edge of the caprock. The three young Comanches fell in behind them. As they rode, bands of bison scattered and regrouped then stood watching and sniffing. Wolves sat on their haunches in the distance, tongues aloll, waiting. Vultures gathered in garrulous flocks.

They rode toward their camp. On the horizon before them, the dark irregularities of the caprock brakes rolled away to the east. Laughing and shouting above a stiff wind, they descended a gentle swale and rode headlong into a party of seven white buffalo hunters.

Cuts Something tried to turn his horse to favor his bow arm, but Short Lance, riding up from behind, had not yet seen the white men; he slammed broadside into Cuts Something. Both horses went down. Cuts Something fell free and rolled to get up. The fall knocked his breath away; panic seized him as he tried simultaneously to breathe and to grab his bow. Both horses quickly regained their feet. As Short Lance rolled to get up, the white man driving the wagon drew a revolver and shot the young warrior through the chest.

Curses flew in three tongues; horses reared and bucked. As Cuts Something wrapped his fingers around his bow, the big rifles spoke, and he felt the shock waves, and spumes of dust flew up near his feet and on the rise behind him. He grabbed an arrow and saw Elk Rub, still on horseback, nock an arrow and shoot the man in the wagon seat through the clavicle. The man lurched and clawed at the arrow and fell forward into the mules. Cuts Something nocked his arrow and searched frantically for a target. Otter Belt and That's It screamed and shot arrows, but the white men had dismounted and taken cover behind the horses and wagons.

Arrows bristled from the sides of horses, mules and wagons; some of the white men shot huge revolvers while others fired and reloaded single-shot rifles. Cuts Something dropped to one knee and shot beneath the wagon, taking one of the hunters in the groin. He yelled at Elk Rub to get away. The boy shot another arrow then vanished from his horse's back as the thunder of another volley rolled over the grass.

Cuts Something's horse had fled. Short Lance lay on his side, blood gurgling from his nose and mouth. Cuts Something scrambled toward his son's horse, but another volley knocked it down sending a plume of dust into his eyes. He leapt to his right and rolled up and out of the swale. Someone grabbed his arm, then Otter Belt shouted, "Get on!" By feel alone, he mounted the horse behind the young warrior then blinked his eyes free of dust in time to see That's It riding by the far side of the wagon, behind the white hunters. That's It leaned to his horse's lee side and shot two arrows under its neck and into the backs of two white men. The three others scrambled under the wagon.

"The boy is still down there!" Cuts Something screamed.

"He is dead; I could put my arm through the hole in his chest. We cannot get to him; they will kill us for sure."

Cuts Something thought of his son's body; if the white men scalped the boy, he would not be allowed into the spirit world. Cuts Something's tears fell onto Otter Belt's back. They rode out of rifle range. They saw That's It, a speck on the horizon now, circling to join them.

Cuts Something had been sure that Yellow Beads had wailed at the top of her lungs the entire trip back from the Llano. Yet when she came within earshot of the main encampment, her wails rose to a level the men would have sworn was impossible. Elk Rub was the son of She Invites Her Sisters.

They rode into camp; an explanation was unnecessary. The People came out of their lodges and wails and curses went up and set the camp dogs to howling. So great was the din that Cuts Something had to scream his intentions to raise a war party to kill and skin the white men and recover the bodies of Elk Rub and Short Lance. Already more than a dozen warriors had gathered their weapons and sent their women to fetch war horses.

Cuts Something did not go into the lodge of She Invites Her Sisters. He heard her shrieks well enough and knew that she was already slashing with a knife at her bare breasts and thighs. He had recovered his horse, but sent Fast Girl to fetch a fresh one. He ran to retrieve his shield. He had no time to make medicine or seek visions. If the People were to recover the bodies of their dead warriors, they would do it tomorrow or not at all, for the wolves worked quickly; and he did not believe the white men would bother to bury dead Comanches.

Just after midnight some twenty Comanche warriors rode out of camp, westward toward the canyons and the Staked Plains beyond.

CHAPTER 12

From Logan Fletcher's perspective, the week was passing much too quickly. In two days, he, Bob, Ezra, Romack and whoever else they could round up to help with the skinning chores would be heading southwest for the Texas Panhandle. Logan felt that with each passing day another heavy blanket of dread was spread over him, and that any day now, he would suffocate under the accumulated layers.

At night he slept beneath Romack's wagon. Even with its constant drunken raillery and nightly cuttings, Dodge City felt like a sanctuary. From where he lay, propped up on his well-used but newly purchased saddle, he could look beyond his feet, down the muddy main road to the open prairie. Evil and death lurked out there. Evil and horrible death. Quick death, if you were lucky — like Muntz.

Sometimes, Logan's dread overcame him so that he could not look beyond his feet, and he felt exposed with them near the edge of the wagon. Then he would curl up with his rifle beneath his blankets and the two buffalo robes Bob and Ezra had given him. Even the sporadic pistol fire and shouted curses were reassuring. Most nights he did not fall asleep until after Bob returned slightly drunk after midnight and crawled into the wagon with comic effort at quietness, only to lapse immediately into thunderous snoring. Logan welcomed the noise and would then stretch his legs and fall asleep.

Romack disappeared the moment they rode into Dodge City. Ezra and Bob seemed completely unconcerned. Ezra purportedly had taken a room, although Logan could not imagine where in Dodge City one might find accommodations. As far as he could see, most visitors slept drunk in ditches or along whatever passed for walkways and alleys. In regard to Ezra, Logan suspected some manner of fornication, but tried to push the thought from his mind. *If there be any virtue and if there be any praise, think on these things,* he reminded himself.

Despite his terror, Ezra and Bob seemed to take him seriously, which made him all the more drawn to them. Logan feared insignificance nearly as much as he feared Indians. His employers suffered fools poorly, whereas they seemed to listen intently to his concerns and opinions. Even when they disagreed with him, they rarely dismissed his ideas without careful explanation.

They did not treat him as an equal; the employer to employee relationship remained intact. Still, he found their apparent confidence in him surprising. From the day he acquired his rifle, which he had not yet shot, Bob and Ezra had advised him casually on the care of his weapons, ammunition selection and reloading, the management of lumpen skinners, hide buyer dealings — all as if it were a foregone conclusion that he would soon litter the prairie with hundreds of bison carcasses.

To his utter amazement, Bob sent him with a rough budget to buy two span of mules and the needed tack, telling him, one mule man to another, that although Ezra knew horses, he could not be counted on for sound judgment on the procurement of mules. Logan spent the better part of two days looking at mules and haggling with traders. He finally settled on two span owned by a trader named Wicker, who stayed so drunk he could rarely remember a price he had quoted fifteen minutes earlier. Nor could he follow the simplest arithmetic. At first, Logan could not imagine how the man managed a living; then he considered the average Dodge City customer. After several frustrating attempts at establishing a price, Logan convinced Wicker to carve all quotes onto a keg full of salted tongues. Logan bought the two span for sixty dollars only to discover that Bob and Ezra had in the meantime purchased a huge metal-lined Conestoga wagon from Myers and now needed another three span to pull it.

Powder, lead, jerked meat, sugar, flour, corn meal. Logan watched the accumulation with satisfaction and excitement during the day and pondered it with dread at night. He envied Bob and Ezra; they were seasoned plainsmen. They understood the upcoming danger, he supposed, but felt up to it. He wondered how they felt at night, alone.

Two nights before their departure, he awoke with a feeling of dread bordering on panic. He peered through the spokes of the wagon wheel at the night sky. He wanted to sob. Bob snored above him. So this was manhood? He prayed for protection until tears streamed down his face. He wanted to be home in Kentucky, lying on his feather mattress, listening to his father's snores. Throughout his boyhood, he had yearned for manhood and competence. Now, he was about to ride into Indian country with three men he had known for barely a month.

He thought of the scalped Pawnees and of Muntz and Krebs. He had fought many times with his fists, but always the objective had been to end the fight quickly by bloodying an opponent's nose or mouth. On these plains, fights ended with gruesome death. He felt certain the Pawnee that killed Muntz could have torn him to pieces with his bare hands.

Yet another breed of red men — three or four of them, Ezra estimated — had annihilated the six Pawnees. These were the most feared Indians on the Southern Plains. In a few days, he would be riding into this people's stronghold. He wondered how this could be the Lord's plan for him. Yet everything had lead directly to this point, it seemed. Surely he had not survived the Pawnee attack in order to retreat to the settlements.

He prayed again for strength, wisdom and protection. The wind stirred dust in the street. He drew his legs up as tightly as he could, and pulled a buffalo robe over his head.

Cuts Something and his warriors found the white hunters' camp, and to their dismay, many campfires. The small group Cuts Something and the others encountered the day before evidently had been part of a much larger group, although Cuts Something cautioned the younger warriors that the whites might have built the many fires to deceive the People. That's It wanted to try for their horses then attack at sunup. Then Otter Belt returned and reported that there was indeed a substantial force of well armed and alert white men at the camp. Worse yet, all of the horses were picketed near the center of camp, and they could not find the bodies of Elk Rub and Short Lance.

Even in the dark, Cuts Something knew that all eyes were upon him. He called out the names of four of the younger warriors. "Ride before them and draw their shots, but stay far enough away that they do not kill you. Keep the rising sun in your face. The rest of us will ride out of the sun and kill as many of the white men as we can." The four young men stayed behind as the other warriors rode away in the dark.

At dawn, Cuts Something saw that the buffalo hunters had picked a near perfect location for their stand; their position at the top of the low butte afforded an unrestricted field of fire in all directions, and there were no contours to hide approaching attackers. He saw something else: two severed heads on spikes near the eastern edge of camp. The white men knew the People would ride out of the sun. In front of the spikes lay the two dismembered bodies; already, wolves were howling and skulking nearby, working up courage. He could not see the faces on the spikes, but he knew them very well. The braids swayed stiffly in the wind.

He numbly sat his horse. That's It let go a low moan. The other warriors gasped. This was a bad sign. The sun lighted the severed heads and the People saw that Elk Rub and Short Lance had been scalped; soon the bodies would bloat.

Cuts Something knew that if they simply rushed the camp the white men would cut them down. Whatever he was going to do, he would have to do very soon. His badger medicine had carried him many times; perhaps it would again. They would be in sunlight shortly; and already they were within range of the big guns. His warriors were all anxious to go; That's It ground his teeth and muttered curses at the white men.

The first shots came from the far side of camp, starting as sharp reports and then rolling toward them, building like low thunder. The young warriors were taunting the white men as ordered, trying to draw their attention.

By the second volley, Cuts Something had prepared himself to die. He yelled, 'Hah!" and dug his heels into his horse's ribs, ducked low, and led the two dozen warriors out of shadow in a tight wedge formation. The riders cast grotesquely tall, elongated shadows upon the prairie and the low butte before them. At the first sight of a raised barrel, the formation spread at once then closed and melded, spread again and reformed like some living, but amorphous thing. The riders whooped and screamed, and the heavy guns drowned their voices. They closed to within fifty yards before the first Comanche was knocked from his horse. They rode screaming and cursing past the mangled, headless corpses and the hideously grinning countenances and into camp. Some of the white men frantically reloaded their rifles; others aimed. Another volley knocked over two Comanche horses. The warriors shot arrows one after another from beneath their horses' necks, but few found their marks, for the white men had taken cover behind wagons and mules.

The shots rolled together; horses and mules lurched and bucked. The People formed an ever widening circle, riding one at a time through camp, loosing arrows, never exposing themselves, and the frustrated buffalo hunters shot poorly at the bobbing, weaving targets. Yet the warriors did little better. Two more Comanche horses went down, but the riders hit the ground running and were picked up by other circling warriors. The circle dispersed then reformed into two circles rotating in opposite directions, moving in synch like gears. Another exchange of arrows and heavy bullets resulted in no blood or scalps. The Comanches dared not dismount to recover the bodies of Elk Rub and Short Lance. To have done so would have been suicide.

Cuts Something made a final pass and put an arrow into the hip of a white man, then rode out of rifle range. The others followed and then assembled and shouted curses at the white men. They had lost no one despite the desperate fighting. A warrior named Bone Pipe had been knocked from his horse, but the bullet had struck the top of his shield. Four horses were dead or dying. The warriors, gasping for breath, talked excitedly and gulped from their water bags. Cuts Something, too, felt the rush of battle but could not forget the bodies left on the butte.

"Your badger medicine is strong!" That's It shouted. "They knew we would come, yet we lost no warriors. I think we killed some of the white men."

"Elk Rub and Short Lance were scalped."

"Yes. Had any man dismounted to get the bodies, he surely would have been killed."

Cuts Something sat his horse and kept his eyes on the white hunters' camp. "What good would it have done? They were scalped. Their souls can never rest."

"I do not think we will get scalps here," That's It said. "There are too many white men; only the protection of the spirits kept us alive."

"We must have white scalps."

Giving the hunters' camp a wide berth, they rode to meet the younger warriors. They found the young men huddled nearly a mile from the butte. One of them, a boy named Tall Wolf, had overestimated the distance to the white men and had taken a .50-caliber bullet just below his knee. His shattered tibia protruded raggedly. Cuts Something dismounted and knelt to comfort the boy who was very pale and clammy. The boy's lips were taut and colorless. Cuts Something had seen these symptoms many times before in victims red and white and black; the boy would die shortly. Tall Wolf grappled at his chest, and Cuts Something guided his hands to his medicine bag. The boy clutched it tightly.

"Hawk medicine," Cuts Something said. "Tall Wolf has hawk medicine." The other boys' normally copper faces were ashen. Vultures gathered above the hunters' camp.

Cuts Something stood and mounted his horse and rode into view of the white men. He issued curses in Comanche and Spanish. He called the *tahbay-boh* old women and skunks and vowed to cut their throats and feed their balls to his dogs and hang their scalps in his lodge. The others joined him; they shook their fists and screamed curses, all the while performing feats of horsemanship they knew to be beyond the ability of any white man.

The sporadic puffs of smoke from the hunters' rifle barrels did not concern them; they maintained a distance of several hundred yards. The white men's bullets struck the ground fifty yards short.

Suddenly That's It's horse went down with blood flying from its nostrils. Cuts Something heard a hissing sound near his head and the boom and swell of another volley. He instinctively turned his shield up at an angle to protect his head. The other warriors were screaming to pull back when a tremendous impact on his shield knocked him from his horse. He rolled away from the hunters and Otter Belt and Bone Pipe picked him up by his arms and dragged him away, battering his heels against the ground.

Safely out of range, they gently laid him down. He could not feel his shield arm, but he was relieved that it was still attached. That's It bent over him. "Your shield saved you!" The other warriors encircled him, wide-eyed, shaken that their old chief had been knocked from his horse. He knew the fighting was finished for now. He turned to look at Tall Wolf who lay motionless, still clutching his medicine bag. From the distance came the whoops and shouts of the white men who held their rifles over their heads in triumph.

Cuts Something's arm hurt so badly he could not sleep. But then no one could sleep for the wailing and shrieking of the women. He had not seen his two older wives since his return, although he heard them constantly. Fast Girl, wide-eyed and solemn now, had been clumsily caring for him. He wondered how badly She Invites her Sisters had disfigured herself in her mourning for Elk Rub. He supposed the pregnant Yellow Beads might show more restraint.

His elbow had been horribly swollen by the time they returned from the Llano to the main encampment, and over the past two days it had turned various shades of brown, black and blue. Fast Girl begged him to see her uncle, Low Tree, purportedly a shaman, but Cuts Something had little use for the man. For that matter, he had seen little in the way of medicinal power since most of the People agreed to move to the reservation. The Antelope and Buffalo Eaters, he suspected, still had effective medicine men. Perhaps in their new freedom, one of the Wanderers would rise to the position. Low Tree, now an old man, had shown little ability back in the days when the People raided the Texas settlements with impunity.

The raid against the buffalo hunters had gone poorly, yet Cuts Something had little reason to doubt his medicine. They had attacked a large, well armed camp and had lost only one warrior and five horses. His shield had turned the white man's bullet. His arm would heal soon enough. The Wanderers had laid away a huge quantity of buffalo meat and robes. There should be no hunger over the cold time.

But he had lost his son, and worse yet the boy had been scalped and dismembered; he would exact revenge or die trying. Already the men were urging him to lead a revenge raid, and the women wanted captives for torture.

At length he pushed himself up with his good arm and stepped outside to a cold overcast dawn. Fires already burned in most lodges, and he could see She Invites Her Sisters's silhouette in her lodge as she rocked silently back and forth in her grief. At present, she was not wailing. Cuts Something enjoyed the momentary quietude. He hoped she would fall asleep soon.

The pain in his arm nauseated him. He went back into his lodge and pulled the rawhide string to summon Fast Girl who appeared shortly to feed his fire. She was about to leave, but stepped back to allow That's It to enter. Fast Girl left, and That's It sat across the fire from his old friend. They sat in silence, staring into the flames. She Invites Her Sisters began to wail softly. With his good arm, Cuts Something drew his knife and looked at That's It. That's It held one of Cuts Something's long braids taut and Cuts Something severed it close to his scalp. That's It then took the knife and cut off one of his own braids and threw it into the fire. The two friends sat and wept bitterly.

CHAPTER 14

Given the choice, Logan would have stayed beneath his blanket and two buffa-lo robes. Though the sky had been clear when he went to sleep, he knew even in the darkness beneath the wagon that the morning was overcast. He smelled rain. Or snow. In any case, it was cold enough that he dreaded sliding the first leg from beneath the covers. Bob's snoring was a comfort. As long as it contin-ued, Logan could lie and luxuriate.

Bob rolled and sighed. Logan pictured him lying on his back, blinking at the stars, already planning the day ahead. Logan did not move. He hoped Bob would fall back to sleep. He should have known better.

"Logan, you up?"

"I'm up." He kicked the covers away and pulled his boots on.

Bob was the only black man Logan had known that did not address him as sir or Mister Logan. Bob was not allowed in white establishments — or at least he did not try to enter them. Yet even the roughest skinners deferred to him. The day they arrived in Dodge City, he and Logan turned into the alley behind the barn and nearly bumped into a pair of filthy hunters.

"Pardon me, suh," Bob said.

One of the two, a tall skinny man with long greasy red hair and broken teeth, was indignant. "Watch where the hell yer goin', ye goddamn ignorant darkie."

The man's partner, a rotund, red-faced Scot looked sheepishly about. "Uh Jackie, that would be Nigger Bob Durham." The skinny man blinked, then walked on. "He still oughta watch where he's goin'." The Scot nodded cordially and followed.

"My apologies gentlemen," Bob said.

Logan never thought of questioning the authority of a man who had ridden a mule from the Texas settlements deep into Comancheria to rescue his stolen wife from the Kiowas.

Bob's feet hit the frozen mud. "Get the coffee goin' and I'll go kick Ezree awake," he said.

Logan pulled on his coat and rolled from beneath the wagon. He had rinsed most of the blood from his coat in the Arkansas River. He buttoned it to his chin and enjoyed its warmth. He sifted through the kindling box in the back of the wagon and gathered an armload of bois d'arc, cottonwood, elm, and dried bison flops and carried it across the alley to the fire ring they had established. He no longer took firewood for granted. In Kentucky, there was firewood when there was nothing else. Oak, hickory, pine. But on the plains, firewood was an unexpected gift. He whittled off a handful of shavings then pulled from his coat pocket a handful of dried bluestem. He mixed the grass and kindling then fired the grass with flint and steel.

He had the coffee boiling when Romack, whom he had not seen since the party rode into town, walked unsteadily into the firelight carrying a pouch of bacon.

"Where's the boss men?"

"Bob went to wake Ezra up. Where you been?"

"I'd tell ye, but it'd be too much for them tender ears." He pointed his finger at Logan's chest. "And don't go quotin' the Good Book at me. Just 'cause you're the boss men's fair-haired boy don't mean I won't haul off and jerk a knot on ye."

Logan found the outburst surprising. Romack had always seemed personable. For an instant he considered giving the cook a kick in the ribs. He had no use for a drunkard and had whipped more than few backwoods ruffians. He decided against it, fearing that Bob and Ezra would fire him for further incapacitating their cook. Besides, he didn't feel like bouncing his cold fist off the side of Romack's oversized head. His knuckles would hurt for days, and the bacon might burn.

"I'd say you got up on the wrong side of the bed this mornin'. Head hurtin' you is it? Take heed to yourself, lest your heart be overcharged with surfeiting and drunkenness. Luke 21 verse 34." The hung-over grouch had asked for it.

"I'm glad to know that if we run across a murderin' horde of Comanches, we'll have us a preacher along to see us on to glory."

"I done told you I ain't a preacher. I'm just a God-fearin' man; that's all."

Romack sliced off a strip of bacon. "God-fearin' boy, I'd say."

Logan sighed. "Earl, get you a cup of coffee. Maybe it'll make you feel better and you won't be so cross."

"Believe I will. Better do somethin' before I have to whip your bony ass."

"That might be a job, now." In the firelight, Logan could see that Romack's left ear was a scabrous mess and that his lips were puffy and blue. Though his face was badly swollen, he looked like he had lost twenty pounds. *For everyone that exalteth himself shall be abased and he that humbleth himself shall be exalted.* Logan walked back to the wagon and took two tin cups from the cook box. He poured them full and handed one to Romack who was on his haunches tending the bacon.

"Thank ye."

"How long does it take to get to Texas?"

"About eleven days, they tell me. I ain't never been there. I wish we would wait and go with that Myers bunch, but I can't sit around here all winter not gettin' paid."

Logan stopped short of commenting on the idiocy of spending hard-earned money on whisky and women of ill repute.

"I smell bacon from here!" Bob yelled from the pitch dark barn.

From the loft, someone shouted, "Shut the hell up!"

"Oh yeah!" Bob said in a loud whisper. "Shhh. . . . " He and Ezra stepped into the muddy alley. Bob held his finger to his nose and walked on his tiptoes.

Ezra produced a cup from somewhere beneath his buffalo skin coat and filled it with coffee. "Well boys," he said, "by Christmas, we'll either be rich or dead and scalped."

There were few cook fires burning around the hide sheds when they rode south out of town. Logan rode a tall awkward gelding named Rufus. Two of the three skinners Ezra hired — Hunt and Corbin — were asleep in the back of the kill wagon; the third, Mullins, drove unsteadily. All three skinners, like Romack, had hired on because they were destitute and could not wait for the Myers expedition to depart. Though Bob and Ezra owned scabbards, they rode with their rifles laid across the front of their saddles. Logan considered this a grim sign, though he did the same and did not ask about the practice for fear of appearing green. He had kept the Pawnee scabbard which, along with the decorated rifle, had been the subject of much curiosity among the Dodge City ruffians.

Somehow — Logan suspected that Ezra was involved — word had gotten around that Logan had killed the rifle's Pawnee owner. He had been too sheepish to set matters straight, and now worried that Romack would hear the embellished story. The cook would never let him live it down.

Try as he might, he could not imagine shooting an Indian. He had no moral objection to killing attacking savages. He simply wondered how it would feel to look at an Indian that had died by his hand. He did not know how many Indians Bob and Ezra had accounted for; dozens, he supposed. Ezra purportedly had ridden with Captain Ben McCulloch at the battle of Plum Creek when Rangers and the Texas Militia ambushed and killed dozens of Buffalo Hump's warriors as they made their way back from the coast with nearly a thousand stolen horses and mules and many captive white women. Ezra loved to tell the story and Logan loved hearing it, although he had loved it somewhat less since the Pawnee attack.

According to Ezra, Buffalo Hump's raiders broke into a warehouse at Linville late in the summer of 1840 and came back up a broad war trail wearing women's hosiery, hoop skirts and top hats. They had woven calico into their horses' tails and wore all manner of cheap jewelry. "Made damn fetchin' targets," Ezra said. He was always vague when it came to the number of Comanches he personally dispatched that day.

"You can't keep count," Bob would always say.

Logan gathered that Plum Creek lay well south of where they would be hunting. He took comfort in that fact; he hoped to avoid anyplace where Comanches might harbor an unusually large grudge.

Five miles out of Dodge City, Logan's death grip on the Ballard had exhausted his forearm so that he could not have lifted the gun had they been ridden upon by a thousand Comanches. Further on, he noticed that Bob gripped his Sharps very lightly, sometimes simply balancing it with his palm on the stock. Despite his initial awkwardness and Rufus's murderous gait, Logan soon mastered the technique himself.

They rode southwest toward the Cimarron River. For the first few hours, Logan half expected to encounter Indians over every hill, but as the morning wore on, his mind wandered, and he remembered why he had grown fond of the plains. Bob and Ezra rode ahead; Logan rode a respectful distance behind, generally alongside Romack's wagon. The old cook, still sullen, seemed little interested in conversation. The two sleeping skinners snored loudly despite the cold weather and their lack of heavy coats.

A nearly featureless plain lay before them; sage, little bluestem and prickly pear cactus and occasional narrow creeks lined with plum and cottonwood. The slate sky spat snow, and steam rose from the mouths of the horses and mules. For breakfast, the crew had eaten most of the bacon and had drunk three pots of coffee. Logan was wide awake now and found the brittle air bracing.

They passed many piles of buffalo bones picked clean by scavengers, and from the north, along the Arkansas, came occasional thumps from heavy rifles. "Just cleanin' up the dregs," Ezra yelled.

At times, Ezra and Bob rode out of sight, leaving Logan with unnerving thoughts of a skirmish without an experienced Indian fighter. He thought briefly about waking the drunken skinners, then decided against it. Why have such a glorious morning spoiled by a wagonload of half-wits? Meadowlarks flushed, and tiny gray birds flitted in the tallgrass. Occasionally Logan glimpsed the white crests of blue quail running ahead of the horses and mules.

They encountered no bison. Twice Logan saw antelope within rifle range — at least he thought they were within range — but Bob and Ezra were scouting well ahead and he did not want to shoot without their permission. By noon, the skinners were all awake and talking and laughing stupidly at every remark. Ezra rode in from the southwest. "Logan, there's a flock of chickens flushed and flew into a draw on the other side of that little hump," he said pointing westward. "You ought to take the shotgun over there and see what you can do."

"That's *my* goddamn shotgun," Romack snapped.

Ezra spat. "Well then, take *Earl's* shotgun over there and shoot us a chicken. We'll stop here and Earl can fry the rest of the bacon." Romack glared straight ahead. Ezra shook his head. "By god, I hope you get to feelin' better before long. Hell I can cook and so can Bob." Romack spat a stream of tobacco juice onto the back of one of the mules.

Logan took the huge, unwieldy ten-gauge double-barrel and slung the powder horn and possibles bag over his head and shoulder. He charged each barrel while the skinners chewed their tobacco and watched dully, unblinking like cattle. He supposed that at some point, in the interest of cohesion, he should make small talk with the three. He was beginning to remember Krebs and Muntz fondly.

Logan rode up the low hill and picketed Rufus near the top. He walked into the draw carrying the shotgun at port arms. In Kentucky, he had shot many ruffed grouse with his Enfield as the birds trundled along creek banks picking up grit. But the prairie grouse rarely allowed a close shot. They usually flushed well ahead of the hunter.

He walked westward along the draw, ready for a quick shot. A harrier hovered six feet above a long strip of sand sage. He wondered how the raptor would affect the prairie chickens' behavior. He had been quite comfortable on horseback, but now his exertion raised a light sweat. He stopped to unbutton his coat, and as he cradled the shotgun, a flock of eight grouse flushed before him at the edge of shotgun range. The birds flew down the draw and out of sight.

He fought the urge to swear. He took a step forward and two prairie chickens flushed at his feet and flew straight away. His first shot missed low — fortunately; it would have pulverized the bird at such close range. He dropped a bird with the second barrel, marked the fall and kneeled to recharge the shotgun. He worked the ramrod and kept his eyes on a clump of sage next to the place where the bird had fallen.

After a brief search he found the bird dead in the sage. He picked it up and smoothed the feathers. This grouse seemed slightly smaller and lighter in color than the birds he had shot near Salina.

He climbed out of the draw, and looked in what he thought was the direction of the wagons but saw nothing on the deceptively contoured prairie. He heard nothing. He briefly considered striking out in the most likely direction, but decided instead to retrace his steps in the draw.

As he struggled up the hill toward his horse, he wondered at his lack of nervousness. He was, after all, alone in Comancheria. Yet he found it difficult to keep that fact in mind. The prairie seemed clean and pleasant after the Dodge City squalor. He grimaced at the thought of the stench there in high summer. He climbed out of the draw and led Rufus back to the wagons.

Bob had rejoined the group. "Where's the other bird? I heard two shots."

"Flew away with his heart shot out. Ever seen a dead bird fly off?"

Bob laughed. "Many times. Why there's dead chickens flyin' all over Kansas Territory."

Romack looked up from his skillet. "You're awful handy with my powder and shot." The skinners stood about eating the last of the bacon and sipping coffee and watching Logan who did his best to nod pleasantly. None of the skinners spoke.

"Give Earl his shotgun back," Ezra said. "He's been worried sick over it."

Logan stepped away, drew and skinned the bird then gave it to Romack. The cook halved and floured it and laid the pieces in the hot bacon grease. "Half of this bird's mine," he said.

After their meal, they rode on. Romack's disposition improved steadily. He began to remark on the landscape and the weather and sorry crew of skinners.

"That bird must've set well with you," Logan said.

"Did for a fact. I've been feelin' green for three days." He spat. "I'll make us a little bread tonight if Bob'll leave me alone."

They made a late afternoon camp along a small creek. The creek barely flowed, but there were small, clear pools full of minnows. The clouds had begun to break away and sat orange and red and dark gray above the western horizon. To his vexation, Logan caught himself worrying more about supper than about Comanches. There was little work to do; he had already curried the mules and had carefully checked beneath collar pads and harnesses for sores and raw spots. He stood cradling his rifle, looking about, anticipating the hunting. He noticed a peculiar absence of wolves. Bob and Romack argued over the preparation of the bannock. He heard Bob's voice indistinctly then "pig-headed fool."

It would be dark soon. He had been assigned third watch; the wee hours. He wondered how he would feel then.

CHAPTER 15

Cuts Something watched the saddle maker Moon Dog at work. Watching careful handwork always soothed him. He and Moon Dog were roughly the same age; Moon Dog had been a slave since Cuts Something's father carried him nine summers old and terrified out of northern Mexico in the days when the People rode unchallenged from the Arkansas to the Del Norte. Per custom, the boy was castrated and renamed; Cuts Something's father, who grew quite fond of Moon Dog, always regretted the castration and held that Moon Dog would have made a warrior. Small captive boys usually were adopted and often made fine warriors, but Moon Dog had been too old for adoption, or so the reasoning had gone the day he was dragged kicking and screaming into camp. After gelding, he quickly became a reliable worker, resourceful and completely trustworthy. Cuts Something loved him dearly.

Cuts Something sat in the shade of a cottonwood tree and watched Moon Dog sewing the wet buckskin onto a carefully cut and fitted elm frame. The Mexican used a Comanchero needle and green sinew. He was sitting on well-beaten ground, and his hands mesmerized Cuts Something. The saddle sat on a low scaffold built to a comfortable working height. After a while, Cuts Something took out his pipe and tobacco and with his good arm and hand began awkwardly stuffing the pipe. Moon Dog noticed his friend's difficulty and without speaking, stopped his work and prepared the pipe. Cuts Something fired the tobacco with an ember from the small fire and nodded his thanks to Moon Dog who had already returned to his work.

They sat in silence. The only sound other than the dry, rustling cottonwood leaves came from the sinew being pulled through the wet buckskin. At length, Moon Dog looked up from his work. "You will be well soon. What will you do then?"

Cuts Something thought about the question for several minutes. He finished his pipe and set it aside. He knew that everyone in camp was watching him closely, waiting for his response to Elk Rub's death and the disastrous raid on the white buffalo hunters' camp. "I have not decided the best way to avenge the killings. The women are screaming for scalps and captives. But the white hunters cannot be taken alive. They fight bitterly." Since Elk Rub's death, he had spoken little with She Invites Her Sisters. After a week of hysterical mourning, she had quieted somewhat, but she remained pale and weak from self-mutilation. He had no desire to see her breasts. As the pain in his arm subsided, he felt the stirrings of the old bitterness and the hate that had fueled his youth. He felt it most often early in the day. His agitation had lately driven him to seek the soothing sight of Moon Dog's steady hands. But at night, when his arm throbbed and the cold seeped into his joints, fatigue and despair replaced anger. His vision on the mesa had shown him nothing of impending disaster — or at least he had seen nothing — although the images of the fading bulls sometimes troubled him. The nights were growing cooler. For the past several nights he had been unable to sleep outside for more than few hours before cold and aching joints and the horribly throbbing arm sent him crawling into his lodge. On the worst nights, Yellow Beads prepared a sedative of boiled silver leaf which enabled him to sleep for a few hours at a time.

"Perhaps the Texans would not expect a raid on the settlements just before the hungry time." Moon Dog's words jolted Cuts Something from his thoughts."

"What did you say?"

"The Texans. Would they expect a raid just before the hungry time? Do they expect raids anymore?"

Cuts Something had long considered the settlements far too dangerous to approach. If the Rangers did not catch you outright, they came later, unexpectedly, and killed everyone and everything. But then he had heard little of the Rangers since the white men had stopped fighting among themselves. Perhaps they had grown fat with their success. Or perhaps, as the Kiowa, Sun Boy, had asserted, the soldiers and the white's Great Father so feared the Rangers that they had taken their guns and horses. Perhaps a small raiding party could strike at sunset — as the People did in the old days — and kill and scalp the white men, steal the children and bring the white women back for sport. The Wanderers had enjoyed no white women since they ransomed the last three back to Lowery and the soldiers shortly after they arrived at the reservation. They had caught a few traveling along the Arkansas, but those women probably were not Texans. Their men had fought weakly and the sniveling women were ruined within a few hours.

A raid into the heart of the settlements! What could make the Texans angrier? The soldiers would not pursue the People during the hungry time. He could take his scalps and captives, and, if by spring his wives had not cut them up or burned them to death, he could offer them back to the fool, Lowery, for a few horses. Then, the Wanderers could join Quanah and the Antelope on the Llano where the whites would never follow. He would miss the river brakes country, of course, but the People were adaptable. After all, had they not once been mountain people?

"I will think about this," Cuts Something said. Moon Dog continued his sewing. Cuts Something repositioned himself so that the sun shone directly on his sore arm.

Cuts Something watched Sees How Far It Is strip the bark from the length of bois d'arc. His arm had pained him terribly when he and That's It and Sees How Far It Is rode to the Canadian to look for the perfect tree. But the pain had been worth it.

The old man worked the hard, dense wood. He worked all morning and into the afternoon. By mid afternoon, the shaft felt comfortable in Cuts Something's hand. Satisfied with the girth, Sees How Far It Is cut the shaft to a length of three arms.

The three friends talked quietly and gravely among themselves causing much conjecture among the other members of the band — especially the other warriors. They took turns hefting the shaft and made further adjustments. The work continued the next morning until the old man at last laid the shaft against his work scaffold to dry and harden in the sun. The other warriors watched from a distance, stealing glances while they smoked and talked among themselves. Occasionally, someone would find a reason to walk near the scaffold, but no one asked Cuts Something about the pole or about his activities with his closest friends. Otter Belt pointed out that the blackness was fast leaving the old chief's arm. Some of the women joked among themselves about Fast Girl's shrill yelps they had been lately hearing.

CHAPTER 16

Logan sat on his haunches in the dark beyond the glow of the campfire coals, watching. He heard nothing but the sound of the horses feeding and moving over the frosted grass. The clouds had dispersed revealing the firmament. He marveled that wild red men could be looking at the same night sky. He stood and listened, then moved about the perimeter of the camp. He considered easing back to the fire for another cup of coffee. He could sip while he watched the horses. He decided against it. His eyes had adjusted to the darkness and the light from the low coals would necessitate another adjustment.

He understood now that death could come swiftly and horribly at any instant, but it seemed impossible now just as it had before the Pawnee attack. He had always loved autumn. In Kentucky, the poison ivy died in late fall, and one could move about then without sweating. He always felt most alive then. He forced himself to think again of the Pawnee encounter and the way his stomach had felt and the smell of the corpses, yet now it all seemed quite remote. He was warm and alert; the night was bracing; he could see the horses' breath in the moonlight. He gave in and laid his rifle on his shoulder and walked quickly and softly toward the campfire. He poured the coffee and carried the steaming cup back into the darkness. He moved to the shadow of a juniper clump and took a tiny sip. The near scalding coffee felt as good as it tasted.

A coyote yipped a hundred yards upstream. Logan tensed slightly. Another answered from the distance, and he began to feel his pulse in his temples. Were they really coyotes? Probably. But perhaps not. He did not move. He felt badly exposed despite his position in the shadows. Another yip from the creek; another answer. He set his cup down and eased his rifle to port arms. For God's sake, he thought. They weren't even in Texas yet. Two more yips from the creek. He waited, barely breathing. Then another, and more voices joined the serenade which quickly rose to the ludicrous din that only coyotes produce.

He relaxed, laughed softly, and took another sip. The eastern horizon showed faint traces of pink. He heard Romack coughing to clear his throat of phlegm. Breakfast would be ready soon. A bobwhite called *koi-lee* from the low hills to the west. Ezra spoke from behind him. "All quiet?" Ezra was relieving himself on a clump of prickly pear.

"I didn't hear no red men."

"Maybe you didn't; maybe you did."

Logan laughed softly although he saw little humor in the comment. He turned and started for camp. He noticed a peculiar tightness between his shoulder blades.

They rode on for the Cimarron. The country grew more arid and broken with draws and dry creeks. They encountered much bison sign but no bison. Antelope moved in and out of focus against the heat waves and small raptors hovered on low currents eight feet above the grass. The wagons bounced and pitched violently at creek crossings but sustained no apparent damage. The nights were mostly clear and cold, and Logan stood the last watch each morning without incident. He crouched in the shadows, the darkest spots he could find. He sat unmoving, wrapped in his buffalo robe, watching, listening. The prairie nights were never silent, and he strained to sift the noises; the coyote yips and the rustlings of night things. Windy nights were worst, for he could hear nothing but gusting wind and pitching branches and grass. On those nights he sat motionless, watching the horses while the clouds scudded wildly overhead.

On the seventh morning out of Dodge, they crossed the Cimarron at a wide shallow ford and rode into Indian Territory. Logan rode alongside Romack while Bob and Ezra ranged well ahead.

"We'd better find some meat before long," Romack said. "Them damn skinners is about to eat us right out of business. No tellin' how much they'll eat after they get off their asses and do a little work." He spat. "That goddamn Mullins is a losin' proposition all the way. He eats more meat than a dozen men can shoot and skin."

Logan cringed whenever someone took the Lord's name in vain, but he knew better than to bring up the matter with Romack. Logan told himself that the cook's swearing was such a habit that he did not realize what he was saying. Perhaps, he thought, if a person was unaware of his sins and was too innocently pigheaded to be educated, the less egregious sins could be overlooked.

He and Romack were fast becoming friends. Logan thought it fortunate that Ezra and Bob had been unwilling to take up much valuable wagon space with whiskey. Most nights by bedtime, Romack and the skinners had been at least pleasantly fortified, but they seemed to be showing some restraint in lieu of their modest supply. Still, at the present drinking pace, the whiskey would be long gone by the time they made the Canadian River.

Logan glanced back at Mullins who drove the kill wagon while the two other skinners slept, mouths wide open, atop the supplies. Mullins did indeed have a huge appetite. He was as tall as Logan but very thin. Logan had found Mullins the only one of the three skinners capable of anything resembling a coherent conversation.

"I believe old Mullins might make a good hand, though," Logan said. "Them others is liable to lop their fingers off, I'm afraid."

"And every one packin' a rifle or a pistol. That'll give you somethin' to think on."

"How long you think we'll be out?"

"Not long if there's the buffalo in Texas Bob and Ezra thinks there is. We'll kill out in a few weeks and head back, I imagine. Or else if them boys get set up at the tradin' post by spring, we might stay out for a long time. We could take a wagon load of hides in and bring a load of supplies back. Somebody said Myers is buyin' every hide he can get his hands on. They'll take hides year-round now. Somebody smarter than me figured out how to tan them old dried summer hides."

A rider came into view to the southwest. The procession continued, but all wakeful eyes tracked the rider continually changing shape behind the heat waves. Romack spat then squinted. "Ezra. He looks to be in a hurry."

"I wonder where Bob is," Logan said. He felt a tinge of panic, but did his best to appear cool. He launched a quick, silent prayer for Bob's safety.

Ezra rode alongside. He pointed to Logan. "Four little bunches," he said excitedly. "Bob's already workin' a bunch." He left again and Logan followed. Romack slowly turned the mule team and the procession followed at a distance.

For the first time since he had come to the plains, Logan felt exhilaration. Not fear or tedium or despair or boredom. He followed Ezra closely, wondering all the while how anyone could find the same place twice on the plains. After a half mile of riding, he began to hear Bob's Sharps.

They crested a low rise, and Logan saw in the distance the black specks that were the scattered bands. Ezra did not ride directly at them. Rather he turned his horse into the wind, and they rode keeping their distance until they were north of the northernmost band whereupon Ezra dismounted and picketed his horse. Ezra's eyes were wide. Logan had never seen him this way; he realized that he had never been hunting with Ezra or Bob; he had only seen the aftermath.

"Don't just go to shootin'" Ezra said, whispering unnecessarily. The bands were still well out of earshot. "Do what I do except don't shoot until I tell you, okay?"

Logan nodded. His mouth was dry, and he needed to make water, but he did not want to ask Ezra to wait. Ezra pulled from a small scabbard a pair of yard-long sticks tied together in the middle with a rawhide string. He glanced at Logan. "Goddamn, you don't have a rest, do you?"

Logan stared at him.

"A rest; for your rifle."

"I never thought about it."

"You'll just have to prop your elbows on your knees. We'll get you fixed up before the next hunt."

Ezra climbed to the top of the draw then slid quickly back down on the seat of his pants. "Let's go a little further down this draw," he whispered. Bob's gun boomed in the distance. They jogged along the draw for fifty yards then scrambled out and crawled on their bellies through the sand sage. The wind nearly blew Logan's hat off.

He followed Ezra. He could not see the buffalo and did not raise his head for fear of spooking them. He wondered how he and Ezra could shoot lying face down in the sage. They crawled for what seemed to Logan another half mile before Ezra cautiously sat up. Logan did the same and choked on his gasp. A dozen bison grazed peacefully eighty paces away. He had not expected to be so close to their quarry.

Ezra saw his surprise. "Sumbitches can't see nothin'," he whispered, "but you gotta keep downwind of 'em. See that big old cow in the middle?"

"I see her." The sweat on his face was drying fast in the wind.

"I aim to gut shoot her soon as she turns. Then we'll kill the whole goddamn bunch. But don't shoot 'til I tell you."

Ezra spread his sticks into an X which he set upright before him. He took from his coat pocket a swath of rolled buckskin and wedged it into the resulting crotch then laid the barrel of his rifle atop the buckskin and took aim. Logan sat cross-legged and waited. The bison milled about. The bulls occasionally raised their noses to the wind and stared at the hunters. Ezra adjusted the base of his rest to raise his rifle barrel. He hooked his left thumb over the barrel. "Sumbitch'll jump on you if you don't hold her down," he whispered, aiming. Logan barely heard him above the wind.

The gun's report nearly stopped Logan's heart. He had been watching the cow and wondering why Ezra would want to gut shoot her instead of killing her outright and had for the moment forgotten about the gun. There was a moist slap and the cow shuddered. The rest of the band jerked their heads up and milled about nervously for several seconds then resumed grazing.

Ezra quietly reloaded. "Just watch," he whispered. The old cow stood rigid for several seconds then dropped her head and staggered. Two of the younger bulls sniffed and nudged her. The others watched then moved closer to her. An old bull nudged the cow repeatedly then raised his head and bawled mournfully and pawed the ground. Ezra aimed and fired and one of the young bulls dropped instantly. Its legs churned convulsively. Ezra reloaded and shot a second bull with the same result. The band stomped about nervously.

"Shoot that old bull on your end," Ezra said casually.

Logan rested his elbows on his knees and took aim. The bull stood nearly broadside. He set the rear trigger, drew a breath and slowly exhaled. The heavy barrel wobbled. He could never hold steady after exhaling. He took in another breath and held it. He found a spot just behind the beast's shoulder and squeezed the trigger. He did not hear the blast, but the recoil took him completely by surprise, rocking him backward so that he had to put his hand down to avoid falling onto his back.

The bull shuddered, then staggered but did not go down. Logan groped frantically for another cartridge.

Ezra laughed softly. "Hell you hit him all right."

"Don't I need to shoot him again?"

"Hold on; he ain't goin' nowhere. You hit him in the lungs. See that blood on his nose?" The bull took several steps and stopped again. Ezra laid his barrel back on his rest. "Pick out anothern and shoot it."

Logan reloaded and shot a cow. She fell over, got up again, then went to her knees. As he reloaded, he noticed the wounded bull lying on its side. Ezra finished the gut-shot cow. "I don't know why it is, but if you drop the first one dead in its tracks, the whole bunch is liable to run off. But if you gut shoot the old cow and make her sick, the rest of 'em will stand around and let you shoot 'em." Logan's cow tried again to get up, but fell onto her side.

They finished the band of thirteen bison then walked among the carcasses. Romack and the skinners approached in the wagons. "It's good to be out again," Ezra said. "I wonder how old Bob did."

Logan felt as if he had been punched in the jaw, and his shoulder throbbed. "These rifles kill on both ends, seems like."

Ezra laughed. "Just wait 'til we get to the Canadian. You'll rattle them bones sure enough."

The wagons arrived. The skinners clamored out and started for the carcasses. "By god, now, Mullins," Romack said, "Be sure and peel the hide off 'fore ye start eatin.'"

Mullins ignored the comment. Bob rode in from the south. Ezra looked at him questioningly. "Lebum," Bob said. "Don't start eatin' yet, Mullins." The tall skinner looked at Bob flatly then came down on the steel skull spike with the sledge hammer.

Night fell freezing cold. The hunters ate close to the fire. Mullins singed the soles of his boots. After supper, Logan unrolled his soogan, crawled beneath the blankets and robes, and fell at once into a deep sleep. For the first time since the Pawnee attack, Indians did not visit his sleep. He thought he had just closed his eyes when Bob shook him awake for the early morning watch. Bob handed him a cup of coffee then crawled into his own bedroll.

Logan warmed himself by the coals then took his rifle and buffalo robes and walked into the darkness. For his vantage point he selected a dark spot in the sage against a low rise that hid his silhouette. He sat on one robe and wrapped himself in the other. He could see camp, the horses and mules, and the unbroken prairie beyond. He sat and watched and listened and thought about hunting.

C H A P T E R   1 7

Cuts Something drew his bow and let the arrow fly. It sailed a foot over the back of a young mule deer doe. The little deer bolted and disappeared into head of the juniper-studded draw. Cuts Something shut his eyes tightly then reopened them and squinted to focus. The pain in his elbow made him dizzy. Yet he knew that he was improving. A few days earlier he could not have drawn the bow. He walked into the brush to look for his arrow. He found it after a short search and walked back to his horse. Had some of the younger warriors been present, they would have chided him for not shooting the deer with a rifle. Cuts Something had no problem with guns — many of the young men shot them quite well — but he never seemed to have the right kind of bullets. He had quickly learned that one did not simply use whatever ammunition was at hand. Guns tended to foul and to grow a dark red dust after a time, and once a gun failed no one seemed to have the slightest idea about how to repair it. Surely, he thought, white men knew how to repair their weapons.

He knew how to repair his bow and lance, and they always worked when called upon. If the arrow missed the mark, it was not the fault of the arrow or the bow. Guns, on the other hand, were noisy and often spooked game. He had seen young men take deer and antelope at incredible ranges with guns. So incredible, in fact, that he had not been able to see the target. What good was a rifle, with all its killing range, if he could not clearly see the target? He could see as far as his bow could effectively shoot, so he reasoned that his bow was quite adequate for his needs. He did not want to stop making arrows.

He rode up a narrow game trail toward the head of the canyon. He did not feel like hunting. His arm hurt terribly. Yet he felt a lightness of spirit as if some burden had suddenly been lifted. He wanted to be high, near the spirits. His horse picked its way very carefully. He rode higher. The country changed from broken woodlands to sheer sandstone cliffs and talus slopes dotted here and there with tenacious shin oak and juniper. Ever-vigilant turkey vultures circled overhead. The morning warmed, and his arm felt better. He rode higher until his horse clamored up the last of the steep, narrow trail and onto the caprock. He sat his horse and looked eastward over the rolling, eroded plains and the scattered bands of buffalo, some grazing, others moving slowly in columns toward the canyons and water. He dismounted, tied his horse to a clump of juniper and sat on his blanket and lit his pipe. A slight breeze raised goose bumps on his arms and blew away the swarm of gnats that had been bedeviling him.

He worked to summon hate, but could not. When he was young, he could summon hate anytime and often did, and the talent had served him well over the years. As the women's hysterical mourning subsided, so did his ability to summon rage. Yet he knew he must summon it again. Lately he had been much better at summoning grief over Elk Rub's death and for the passing of the old days and his youth.

He would strike at the Texans and he would kill again. If the raid went well, the women would once again enjoy cathartic torture of captives. There was no other way. The People could not simply live out their days in these canyons. If he would not lead a revenge raid then he was nothing — in his own eyes or in the eyes of the People. Yet revenge assuaged only anger. It did nothing for one's grief. Only the passing days helped with the grief. He would raise his war party, strike at the heart of the settlements, return with his scalps and horses and captives. The People would winter on the Pease, and after the hungry time they would join Quanah on the Llano. Perhaps Yellow Beads would bear him a son. Hope lingered.

He finished his pipe, mounted and started back down the narrow game trail.

* * *

Cuts Something took the huge stone spear head from his parfleche bag and laid it in Sees How Far It Is's hand. The bois d'arc pole had dried and hardened nicely in the sun. The old man slid the fluted portion of the spear tip into a notch he had cut in the end of the shaft. Sitting cross-legged with his work in his lap, he secured the head by tightly whipping the lance head with green sinew. He finished and handed the lance to Cuts Something who hefted it thoughtfully. "Heaviest lance I have ever held," Cuts Something said.

"The most terrible weapon I have ever seen," the old man answered. "Think of the beasts that lance head has felled. There is surely power in it."

Cuts Something propped his weapon, point up, against the meat scaffold to allow the sinew to dry and shrink. No one in camp except That's It and Sees How Far It Is came near the lance. The women did not look at it.

Two days later, Sees How Far It Is daubed onto the sinew wrapping a glue made from boiled chips of buffalo hooves and horns and hide shavings. Again he set the weapon aside to dry and cure.

Cuts Something rode daily to his vantage point on the edge of the caprock. He did not fast. He smoked his pipe. If the spirits chose to reveal some piece of wisdom, then so much the better. His task was clear; he needed no further urging.

After Cuts Something's fourth trip to the caprock, Sees How Far It Is pronounced the lance ready. Cuts Something and That's it applied their war paint and sent their wives to fetch their war horses. Two girls saw what was happening and ran to summon Otter Belt who joined the older warriors. The three warriors, their faces streaked with black paint, rode four times through the encampment loudly summoning every warrior with the courage to strike at the Texans and exact revenge for the deaths of Elk Rub and Short Lance and Tall Wolf.

Warriors came from their lodges and sent for their horses and painted their faces. Soon a war party of three dozen men rode single file around the encampment. They made four revolutions and then each peeled off to his lodge and there picketed his horse. The warriors crowded into the council lodge to pass the pipe and sing war songs while the women, children and slaves gathered wood for a huge fire.

Just after dark, the fire hissed and danced twice the height of the tallest man and the People danced to the rhythms of beating drums and to the war chants of the warriors and the songs of the women. They danced and sweated from their exertion and the heat of the fire. While the young men rested, the old men leapt stiffly into the circle and told of their coups against the Texans and dared the sun to strike them dead if they did not speak the truth.

They danced into the wee hours; the women continued while the warriors drifted away to gather their horses and weapons. Just before first light, the war party rode single file out of camp, southeastward toward the Middle Brazos.

They saw no more bison in three days of riding. Logan began to think again of Indians. He could not imagine how they would ever find buffalo in Texas; the plains looked as if they could swallow a hundred million buffalo. They saw many antelope, however, and took one or two nearly every day. Logan found long range marksmanship far more difficult than he had imagined. Squirrel hunting in Kentucky had not prepared him for prairie distances. Was he looking at a fawn at two hundred yards or a full grown doe a quarter mile distant? The wind could blow even a 600-grain bullet askew, especially at the longer ranges. Yet he felled four antelope and most days worked flocks of prairie chickens with the shotgun. Several times, Bob and Ezra came in from creek bottoms with turkeys.

Although he enjoyed riding beside Romack, he had lately been riding ahead with Bob and Ezra. He still did not understand their method of navigation, and neither of the two older men gave him a satisfactory explanation, so he always stayed close to one or the other.

He tried at first to memorize terrain features, but soon found the approach useless; he spent so much time concentrating on details that his tenuous sense of direction was completely upended five minutes from the wagon. He suspected that the two simply kept track of their general direction, major land features and the wagons' direction of travel. He asked Bob about it. The graying plainsman considered the question for several minutes. "Yeah, I reckon I do that." he said.

After four days of riding with Ezra and Bob, Logan began riding out short distances on his own. Unlike the two older men, he did not scout ahead for hazards or for buffalo or for the best route to travel. He simply wanted to learn to get around; the thought of being lost on the plains terrified him almost as much as the thought of Comanches. At least the Comanches would eventually drive a stake through your skull, which would be far better than slowly dying of thirst. Or so he thought most days. But the Comanche practice of castration bothered him. He wondered: did they castrate you before or after they killed you? Again, he got no satisfactory answer from his superiors. "Sometimes," Ezra answered. Logan wondered how anyone could know for sure and be alive to tell about it.

Bob and Ezra seemed to approve of his short forays. Upon each return, they asked him what he had seen. Romack nearly always greeted him with the same comment: "I thought sure we'd lost yer bony ass this time. Mullins has already laid claim to your share of the grub." The skinners always watched his departure and return with the same dull expressions.

Once, while he was out chasing a flock of prairie chickens, he lost the wagons and had to choke down his terror to avoid a mad, screaming dash. He had flushed the birds several times, and, intent on pursuit, lost track of his party's direction. It was still early morning when he realized his mistake. He told himself that he had plenty of daylight left. After a half day of despair, he rode onto several low hills and scanned the plains to no avail. He could not imagine how two wagons and several horses could disappear when he could see thirty miles in all directions. Two hours later, he topped a low rise, looked about and saw nothing but empty prairie. He heard a cough behind him and turned and saw the wagons only 120 yards distant. He did his best to ride nonchalantly in with his five prairie chickens. His companions said nothing, but he felt sure they knew that he had been lost. He suspected too that Bob and Ezra had seen him wandering lost on the prairie and had not seen fit to rescue him. When he rode up to the wagons, Ezra's smile seemed overly wide. "Did some good?"

"Some."

"Lotta ridin' for five little birds," Romack said. "I thought sure ye had somethin' big down."

"I'll eat yourn then."

Romack laughed and hit the right front mule with a stream of tobacco juice. "I don't believe ye will. Not long as ye usin' my shotgun. I do like chicken every now and then. Next time, see if ye can't lose yer bony ass a little longer and shoot the whole flock."

"We won't have to fool with chickens much longer," Bob said.

Romack spat out his chew and worked to rid his tongue of the errant flecks. "Welp," he said, between spits, "that's what I keep hearin'."

Sixteen days out of Dodge City they rode into the brakes of the Canadian and looked southward over the narrow green river and the sandy, grassy bottom.

"Sweet Jesus," Romack whispered. "I ain't never seen nothin' like it."

None of the rumors or the stories or anything he had known had prepared Logan for the sight before him. Tens of thousands of buffalo — or hundreds of thousands, he could not say — covered the river bottom, the brakes, and the prairie to the horizons.

"Oh, I seen it like this up around Fort Dodge," Ezra said, "but it's been a long damn time."

Logan could think of nothing to say. Columns of bison came out of the southern brakes to the river while others moved into the hills and draws or onto the plains beyond. Packs of wolves skulked about the bands. Bulls bellowed and butted heads and rolled in the sand, yet all the herd and the wolves and the coyotes seemed to Logan like one expansive living thing. "Only God Hisself could make this."

Ezra smiled and kept his eyes on the spectacle. "God's work or not, they won't be here five years from now. Better see it while you can. Your sons and daughters won't believe it. Nobody will. You can't tell it right. You gotta see it."

"I don't see how they'll ever be killed out."

Ezra shook his head knowingly. "Logan, I'm tellin' you, they'll be gone in five years if they last that long. I done seen it once. Bob, you're bein' awful quiet over there. This is what we came for."

Bob sat his horse. "I's just thinkin' 'bout how this country's gonna be changed when we get done with it. We always knowed this was here and knowin' it made it easy to keep killin' up at the Arkansas. But when somethin's gone it's gone and when you look at the last of it, you get to wonderin' about what you're doin'. What are we gonna do when we're done killin' buffaloes?"

Ezra looked mirthfully at his partner. "Hell, go north, I reckon. The whole northern herd's still there. The Sioux and Cheyenne ain't killin' 'em off. The heathens ain't got enough sense to do any different than they been doin' since the world was made."

"Then what?"

"We'll do like we said and go into business doin' somethin' else — we might run cattle right here."

"Folks won't know what to think about us. And we won't know what to do with ourselfs. Back when I was runnin' freight, I always knowed this was here. How's it gonna be when it ain't?"

"Well hell, Bob. I s'pose we could go back to St. Louis and open a saloon and run whores if you've lost your stomach for killin' buffalos. But then you won't be able to let yourself drink at your own saloon."

Bob shook his head solemnly. "I'm just sayin', Ezree; that's all. Won't change nothin' no way. These buffalos is goin' away if we do the killin' or if somebody else does the killin'."

"Well I'm sure glad to hear you talkin' sense finally. I'm fixin' to do somethin' I ain't done in I don't know when."

Bob smiled. "Fixin' to kill your horse is what you're fixin' to do."

Ezra slid his rifle into its scabbard. "I won't be needin' her for this." He drew his Colt Navy and started down the hill toward the river. The bison paid him no attention until he was nearly among them, and then a ripple of panic appeared and moved around him like a bubble as he rode through the herd. He lashed his horse, starting this way and that until he cut a bull from a family group. He ran his horse alongside his quarry, a moving speck viewed by his observers. They heard the claps from his pistol as he emptied the cylinder; then again, this time more deliberately.

Bob tamped tobacco into the bowl of his pipe. "He got one down. Might as well just camp right here tonight."

Romack set about gathering wood. The skinners stayed in the kill wagon, watching the herd. "I don't guess you three could pick up a stick of wood," Romack shouted.

The skinners all turned at once. "We never hired on to be no goddamn cooks," Mullins said. Corbin and Hunt looked at Mullins then back at Romack.

Bob lit his pipe. "Be rough afoot in this country." The skinners did not move. Bob jerked his pipe from his mouth. "Love of God! Get up and get some wood!" He spat. "And see if you can't get scalped while you're at it."

The skinners got out of the wagon and shuffled about. Mullins grumbled something about taking orders from a nigger.

"I'll have to watch them three when we get back to Dodge," Bob said casually. "They can't do without me out here, and they know it."

Ezra rode into camp. He held up the tails of three bulls. Bob blew pipe smoke as he laughed. "I reckon the wolfs is grateful," he said.

Logan lay curled beneath his robes, but sleep proved elusive. He felt as if a million buffalo were in camp with him. He listened to their bellowing and splashing in the river and the dull thud of their butting heads. Even as he drifted toward sleep the beasts stayed with him, and at times their bellowing or bolting woke him. Wolves and coyotes howled constantly.

Wolves fascinated him. There were said to be a few wolves left in Kentucky. As far as he knew there had never been coyotes there. Occasionally rumors of wolves had arisen near his home, and the resulting excitement revolved around the opportunity to kill any that might remain. He had seen hundreds of wolves in the past month — thousands maybe. When a number got so large, one could no longer differentiate between hundreds and thousands. Yet he had never seen a wolf up close. Although Bob and Ezra seemed to dislike wild canines, they never shot at them. They probably did not consider them worthy of the lead, powder and trouble. He wanted to at least touch a wolf. Perhaps, he thought, he would shoot one sometime when he was hunting alone.

Hunting alone. At night, alone with his thoughts, the prospect terrified him. Yet he found that when he actually struck out on short hunts for prairie chickens or antelope, he could concentrate on his hunting with little thought of Indians. Certainly he remained alert; he simply pushed his terror to the back of his mind. With every passing day, the country seemed less menacing. But at night the fears returned, and he caught himself curling into a tight ball beneath the cook wagon. He did not envy the skinners who slept in the open.

To his surprise, he enjoyed early morning watch, and in fact felt uneasy whenever one of the skinners spelled him. Sometimes, when Mullins or Corbin or Hunt stood watch, Logan would awaken and lie uneasily, listening, supposing that the fool was asleep or dead and scalped and that camp was about to be attacked by murdering, hating savages. On watch, he felt a measure of control. He trusted Bob and Ezra completely.

This first night on the Canadian he wondered how many hides and tongues they could take in a single day. Surely the wagons would be full in a couple of weeks. Then they would make the arduous trip back to Dodge; then back to

the Canadian. It seemed they would spend more time traveling to trading cen-
ters than actually hunting. Surely Ezra and Bob had thought through these
problems.

Although he prayed fervently every night, the mission his father had
assigned him seemed anything but urgent. That his plan to spread the Gospel
and make disciples of men had become a purely intellectual concept disturbed
him. The fact that it disturbed him only slightly worried him further — whenever he thought about it. His days were filled with hunting and riding and concern about Indians and talk of the same. Among his party, there was much talk
of women and women's anatomy and whisky. He did not take part in these
conversations, although women often occupied his thoughts. There was no
one to witness to except the skinners who disgusted him so that he had not yet
forced himself to engage them in real conversation. Kentucky and his father
and Brother Ramsey and the flock, the camp meetings and revivals and the
riverboat healings all seemed like scenes from another man's life. What he
knew viscerally was that he was part of a small party in a savage-infested
wilderness and that he hoped he made a bit of money and lived to spend it.

Surely, he told himself, he had not come this far to be scalped and left for
vultures. Then again, why not? Undoubtedly, the plains were littered with
corpses of Christians who had struggled and persevered in the face of tremendous danger right up to the moment they died horribly. The Plains: the buffalo,
the raw weather, the worry, the hunting. These things he now knew as much as
he had ever known anything. Sometimes he struggled to remember the sound
of his father's voice or the smells inside their cabin or the sound and feel of
Greasy Creek or the shape of Claudine Monroe's mouth and the scent of her
hair, and often he could not. What he now knew overpowered what he had
known. How could he remember the sound of his father's voice or the scent of
a favorite girl's hair when fear, rifle blasts and the stench of punctured intestines assaulted his senses daily? Most nights he wondered what ludicrous reasoning had brought him to this place. Had his father understood that he could
be sending his only son to die alone and have his bones picked clean by scavengers, to lie with no eulogy, no words said, just another dead traveler bound
to disappear from all memory?

"Time to get up." Bob shook him gently and passed a cup of hot coffee near
his nose. "Wrap up. She's a cold one this mornin'. Cold and clear."

Logan opened his eyes. The smell of the coffee and Bob's pipe and the
bison's racket along the river reminded him where he was.

"You lookin' tired," Bob said. "Just sit here wrapped up and drank your coffee a minute to wake up. Just don't fall back asleep." Bob climbed into the wagon and covered himself. He was snoring before Logan could take three sips. Logan refilled his cup and walked out of camp to find a dark place from which to watch the horses. He found his spot against a clump of chittam. He sat on one robe and draped the other about his shoulders, laid his rifle across his lap and sipped the coffee. He felt better already; the noise in the river bottom made him anxious to begin hunting. He wondered at the way the nights' despair always passed. He said a quick prayer of thanks. Perhaps a cup of coffee, his rifle, a good view, thousands of buffalo and a brittle cold, clear morning were enough for now. He worried little about Comanches. Unless they had perfect night vision, he would see them coming well before they could see him.

He watched the horses and looked over the dark river valley. He could discern movement but not individual bison. At times their motion made it appear that an acre of river bank had detached itself and was moving into the brakes.

He caught a flash of movement among the horses; low movement like a man crawling. He set his cup down and eased his finger inside his rifle's trigger guard. He started to raise the rifle then stopped. Should he alert the camp or wait for a clear shot? Why had he not asked Bob or Ezra how to handle such a situation? More movement. He relaxed his grip and exhaled. "Wolves," his whispered to himself. "Just wolves." He wondered why they never attacked the horses. They seemed content to slink around camp and the horses paid them little attention. "Let my coffee get cold worryin' about wolves," he muttered. The back of his neck hurt from the momentary tension.

From his lie in the sage, Logan watched a band of a dozen or so cows and yearling calves and one old bull. One band in a sea of bands, but Logan had quickly learned to separate the thousands of beasts into family groups. They all faced him and lifted their noses in suspicion, but he had carefully positioned himself downwind. His slow, deliberate movements did not appear to alarm the beasts. But none would turn to offer him a shot. He supposed that one could shoot a buffalo head-on, just beneath its chin, but he remembered Ezra's lesson: Pick the oldest cow and gut shoot her first. When the others become confused by her behavior, knock two or three down with spinal shots, then kill the rest at your leisure. That was fine, but now he did not have a decent gut shot. The thumps from Bob and Ezra's rifles did his patience little good.

At last, a yearling bull turned broadside — an easy shot. But the old cow continued to face him. His impatience got the best of him. He set the front trigger and shot the little bull just behind the shoulder. The wounded beast bolted and the entire band scattered like a covey of quail. Logan leapt to his feet and reloaded, trying all the while to keep an eye on the scattering buffalo. He finished loading and realized that in a matter of seconds he had completely rid several hundred acres of bison.

For all he knew, he had stampeded Bob and Ezra's band as well; their shooting had stopped. Most of the bison had gone downriver. A quarter mile upriver, the young bull lay on its side kicking in its death throes. Logan memorized the spot then walked downriver. On the way, he cut two yard-long cottonwood sticks and tied them together with a strip of rawhide to form a rest like Ezra's. He was not at all sure that he could make a spinal shot. For that matter, he was unsure as to the location of a buffalo's spine. Did it run along the top of a bull's hump or did the hump grow above the spine? Why did he always think of questions when his bosses weren't around? He decided that he should have paid more attention to bison anatomy when he was a skinner.

A hundred and fifty yards downriver, several hundred bison turned to look in his direction. He dropped to his belly and crawled toward a low spot which, much to his surprise and discomfort, held several inches of cold, muddy water. Yet with the bison so nervous, he dared not crawl to higher ground. He eased his rest into position then laid his rifle barrel on the intersection and waited shivering in the cold water. His testicles felt the size of number eight shot. The nearest buffalo continued to stare in his direction. His teeth began to chatter. At last the buffalo lowered their heads to graze. He watched the mature cows. One finally turned slightly and he shot her through the paunch. He heard the fleshy slap of the bullet; the cow shuddered and dropped her head. Several others gathered about her sniffing and nudging. Logan shot the nearest bull just below the top of the hump. A patch of hair flew off the hump and the beast went to its knees. The others stamped their feet and mulled about nervously.

Squeeze, reload, take in a breath, squeeze. He lost track of his shots. Sweat dripped from the end of his nose. He squinted in the acrid smoke. He finished the nearest band then crawled quickly out of the water to another small band and wiped it out. The gun barrel raised blisters on his fingers. He opened the breech, swabbed the barrel, then propped the gun against a clump of chittam to cool. Among Dodge City ruffians, he had heard that a truly salty hunter cooled his rifle barrel by urinating on it. Bob disapproved of the practice having once pissed on his Sharps only to watch the sizzling urine run along the barrel and into the breech where it mixed readily with powder residue.

Ezra and Bob rode up behind him. He stood and water ran down his legs onto his boots. The two gawked at him. "By god, now there's a hunter, Bob," Ezra said. "He hides underwater."

Bob looked over the killing field. "From all the stir, we thought maybe you was walkin' amongst 'em clubbin' 'em on the head. We appreciate you runnin' all them buffalos our way. Only thing is, they never stopped to be shot at."

Logan's feet were cold. He was completely soaked and covered in grass seeds and bits of debris. Ezra bit off a chew of tobacco. "Better get back to camp and dry out so you don't take sick on us."

"There's anothern upriver a piece," Logan said.

The skinners rode up in the kill wagon. Logan looked at them contemptuously. He walked upriver toward his horse.

"By god," he heard Ezra say, "the pup didn't do too bad, did he?"

Ninety-one buffalo in the first two days of hunting along the Canadian. They had so many hides stretched and drying that it was becoming difficult to keep the coyotes and wolves out of camp. On the third night, several wolves ventured to the outer edge of camp to eat the fat scrapings. Romack shot at them with his shotgun. There were yelps, but a dozen or more gray wolves prowled the camp perimeter all night, sniffing and popping their teeth. Next morning the men found three hides badly chewed.

Bob was furious. "I'm fixin' to start shootin' every wolf I see!"

"You'll go through your lead and powder in a day," Ezra said. "I say we just keep a big fire goin' at night and take turn watchin' for wolfs. Me and you and Logan can swap off the regular watch."

"Maybe we oughta just shoot some wolfs and hang 'em up or leave 'em lay out there to scare the other wolfs off," Logan said. He was thinking of the effect the sight of the mutilated corpses still had on him.

Bob snorted. "Why the live wolfs would eat the dead wolfs and lay out there waitin' for us to shoot some more. And I hate thinkin' 'bout them skinners walkin' around out there in the dark with a shotgun."

"Well if they had any sense, they'd be doin' somethin' else for a livin'," Ezra said. "I don't know too many smart skinners."

Logan contemplated the vile habits of prairie predators, animal and human. He nodded in agreement to Ezra's assertion, then remembered that he had joined the outfit as a skinner. He did not know how to take the comment but made no issue. Ezra had said that he did not know *many* smart skinners. Perhaps, then, he knew of a few.

Bob and Ezra decided to deal with the wolf problem by moving camp daily. Their hunting involved little strategy. With so many buffalo crowded into the river bottom and the surrounding brakes and plains, they merely had to pick a few bands, approach with reasonable caution, and wipe them out. Logan's rifle had pounded his shoulder into a patchwork of black, blue and various shades of brown and green. Fortunately, the cool weather continued and his coat helped pad his shoulder.

Bob assured him that the pain would go away shortly, but Logan remained unconvinced. He could not see how his bruises could heal while being pounded a hundred times a day.

On their sixth morning along the Canadian, Bob stopped suddenly, still within earshot of Logan and Ezra. "Somethin' spooked these buffalos over here," he said. Ezra and Logan jogged over to look. A half mile distant, a distinct ripple moved south to north through the bison herd.

"Somebody's ridin' across the river bottom," Ezra said, squinting.

Bob hurried to his picketed horse then returned with a pair of field glasses. He raised the glasses to his eyes and jerked his head uncertainly and fumbled with the focus ring. "I can't see nothin' with these things. I oughta just let you have 'em." He handed the binoculars to Ezra who repeated the performance.

"I don't see nothin' but dirt — wait — no, goddamnit, that's them hills."

"I'll find 'em," Logan said. He knew how to use field glasses. His Uncle Jess, a former Confederate infantryman, had brought two pairs of field glasses home from the war. According to his much-doubted story, he had taken the glasses from two dead Union officers at Tebbs Bend. Upon his return, he gave one pair to Logan who then spent hours sitting on the cabin roof glassing birds or occasional wagon traffic along Greasy Creek, and especially Claudine Monroe's house, hoping she would forgo the privy for the edge of the woods.

He found the disturbance then brought the field glasses smoothly to his face.

"What you see, son?" Ezra asked nervously.

For several seconds Logan could not answer, and not because he had not found the source of the bisons' panic. What first caught his attention were the thick, black braids bouncing against bronze arms. Then the whole scene came into focus: the white shields and naked torsos and two lances, each longer than a man and the bows slung across broad backs. And something else.

"Logan? You seein' it?" Bob asked.

"Yeah." His mouth suddenly tasted very bitter and dry. "Four Indians."

"Love of God!" Bob said. He nodded resolutely. "We knowed it 'fore we come this way."

"They got a woman with 'em."

"A squaw?"

"No. She's a white woman. Tied on a horse."

CHAPTER 19

Eunice Perry was only mildly concerned that her husband had not yet returned from the five-acre field just above the Big Keechi. He was usually in by dark, but the rich little field had produced an abundance of corn to be shucked and hauled to the crib. Her husband had saved this little field for last and now wanted to get the gleaming yellow ears in before the first hard frost. She smiled thinking of how much Clayton enjoyed the sight of a wagon full of clean, shucked ears.

Her biscuits were done; she put the lid back on the Dutch oven, whisked off the ashes, and with a poker, positioned the oven close to the coals so the biscuits would stay warm without burning. Perhaps, she thought, she should fix her eight-year-old son a plate; she might even have time to feed her infant daughter before her husband finished his work. Then she and Clayton could enjoy a peaceful meal.

She glanced again out the open door. It would be hard dark in a quarter of an hour. She stood in the door for a moment and let the October breeze cool her. She raised her arms and then her skirt so the breeze could cool her sweaty legs. The cook fire made the little cabin oppressively hot. She stepped out onto the front step and luxuriated in the coolness. She looked anxiously toward the creek bottom, expecting to see any second the mule's ears and then the top of her husband's head as they came up the hill.

She decided to go back inside and prepare her son's plate. He probably had tired by now of playing with her thimbles and would be hungry. She wondered why the dog had not tried to take advantage of the open door. She turned to go inside and smelled a curious odor: old wood ashes — and something else; something musky she could not place. She stepped inside only to be jerked violently by her hair. She screamed and groped at the back of her head as she fell backward. She landed on her back and looked up into a young face streaked with black paint. The coal-black eyes were wild and hard. Thick, greasy braids dangled nearly to the young man's waist. He was naked save for breechclout, leggings and moccasins and he held in his hand a small, crude ax decorated with feathers and something else she did not recognize. She tried to scream, but couldn't get her breath.

The young man leered and stood straddling her like a wolf over prey. He looked up and spoke in a tongue she did not understand, and she became aware of three other men standing at her head. Then another stepped out of the shadows, this one older, stocky and powerfully built. He wore a horned buffalo headdress and carried a heavy lance. From the butt of a lance hung a fresh scalp, and Eunice Perry knew now why her husband had not come home for supper.

She sobbed and tried to roll onto her belly to hide her face, but the older man kicked her in the ribs and held the tip of the lance at her throat; she felt its stony coldness and the jagged sharpness. She could barely breathe, as if someone were standing on her chest. She sobbed, "Oh, no, no, no; God, please no." The men laughed.

She remembered her children. She could not let the men know that her children were in the house. She prayed that the baby would not wake; that Stephen would not come outside. Perhaps the savages would simply take her and leave. She could bear anything as long as her children were safe.

The feral scent of her captors nauseated her. She recognized the smell of sweat but it did not smell like her husband's sweat.

One of the Indians grabbed her arms and pulled her away from the door. She heard the others ransacking the cabin and Stephen screaming, "Get away! Get away!" Then "Mama!" She pleaded, knowing that the savages understood her pleas if not her words. Then she saw her son. An older Indian with a horribly pocked face had him by the waist, dragging him kicking and screaming. The boy bit the Indian's arm and earned a vicious backhand.

Eunice Perry fought, kicking and clawing. Her legs were strong. As a girl she had been fleeter than most of the boys and now as a young woman she was taller than most men and taller than any of her captors. The stocky leader stepped in front of her and before he could raise his arms, Eunice Perry went at him with her fingers, gouging and ripping as if she meant to tear his eyes from their sockets and pull his face from his skull.

The Indian screamed in pain and the others laughed. The man came up under her chin with the butt of his lance and the force lifted her off the ground and sent her dazed and choking onto her back. The other Indians laughed harder still.

Eunice Perry looked into the bloody face of her tormentor. She did not see anger or pity in his tight-lipped smile; only contempt. She looked upward and away from his face. A clear night, she thought. There'll be frost in the morning. She felt a tremendous downward pressure and tightness in her left shoulder. Then to her astonishment she saw the lance shaft protruding upward from her shoulder and the scalp dangling from the butt. She tried to pull the lance free with her other arm, but the stone tip was completely buried in the earth beneath her.

Now she did not hear her son's hysterical screams or the Comanches' laughter. She did not notice her clothes being cut and ripped away or her legs being violently pried apart. She furrowed her brow in concentration. The biscuits would be hard as a rock by now, she thought. She wondered: Is that the baby crying? Why yes, she is crying. She's probably hungry. I've got to get up from here and feed that child.

C H A P T E R 2 0

The Indians were half a mile ahead, riding northward, and, as far as Bob and Ezra could tell, were unaware of their pursuers. Logan had assumed that the pursuit of savages always involved skilled tracking. Thus far, he had seen nothing of the sort. His older companions simply held a general course and seemed to hope for a sighting. He expressed his surprise and Bob pointed to the buffalo-trampled ground and asked if he wanted to try to find the hoof print of an unshod horse.

They rode on, keeping to the low contours. Bob and Ezra speculated on the odds of encountering a rearguard; they decided that the Indians were far enough north to feel secure. At times the three dismounted and skulked afoot to some vantage point before pushing on. Twice they glimpsed the Indians. Other times, they saw only their dust. Logan wondered what would happen if they caught up with the Indians. Would they try to kill them and take back the woman? Or would they look for an opportunity to steal her back? For that matter, did one, without exception, pursue Indians who were in possession of a white woman? Bob and Ezra had not discussed the matter. They simply mounted and rode, a tactic that seemed out of character since prior to that moment, the apparent approach to dealing with savages had been to avoid them. Then there was the matter of the woman; he told himself that he mustn't forget that detail. He had heard many stories of Indian treatment of white women. He had seen first hand the Comanches' treatment of captured men.

Riding through the hills and draws, at times jumping narrow drainages, Logan pondered but could not take to heart the fact that in few minutes he might be involved in a desperate fight with four savages who probably could outfight any white man he had ever known. He thought again of the ferocity of the Pawnee that had smashed Muntz's skull. He wondered how he would respond to such an attack, and even if he would see it coming in time to respond at all. These Indians, he supposed, were Comanches, the kind of Indian that had slaughtered the Pawnees who had slaughtered Muntz and Krebs the way he himself would kill a snake. He desperately hoped that he would remember to use his weapons and would not simply shit in his britches.

Through the field glasses, these Indians looked surprisingly tall and dark, and he had not imagined the long, thick braids hanging to the men's waists. These undoubtedly were the rudest of all heathens.

They moved away from the river bottom and into rough sandhills. Aside from the low clumps of sage there was not a single shrub, let alone a tree. The buffalo hunters wore no chaps and the sand bluestem, warmed by the mid-morning sun, glistened with melting frost that soaked them from their waists down. Though Logan felt clammy and cold, sweat ran down his sides.

Ezra and Bob stopped and Logan barely halted Rufus in time to avoid plowing into them. Both were looking up at dozens of vultures wheeling and circling beyond the next hill. "I bet we ain't camped five miles from a Indian camp," Bob whispered. Ezra, wide eyed, checked his weapons and nodded.

"What has buzzards got to do with Indians?" Logan asked. He hoped the vultures were circling dead or dying Indians. Then again, perhaps some tribe more horrible than the Comanches had swept down upon the camp to slaughter everyone. God help the poor white woman.

"Them Indians throw their meat scraps all over the place," Bob said. "Their dogs don't leave nothin', but them buzzards is always hopin'. I ain't never seen a Comanche camp more than two days old didn't have buzzards flyin' over it."

Bob and Ezra dismounted, handed their reins to Logan and scrambled up the hill. They made the top, took a quick look, then crawled over. Logan had not expected to be left alone within earshot of an Indian encampment. He strained to hear, but heard nothing but his own pulse and the wind in the grass and faint, raspy birdsong and the horses' breathing. He needed to make water — he felt as though he would burst — but when he dismounted, he made very little. Within thirty seconds he felt the need to go again. His mouth was cotton dry, but the thought of drinking water made his stomach roll.

Bob slid back down the bank on the seat of his pants with the lumbering Ezra close behind. Both men were wild-eyed and obviously bursting to talk about what they had seen.

Bob wiped his brow with a bandanna. "Only four or five lodges. Must be some kind of huntin' camp — else there'd be more lodges."

Logan still hoped the buzzards were circling dead Indians. "Comanches, are they?"

Ezra shook his head. "Lookin' at them lodges, I'd say Kiowa. Ain't much difference in a Kiowa and a Comanche. Sometimes you get 'em together. Anyways, if we don't get busy, we're fixin' to hear that woman start squallin'."

"Seem like we have to wait 'til dark," Bob said. "And what we gonna do 'bout their dogs smellin' us?"

Sweat dripped from the end of Ezra's outsized nose. "I say we just rush 'em like we done that time on the Little Caddo."

"Ezree, we was with a whole comp'ny of rangers when we done that. That fool McCulloch still like to got us all killed. We talked about it for years."

"But there was prob'ly forty lodges full of Comanches too. We wait 'til dark and they ain't gonna be nothin' worth bringin' back." He rolled his eyes. "And what in hell are we gonna do with a woman? End up haulin' her to Fort Dodge, I imagine." He spat. "Hell."

Bob looked at the vultures. "Seein' as how there's a Kiowa camp right here, I'd say we best be thinkin' 'bout movin' anyways." He sighed and swallowed then closed his eyes and laughed softly. "I guess we best get ready and hit 'em. I don't see no way to sneak in there and get the poor old thing. Logan, you ain't gettin' sick on us, are you?"

"No sir," he lied. "I don't know nothin' about fightin'. I'm afraid I'll get every one of us killed."

"We liable to all get our balls fed to us, but it won't be your fault," Ezra said gently.

"You just as well put your rifle away," Bob said. "Use your pistol for this. Just come in behind us and shoot ever thing that moves 'cept for that woman. And if you ain't sure, why go ahead and shoot anyways."

"I never shot this pistol you give me." Logan did not think he had the strength to draw the pistol, let alone shoot it with any accuracy. He had inherited the huge Colt Dragoon from Ezra who had abandoned it for the newer and much lighter Colt Navy.

"Son, there ain't no choice," Ezra said. "We can't leave no woman with them butchers and we need every gun we got. You gonna be able to stay on your horse?"

Logan could see the fear on both men's faces. They swallowed after nearly every word. He nodded weakly.

"Which way's this wind blowin' Bob? We need to come in from downwind so them dogs won't smell us 'til we're right on top of 'em." He turned to Logan. "We can't leave no Kiowa alive. We do and we won't see the end of the day. I just hope most of the bucks is out huntin'."

"Seems to me like we're right where we need to be," Bob said. "Wind's right in our face. Good thing too, else them dogs would've already smelled us and we'd be scalped and on fire by now."

"We could leave her," Ezra said. "You know what our odds are."

"Yes suh, and we can all three partner up in hell, too," Bob said. "We knowed what was here when we come."

Ezra smiled thinly. "I never said we should. I said we *could*. We could use some of your prayin' about now, Logan. We might need some of your healin' before we're through. Goddamn, I wish there was another way." He spat.

Bob drew his ancient Colt Walker, nodded to the other two and started his horse up the hill. Logan drew the heavy pistol; his wrist was so limp he had to rest the barrel on his saddle horn. He prayed for safety and deliverance from the hands of the savages and for the woman and for His tender mercy should they perish. He prayed on as they eased their horses over the hill and into the next draw, and he did not care if Ezra and Bob heard him.

Halfway out of the draw, without looking back and without speaking or looking at one another, the two older men spurred their horses and rode upon the Kiowa encampment. Logan ground his teeth and raised his gun barrel from the pommel and rode out of the draw behind them. They rode down a hill and into the camp which lay in sparse cottonwood and hackberry along a narrow creek. The sight of the buffalo skin lodges shocked Logan, their height and girth, and the wildness they projected like abodes of devils.

Twenty yards out, the camp dogs erupted. They howled hysterically and charged out to meet the attackers; huge gray mongrels, rib sprung and wild. They charged viciously then broke off their attacks at the last second to run, tails tucked, a short distance away to howl or charge again.

Logan searched frantically for a target. He heard nothing but hoof beats and the dogs' howling. Then there were screams and suddenly figures were running just ahead of Ezra and Bob as if they had magically risen from the earth. The loudness of the first shot startled Logan, and then both men were shooting and Logan saw figures pitch forward. Yet he could find no target for himself. Bob and Ezra screamed curses and shot their pistols, and before Logan had gotten off a single round, they were through camp and turning their horses and changing pistols for another pass.

A shriveled figure, more ghoul than flesh and blood arose beside him and he recoiled in horror. He shot twice and both times sand flew behind this specter so grotesque that Logan knew not if it was male or female. He shot again and blinked at the recoil. When he opened his eyes the apparition had vanished. He did not search the ground for remains.

Then silence. Ezra asked Bob if he was shot and Bob answered that he was not. A dozen or so bodies lay about camp, some quite small. Among the feral odors, there was a rancid human scent Logan knew very well.

Bob rode from the far end of camp to meet him and had already tied his neckerchief about his nose. He shook his head. "Lawd, I b'lieve we wasted our bullets. These devils was sick. Cholera. I reckon. We best git." He gagged. "Oh lawd, I can't take this smell."

Logan looked about, dazed. "We killed a bunch of younguns. And women."

Bob gagged again and shook his head. "Well hell now, there ain't a one of these wouldn't cut your throat in a heartbeat. You ain't got time to worry 'bout it. You just gotta shoot. We got some men too, but they weren't in no shape to fight. I thought they was actin' funny. Not a one put up a fight, and that ain't like a Kiowa."

Ezra shouted from the creek and they rode toward him. He seemed to be looking at someone on the ground. "I found her," he said. "Looks like they never got around to really workin' her over. There's a white fellar too. He ain't in too good of a shape."

On the ground with her legs curled beneath her sat a sullen, dirty teenage girl in a faded yellow cotton day dress. She regarded them all flatly with green eyes. She appeared unhurt. Ezra hunkered before her. "Are you hurt girl?"

"No sir," she said hoarsely.

"What's your name?"

"Lizbeth Keltner. I come from Ioni Creek. Where am I at now?"

"Miss Lizbeth, you're a far piece from home," Bob said solemnly. "Worked you over some did they?"

"Nope. They tied me to that horse, but they acted like they was gettin' sick.

I think they started to kill me or just leave me once or twice, but they brung me on. They seemed like they was in a hurry; we didn't hardly stop for nothin'. I done lost count of how many days we was ridin'. We got here and they throwed me down and kept goin'."

The girl's quiescence astounded Logan. He wondered if she was all there.

"I reckon my folks is wonderin' where I'm at," Elizabeth said.

Bob laid his hand on Ezra's back. "Ezree, we gotta get outta here. This place is full of cholera." He pointed toward the lodges. "Them we shot would've been dead in two days anyway." He pinched his nostrils. "Lawd this smell. Nothin worse than sick people shit."

They heard a groan from back in trees. "Lord, I thought the poor bastard was dead," Ezra said. "Prob'ly wishes he was. We oughta go ahead and shoot him. His bag's swelled up the size of a hornets nest."

The white man lay naked and spread eagle, tied to four stakes. Bob ran to get his canteen, and Ezra cut the rawhide thongs. "Don't try to get up," he said. "We're gettin' you some water."

Bob knelt and the man drank weakly at first then so greedily that Bob jerked the canteen away. "Careful, now; you'll founder."

"I never would've believed a man could live through what this feller's lived through," Ezra said. The man lay on his back, staring upward.

Bob leapt across the clearing to block Elizabeth's view of the man's genitals. "Lawd what's wrong with us? Logan, take Miss Lizbeth on up to where the horses are."

"Yes sir; yes ma'am; you best come on and go with me." He hoped his knees would not buckle. He was more than happy to get away from the unfortunate captive.

"What'd they do to him?" Elizabeth asked, wide-eyed. "What's made him swell up so?"

Logan's throat constricted. He could not fathom having a conversation about a man's privates with any female, let alone with a girl he did not know. He hoped a short explanation would do. "I think they burnt him there some way."

"He looks like a bull, don't he?"

"Huh?"

"A bull — all swelled up like he is."

"Lord!"

"Don't you think he does?"

Heat rose in Logan's face and ears. "This ain't somethin' you oughta be seein'." He didn't think he should be seeing it either. Thinking of the man's condition made him feel like he was peering off the edge of a cliff.

They walked through the trees to the horses. Bob walked up and nodded to Elizabeth. "Ezree's lookin' for that man's britches. We best check in these lodges. Might be some other white folks about."

Logan nodded matter-of-factly for the girl's sake; he could not imagine sticking his head into a Kiowa lodge. Yet he could think of no way, short a display of abject cowardice, to avoid the task. He drew his pistol again and walked unsteadily to the most distant lodge, gathered himself and pulled the door flap back and peered into the gloom. The smell of wood smoke, sweat and grease hit him in the face as if pushed by a strong breeze. Three pallets of buffalo robes were stacked neatly against the lodge wall and the little fire pit in the middle of the lodge glowed weakly, raising a thin column of smoke. Spread about on the trampled grass floor were rude cooking utensils, brass and copper cups and bowls, and implements of bone and horn.

Logan was moved by the domesticity of the scene and the realization that this skin lodge had been a home, that people had slept there and had risen to eat and make a life. He let the door flap fall and moved to the next lodge.

Bob evidently had finished his lodge investigations and now busied himself cursing and shooting at camp dogs bold enough to return and bare their teeth at him. The more timid dogs howled in the distance.

Logan parted the door flap on the second lodge and stepped back to catch his breath. He breathed deeply then pushed the flap aside and stepped inside. The close air reeked of the sickness he had become accustomed to those five days on the Missouri River. The fire pit was cold; the earthen floor had been churned into a quagmire. Utensils were scattered about in the mud. Against the lodge wall to his left, a matted mess of black hair protruded from a stack of buffalo robes.

Logan approached warily, expecting at any moment some painted devil leaping from the pile of robes. Yet there was no movement, and as he drew closer he heard labored breathing. He bent over the robes. Beneath the black hair were a young woman's dark eyes, wide with terror and glistening with fever, and cheeks shriveled so that her lips had drawn away exposing her teeth. The young woman turned her head slightly to look at him; she made no effort to escape. Logan kept his pistol on the woman and pulled back the robe. His hands shook violently. The woman wore a simple buckskin dress horribly stained by her own fluids, and in her arms she held a naked infant obviously dead and stiff. "Oh Lord," he whispered, inhaling raggedly. The woman tried to pull the infant away, but in her weakness she seemed barely able to move even her eyelids.

He remembered Bob's warning against leaving any Kiowa alive. Yet he could not see how a single sick woman could cause the slightest harm. He started to leave her; he wanted to run screaming and jerking his hair. He briefly considered putting her out of her misery. Only God knew the suffering she had already endured.

Yet he could not shoot her. He laid his hand on her forehead. The heat startled him. The woman whimpered and tried to turn her head away from him. "God forgive me for scarin' you this way," he whispered. He kept his hand on her head and prayed on the blood of the Lamb. He prayed for healing and he recited the scripture that had been passed down from his father: "And when I passed by thee, and saw thee polluted in thine own blood, I said unto thee when thou *wast* in thy blood, Live; yea, I said unto thee when thou *wast* in thy blood, *Live!*"

"All clear, Logan?" Bob yelled from outside.

Logan covered the woman and stepped outside and gulped air that a few minutes before had seemed intolerably fetid. "Clear."

"I was about to think you was taking a little nap."

"Just lookin'. A man don't get a chance to look in a Kiowa lodge every day."

Bob laughed and arched his eyebrows. "Now ain't you somethin'. Awhile ago, you was shakin' so you couldn't hardly stay on your horse."

Logan looked at Elizabeth. She stared back at him. He would have preferred that she not hear Bob's comment. He wondered about her age.

"I found his britches," Ezra yelled from the creek.

Bob started in that direction. "You keep Miss Lizbeth up here. I'll go and help Ezree."

Logan and the girl stared in the direction of the creek. They did not talk. Logan cleared his throat after every swallow.

"Logan, bring Rufus down here," Ezra yelled after a few minutes. Logan walked his horse to the creek. Bob and Ezra had the man on his feet. Each supported him by an arm. They each grabbed one of the man's legs and lifted him onto Rufus's back. The man screamed.

"What's he squallin' like that for?" Elizabeth's voice startled Logan. He had not realized she had followed him back to the creek.

"Girl, you'd squall too, if you was him," Ezra said. "Bob, we'd best tie him on. I don't see how he's gonna stand it."

"We gotta go," Bob said. "Be a miracle sure enough if we don't take sick. We done been here too long. Them bucks is liable to come back too. You know good and well they heard the shootin'."

Logan looked at the dead scattered about the encampment. He could not bring himself to look at their faces. "Ain't we gonna bury these dead Kiowa?"

Ezra snorted. "Hell son, the dogs would have every one of 'em dug up before we got a half mile from here. Bob's right. We best get right now. That's why there ain't but four lodges here. The other heathens saw what was goin' on and pulled up and left. That's why them bucks throwed this girl down and kept goin'." He looked at the carnage and then spat. "Girl, climb up on this horse. I don't know what you're gonna do for shoes."

The four skinners sat like vultures, staring at Elizabeth. Ezra dismounted and pointed his finger at the four. "I'll kill and skin the first sumbitch that touches this girl."

Romack set the lid on his cast iron kettle. "What in hell have you three got?"

Ezra helped Elizabeth from the horse. The tortured man had hollered most of the way back to camp. Now, evidently exhausted, he moaned softly.

"I believe Miss Lizbeth's all right," Bob said. "I don't know about this feller. You ain't never seen nothin' like it."

Romack made a pallet while Logan, Bob and Ezra pulled the tortured man off Rufus. The skinners showed no inclination to help. They kept their eyes on Elizabeth who now sat in Romack's wagon and glared back at them while she dug in her ear with her finger. The three eased the man onto the pallet. Logan glanced at Elizabeth and noticed for the first time the freckles on her nose.

Ezra looked at the man lying on the stiff buffalo robes. "I can't think of nothin' to do for him, Earl, after them Kiowa women done him that way. I reckon we'll just have to wait for him to die. I want you to look; we couldn't even button his britches."

Logan realized that the sick woman he tried to heal might have been one of the man's torturers.

They all turned their attention to Elizabeth. "How old are ye, young lady?" Romack asked.

"Seb'mteen."

"Come from down on Ioni," Bob said. "They ain't been hit down there in a spell."

Elizabeth wiped her runny nose with the back of her hand. "They caught me at the branch. I was doin' the washin'," she said. "They acted sick. Never did hurt me."

"How about your family?" Logan asked.

"They'll be wonderin' where I'm at. I hope they don't think I run off."

Ezra cleared his throat. "Uh, honey, I don't 'magine your folks is alive no more."

"My mama'll be worried sick."

"Lizbeth, are you hearin' me? I hate to give you bad news, but you need to figure out what you're gonna do."

Elizabeth's legs dangled off the back of the wagon. She gently swung them up and down. "Everybody up and down Ioni Creek is prob'ly out lookin' for me. I bet Daddy's fit to be tied."

Romack coughed. "Well . . . I guess I can make some sorta shoes out of a scrap of hide. Them little feet'll freeze off if I don't."

Bob looked at Ezra. Ezra looked at Romack. Logan looked at Bob. Elizabeth stared straight ahead. The man on the pallet continued to moan. Bob and Ezra stepped away, and motioned for Logan to join them. "Somethin' ain't right about that girl," Ezra whispered a little too loudly. If Elizabeth heard his comment, she gave no indication. "I wonder if them Kiowa done somethin' to her. Cause she ain't hearin' what I'm tellin' her."

Bob nodded grimly. "She's either a tough egg or she's off plumb. Why she ain't cried once since we seen her." He looked furtively back at Elizabeth. "Who ever heard of a girl caught by Kiowas not cryin'? What are we gonna do with her?"

"We could take her to Fort Sill or Dodge," Ezra said. "But I don't see no sense in doin' it 'til we're ready to take in a load of hides. She ain't got no family no more. If we go in now, we'll miss our chance to get the jump on everybody else. I don't see no sense in it."

Logan looked again at Elizabeth. He was anything but sure about the logistics imposed by a girl in camp. "We gonna have to watch them filthy skinners," he said.

Ezra smiled. "We stay here a little longer and we might have to start watchin' you. Hell we might have to all start watchin' one another."

Logan did not appreciate the comment, but silently acknowledged his difficulty concentrating on anything but Elizabeth. He nodded toward the pallet. "What about that man?"

Bob sighed. "I reckon we'll just haul him around 'til he dies. But I don't see no sense in movin' yet. There's plenty of buffaloes here and I don't 'spect any more trouble outta them Kiowas. They're either dead or about dead."

"Maybe he don't have to die," Logan said.

Ezra rolled his eyes. "What's that supposed to mean?"

"I mean he might die and he might not too. I gotta try." Logan knelt near the man's head. Ezra shuffled wearily to the other side of the pallet and hunkered to watch Logan. "What in Christ's name you aim to do?"

"In Christ's name, I aim to heal him. It's a gift I have. I done told you about it."

Elizabeth stood up in Romack's wagon. "I need to be gettin' on home." She waited for a response. "Y'all gonna take me ain't you? My mama's bound to be havin' a fit."

CHAPTER 21

Three miles from the main encampment east of the red canyons, Cuts Something halted his raiders. It was nearly dark, and he wanted to enter camp in the full morning sun. He dismounted and arched his stiff back. Some of the younger warriors untied the three captive white women and tied them spread eagle to stakes. They bound the white boy's hands behind his back and allowed him to sit or lie down as he pleased. He no longer resisted, but stared silent and unblinking.

The raiding had gone very well. The large party had split up and struck several small farms and had taken a number of scalps, horses and mules and the women and the boy. Cuts Something had hoped to bring back a few girls to help the women with their work. Considering his wives' disposition, he doubted the white women would last long. The young men, looking forward to extended sport, had voiced their hope that their women would not immediately cut up or set fire to the captive women.

The boy, on the other hand, was young enough that he might make a warrior if he survived the initial beatings the Comanche women undoubtedly would give him. If he turned out unsuited for fighting and raiding, he could always be castrated and enslaved. Time would tell. He looked hearty enough. Much to That's It's amusement, the boy, upon seeing his mother's plight, had done his best to pull Otter Belt's ear off.

Cuts Something watched the young men violating the captive women; they never seemed to tire of it. Of course he had been much the same, but age had ground off some of his edge. Age and that night on the Tongue River when a captive Texan woman, after she had given up trying to bite a plug out of his face, spat in his eyes and snarled in Spanish, "Your people are dead!" He back-handed her, but his lust left him at once. No captive woman had ever been so brazen, and no amount of beating and humiliation could break her. All night long she lay tied out, naked, wailing strange songs he assumed were her death songs. She laughed deliriously, and at last That's It, fearing the woman was either mad or a witch, got up and shot three arrows in her chest, then lay back down and slept.

But the incident haunted Cuts Something and thereafter he found himself little aroused by the struggles of captive women. Surely it was bad medicine when a warrior could not satisfactorily break a captive woman.

So he had been pleasantly surprised at his sharp arousal on the Big Keechi. The woman scratching his face only made it sharper. He regretted having to pin her with his lance; he would have liked to have taken her along with the other women, but she was of the same ilk as the woman on the Tongue. He killed her quickly after he had taken his pleasure. He saw no reason to leave her for further suffering. After all, he told himself, unlike some of his contemporaries, he was not a cruel man.

That's It had a small fire burning. Cuts Something sat wearily and prepared his pipe. He hoped the young men would settle down soon; he wanted to sleep undisturbed until dawn.

Cuts Something awoke shortly before sunrise. That's It already had the fire rekindled. They roused the young men. Cuts Something wanted to be above the main encampment just after sunup. The audacity of his raid would further raise his stature, and now the Texans would know that the People could not be herded like cattle onto a reservation. The Wanderers had gone on a revenge raid; scalps had been the objective and now they had them.

Cuts Something initially divided the horses evenly over the protests of two young men who felt they were being slighted as they had actually secured most of the horses. He himself had more horses than he knew what to do with, so he quieted the two by allowing them to divide his share.

They colored their faces vermilion and painted yellow and vermilion streaks on their horses. They hung the fresh scalps from their shields and weapons so as to make them most conspicuous. They tied the boy and the naked, whimpering captive women onto the horses and rode briskly toward the main encampment.

They stopped on a low rise just above and within earshot of camp. They sat their horses. When the early morning sun lit the lodges and the camp began to stir, Cuts Something whooped at the top of his lungs and screamed that he had led the People on a raid into the heart of the Texas settlements. He and his warriors had struck ferociously and now had many scalps and horses and the deaths of Short Lance and Tall Dog and Elk Rub had been avenged, yet not a warrior had been lost.

Shrill cries rose from the encampment. The People poured from their lodges. Cuts Something repeated his boasts, and the war party started single file toward camp. Halfway down the hill they were met by She Invites Her Sisters who held a long, notched pole upon which the warriors hung the scalps. That done, they rode single file into camp amid much whooping and boasting, and each warrior peeled away from the column and rode to his lodge.

With the help of several older boys, She Invites Her Sisters planted the scalp pole near the center of camp. Firewood was gathered and stacked nearby.

The women pulled the captives from the horses; from inside their lodges, the warriors heard the angry cries of their bereaved women and the shrieking and sobbing of the white women.

Too excited to rest, Cuts Something emerged from his lodge to watch the festivities. Two of the captive women were being dragged about by their hair; hardwood sticks were heating in the fires. The largest and most intractable of the captives, a broad-shouldered woman with dark red hair, stark naked and enraged, had Fast Girl by the hair. She swung her about with one hand while pounding her with the opposite fist. The hapless girl shrieked and flailed her short arms. The men roared with laughter while the stunned Comanche women allowed the beating to continue for several seconds before converging and beating the Texan to the ground. Once free of the woman's grasp, Fast Girl rolled about in the dust, crying, kicking and covering her face with her arms.

Cuts Something watched the tussle with mild amusement. He thought briefly of dragging the red-haired woman back to his lodge; his wives — Fast Girl especially — would approve of the woman's further degradation. He decided against it. Fast Girl's beating left him with a slight sense of foreboding. Perhaps, he thought, they should move soon. He went back to his lodge and fell immediately to sleep.

*   *   *

Just after dark, the Comanche women lighted the wood pile and tied the three captive women to a pole a near the fire. Their faces painted vermilion, the warriors emerged from their lodges and sat in a circle around the fire. Four drummers began their rhythmic beating and the women began chanting softly as they danced around the captives. The chanting and dancing increased in fervor, and periodically one of the warriors would leap into the circle of firelight and recount his exploits through voice and exaggerated gesture.

Cuts Something's legs hurt so that he did not think he could stand, let alone dance. To his great relief, his muscles loosened nicely after a bit of animated telling.

The celebration continued. Frequently a Comanche woman or one of the older children would leap at the tied captives and feign a scalping or dangle the fresh scalps of the captives' loved ones before their faces. Two of the captive women cringed and cried piteously, but the large woman, now with horrid welts on her face and burns on her naked body, glared at her captors. Brandishing a knife and with one eye swollen shut, Fast Girl jumped at the woman and stopped just short of cutting her throat. The woman blinked; nothing more.

Cuts Something watched the big woman with interest. He felt sure the two timid women would die shortly. The big woman, however, would make it through the winter easily so long as they kept her fed. His wives would get much work out of her. Then he could sell her back to the Texans come spring. Were he a white man, he would pay a considerable sum for her. Of course he could keep her for a wife but he did not think he had the energy to deal with her.

He turned his attention to Otter Belt who was going on at length about a coup he scored with his hand ax.

Cuts Something was glad for the unseasonably warm days. He sat in the late morning sun, feeling his muscles relax. The raiding and dancing had exhausted him. Earlier that morning he had been unable to stand erect and had to summon She Invites Her Sisters to build up his fire and rub his lower back until he could step outside with dignity.

He watched his two older wives fussing over the small captive boy. The women were quite taken with the little boy's yellow hair. They ran their hands through it and cooed to him as if he were a pet. Whenever he tried to jerk away, they slapped him lightly as if correcting a recalcitrant dog.

He wanted to move camp soon. They had plenty of buffalo meat, and his stature was now as high as it ever had been. A strike against a single Texas farm carried far more prestige than months of raiding unarmed Mexican villages. In addition to leading the People to heretofore unheard-of numbers of bison, he had successfully struck deeper into the heavily armed Texas settlements than anyone had struck in many summers.

He would move camp as soon as he felt up to a two-day ride. In the meantime, She Invites Her Sisters was telling everyone that her husband was busy making medicine and seeking guidance from the spirits. That's It, in no shape at all for an arduous ride himself, happily corroborated.

A commotion at the far end of the encampment jarred him from his thoughts. There were shrieks and whoops and much laughter. He was curious, but did not feel like getting up. Shortly, several boys came running from the direction of the disturbance, laughing and jabbering excitedly. Cuts Something called them over and asked them what had happened. Fast Girl, they said shyly, had again gotten too close to the big Texan woman.

CHAPTER 22

"I don't believe he'll do a drop of good," Ezra said.

Bob was watching Logan. "There was a widder woman down to Natchi-dotches had the gift," Bob said. "I seen her heal folks. Least they got well anyways."

"If she was such a healer, how come she was a widder?"

"Everybody's got to die, Ezree."

"Well." Ezra shifted his weight from one knee to the other. "I'd say them people was fixin' to get well anyway."

Logan tried to ignore the older men's conjecture. Getting Elizabeth out of his mind was proving even harder. He knelt and placed his hands on the man's sallow face. The man's eyelids fluttered at Logan's touch. He sobbed and Logan felt his breath on his palms. Logan prayed silently. He prayed on the blood of the Lamb that His healing power would flow through his own feeble hands. He quoted aloud from the book of Ezekiel and exhorted the man to live. The man sobbed again exposing his toothless gums.

"I don't see how he's gonna live all swelled up the way he is," Ezra whispered to Bob. Logan prayed on. He finished and looked at his companions. He fought self-consciousness yet heat rose in his face. Bob and Ezra stood awkwardly looking at their feet. The skinners stared. Elizabeth had gotten out of the wagon and now sat on a buffalo robe toasting her bare feet before Romack's cook fire. She seemed far more interested in the dried meat she was chewing than in divine healing.

Logan walked to the fire and poured a cup of coffee. His ears burned and he knew the ridicule that awaited him if the man did not recover. He sipped his coffee and looked about too casually, as if Elizabeth were not sitting there.

Bob and Ezra continued to stare at the tortured man. "If he's gonna get well, I hope he don't take too long doin' it," Ezra said.

"Earl, them shoes makes that gal look like a Lipan squaw." Ezra was watching Elizabeth dragging a bucket of water from the little creek.

Romack dumped a palm full of coffee into his pot, started to dump another, but paused instead. "Well hell; now you've made me lose count. I ain't heard her fuss about them boots one time." Elizabeth had gone barefooted about camp for two days while Romack fashioned a pair of crude, ill-fitting parfleche boots. She seemed delighted despite the fact that the boots bagged around her ankles and curled beneath her toes.

The men all agreed that Elizabeth was an energetic and resourceful worker. Romack doted unmercifully over her. Ezra and Bob continued to deflect her questions about when she would be going home. Logan, although he spent nearly all his wakeful hours and a good many of his sleeping hours thinking about Elizabeth, could not bring himself to return her gaze let alone make conversation with her. He had managed the past two mornings to at least nod in response to her greeting.

His shooting had become so mechanical that he could annihilate a band of bison while imagining what he might say to Elizabeth if an opportunity for conversation arose. She was tall and angular, and, at present, filthy and disheveled, but obviously a young woman. Logan's grooming standards had fallen considerably over the past several weeks. Whatever task he performed, he imagined that Elizabeth watched and admired from a distance. He had become so self-conscious around camp that he could hear himself gulping whenever he ate or drank. Bob and Ezra had taken to watching their language around the girl even though she had already given Mullins several impressive cussings for trying to follow her on one of her "little walks." The other two skinners seemed to have taken Ezra's warning to heart.

Eight days had passed since Logan's healing attempt, and the tortured man still looked near death. He had not spoken a word, although the day after Logan's healing effort he rolled off of his pallet and managed to relieve himself and had taken care of the chore ever since.

Logan sat down with his plate of beans and tongue. He was more than ready for venison or prairie chicken, but they had been too busy shooting buffalo to hunt other game. He ate without tasting and furtively watched Elizabeth going about her work at the edge of the firelight. He glanced about and saw Ezra watching him. Logan could not discern the older man's expression in the poor light.

The man on the pallet coughed and moved his head back and forth restlessly. "Them bitches," he sobbed. "Them heathen bitches come after me with them sticks." He sobbed and muttered something unintelligible. Everyone else in camp sat bolt upright to listen. "They got them sticks out of the fire," he said. "Them bitches just kept jobbin' me with them hot sticks." His sobs became whimpers.

Logan looked at the faces in the firelight. Ezra shook the grounds from his cup. "I believe he'll die yet," he said."

"It just tears me all to pieces to hear a man carryin' on like that," Elizabeth said from the shadows.

Logan had just propped his rifle against a cedar stump to let the barrel cool when he saw Romack riding one of the mules toward him. He had been expecting the skinners; he had eight bison down and had been doing mental arithmetic to determine if he would be better off being paid by the hide as opposed to the current arrangement of two dollars per day. Romack rode through the killing field. He looked at the dead buffalo and arched his eyebrows. He looked grim. "I'm afraid that girl's got sick on us," he said. "She walked outta camp this mornin' and never came back." He spat and wiped his chin with his sleeve. "After a spell I went lookin'. She heard me hollerin' at her and hollered back and told me to get away. I went back and got Ezra and Bob, but they can't do nothin' with her neither. She dared 'em to come any closer; said she'd jerk ever one of us bald headed. Bob thought you might be able to talk some sense in her."

"How am I s'posed to do anything with her?"

"You two 'bout the same age, and she saw you the other day tryin' to heal that feller. We ain't seen her, but she sounds crazy as a wildcat — like she's been heavin'. I bet them damn Kiowa made her sick. Prob'ly made ever one of us sick and we just don't know it yet."

"Will you get them skinners for me?"

"I'll get 'em. Go talk to that girl."

Logan rode back to camp and yelled for Bob and Ezra who answered from the hills a short distance above him. The two looked completely out of sorts. As best Logan could tell, Elizabeth was out of sight just beyond a shin-oak motte at the head of a narrow draw. Bob and Ezra were squatting on their heels trying to talk to her.

"Are you too sick to come out by yourself?" Ezra shouted.

"Get on now! I'll be along in a while," came the hoarse reply.

Bob stood. "Miss Lizbeth, Logan's here. He's gonna walk on up there now."

"Bob! I can't just walk up there," Logan whispered loudly. "She's prob'ly got her drawers down around her ankles. She'll smack me cross-eyed."

"That's why I'm tellin' her ahead of time. If you can't do no good, we're all gonna have to run up there and drag her down to camp."

Logan had fantasized about many situations involving Elizabeth, but he had not imagined anything like the present predicament. The thought of Elizabeth shriveled like the Kiowa woman made him heartsick and queasy. He walked half the distance to the oak motte. "Lizbeth, it's Logan. You doin' all right?" He realized suddenly that his stupid question constituted more words than he had spoken to her over the past week.

"Logan Fletcher, don't you come no closer! I'll jerk a knot on you! I swear I will!"

The wind shifted slightly and he smelled her sickness. "We're just tryin' to help you, now. I know you don't feel good, but you can't stay up there. There's Kiowas about."

She did not answer for several seconds. He hoped his remark had swayed her. Then he heard her retching. He could stand it no longer. He ran up the draw. When he got to her, he gasped at the sight of her on her hands and knees, tears streaming from eyes that were already retreating within their sockets. Her face was drawn, her cheeks sunken. She gave him a sidelong glance but made no attempt to chase him away.

"Lord Lizbeth. Are you through for a spell, you think?"

She nodded weakly, and he took her by the arm to help her stand, but her legs buckled.

"I'm fixin' to carry you, okay?"

She pulled weakly away and lay on her side and drew her knees up. She sobbed. "I ain't never been so sick."

"I'm gonna pick you up now, okay?" She did not answer. He bent to pick her up. She was tall and would be awkward to carry. He stopped suddenly. "Uh, Lizbeth, we're gonna have to pull your drawers up. Can you do it by yourself? I promise I won't pay no attention."

She groped weakly. He grabbed her rough, woolen pantaloons, looked away and jerked them up as far as he could. "I won't tell a soul," he said. He picked her up and carried her down the draw. Her teeth chattered, and she held her arms tightly against her breast. Her lightness surprised him.

Bob and Ezra stood wide-eyed at Logan's approach. "Gracious lawd! Bob said. "That child's bad sick!"

"Hell, Bob! Don't be so loud," Ezra whispered. "You'll have the girl givin' up the ghost on us. We'll get her a pallet fixed and Earl can get the fire goin' big. She acts like she's freezin' to death."

Logan stumbled then righted himself. "What about them filthy skinners?"

Bob looked closely at the girl's face as he walked. "Son, we got worser problems than them hooligans."

Romack already had the fire blazing. "He looked up from his work. "I's afraid of that," he said.

They eased Elizabeth onto the pallet then covered her. She continued to shiver. Ezra looked at the tortured man and shook his head. "How's he doin'?"

"About the same," Romack answered. "Reckon she's empty?"

Ezra snorted. "If she's sick with cholera, she won't be empty 'til she's shriveled as a year-old carcass."

Bob frowned. "What was it you was sayin' to me about talkin' too loud?"

"Looks like she's freezin' under them hides," Romack said.

Ezra nodded grimly. "Wringin' wet with sweat at the same time. It's cholera all right."

"I ain't feelin' too good myself," Romack said. "I believe thinkin' about her bein' sick is makin' me sick."

Ezra stuffed his pipe. "We're about to have a bad problem. None of us ought to be around this girl." He looked mirthfully at Logan. "'Course now, Logan here will fix everything. I wish he'd get busy with this girl."

"I aim to. It tore me up seein' her the way I did."

Ezra softened. "Son I don't mean to be makin' sport of your beliefs. But we're fixin' to be in trouble here. You seen what cholera done to that Kiowa

camp." He looked at Romack who was banging the coffee pot on a rock to settle the grounds. "And I believe Earl's tryin' to get sick on us."

Bob took off his hat and stared into it as if contained the answer to their
predicament. "When I was a youngun in the pine woods, yeller fever come
through and 'bout got every one of us. We finally had to burn everything and
clear out or it woulda got us all, I b'lieve."

"What're you sayin'?" Logan asked tensely.

Ezra blew a puff of pipe smoke. "What we're sayin' is there ain't no use in
all of us dyin'. I ain't sayin' we leave this gal to die — a man's gotta live with
hisself. I'm just sayin' there ain't no sense in all of us stayin'."

"I say I can help her," Logan snapped.

"I ain't sayin' you can't," Ezra said. "But you might be prayin' over the whole
outfit before Lizbeth gets well — if she gets well in the first place." He nodded
toward Romack who sat down heavily and wiped the sweat from his brow.

"So who's stayin'?" Bob asked.

Ezra shrugged. "It don't matter. I'll stay. I've been in the middle of a mess of
it before and I made out fine."

"Ezree, that ain't right. We oughta draw cards or sticks or somethin'."

"I'll stay," Logan heard himself say. "I got the gift. I ain't got no choice. I
lived through a mess of cholera on the Missouri. That's when I knowed for sure
I had the gift. I'll stay or my daddy'll roll in his grave."

Bob shook his head. "We ain't leavin' no boy out here by hisself."

"I gotta stay; I ain't got no choice."

"You ain't doin' it."

"You can't stop me."

Ezra looked incredulously at Logan. "By god, son, you're hired help. You'll
do as you're told or walk back to Dodge City."

"I'd say a man can do as he pleases after he's been fired." Logan was arguing
on momentum alone. He knew that if he stopped, he would lose his nerve.

"Ezree, you ain't gonna make that boy walk back to Dodge and you know
it. If he wants to stay, we oughta let him try. Why he might *have* the gift.
What're we gonna do but sit and watch her shrivel up?"

Just then Romack ran out of camp; seconds later they heard him heaving.

CHAPTER 23

Cuts Something rested his back against the meat pole, drew his legs in and wrapped his robe tightly about him. Two robes beneath him insulated him from the cold ground. He was glad to be back on the Pease, in the brakes he always would think of as home — as much as anyplace could be home to a Comanche. The night was clear and cold, the camp quiet save for the low murmuring of several young men gambling and the dogs' occasional yapping answer to the wolves howling north of the river.

There would be no hungry time this winter; the People had secured more than enough meat in the red canyon country. Cuts Something could not remember when his people had put aside so much meat. Not even Sees How Far It Is could remember the People ever being so well provisioned, although all Comanches had heard the stories about times before the Texans ventured onto the plains. Cuts Something often wished he had lived in the time before the white and Mexican sicknesses decimated the People. His father and uncles had told him that the People once had numbered many times what they now numbered. No wonder, he thought, the People then lorded unchallenged over the plains and rode easily into Mexico to take whatever they wanted. He could scarcely imagine the power that must have accompanied such a population of warriors.

But they had been so few in his lifetime; and fewer still after the skirmishes with the white hunters. Increasing their numbers with captive children was now very dangerous, although the small yellow-haired boy showed promise. Already he was learning the tongue of the People and had begun playing with the Comanche boys. Most of the adults, especially the women, now regarded him with affection, calling him Short Tail.

One of the captive women had already died; another lay near dead and not worth feeding. The big woman, however, still had to be tied up at night. She ate her food and went petulantly about her assigned work. Fast Girl had at last learned to avoid her. None of the women went out of their way to provoke her.

That's It had forced her into his lodge and claimed to have enjoyed her immensely, although he had not bothered her since. Cuts Something occasionally considered trying her but thus far had judged her not worth the trouble. Certainly he could beat her into compliance, but in middle age he had found that such a struggle left him with little lust. The woman bit a plug out of Otter Belt's chest and the young warrior had been determined to slit her throat, but Cuts Something remained adamant that she would be kept alive for sale after the cold time. If the Texans would not buy her back he could always get two or three good horses for her from some unsuspecting Kiowa. In his experience, Kiowas often lost their heads over captive women.

He still mourned Elk Rub's death and missed him terribly, although the revenge raid had done much to assuage his pain. He had recently spliced horsehair into his shortened braid to regain the length he had cut off in his mourning. For the most part, She Invites Her Sisters had stopped wailing after he brought her the Texans' scalps. The white man who killed Elk Rub might not have been a Texan, but the Texans were somehow always responsible for the People's sorrows. Cuts Something dozed.

He awoke miserably cold and got to his feet with great effort. His teeth chattered so that he had difficulty making water. He crawled into his lodge and into his stack of buffalo robes. Still shivering, he tugged the rawhide string that ran into She Invites Her Sisters' lodge. He was barely warming when his oldest wife staggered sleepily in and rebuilt the lodge fire. He could see its light through his closed eyelids and imagined his wife's shadow against the lodge wall and her breath visible in the cold air.

After a good sleep he could arise at his pleasure and warm himself before the fire. His work was done until the grass greened again, and he looked forward to the days of sitting with That's it and Sees How Far It Is, making arrows and eating as often as he pleased. Perhaps he would ride up to the Canadian to look for wood for a new bow. Perhaps not.

He was only dimly aware of his wife's substantial bulk as she wormed into his stack of robes. He was deliciously warm now and felt the fire's warmth on his face and heard the faint popping and smelled the juniper smoke. Nothing from the four reservation years entered his mind.

C H A P T E R   2 4

Logan had expected rain, and when it came in big, cold drops, he could do nothing but build the fire up and keep it roaring lest the rain drown it. They had no shelter save for the nearly bare cottonwood limbs overhead. Logan sat with his back against one of the trees and wrapped a robe about his shoulders and watched the rain drip from his hat brim. He had dragged Romack and Elizabeth beneath the trees and had turned them on their sides and covered their faces fearing they would drown in the deluge.

In the two days since Bob and Ezra left them at this river bottom campsite, Elizabeth and Romack had only worsened despite Logan's nearly constant praying and recitation of Scripture. He asked the Lord to make the rain cease, but he did not believe He worried much over physical comfort. He had more important things to attend to, such as, Logan hoped, healing people dying of cholera.

He himself had been very queasy the first day and a half alone with Elizabeth and Romack. He had been sure he was taking sick, but the feeling left him. He decided the sight and smell of the sickness had gotten to him as they had on the river boat.

Were it not for the cold rain, their camp would have been reasonably comfortable. Daily, he walked into the hills to a food cache site where Bob and Ezra left dried buffalo meat or fresh tongue or prairie chicken still in feathers in a hole they had dug and covered with a large rock. Logan noticed the site had already attracted scavengers. Coyote and skunk diggings were all around the entrance, but thus far the rock had protected the cache.

Throughout the days, he could hear his party's guns miles upriver. He wondered how the tortured man was doing and how long cholera took to kill someone. The people on the river boat either died within hours of the first symptoms or began recovery within two days. Elizabeth and Romack had lain deathly ill for two and a half days now. Both moaned and talked out of their heads, and Logan doubted they heard his words of comfort and encouragement.

The pallets were horribly soiled. Twice he had washed Romack, but thus far he had been unable to look beneath Elizabeth's top robe. Yet he knew that eventually he would have to overcome his discomfort with the task. He fell asleep in prayer in the rain beneath the cottonwood trees.

Elizabeth's shouts woke him late in the afternoon. The rain had ceased and the air smelled clean with a hint of juniper and cured grass. Elizabeth yelled for her mother and someone named Ella. Logan went to her and placed his hands on her face and repeated his prayer of healing, quoted again from the book of Ezekiel and spoke words of comfort. The girl calmed but jabbered incoherently, eyes closed, sweat running down her cheeks and forehead forming a pool beneath her larynx.

He left her and fetched from the river a copper pot full of water which he heated on the fire. He cut a swath of buffalo robe and carried the pot of warm water to Elizabeth's side. "Lizbeth, I need to clean you up. I promise I won't pay no attention. You'll feel better when I'm done."

The girl pursed her lips and furrowed her brow. Logan pulled back the robe and gasped at her filthy condition and the sight of her legs which only two and a half days ago he had admired in spite of himself. They had been muscular and shapely then, but now were shriveled skin draped loosely over bone. He breathed through his mouth and cleaned her.

For three days afterward, he smelled sickness wherever he went: in camp; at the river; in the hills overlooking camp. His food gagged him. He went to the river and bathed, shivering, scrubbing himself raw with wet sand. He scrubbed his clothes and hung them to dry away from camp and shivered naked beneath his robes.

At night, shriveled corpses with reeking open mouths and bones showing through torn skin visited him in his sleep, and he woke sweating and exhausted. He dribbled water down the throats of the sick and each morning expected to find one or both dead. They looked unchanged and he wondered if they had worsened so gradually that he had not noticed.

On the fifth morning, Elizabeth, upon feeling water on her tongue, began searching with her lips. She gulped so greedily that Logan pulled the cup away for fear she would choke. She gasped and moved her lips as if drinking. He sent up a prayer of thanks and put the cup back to her lips with trembling hands. She drank three full cups then slept without moaning or calling out. Romack appeared unchanged.

At midday, he returned from the food cache to find Elizabeth with her eyes open, staring upward, her mouth open slightly. He dropped the food and sobbed and started toward her on weak legs. "Lord . . ." he sobbed, "Lord, I tried my hardest." He wept, rocking back and forth on his knees. He wiped his eyes and looked at her; then wiped his eyes again. He crawled to her on his hands and knees and examined her face from six inches away. Her eyes were no longer turned upward but were instead fixed on him. She moved her lips as if trying to speak, but managed only a hoarse, unintelligible whisper.

He ran to the river with the copper pot and fell on his way back and spilled most of the water. After a second trip, he kneeled and put the cup to Elizabeth's lips. She drank unsteadily then slept again.

When she woke, Logan fed her a cup of weak broth — dried buffalo meat and river water. He fed her again before he went to sleep and then again during the middle of the night. Next morning she raised her head slightly as he lowered the cup to her lips. She tried to whisper something. He lowered his ear to within inches of her lips. "I heard you sometimes," she whispered.

"That's good," was all he could think of to say.

"You really think you're the one done it?" Elizabeth was sitting with her back against a tree sipping the buffalo meat broth. Her voice was still hoarse and weak.

"Done what?"

"Got me well."

"Lord done it. I'm just his instrument."

"It's funny how outta all of it, the only thing I remember is you puttin' your hands on my face and prayin' over me. Ain't it funny?"

Logan's ears burned. He hoped she did not remember him washing her. "Might be somethin' to it," he said. It seemed to him that after all he had been through with Elizabeth, he should not feel so uncomfortable around her.

Elizabeth gave her head a good scratching then ran her fingers through her damp hair. "That bath done me some good. Lord that river's cold though. I like to not been able to crawl out it wore me out so." She pulled the robe more tightly around her. "Clothes oughta be dry before long."

"Where'd you hang 'em?"

"I ain't tellin'. Don't you reckon Mr. Romack's gonna make it too?"

Romack had started taking water on his own earlier that morning. Though his face was horribly shriveled, he never had looked as bad as Elizabeth had looked. Nevertheless, Logan felt sure the old cook had been very near death.

Elizabeth dug her toes into the cool, shaded sand. The afternoon sun was pleasantly warm, but the clear sky portended a cold night. "My folks ain't never gonna b'lieve what all's happened to me. That brother of mine will accuse me of lyin' for sure."

Logan nodded; said nothing.

"He ain't but thirteen. Rough as a cob. I guess y'all gonna take me back after you get a load of hides."

"We'll take you to Fort Dodge, I imagine. Your folks can come get you there." He wondered if that statement constituted a lie. Her folks were almost certainly dead and scalped. He supposed that since he had not personally seen them dead and scalped that he bore no obligation to force his grim opinion upon her. She might fall into despair and relapse, even though she had thus far completely ignored Ezra's blunt comments about her parents' probable fate.

She took a big gulp of broth. "I wish I felt like fixin' something. I believe this is the awfullest stuff I ever put in my mouth."

"I guess you're feelin' better sure enough," Logan said.

Just after sunup, two days before Christmas 1873, after eight days of exile, Logan Fletcher helped Elizabeth and Romack onto Rufus's back. He took the reins and led the horse upriver toward the sound of heavy rifles.

CHAPTER 25

Logan appreciated the early spring warmth. He did not appreciate the accompanying flies and gnats. He slid his hand beneath his hat and felt two itching bumps beneath his sweaty hair. He wondered what sort of insect could have bitten him through his hat. Fleas would shortly become a nuisance, serious or minor, depending on the standards of the host. Logan felt certain that most of the men he had met over the past half year would barely notice a major infestation.

He was sitting beside Elizabeth in Romack's wagon while Bob and Ezra dickered with three hide buyers. As usual, Elizabeth was talking about her family, and Logan was nodding and thinking with dread of the day when Elizabeth would allow reality to set in. All around, members of the Myers party out of Dodge were loafing and drinking or laying sod roofing on pole and picket structures. Already there was a saloon and a store the hunters called Rath's. Word was a freighter named Dirty Face Jones was on his way from Dodge City with a load of whores and was due to arrive any day. A mile southwest lay the ruins of the original adobe-walled trading post that trader William Bent abandoned and blew up in 1849 after Comanches killed several of his oxen.

Bob and Ezra had expressed hope that a dress could be procured from one of the whores. Elizabeth had scrubbed her dress nearly to threads getting the cholera stench out. Now the smell of her hair and skin had Logan squirming in his seat. He did not enjoy her talk of her family, but he did enjoy sitting where he could smell her.

The men all agreed that Elizabeth was quite sensible and capable whenever she could be distracted from thoughts of her family. She had the sharpest eyes and keenest ears in the group. On the ride in from camp she pointed out three distant antelope visible only by the tips of their black horns protruding above the grass. One of the antelope now lay gutted in the back of the wagon and would bring a welcome change in diet. Two days earlier in camp, swinging Romack's spade, Elizabeth killed a prairie rattler that had crawled into a tangle of dead juniper to warm itself in the sun.

As far as anyone could tell, she had recovered completely from her bout with cholera, a fact obviously not lost on the skinners and hunters working and milling about the trading post. Nor had Elizabeth's health gone unnoticed by the torture victim, Burress, who had also fully recovered only to have his three remaining teeth knocked out by Romack, who had been enraged by the skinner's aggressive ogling. "You shoulda' just let that sumbitch die, so I won't have to kill him," the old cook sputtered at Logan.

The now toothless Burress, the sole survivor of a small High Plains hunting expedition, had proven to be the best skinner in the group. His usefulness had saved him from even further bodily harm after he found Bob's whiskey cache and then, roaring drunk, stepped into Romack's Dutch oven full of beans.

The skinner Hunt had taken sick in camp and had died within hours while Logan was nursing Elizabeth and Romack back to health.

"I wish we had us a pig," Elizabeth said, shooing flies from her face. "A pig sure would go good about now. And some shucky beans."

"Welp." Logan thought that any digression from the subject of her family should be encouraged.

"I don't see how we'd keep pigs though. I ain't seen no mast on the ground."

"I've always found mast right sparse in spring."

"You know what I mean. I suppose we could feed 'em slops."

Logan laughed softly and looked over the mules' backs. "A pig would starve to death on the slops you and Mullins leave." Elizabeth's appetite had become a favorite joke among the men and a source of delight for Romack.

"My daddy always said I was gonna be big as a barn if I didn't quit eatin' so much."

Logan winced and rested his chin on his fist.

"I never did get fat though. I just kept growin' up and up and up. I'm a head taller than Mama and about as tall as Daddy. Mama's got some big people on her side. Uncle Harlan was a six footer — until that tree fell on him."

"How tall was he then?"

Elizabeth cocked her head. "Well . . . still six feet, I suppose. It was a long casket they buried him in. You're about that tall ain't you?"

"I believe."

"Looks to me like you'd blow away though," she said matter-of-factly. "Lord these flies!"

Logan listened to the flies buzzing furiously on the antelope carcass behind him. He was more than ready to leave. He did not like the dozens of pairs of eyes on Elizabeth. He had been sure that no place could be as squalid as Dodge, but looking at the vermin-infested humanity around him, he decided that he had grossly underestimated man's capacity for squalor.

Notwithstanding her battle with the flies, Elizabeth seemed oblivious. He knew too that he probably looked little different from those around him. He hoped that Bob and Ezra would soon finish their trading.

Yet from a business standpoint, the trading post was a godsend. In two months they had taken over nine hundred hides and several kegs of tongues. Their original plan had been to take a wagon load to Dodge City, sell to hide buyers then re-supply and hurry back to the Panhandle. Now, with the trading post reestablished on the Canadian, they could stay out indefinitely making only occasional trips to re-provision and sell their hides and tongues. Demand for hides was such that buyers were actually visiting the less remote hunting camps to do business.

Most hunters, however, were basing operations at the trading post for security and venturing out during the day to hunt. Mullins and the other skinners had wanted to do the same, especially after they heard the news of the soon-to-arrive whores. But Bob and Ezra did not believe they could keep their supplies, money or Elizabeth safe among such rough company. Looking about the close confines of Adobe Walls, Logan agreed with their decision. They had seen no Indians or Indian sign since their encounter with sick Kiowas. He wondered again at his ability to forget about Indians. He knew how quickly the horror could return.

Elizabeth jabbed his arm with her finger. He looked to his right. A gaunt man wearing filthy homespun pants and a greasy, sweat-stained buckskin shirt stood next to the wagon, drunkenly regarding Logan and Elizabeth. The man's left eye was missing, revealing a twitching socket, and he held in his right hand a nearly full bottle of whiskey. His other hand lacked the two middle fingers. Logan stared at the man's long, dirty fingernails.

The man studied Elizabeth. "How much?"

"What do you mean how much?"

"For some of that girl."

"I ain't no whore!" Elizabeth snapped. "And even if I was, I wouldn't have nothin' to do with you." Her face was flushed; her green eyes hard.

"We got her back from some Kiowas."

"You and that nigger did?" The man's face hardly moved when he talked. His lips moved just enough to reveal one brown front tooth.

"There was three of us."

"I b'lieve I heared of that nigger. Reckon he'd sell his part?"

Elizabeth grunted in outrage.

"We don't own no part of her. We're takin' her to Fort Dodge before long."

The man took a drink of whisky. He kept his eyes on Elizabeth. "Where is he?"

"Who?"

"That nigger. He'd prob'ly sell his part of that girl, don't ye reckon?"

"You get, you nasty drunkard!" Elizabeth snarled. "We ain't talkin' to you no more."

The man paid her no mind. "I got a bunch of hides."

Logan suddenly felt very tired. He could not leave without Bob and Ezra, and he doubted he could reason with a drunken imbecile.

"Logan Fletcher, do somethin' about him."

"Now look here. I done told you she ain't for sale, no part of her. If you don't get, I'll have to come down outta this wagon." He noticed men stopping their work and conversation to gather and watch.

The man took another drink. He had yet to take his eyes off Elizabeth. "And do what?"

"That's it." Logan slid from his seat and before he could raise his fists, the man came up hard beneath his chin with the bottle. Logan staggered backward into the wagon and tried to right himself, but the man held him against the wagon with a large blade. Logan could feel the keen edge against his throat; he had not imagined that a drunk could move so quickly.

"Whassamatter pup? Can't ye stand up?" The man's breath made Logan's eyes water. Logan looked at the impassive faces standing about and sensed their bloodlust. He could picture himself lying in the dust with his throat slit and the onlookers staring stupidly for a few moments before shrugging and going back to work or back to their conversation or bottle. "Let's talk 'bout that girl now, why don't we?" the man said, still barely moving his lips.

"She ain't for sale," Logan croaked. He wondered if Bob and Ezra had passed out drunk somewhere.

The man's empty socket twitched and his expression changed suddenly as he looked up. He smiled.

"You go on," Elizabeth said coldly. She held the twin bores of Romack's shotgun in the man's face. "I'll kill you right here in front of everybody."

Ezra pushed his way through the crowd and calmly took in the scene. "Logan, bring the wagon over to the store and help Bob load up." He looked at the one-eyed man then at the crowd. "Don't let me catch any of you botherin' these younguns again."

The man looked at his broken bottle then started for the saloon. The crowd momentarily stared at Ezra then slowly dispersed. Logan climbed back into the seat. Elizabeth sat down and propped the shotgun between them. "I forgot to pull the hammers back," she whispered.

Logan worked his jaw. "That ain't nothin'. I forgot all about my pistol. Wouldn't have done a bit of good no way."

Elizabeth's green eyes were wide. "Reckon he would've really killed you?"

"I believe he would've." Logan felt as if he could lie down and sleep forever. Even with the blade at his throat, he had felt more tired than scared. "Thank you," he said to Elizabeth without looking at her. "That was a good thing you done." He took the reins.

Elizabeth looked warily toward the saloon. "Wasn't he the awfullest lookin' man you ever saw? Whoever heard of somebody buyin' part of a girl?"

Another disturbance broke out just outside the saloon. Logan stopped the mules next to the store. Bob stepped outside. He spat. "No need goin' into it. I done heard." He lifted a keg of gunpowder into the wagon. Logan flinched at the sound of two shots from the direction of the saloon. Bob turned to pick up another keg. "You two are somethin'," he said.

Logan sat his horse and waited for the wind to lay. Already, a faint pink edging grew on the eastern horizon. He knew he should be riding toward his ambush spot in the river bottom, but an odd sound had caught his attention, and his curiosity had gotten the best of him. The sound did not strike him as threatening, but simply as odd. The wind abated and he heard the sound again: *thoo-up . . . thoo-up . . . thoo-up*–a liquid sound like water dripping from an icicle into a puddle. He turned Rufus toward the head of the draw. The wind picked up again, and he rode up the draw and onto a broad, shortgrass flat surrounded by low, bluestem-covered sandhills.

The wind continued, and the sound wafted wildly about, coming and going with the gusts so that he could not place it. Now and again, the sound came from the grass virtually at Rufus's hooves. Logan sat very still. A slight uneasiness came over him; he felt very exposed on the open flat.

By and by, the wind laid again, and he heard all around him the liquid clucking. *Thoo-up . . . thoo-up . . . thoo-up*; then *cack! cack! cack! cack!* and the beating of wings. He knew then that he was hearing some kind of fowl. He squinted and made out dark forms close by in the grass. He looked eastward at the growing light and turned his collar up against the early spring coolness and waited.

He saw a bird fly in backlit by the rising sun. Downward cupped wings, beating, gliding, beating, gliding. A prairie chicken. With the growing light and new recognition, he discerned the dark forms in the grass. He watched, mesmerized. The prairie lightened imperceptibly, and he made out the cocks with their fanned tails and the orange neck sacks. Strutting, booming, stamping their feet in a blur and fighting among themselves. He had seen turkey gobblers in Kentucky strut, fan and gobble for hens in the springtime. He had never known prairie chickens to behave so. Hens came and went and fed casually like purposefully disinterested schoolgirls he had known.

The sun cleared the eastern hills, and the birds cast long shadows onto the greening shortgrass. He saw his own elongated shadow stretching oddly westward. The big rifles began to boom in the river bottom, yet he did not move and the birds showed no alarm. A harrier flew in low and scattered the birds, but they quickly regrouped and the sleek little hawk drifted away to pursue smaller prey.

Rufus took a step, and the birds flushed cackling, a dozen or more, and flew into the sandhills. The sun lighted their white undersides. They banked and the sun glinted on their wings, and Logan watched them until they were nearly a mile distant.

He rode back toward the head of the draw and looked out over the river bottom at the bands of bison and the rough yellow brakes beyond. The grassy hills looked naked save for hackberry and oak and plum in the draws and patches of dark sandsage growing on the gentler slopes. A bobwhite cock issued his morning hail call from the draw below.

Logan knew that he should get on with his killing. Yet he sat Rufus and looked at the Canadian River bottom and thought of Bob's words: *We always knowed this was here and knowin' it made it easy to keep killin' up at the Arkansas. But when somethin's gone it's gone and when you're lookin' at the last of it, it gets you wonderin' about what you're doin'.*

He grappled for a piece of Scripture his father had recited whenever he admired the family's little vegetable garden: *Thou art worthy, O Lord, to receive glory and honour and power: for thou hast created all things, and for thy pleasure they are and were created.*

He rode into the river bottom toward his ambush spot, a sandy wash just east of a small band of bison he had marked at dusk the day before. He hoped the beasts had not moved. The sound of Bob and Ezra's rifles did not help his already guilty conscience. He wondered if they had noticed his lack of shooting. He was, after all, being paid to do a job. *He becometh poor that dealeth with a slack hand: but the hand of the diligent maketh rich.* He hurried on.

By the time he had picketed Rufus and crawled to his ambush spot, sweat was running down his sides and dripping from the end of his nose. The air was rapidly warming. The buffalo had moved only a short distance overnight and still offered good shooting. He took off his coat and placed it beneath his knees and set his rifle barrel on the cross-stick rest. He waited for one of the cows to offer a shot. He luxuriated in the light breeze that cooled him through his sweaty shirt. Bob recently had given him an old, porcupine-chewed cartridge belt, so he no longer had to keep his ammunition in his coat pockets. A cow turned broadside, but he did not take the shot. Languor stopped him more than any concern for the buffalo. His chin still hurt from the altercation at the trading post. He sighed, dreading his rifle's recoil, which never failed to jar any sore spot — even a sore spot on his foot.

Neither Bob nor Ezra had mentioned the trading post incident which left Logan wondering about their estimation of his competence. They had left him with the wagon to look after Elizabeth and at the first altercation she saved him from having his throat slit by a filthy drunk. The second they reached camp, Elizabeth launched a dramatic, rapid-fire account of the incident much to the confusion of Romack and the skinners.

Midway through the first telling, Romack looked up from his fire, scratched his head beneath his hat and said, "That don't sound like Bob to be tryin' to sell ye."

"No, no," Elizabeth said, obviously panicked at the misunderstanding. "That man said he *thought* Bob would sell his part of me."

"Sell his part of ye."

"Yeah. To the man. He was drunk."

"Bob was drunk? Bob don't get drunk. I mean he don't get *drunk*."

The skinners were sitting about waiting to be fed. Wide-eyed, they alternately stared at Elizabeth and Romack and Logan. Romack got the story straight on the third telling. Burress, on the other hand, remained confused. "What's she sayin?"

Mullins turned from Elizabeth to Burress and said in a tone of wonder, "That boy was tryin' to sell her to a nigger and she drawed down on 'im."

The skinners all looked at Logan. Burress blinked. "Who drawed down on 'im?"

"That girl did."

"What'd she draw down on 'im for?"

"He was fixin' to sell her to a nigger."

"Who was?"

"That boy was."

Logan had been too full of contempt to set matters straight. He sullenly ate his beans and biscuits; his sore jaw worked so spastically he nearly bit his tongue in half. On the positive side, Elizabeth had been quite solicitous since the trading post incident, evidently feeling a degree of kinship through shared calamity.

The guns continued booming upriver. Logan took a bead on the paunch of the old cow, cocked the rear trigger, slid his finger to the front trigger, drew and held a breath and gently squeezed.

CHAPTER 26

Cuts Something squatted with That's It outside Yellow Beads's lodge. He knew that such behavior was beneath his position as a war chief; he should have been calmly sitting in his lodge enjoying a pipe. Yet how could a warrior sit calmly while his wife prepared to give birth to a child that might be the son that would secure his place in the continuum?

Of course Yellow Beads might bear a daughter. Daughters were fine. He enjoyed them and they in turn doted over him, yet a warrior required a son if he was to call a long life a success. Were Cuts Something to die that day, he had already lived a long life by Comanche standards.

He could hear the excited murmuring within the lodge and occasionally Yellow Beads's restrained moans. He could feel the heat of the fire and the fervor of the women's work through the walls of the lodge. He stood and arched his stiff back and walked in place to return the circulation to his numb feet.

That's It drew nondescript figures in the dust with his finger. "It could be a long time yet," he said. That's It had a fair-sized herd of daughters but no sons, and none of his aging wives had become pregnant in many summers. He had more than enough stature and horses to take a young wife, yet despite Cuts Something's urgings, he had made no effort to do so. Cuts Something understood his friend's lack of motivation very well. Young women, with all of their energy and attractiveness, were tiresome. Sometimes captive women bore warriors' sons, but at present their only captive was the big white women who had recently fought Otter Belt so bitterly that he had vowed to slit her throat and certainly would have were it not for Cuts Something's plans to ransom her back to the *tahbay-boh*. Although That's It had assured Cuts Something that the Texan woman had been a delicious diversion, he had been sore and bruised for days after the struggle.

Cuts Something wanted to peek inside the lodge to check Yellow Beads's progress, but he knew that he could not. Doing so would have been the worst kind of taboo, although he had no idea why. A warrior simply did not involve himself with birthing unless the mother happened to be a mare. He tapped the ashes from his pipe and refilled it.

"Fast Girl might bear you a son," That's It said.

"Yes." He smoked his pipe and nodded thoughtfully. "If only the girl interested me more."

"She will get better. You should practice with her. She is comely. I would not ignore her too much."

"She would rather play with the children, and she is lazy. I should not have given two good horses for her."

"She will get better." That's It smiled. "Let me borrow her for a while. I will teach her important things."

Cuts Something grunted. "I think too much of you. Perhaps if you were a bitter enemy . . . " They laughed and smoked their pipes.

The day warmed, and the men dozed and swiped at flies. Cuts Something occasionally caught himself snoring. An infant's cries slipped into his consciousness and for a time he struggled in his sleepiness to interpret them. He jerked suddenly awake when She Invites Her Sisters poked her head through the lodge door. Cuts Something's venerable wife blinked in the bright sunlight, wiped the sweat from her nose and blew an errant hair from her forehead. She squinted at the two men until her eyes focused on Cuts Something. "You have a good friend!" she said. She disappeared again.

Cuts Something blinked. "Ha!" he said. He tried to stand on numb feet but staggered and fell on his side. He rolled onto his stomach and gathered his legs beneath him. He was about to stand again when That's It tackled him. Cuts Something rolled onto his back with That's It beneath him holding him in a bear hug. The two kicked wildly and laughed so hysterically the camp dogs began to howl.

CHAPTER 27

Logan leaned back against the kill wagon to watch the skinners work. Eleven buffalo down. He wondered how Bob and Ezra were doing. He knew that he should scout for more targets, but it was a fine April morning, pleasantly warm and breezy with high, scattered clouds against a cobalt sky. He watched the swallows working the air above the river for insects. The river valley and the drier uplands were greening, yet the days remained pleasant with enough breeze to keep the gnats and mosquitoes from gathering.

Bob and Ezra had assured him that summer would be miserable, but for the time being, he could imagine nothing but the present weather. Even the occasional shower was refreshing. They were enjoying a wet spring, or so he had been told. An equal amount of rainfall in his Kentucky highlands would have constituted a horrible drought. The plains made good use of rainfall, he thought. He had never seen such color: reds and yellows and violets, Indian paintbrush, toad flax, plains flax, partridge pea, larkspur, prickly pear, prickly poppy. Indian blanket and sunflowers now grew in soil that had been churned by bison. He did not know the names or even if names existed, but had begun to distinguish one flower from the next.

There were wildflowers in his Kentucky mountains, but they tended to be very delicate, retiring and transient; nothing like the bold grassland flowers.

He wondered what sort of medicinal plants the prairie held and if red men were advanced enough to make use of them, or if they simply relied on childish superstition. *For thy pleasure they are and were created,* he thought.

There was a loud *thunk-thunk* and the skinner Corbin screamed, and Mullins and Burress cursed as they sprinted for the wagon. For an instant, Logan could not find Corbin nor comprehend the scene before him. Then he saw arms and legs flailing beneath the forehead of a furiously bellowing bull bison. The beast raised its head and Corbin's limp body followed, impaled on one horn. Logan aimed his rifle and fired and the enraged bison's body shuddered as it took the bullet through the lungs, but it charged the wagon with Corbin still draped across its face.

Mullins screamed, "Shoot the bastard!" Logan felt strangely calm as he drew his pistol and aimed at the beast's forehead and fired. Only after the bull's knees began to buckle did he realize that the bullet had gone between Corbin's shoulder blades and into the animal's skull.

The bull stood again and came on. Logan jumped aside and the beast rammed the wagon broadside, further crushing Corbin's body. The wagon bucked violently. Logan emptied the revolver into the bull's head and vitals then ran to the other side of the wagon to reload. He looked up from his pistol to see the bison on its side, kicking wildly. It bellowed mournfully and went still. The men approached warily.

"I might've killed Corbin," Logan croaked. He felt numb, unsure of what he had said.

Mullins spat then squatted to look at Corbin's body. "You mighta shot him, but you ain't the one killed him. Ever see a man's head mashed that way? Hell, if you hit him you done him some good, I'd say."

"By god," Burress said. "I want you to look what that sumbitch done to the wagon." The mules had dozed through the entire incident.

Logan looked over the killing field, trying to understand. "Where'd he come from?"

"Never come from nowhere," Mullins said. "Sumbitch was layin' there lookin' dead and Erastus bent over to start skinnin' and the goddamn thing jumped up and went to mashin' him."

Bob rode up and looked at Corbin's body. "Lawd. I knowed them was pistol shots," he said.

They buried Corbin in the brakes so that the Canadian would not wash his body away when it flooded. Logan gave a short eulogy for a man he had found utterly repulsive and had never wanted to know. He wondered whose soul was most imperiled. They stood and looked at the freshly turned grave. "I can't figure it out," Logan said. "I touched his eye with my rifle barrel and he never blinked."

"You must've just nicked his spine," Ezra said. "I heard about a bull up on the Republican layin' looking dead as a hammer. Damn thing got up and tromped all over three Kansa that was fixin' to skin him. Hell. Sumbitch run off and for all anybody knows he's still lookin' for somebody else to mash."

"Might as well let her go," Bob said. "Could've been any one of us shot that bull. Stay out here long enough and somethin' queer is bound to happen."

"I never talked to the man," Logan said, staring into his hat.

Ezra and Bob put on their hats and walked back to their horses. Burress was already in the wagon. Only Mullins remained, staring at the grave. He and Corbin had always taken their meals together.

"I'm sorry 'bout your friend. If I'd knowed that bull wasn't dead . . . "

Mullins spat. "Hell. Don't matter. I never liked the sumbitch no way. You had to watch him like a hawk. He was bad about chewin' up all a man's tobacco."

CHAPTER 28

Cuts Something lay motionless. He did not like what he saw. He had felt quite secure riding up to the Canadian to look for wood for a new bow. He had not expected to encounter white men, yet he had nearly stumbled into a camp full of well-armed Texans. He had been riding along the river looking for bois d'arc when he heard voices close by. Now he regarded the Texans from less than a bow shot away.

Most troubling of all, he recognized the little black man, Durham. This was not a man to trifle with. Durham was a deadly fighter and a skilled plainsman. Cuts Something would not have been at all surprised if the little man looked up and saw him or even smelled him, although much to his relief he lay downwind.

He had first met Durham when the whites were fighting among themselves. He and another war chief, Little Buffalo, led a large group of warriors on a raid of the Texas settlements on the Brazos north of Fort Belknap. Several hundred Comanche and Kiowa warriors swept down upon the few remote farms, one of which belonged to Durham's former owner. The black man fought ferociously, killing several warriors, but not before Cuts Something and That's It managed to take his wife and sons.

Little Buffalo claimed the oldest boy, and when That's It refused to give in,

Little Buffalo, in a fit of rage, lanced the boy while the boy's mother screamed piteously. Cuts Something had always thought that Little Buffalo was overly covetous and dangerously irascible and that his hunger for glory had gotten him killed later that day. A sensible man would never have charged a cabin full of Texans shooting from their gun ports.

After the fight, Cuts Something and the raiders withdrew into Comancheria with much loot and many captives including Durham's wife and small surviving son. Through various trades, most of the captives ended up in the hands of the Kiowa.

To Cuts Something's complete amazement, Durham brazenly rode up to him at a water hole a few days later and explained in Mexican that he wanted to buy back his wife, son and several of the white captives. Cuts Something was so impressed that he agreed to help Durham negotiate with the Kiowa, a people Cuts Something had little use for and barely tolerated.

The shocked Kiowa sold the captives to Durham for virtually nothing — a few small sacks of sugar and coffee — which, in Cuts Something's view, was exactly what they deserved. He had long begrudged every bit of ground in Comancheria occupied by the Kiowa — with their ridiculous Sun Dance — and felt that they should be driven out. But that was not the current arrangement and no one could tell him why. He had even less use for the Cheyenne, but at least they usually stayed north of the Arkansas River.

Cuts Something studied Durham and the others in camp. He did not know the huge white man, nor did he know the boy. But he knew the boy's type, and that knowledge disturbed him deeply. He had seen similar countenances on the lean Texans that relentlessly trailed and harried the People and swept down from the hills to kill and burn. He had been told by his elders that many of these men had come from mountains far to the east to make a life on the plains just as the People had migrated from the mountains to the west. The hard mountain life had sharpened their hunger and mettle, and now they were prepared to fight for the plains as the People had fought to take them from the Apache farmers.

He did not wish to engage these men, yet a warrior had to live with himself. Otter Belt would give him no peace if they did not at least try to steal a few of the Texans' horses and the mules. Cuts Something had never seen more handsome mules.

He began to inch backward, never taking his eyes off the black man who occasionally stopped eating and furrowed his brow as if listening — or smelling. Cuts Something stopped suddenly. A white girl stepped into view.

She was very tall like the woman on the Big Keechi. There would be no reasoning with Otter Belt now.

Durham was going to be serious trouble, he thought, and that boy; they had best kill him now while it would be easy. He knew from horrible experience that killing him would not be easy if they waited.

Logan found a dark place at the edge of a shin oak thicket and with a long stick, probed the shadows for rattlesnakes. Hearing no rattling, he sat down, laid his rifle across his lap and sipped coffee while he watched the horses. It occurred to him that he had never actually seen a Comanche, although he had seen what their presence could mean. Bob and Ezra agreed that Comanches were in general shorter, thicker and more bandy-legged than Kiowas. Bob thought Comanches tended to be lighter skinned, while Ezra admitted that he had never noticed. Both were sure that Comanches were unequaled when it came to horsemanship.

On the subject of torture, neither man felt that Comanche warriors, proficient though they were, had quite as much lust for the practice as their Kiowa counterparts. Comanche women, they felt, could hold their own with anyone. Logan wondered how the two had arrived at these conclusions since as far as he knew neither had ever been tortured by a savage. He kept his question to himself. Perhaps, he thought, they were going on what they had seen and heard during their partisan days on the Texas frontier. He decided that after one had been scalped, emasculated and burnt crisp, the question of which breed of heathen was the superior torturer was pointless. Ezra and Bob also agreed that Comanches hit harder, in greater number and left behind more carnage than the Kiowa, although the two often raided together.

A waning moon lit the prairie below him and shone on the horses' backs. They had lately been moving camp every two or three days, generally westward along the river valley, to avoid the stench and flies brought on by warm weather. They now sprinkled every hide with arsenic water to ward off moths and a broad class of insects Ezra and Bob referred to as "hide bugs." Since they had arrived at their present campsite, Bob had been distant and jumpy; when Logan relieved him for the late watch, the older man seemed very edgy. When Logan asked him if he was okay, Bob responded, "You stay awake and stay hid. We ain't payin' enough attention. Them heathens be stirrin' in this warm weather. We'll be in a mess sure enough without our horses."

Logan sipped his coffee. Even though the night was warm, the familiar scalding heat and bitter taste were a comfort. He tried to ignore the gnats and the frequent, maddening whine in his ears. A screech owl gave its quavering whistle from the river bottom cottonwoods. Logan drew comfort from screech owls too; they were common in Kentucky and their calls had often been on the edge of his boyhood sleep.

Most of the other plains animals seemed different from those he had known as a boy. Even the deer were different. Ezra said the plains deer were mule deer — they had comically long ears and did not raise a white tail flag when they fled. He did not know what kind of deer he had grown up with. They were just deer. Until he came to the plains he had no idea that there were different kinds of deer. Or rabbits. What would his father think of a jackrabbit? Or an antelope? . . . *for thy pleasure they are and were created.* The wolves here were larger and bolder. There were no coyotes in Kentucky, but there were a few wolves still, shy and seldom seen, though occasionally heard in the timbered hollows.

Despite his efforts at purity of mind, Elizabeth frequented his thoughts. She was an unusual girl, certainly, but the thought of her green eyes and perpetually sunburned nose, long fingers and ripening figure made forgetting her foibles easy. Then again, the only thing truly unusual about her was her inability to grasp her family's fate despite Bob and Ezra's gentle explanations. That and her apparent lack of emotional scarring from her capture. Ezra felt certain the Kiowas had violated her and that she had simply buried all remembrance of the incident and that one day it would come out in all its violence and ugliness.

Whenever purity of mind seemed impossible, Logan reminded himself that the apostle Paul had made a small allowance for lust in his letter to the church at Corinth. On the other hand, Logan feared that in his case, neither lust for a wife or for other women would disappear with the taking of a bride. Still, he felt fairly certain the Almighty would not banish a man to eternal damnation over a bit of carnal desire.

This was fortunate since he had been walking around in a near constant state of arousal for the past three days since he had felt and smelled Elizabeth's breath on his face after she pried open his left eye to blow out a bit of debris that had been tormenting him. It had gotten so that he had to concentrate on various repulsive images before he could make water. Fully aroused on the afternoon after the eye treatment, he shot four buffalo before the tooth-loosening recoil reminded him what he was doing.

He recently had discovered that he and Elizabeth shared a passion for well-prepared food. What had started as a desperate attempt to steer conversation away from Elizabeth's family had evolved into nightly rhapsodies on fondly remembered meals, and, more popular yet, fantasy meals planned in tortuous detail down to temperature and presentation. After another meal of bison tongue and hardtack or prairie chicken, gravy and biscuits or tongue and bannock, or fried hump and bone marrow spread on hardtack, but before time for first watch, Elizabeth would initiate the menu planning with a suggestion of some main course. Romack, Bob and Logan would each offer a side dish or dessert. Variations on presentation and subtleties of preparation would be rigorously examined. Heated debates were common.

One night after Elizabeth had taken care of her part of the menu — baked hen, shucky beans, sliced onions and sourdough biscuits — Logan and Romack, who had been assigned dessert, were passionately arguing the merits of blackberries versus rhubarb for pie and cobbler filling. Ezra, who had been listening and spitting constantly stood up suddenly and bellowed, "Shut the hell up, or go camp somewheres else!"

Bob, who had been especially interested in Elizabeth's hen, glanced at Ezra, blinked uncomprehendingly then segued into a learned treatise on dumpling texture. Ezra spat copiously then stomped off to take first watch. Romack allowed that when the plums ripened, he would see what he could do about a cobbler. It seemed to Logan that he stayed in a constant state of aching desire, either carnal or gastronomical.

He sat watching the horses. Dark, low-slung figures skulked among them. Wolves. The placidly grazing horses paid them no mind. Logan wondered what the wolves were looking for; they came every night. He still wanted to get his hands on one to examine it closely. He could easily have shot one, but he knew the entire camp would erupt and the horses might panic.

He watched with interest. One of the figures approached Rufus head on then stopped five yards away. Oddly, the horse moved toward it then stopped a few feet away. The figure backed slowly away and Rufus again followed. Logan waited for his horse to come to the end of his picket rope. Yet Rufus kept going, following the dark figure. Logan stiffened. His pulse quickened. The four other horses were now being drawn away from camp. He raised his rifle, set the front trigger and took aim at the figure before Rufus. The front sight wobbled. He exhaled quietly, drew in another breath. The sight steadied and centered on the dark figure. He would not miss this shot, shaking or not. Then a shotgun blast back in camp made him slap the trigger, and even as he recovered from the recoil, he knew the figures had vanished.

Romack was screaming, "Son of a bitch! You heathen son of bitch!" Logan left his empty rifle and bolted for the horses. He made the seventy yards to Rufus and grabbed his picket rope and turned him back toward camp. In the darkness, something — someone — rushed past him; someone coming from the direction of camp; someone smelling of sweat and grease and wood smoke and moving faster than Logan would have believed a man could move. Whoever it was disappeared into the darkness, and Logan suddenly realized his own foolishness in charging from his hiding place. He crouched low, keeping Rufus between himself and where he thought the Indian might be. He caught the other horses before he remembered his sidearm. He drew it awkwardly and worked the horses back toward camp.

"Well by god Earl, you've blowed a hunk out of your wagon." Ezra was still staggering from heavy sleep.

"I swear he was right here. Buck no older than Logan."

"And you missed him ten feet away with a shotgun."

"How many times have I said I can't shoot this sumbitch. Tryin' to steal Lizbeth, I reckon. Heathen bastard. Hell."

Ezra shook his head and sighed. "I swear Earl, you sure you wasn't dreamin'?"

"Goddamn right I'm sure. Rolled out to piss and there he was hunkered by the wagon. I like to have shit in my britches."

"I heard somebody else shoot," Elizabeth said weakly. Her face was ashen.

"That was me." Logan picketed the horses at the edge of camp. "They was here. I ran into one of 'em out there in the dark."

"Saw him?"

"Heard and smelled him. I could've reached out and grabbed him if I'd been ready."

"You'd have thought you had holt of a wildcat too." Bob appeared suddenly from the darkness. He was breathing hard. "They was here Ezree. They're gone for now though. I heard their horses crossin' the river. They was movin' fast."

Elizabeth took a loud breath and smoothed her threadbare dress against her thighs. "You don't reckon they'll come back, do you? After we run 'em off?"

"I'm afraid they will, Miss Lizbeth," Bob said gently. "Ezree we got to get this gal to the tradin' post."

"Back to that place where that nasty feller tried to buy me? I ain't about to go back to that place!"

"Dodge then," Bob said.

Ezra turned to Bob. "Dodge! Hell Bob, who's to say we'll make it with our hair? Whatever buffaloes we're gonna shoot, we're gonna shoot in the next half year. They ain't gonna be here much longer than that."

"Y'all ain't gonna leave me somewheres are you?"

Bob sighed and slapped the side of his leg. "I swear Miss Lizbeth, you best start sleepin' in the middle of us."

Ezra laid his rifle in the crook of his arm and wiped his eyes with his fist. "Boys, we knowed this might happen. I say we move first light and keep a cold camp for a few nights. Earl, whatever cookin' you do, you need to do during the day; and keep the smoke down." He looked toward the kill wagon. "We best wake them skinners up."

CHAPTER 29

Cuts Something glanced furtively at Otter Belt's wounds. He did not like what he saw. Even after the young warrior had taken several shotgun pellets in the face, he had run away strongly and now insisted that he could still fight. Cuts Something felt certain he would die very soon and very badly.

Cuts Something had seen many similar wounds. One pellet had split the skin above Otter Belt's left eye. At least two others had gone through his cheek, breaking off teeth and leaving open, angry wounds. Already, in the spring heat, the proud flesh had begun to swell. Otter Belt squatted by the small fire and gingerly chewed his pemmican.

Cuts Something had grown very fond of the brash young man and felt badly that he would be dead in a few days. Of course they could hurry back to the main encampment and let the vainglorious old medicine man Hears the Sunset, who purportedly possessed beaver medicine, try to heal Otter Belt. Cuts Something considered Hears the Sunset a ridiculous huckster. Certainly potent medicine men existed — he had seen many impressive healings in his youth — but at present the Wanderers were without such a man, although his beloved old friend Sees How Far It Is could be counted on to take care of minor ailments, if not by supernatural means, then with various purgatives and poultices. Unlike Hears the Sunset, Sees How Far It Is did not require gifts for his services, preferring instead to hold the patient's family captive for much prognostication and reminiscence.

Cuts Something had never seen any medicine man demonstrate power over severe open wounds — especially in hot weather. Such cases all ended the same. Over the years, Cuts Something had become convinced that a warrior should cultivate and depend on his own medicine, his own protective spirits. His badger medicine had always served him well, although Otter Belt's misfortune might cause some of the People to question the badger's power. The thought galled him. How could his medicine be expected to protect an over-eager young warrior who had been warned repeatedly against trying to steal a white girl from a well-armed camp?

Of course he could save face by stealing the Texans' horses and collecting a few scalps. But collecting scalps would be anything but easy. The night before, they had watched the camp, waiting for an opportunity to steal the horses. But Black Durham was too alert. He appeared and disappeared among the shadows. Each time they thought they had him located, he appeared unexpectedly in some new location. He never made a sound.

Then the boy. They knew exactly where he was and felt sure they could slip in among the wolves and ease the horses away. Then the fat white man awoke to piss and saw Otter Belt. The boy shot at them which meant that he had seen them. If not for the calamity in camp, the boy surely would have made a kill with his rifle. The way he went to the horses — shielding himself among them. Cuts Something had stayed back to ambush the boy while the others escaped to the river, but the boy gave him no opportunity. The boy needed killing; Durham obviously was preparing him, teaching him. There was something else too, something about the boy that struck Cuts Something and troubled him deeply, but he could not place it.

"I should have killed that boy," Otter Belt slurred. "Tonight I will take his scalp and cut off his balls."

Cuts Something sighed. "My friend, you are lucky you did not meet Black Durham in the dark, and I do not think that boy will die easily." It occurred to Cuts Something that Otter Belt would be better off had Durham killed him and thus spared him several days of horrible suffering. He dared not voice his opinion, however. Otter Belt, young though he was, had made a fine warrior and deserved consideration. "We should boil some thistle blossoms and make a poultice for your wounds."

Otter Belt spat blood. "Yes."

Cuts Something stood and prodded the two other young warriors awake and sent them away in search of thistles. He did not disturb That's It who was snoring loudly.

"We will find them tonight and get their horses if we can," Cuts Something said as he sat down again. He tossed another dried buffalo flop onto the fire, and it flared up immediately. "Then we will follow them, and when the time is right we will ride out of the sun and kill all of the men and take the girl." He added this last part for Otter Belt's benefit. He did not believe for an instant that they would kill them all. He hoped they could get their one revenge scalp and ride hard for home.

Of course he hoped to steal the girl too. After Otter Belt died, his bereaved family probably would cut up or burn the big captive woman he wanted to sell back to the whites at Fort Sill. He had planned to take care of that business immediately upon his return, but he did not think Otter Belt would make it home. The young white girl looked robust and comely. The *tahbay-boh* would pay handsomely to get her back.

Cuts Something lay back on his blanket. He did not want to think about Black Durham or the girl or that boy. Why did that cursed boy torment him so? All he had wanted was to find some excellent wood with which to make a new weapon and to return and lay up with She Invites Her Sisters. His venerable wife had been rejuvenated by his new son whom, for the time being, they were calling Fox. She had stopped openly mourning Elk Rub's death and had lately been quite desirous.

The plains had again become malevolent. Everything seemed threatening, especially the brakes south of the Canadian River. Everything required close scrutiny. Logan stared at every clump of brush, every motte, every swale until his eyes scraped in their sockets. No matter where he was, he wanted to be elsewhere. They did not hunt the day after the attempted thievery. They moved three times before dark. When they were in a deep draw and had made a small cook fire with the driest wood they could find, Logan felt caged and visualized savages pouring onto them from above. Out of the brakes with a good view in all directions, he felt naked and vulnerable.

He could no longer remember what it felt like to simply ride into the river bottom to hunt or to collect water. He could no longer imagine being unafraid. Always he imagined on the breeze the faint odor of sweat, wood smoke, tobacco and hair and always he heard the soft rush of moccasins and felt the passing rush of a wild man. Every flash of movement stopped his heart and loosened his bowels. He ate without tasting, always wanting to move, yet dreading the exposure and vulnerability movement entailed. He prayed constantly for deliverance. Even while he was busy with some task, the prayers continued in the back of his mind.

Bob and Ezra looked haggard. Elizabeth went about her chores without speaking. The skinners muttered among themselves. Late in the afternoon, while Romack kindled a small fire for coffee, Mullins got up from his seat in the kill wagon and approached Bob and Ezra, who were busy counting and sorting ammunition.

"Damn crazy of us to be ridin' around out here when we could be snug at the tradin' post. Ain't nobody else fool enough to be campin' out here like this."

Ezra finished his count. "Seb'nty-three. Strike out if you've a mind to."

"Well hell, we ain't got no horses."

"Then I'd say you ain't got no argument."

"Goddamnit, I don't see no reason for it."

"Reason is, me and Bob don't aim to share these buffaloes with a thousand other hunters. They'll have everything around that tradin' post killed out in a month if they ain't killed everything already. Stay there and you waste half your time gettin' to where you need to hunt." He spat. "We aim to clean up by bein' where the buffaloes are. That's it. You knowed it when you hired on."

Bob shook a powder keg up and down to check its contents. "I don't b'lieve there's many of 'em. Course it don't take too many Comanches to lift a bunch of hair."

"If we don't run into trouble in a day or two, we'll prob'ly be okay," Ezra said. "They was just a little bunch of hunters ridin' through. Might've done beat it for home."

Mullins spun and walked back toward the wagon. "Goddamn crazy. I'm gettin' outta this outfit first chance I get."

Bob set the keg down then sat on it. "You know, Ezree, the thing that worries me is them Buffalo Eaters live in this country, when they ain't off scalpin' or stealin Meskin women. And there's a bunch of 'em. They liable to clean that tradin' post out."

"Last coffee today, boys," Romack said, lifting the pot. "We need to drown this fire and move."

Elizabeth watched forlornly as Romack dumped a spade full of soil on the fire. Without speaking, she climbed into Romack's wagon and rested her elbows on her knees and her chin in her hands and looked at nothing in particular.

"By god I wish that moon would hurry up and rise. I can't see nothin'." Ezra's huge outline was just visible against the slight paleness to the west. They were camped on the open prairie north of the river brakes.

The darkened camp seemed to Logan surreal and cold even in the late spring warmth. He chewed his dried meat and drank his salty Canadian River water and longed for a fire. He looked for Elizabeth and found her indistinct form still sitting in the wagon seat. "Seems like it would be hard for an Indian to get close without us seein' him," he said, still chewing the tough meat.

"That's the idee." Bob's voice came from startlingly far out in the darkness. "We just as well forget about sleepin' tonight. We need every pair of eyes we got."

"Sleep hell," Mullins said.

"Just keep low and keep still," Ezra said. "If they're around they're lookin' for us."

The horses were a strangely comforting presence picketed in the middle of camp. Logan reluctantly left their warmth and shelter and walked out of camp and sat cross-legged sixty yards east of the wagon. He could hear very little above the stiff westerly wind. The moon rose and bathed the plains before him and the river bottom to his right so that he could clearly see the Canadian's pools and sluggish riffles through openings in the streamside brush and rushes.

The prairie lay apparently flat, yet he knew that it was deceptively undulating and that a skilled horseman familiar with its contours could ease close then bolt and be upon him before he could mount his rifle and take careful aim. But he felt certain that no riders crossing the river below him could escape his attention. He tried not to worry about his back. Bob and Era had that responsibility. Still, he worried and felt the peculiar tightness between his shoulder blades.

He sat and watched and listened as best he could. He wished for something to rest his back against. Whenever the wind abated slightly, quavering howls of wolves and hysterical yowls of coyotes and the occasional sharp bark of a swift fox came to his ears. At times, the slinking forms of the wild canines caught his attention and his pulse would momentarily race.

He found Polaris and then the Little Dipper seemingly standing on its handle. Not yet midnight. He contemplated Elizabeth's chipped front tooth and the way her calves looked whenever her parfleche boots sagged around her ankles. He crossed and uncrossed his legs; stood, and as quietly as he could, stomped circulation back into his feet. Twice he woke himself snoring. Perhaps, he thought, the savages had left after all. Perhaps they were just passing through and were not looking for a fight. The hum of the wind faded into the distance. His mouth fell open. His head fell back then forward.

He awoke with a lurch. Beyond a distinct line a hundred yards before him, the new sun bathed the grass in a bright yellow-orange light. Behind the line and to the horizon behind him the prairie was still in shadow. The buffalo grass and grama bent with the gusts, and from the river bottom came a bobwhite's dawn *koi-lee*. He stood tenuously, leaning on his rifle for balance, and waited for the numbness to leave his feet. "Praise you," he said, "praise your name." The tingling left his feet, and he walked into the morning shadow toward the wagons.

C H A P T E R   3 0

"I wish we had us a good shoat," Elizabeth said. She was sitting against the wheel of Romack's wagon. Her long legs stretched before her.

"And roastin' ears," Logan answered. He strained his eyes in the growing darkness to see Elizabeth's reaction. They had spent the day without incident on the open plains.

"That makes me think of cornbread," Romack said, chewing his hardtack, "and molasses."

Elizabeth sat up straight the way she did whenever she had an idea. "I'd take a drink of milk too. Wonder what buffalo milk tastes like?"

Bob swallowed a bite of jerky. "Ain't nobody I know of ever tried to milk one."

"You can't milk a buffalo," Ezra said.

Elizabeth dug in her ear with her pinkie. "Maybe if you tamed one."

Ezra shook his head. "Can't tame buffaloes."

"Somebody had to tame a milk cow," Elizabeth answered.

Ezra said, "Why, you don't have to tame a milk cow."

Elizabeth crossed her legs. "Somebody had to tame a cow sometime."

"Who did?" Ezra studied the girl as if trying to discern her expression in the failing light.

"Well, I suppose they did. Didn't they? Seems like they would."

Ezra took off his hat, stared into it momentarily then put it back on. "Never thought about it. I reckon they had milk cows in Eden. Logan?"

Logan cleared his throat. "And God made the beasts of the earth after his kind, and cattle after their kind, and everything that creepeth upon the earth after his kind," he answered knowingly. People's ignorance of the Word never ceased to amaze him.

Ezra nodded earnestly. "That's what I thought."

Bob spat. "'Cause if it was Eden, and they had everything they needed, they would have to have milk cows for milk."

Elizabeth could be heard scratching her head in the darkness. "Hmmm. Well."

"Somebody out there," Mullins said from the seat of the kill wagon. Burress, who had been lying in the back of the wagon, sat bolt upright. Everyone else stood at once.

"Where?"

"Out there. Wait — I lost him."

"I don't see a thing," Ezra said tensely. They were all looking northward.

"There. Way out there." Mullins pointed at the northern horizon. "See?"

They alternately squinted and widened their eyes. "Wait. I see," Ezra said. "Damn wolf. Lord have mercy, Louis. You had me shakin'."

"Well, I reckon it *is* a wolf." Mullins said. "Damn, I'm jumpy."

Bob laid his rifle barrel in the crook of his arm. "We best quit carryin' on about eatin' and post watch."

"Lizbeth, get under the wagon and get quiet," Ezra said.

"What if I gotta go?"

"Go under the wagon."

"I hate bein' the only girl!"

"Well."

Logan walked to his assigned spot and sat down. He had little hope of staying awake all night even though he had slept a few hours during the day. Three days had past since the attempted thievery and there had been no sign of Indians. Bob and Ezra agreed that hunting should resume the following day.

Drowsiness overcame him almost immediately. Even thoughts of Elizabeth's calves failed to arouse him. He wanted to lie back and stretch his legs and sleep until morning. The shortgrass felt as soft as feather ticking. The moon rose. He dozed. Someone touched him on the shoulder. He yelped and rolled away then recognized the silhouette. "Lizbeth!"

"Shhhh . . ."

"You s'posed to be under the wagon."

"I don't believe that was no wolf," she said. "I seen it."

"What was it then?"

"Couldn't tell, but it didn't look like no wolf to me."

"Where's Earl?"

"Sound asleep."

"What you want?"

She set her eyes and glared at the ground. "I aim to know what it's like."

"What what's like?"

"*It!*"

"Shhh . . ." Logan's mouth went dry. "Lord. You don't mean that — surely."

"I do."

"Them Kiowas about took care of it for you."

"It ain't the same."

"You ain't kiddin' it ain't. Well. We can't. I can't. Anyways, you're awful sure we're gonna die."

"That wasn't a wolf."

"Lizbeth, we'll land straight in hell."

"I guess I'll have to wake up old Mullins."

"You ain't doin' no such thing."

"You watch me."

"Well . . . Lord!"

"Are you or ain't you?"

"Shhh . . . " His mind spun. *I say therefore to the unmarried . . . It is good for them to abide even as I . . . But if they cannot contain let them marry: for it is better to marry than to burn . . . If we confess our sins, he is faithful and just to forgive our sins.* "Well. I don't want you goin' to Mullins."

"Okay then." She sat down then lay back in the grass. "Are you comin' or not?"

"I ain't ready yet."

"What you mean you ain't ready?"

"I mean I ain't ready yet. I need to lay with you a spell."

She pulled her dress up.

"Lord," said Logan Fletcher. "What'd you do with your drawers?"

"Hid 'em under the wagon."

"I swear." He lay down beside her.

"Whoever heard of somebody not bein' ready?" she whispered.

He rolled on top of her and awkwardly placed his lips on hers. She p
ered stiffly to return the kiss. The density and hardness of her body surpris
him. He groped for her thighs. She stiffened.

"What's wrong?"

"Somethin's eatin' me up." He rolled off. She rolled onto her side and furiously scratched her bottom with both hands. "Now then." She moved a foot to
one side and lay back again.

Logan put his hand on her belly. She stiffened again.

"Now what's wrong?"

"I don't b'lieve I can do it. You got me thinkin'."

"About what?"

"Goin' to hell."

"Well I swear."

"I reckon you're mad now."

"No — just good and ready."

"Sure enough?"

"Yes ma'am."

"Well. I can't."

Logan flopped backward and slapped the ground with his hand. "Lord! Lizbeth!"

She sat up, and smoothed her dress over her knees, pulled up her parfleche
boots and drew her knees up beneath her chin. Logan sat up, relieved that she
was not leaving.

"Maybe that *was* a wolf I seen."

"Reckon? I hope it was. I keep thinkin' about how Burress looked when we
found him in that Kiowa camp."

Elizabeth tucked her hair behind her ears. "I can't hardly remember bein' at
home no more. My family has surely give up on me by now. It's queer thinkin'
your family thinks you're dead. Or gone for good."

Logan nodded solemnly. Her earnestness and innocence made it seem likely her family was still alive. "I keep wonderin' what I come out here for. I
could've took a job in town and done as good as I'm doin' out here. Seems like
anyway. Everything just fell in place. Seemed like the Lord was leadin' me. But
it ain't seemed that way for a long time now. You believe the Lord leads you
places don't you?"

"Why yeah. I reckon I do. I've never thought no different. But sometimes it
seems like He just gets out of the way and lets stuff happen."

ɔwa took you?"

d to be here." He couldn't believe he said that.
ghtly behind her ears. "Reckon? Seems like a shame
here and let go and then take deathly sick and live
ᴧen get caught again, don't it?"

ᴧer my head. I believe though. I done seen too much to not believe.
There's a purpose for everything."

"I won't forget what you done for me."

"Well."

"I'd have died for sure."

"It's a gift." He clasped his hands around his knees and rocked gently. "I might've healed a Kiowa woman at that camp."

"Sure enough?"

Under the just waning moon, Logan could see the whites of her eyes. "Bob and Ezra would have a fit if they knowed, but she looked so pitiful. She was bad off. And holdin' a dead baby. I don't know if the Lord would let a Kiowa be healed or not. I laid hands on her though. She didn't want none of it."

"Maybe he'd let a good Kiowa be healed."

"Seems like. I don't know if there is such a thing though. I believe she'd have cut my throat if she could've."

"Wonder why He made Indians?"

"To hone His people, I'd say. Like the tribes in Canaan done. Bob said they're tryin' to teach the Gospel to them Indians at Fort Sill and they ain't doin' much good. I don't believe it'll take 'til they've been whupped good and showed the evil in their ways."

"Wonder what makes 'em do like they do?"

"Just don't know no better, I'd say." He ran his finger along his rifle stock. "You didn't mean that about Mullins, did you?"

"You mean about goin' to him? I'd never let that filthy cur touch me. You knowed it all along."

"Couldn't take no chance."

"Lord. I've heard it all now." They sat silent for awhile. She cleared her throat. "I meant it about the other though. I don't know what got into me. I laid back there and got all worked up and it seemed like I just couldn't stand it. I couldn't live another second if I didn't get up and come out here."

"Well." Logan sat tongue-tied, trying to think of a way to keep the conversation on its present course.

"Then I got scared when we got right down to it." She sighed and extended her legs, leaned back on her hands and crossed her ankles. "My Mama and Daddy never raised me that way."

"Mine neither."

"I hear Bob and Ezree talkin' sometimes. They think I ain't listenin' but I am. I bet you whored a little in Dodge City."

"I never done it!"

"Shhhh . . . "

"Lord, Lizbeth."

"I didn't mean nothin' bad. To hear Bob and Ezree tell it, it's an everyday thing in town."

"I ain't sayin' I never wanted to." He decided that Claudine Monroe was downright bland compared to Elizabeth.

"We're in about the same shape then."

He had absolutely no response.

She sat up straight and drew her legs in Indian style. "I'll stay out here and help you watch. Mr. Romack won't know a thing. He sets a store by you anyway."

He smiled. "I can stand it if you can."

They sat watching the river valley. Elizabeth tugged at her fingers. "If you wanted to put your arm around me, it'd be all right."

"Well." He laid down his rifle and scooted against her and touched her long hair gathered between her shoulder blades. He had expected it to be stiff with sweat and oil, but it was soft and warm to his touch, and he remembered that Bob had given her a currycomb. He stroked her hair and patted her back, then, in amazement and rapt study, moved his hand to her shoulder. Despite her height, she felt delicate in the way of fleet things, an antelope, a doe or a colt, but not fragile, for he closed his fingers around her shoulder and felt the sinew in her upper arm and with his thumb traced the cord of muscle running up the side of her long neck. She placed her hand on his and he judged it harder and rougher than his own.

She leaned into him, and the wind blew strands of her hair across his face. He inhaled her scent. His legs were asleep; he could no more have risen to face an enemy than he could force himself away from Elizabeth. All threats seemed remote now. He could imagine only life.

She turned and rested her chin on his shoulder. "What's gonna happen, you think?" The wind had laid and Logan could hear her breathing and feel her breath.

"Sun'll come up for sure, I'd say."

She cocked her head. "Oh," she said after a moment, and laughed.

Next day they resumed their hunting. Logan's head ached from lack of sleep and the sweltering heat worsened his drowsiness. After a short morning hunt, they returned to camp and ate fried tongue and bannock and swilled coffee and, despite the day's heat, took comfort from Romack's fire.

That afternoon, they shot nine bison. Mullins and Burress worked so lethargically that Logan had to help with the skinning to avoid being out in river bottom after dark.

They camped that night in the brakes north of the river. They ate bison ribs with their hands and knives then sat exhausted about the fire. There was little talk. Within minutes of finishing her meal, Elizabeth was snoring softly, open-mouthed, with her head against the wheel of Romack's wagon

Ezra looked mirthfully at her. "That gal sleeps with her eyes half open."

"I don't see why she's so tired," Mullins said. "She never pulled no watch."

Bob dug in his pipe with a small knife. "I believe Miss Lizbeth took her a little walk last night."

Romack bristled. "She never done it. I'd have seen her."

"I know you would, Earl," Bob said.

Logan casually drank his coffee. He had pulled his watch and that was that. If Elizabeth had strolled out for a visit, that was her doing. Romack should have kept an eye on her.

"Another few days and we'll be needin' to ride over to the tradin' post," Ezra said.

"How long you think we'll be out here?" Logan asked.

Ezra rubbed his beard. "We got a place to sell hides and buy our supplies close by. I don't see no reason to quit long as we got somethin' to shoot. It won't last. We gotta get while we can get."

Burress perked up at the mention of the trading post. "Wonder if them whores ever showed up?"

"You got pay comin', Thurman," Ezra said. "Go right ahead and buy you a good case of clap."

"I aim to."

"I aim to get good and drunk," Mullins said. "Then I'll be ready for three or four of them whores. I don't 'magine I could stand them tradin' post women sober."

"I hope there's a half clean one in the bunch," Ezra said. "I'm gettin' in shape myself."

Mullins nodded toward Elizabeth. "That girl ain't helpin' none."

"No sir!" Ezra said. "We best leave her alone or old Logan'll have our asses." He spat and winked at Bob.

Logan shrugged and drank his coffee. Mullins grunted.

Bob wiped his knife blade on his sleeve. "Louis, that Miss Lizbeth would bite your nose clean off. You seen what she done to that rattlesnake." He looked at Logan. "How many pieces was there when she got done? I believe she's a ring-tail bobcat when she's riled."

Mullins grinned. "I wish she *would* bite my nose."

Logan felt the heat rise in his face. He burned his throat with a huge gulp of coffee. "Mullins, you're a filthy hog."

Mullins calmly spat. His grin returned. This time there was no mirth in it. "I'll cut that Bible quotin' tongue out, you goddamn pup."

Logan tossed his coffee and stood up. "Bring it on, you heathen oaf." He did not feel tired now. He had despised Mullins from the start, despite himself. Elizabeth continued to snore softly.

Mullins drew his skinning knife. Logan picked up the small spade Romack used to dump hot coals on the Dutch oven. "Come on in here Mullins. I'll knock them vile brains out."

Elizabeth raised her head, squinted drowsily at Logan then laid her head back and continued snoring. Bob seemed to be studying the coals. Ezra stood up wearily. "Here now, goddamnit. Louis, I oughta let the boy brain you for sayin' what you said. You knowed you'd rile him before you said it. And I told you about that girl. Touch her and *I'll* brain you if she don't geld you first."

Mullins kept his eyes on Logan. He slid his knife back into its sheath. "Watch yourself, pup," he said coldly.

"Logan, lay the shovel down," Bob said casually. Logan dropped the spade and sat down. His rage surprised him; he knew he would have taken Mullins's head off had the fight progressed. He stared into the fire. Mullins muttered something to Burress who was sharpening the knives. The toothless skinner laughed stupidly.

Ezra cleared his throat. "So how does brainin' a man square with the Good Book? Of course now, I suppose you can heal him after you learn him some manners."

Bob had to stop laughing before he could light his pipe.

* * *

about his confrontation with Mullins. He had been
an over exchanged words. The fact terrified him.
ged, he thought. He wanted to believe he had been
..onor, but he knew that instead he had been driven by a
jealousy — or something baser — and contempt. Mullins had long
annoyed him, had drawn his disdain from the beginning. The man represented
everything Logan held in contempt. Then there was Elizabeth who called upon
that reptilian thing in him that slithered forth to coil about and suffocate his
conscience. That's what it was, he thought. The serpent. When he picked up
that spade he ground his teeth and felt in his chest a longing that terrified him.
A lust: *But these are natural brute beasts made to be taken and destroyed, speak evil
of the things they understand not; and shall utterly perish in their own corruption . . .*
He sweated atop his blanket. The breeze died and the gnats and mosquitoes
descended. He recalled Bob's comment about summer being more miserable
than winter. They had been moving almost daily to escape the stench of rancid
flesh scraped from the hides; *And thou shalt remember all the way which the Lord
thy God led thee these forty years in the wilderness, to humble thee, and to prove
thee, to know what was in thine heart, whether thou wouldest keep his command-
ments or no . . .*

He sat up, ran his fingers through his wringing wet hair, put on his hat,
picked up his rifle and walked out of camp. He walked into the hills in search
of a breeze. The moon was well beyond full, and he walked slowly and very
deliberately to avoid working up further sweat. He worried little about Indians.
He always felt safer away from camp, in the shadows away from the fire. Even
now, with the fire down to coals, he could look back and see camp as if it were
a beacon.

He climbed the hill in search of moving air and relief from swarming
insects. He struggled with images and remembrances of Elizabeth's firm loins
and chapped lips and the strong scent of her hair, and the explosive tension he
had felt in his upper back and chest when he wielded the spade with every
intention of taking Mullins's head off. He recalled other moments of exquisite
rage when he painlessly crushed or tore away massive objects, unsurprised
when his fist went through the hardwood spoke or when the cabin door came
loose from the leather hinges. Nor would he have been surprised when a
smooth, vicious swing of the spade killed a big man cleanly — only surprised

later that he could summon that kind of virulence. *Then when lust hath conceived, it bringeth forth sin: and sin, when it is finished, bringeth forth death . . .* He blinked; *Cursed be their anger, for it was fierce, and their wrath, for it was cruel: I will divide them in Jacob, and scatter them in Israel . . .*

He walked and prayed; prayed for deliverance from his lust; for his lust fed his anger. He climbed onto a low butte and looked over the river valley. He sensed no direction in his life. No assurance. He knew he could easily be skylined on such a bright night, but cast aside all concern. He prayed for guidance, remembering the jolts under the brush arbors at the camp meetings in Kentucky, and the shouts and weeping and catharsis and the purity. Yet he felt he had walked out of a world inhabited by God into some howling wilderness forsaken by its creator, where there were no Christian burials and even the buried dead were dug up and defiled by coyotes and wolves. And his gift? Had he squandered it?

He dozed. The wind stirred. He stood and took off his hat, unbuttoned his shirt and raised his arms to let the breeze flow over him. The river bottom cottonwoods whispered; his sweat dried. He wished he had his bedroll with him. He walked slowly and quietly down the hill. He did not want to spook the camp. The still-glowing embers came into view.

"Good way to get your ass shot off." Bob grabbed his arm and shook him playfully.

"I was burnin' up. Went lookin' for a breeze."

"Find one, did you?"

"A little one."

"Best get to sleep. Soon be time for your watch."

Logan lay on his blanket and rolled his coat to make a pillow. The breeze stirred. He put his hands behind his head and slept soundly.

CHAPTER 31

Logan awoke dimly aware of wretched screaming. He propped himself up on his elbow and looked about. It was dark still, and the coals barely lighted the camp. Elizabeth was hunkered beneath Romack's wagon, shrieking, "Oh Lord! Oh Lord! What is that?" Ezra was cursing and rousing Romack and Mullins and yelling for Bob. The screams came in bursts, close, a couple hundred yards away perhaps; loud and anguished, pleading, masculine yet high pitched; rising then fading to a gurgle.

Ezra yelled, "Get that girl and get away from the fire!" He slid to one knee and grabbed Logan's arm. "Logan, get the hell up and get that girl! Where the hell is Bob?"

Just then, Bob ran into camp, breathing hard. "I think they got Burress. I saw him walk out of camp a while ago — I figured he was goin' to take a piss."

"God almighty!" Ezra looked wildly about.

"God almighty's right," Bob said. "Logan get movin' — get that girl! Bob's eyes widened again. "Oh hell, I better get them horses!" He ran back into the darkness.

Logan took Elizabeth's arm. "Come on. We gotta get you hid."

Her face was ashen. "I hope they just kill me this time," she said hoarsely.

"They ain't gonna get you," he said with little conviction. "Come on." He had no idea where to hide her.

"Goddamnit," Mullins screamed, "he was right here a hour ago. Right here!

I knowed we oughta get to that tradin' post!"

Bob burst back into camp leading three horses. "Logan, let Earl hide Miss Lizbeth. We gotta get movin' or them heathens'll have Burress cut all to pieces."

Ezra was already mounted. "Come on goddamnit!"

Logan grabbed his pistol and rifle and climbed onto Rufus. He needed to make water; the pressure in his bladder only added to the urgency. The darkness looked hellish and impenetrable and he imagined dozens of Comanches hiding just beyond the camp perimeter. Then came another burst of screams. Elizabeth covered her ears. Romack jerked his shotgun from beneath the seat of his wagon and pulled Elizabeth into the shadows.

Bob mounted his horse. "Louis get them mules hid."

"Goddamnit I ain't goin' out there," Mullins answered from beneath the kill wagon.

"You fixin' to wish you had, if I have to come down off this horse."

"Forget him," Ezra said. "We gotta move." They rode southeastward toward the screams which were becoming more wretched and hysterical by the second. Logan drew his pistol and followed Bob. "Dear Lord," he said.

As they rode, the screams seemed to move, yet Ezra held a southeasterly course. The wind had picked up again, and the grass and cottonwoods whipped wildly and their shadows played against the moonlit hills. After a few minutes, Logan realized he could not possibly discern all of the movement. He simply looked straight at the back of Bob's head.

They rode into the river bottom then eastward along the edge of the brakes. Several times, Ezra and Bob stopped, and they listened until the screaming resumed. They were very close when the screaming abruptly stopped. They heard horses fleeing in the hills above them.

"Damn," Ezra said softly, "I don't know why we ever thought we'd find 'em in the dark."

"Had to do somethin'," Bob answered. "Couldn't just sit up there and listen to him squall while they was cuttin' him up."

"Well I'd say they got it done."

"We all thought they was gone," Ezree.

"Me and you should've knowed better. I just hoped they wouldn't find us. I don't see how we're gonna find poor old Burress now."

Logan thought about his own trip into the dark hills. The realization that red men had been watching him, waiting for a chance to take him, made his skin crawl. He tried to spit, but couldn't. "Maybe we oughta holler for Burress."

Ezra snorted. "Let me and Bob ride off and hide before you commence."

"Aw. Well."

"Ain't nothin' to do but wait for light," Bob whispered. "I worry about Earl and Miss Lizbeth."

"They oughta be all right if they stay hid," Ezra said. They rode into a hackberry stand and dismounted and stood holding their horses' reins, listening. They did not talk and after a while their heavy breathing quieted and there was only the sound of the wind in the grass and trees.

Logan wondered how any white man could survive on the plains. It seemed that his own horror and hyper-alertness always dulled after a few days of tedium and fatigue. He had been very lucky. No, he thought. Not merely lucky. Luck had nothing to do with it.

The eastern horizon lightened then turned faintly pink. Minutes passed. A growing orange corona lighted the hills, and the low scrub projected long, distorted shadows. They rode in the direction of Burress's last screams, then separated, each taking a different draw. They searched several draws to no avail. Logan began to wonder if the Indians had carried Burress away. He rode back into the river bottom to find Ezra waiting. Bob appeared at the mouth of a nearby creek.

Ezra's face was chalky; his eyes looked peculiarly bulbous. "He's up there," he said pointing up a sandy wash.

Bob sat his horse. "He alive?"

"Yeah, but he don't know it."

Logan started for the mouth of the creek. "I gotta get to him."

Ezra spat. Most of the amber juice fell on his beard. "You won't save him this time, son. He's missin' some parts he'd need."

CHAPTER 32

Otter Belt's wounds were beginning to smell. Cuts Something discreetly tried to stay upwind of him. They had tried various poultices made of thistle and snakeweed, but the young warrior's face was now grotesquely swollen, and though he remained stoic and capable, his growing pain was obvious. At Cuts Something's urging, Otter Belt had been sipping a brew of boiled silver leaf which helped him relax and sleep.

They had been away from the Wanderer encampment much longer than expected. They had been trailing the white hunters for four days now. They had eaten all of their pemmican and dried meat and now were living on game and whatever plums and hackberries they could gather. They sat watching grease drip from a roasting hunk of venison.

Cuts Something did not want to engage the black man Durham with so few warriors. He did not fear Durham, but the man was dangerous. An experienced warrior would wait until he had a decisive advantage before attacking. But there was the matter of Otter Belt's impending death. Revenge beyond the torture of the white man had to be exacted. Otter Belt, perhaps sensing his own fate, had tortured the man with a savagery that left Cuts Something and That's It slightly shaken. No Kiowa ever did a more thorough job. The two old warriors had been jarred not by the white man's agony, but by Otter Belt's ferocity.

Durham would surely come for them now. Perhaps the huge white man and the boy would come too.

The boy. Why did the boy devil him so? Cuts Something had watched him leave the Texans' camp and walk into the hills. While the other warriors watched the camp and worried about the skulking Durham and tried to find a way to take the girl, Cuts Something shadowed the boy, at times moving close enough to hear his sighs. The boy had moved onto the flat butte and Cuts Something had watched from a clump of juniper. The boy looked to the firmament and Cuts Something heard his soft exhortations and lamentations. He did not understand the boy's tongue, but he knew very well the nature of his quest. He watched him stand and raise his arms and turn slowly in circles — this was not typical *tahbay-boh* behavior. Cuts Something gave up his plans to take the young man there in the darkness. Perhaps he was a shaman; there was something different in him. Perhaps he could be taken nonetheless, but Cuts Something wanted to watch and wait. He wondered what kind of medicine the boy might possess. He had seen the boy's quick reflexes and did not want to rush him when he was so well armed and in the process of summoning his protective spirits. There would be other opportunities.

Cuts Something sliced off a piece of venison with his knife. The others did the same, all but Otter Belt who sat alone with his thoughts in the shade of a huge cottonwood tree. Cuts Something looked with sadness at the young man. The wounds probably would prevent him from enjoying another meal.

That's It wiped his chin with the back of his hand. "I do not believe Black Durham will come soon. He is too concerned with the girl."

"Yes," Cuts Something said. The other warriors listened solemnly. Cuts Something nodded toward Otter Belt. "We cannot go home yet." He chewed his venison. "We need to get their horses."

"And the girl."

"Yes." He smiled at That's It. "Perhaps she will not be as mean as the big red-haired woman."

"The big woman will not be mean much longer. Otter Belt's wife will want to burn her."

"I want to sell her back to the Texans. I fear that she will cut your throat one day when you take her to your lodge." Both men laughed. The young warriors watched and listened then laughed nervously.

Cuts Something looked again at Otter Belt who sat staring across the river bottom into the northern brakes. Black Durham would come. He would not come immediately as he had done when he heard the tortured man's screams. They had tortured the man as long as possible before leaving. Engaging Durham and his friends in the dark would have been too risky with so many young warriors. With more experienced fighters, Cuts Something would have laid an ambush.

Perhaps Durham would take the girl to the trading post and then come. He might be vulnerable as long as he had the girl to worry about. If they could only steal his horses. He would be manageable then.

Cuts Something enjoyed the venison but he longed for a nice fatty hunk of buffalo meat. Perhaps the young men could ride in the river bottom later and take a calf or a fat young cow. He wanted to conserve himself for the coming fight. Better to let the young men expend some of their boundless energy to provide the camp with meat. He worried about his young warriors. Black Durham would kill any of them like he would crush a horsefly. He or That's It would have to handle Durham. "We need to find them again," Cuts Something said without looking up. That's It grunted in agreement.

They needed to kill that shaman boy too. He was trouble. He needed killing in the worst way. Cuts Something now regretted not taking him the night before on the butte.

Otter Belt now lay curled on his blanket. He moaned softly in his sleep.

They waited for Burress to die and then late in the morning they buried him as best they could, knowing that the wolves would find and dig up his body before the next sunrise. The scent of blood was everywhere and there was little they could do. They gathered his severed appendages and buried them with the body.

Logan unbuttoned his shirt. He had worked up a heavy sweat digging the grave. "I can't b'lieve the Lord healed him once just so he could die that way. I shoulda just let him be."

"Son," Ezra said in obvious exasperation, "he might have got well anyways."

"He looked good as dead to me," Bob said.

Ezra regarded the fresh grave. "Well boys, don't be savin' me if I'm missin' any parts. Logan, if you want to say some words over me, make damn sure it's a eulogy."

"I ain't got no choice. I'm called."

Romack tossed his spade into his wagon. "Well, I'm called to save my own ass. What're we gonna do?"

"I believe we oughta go on to the tradin' post 'til them heathens get tired and go home," Bob said. "We gotta think about Miss Lizbeth. Else I'd be all for takin' some greasy scalps." He spat. "Might take some yet."

"Goddamn, it galls me to have to hide behind mud walls," Ezra said. "Earl, pack your stuff. We best get movin.'"

"Y'all ain't leavin' me there are you? That nasty feller might still be there."

"We ain't leavin you, Miss Lizbeth," Bob said gently.

"They'll be more than one nasty feller there," Ezra said under his breath.

Logan helped Romack load the wagon, and they rode out of the brakes and onto the shortgrass plain to avoid ambush. Bob and Ezra rode well ahead while Logan rode beside the two wagons. Mullins handled the kill wagon while Elizabeth sat next to Romack in the seat of the cook wagon. Each time Logan rode by, he heard the two detailing elaborate meals neither would ever enjoy.

Meadowlarks and grouse flushed before them, and plumes of caliche rose as they skirted a prairie dog town. Antelope stood motionless in the distance and harriers hovered just above the shortgrass. Along the edge of the caprock, cliff swallows billowed by the thousands into the cloudless sky in great circling columns. Occasional small bands of bison stared densely, sorely tempting the hunters.

They rode on. The country lay gently rolling with occasional low grassy buttes and swales. The ankle-high buffalo grass and blue grama swayed with each gust of hot wind. Logan caught himself dozing despite the wind and Rufus's torturous gait. Each time the wind abated, clouds of gnats and biting flies swarmed about his head, deviling him. The horseflies found his neck and he ground his teeth and talked himself out of screaming and flailing wildly and running Rufus just to escape the torment. He welcomed the cleansing gusts, giving a soft thank-you each time the wind rose and dried his sweat.

Ezra had said they should reach the trading post shortly before sundown. Logan dreaded the flies and close air and the company at Adobe Walls. He doubted there would be a clean place to sleep, yet he felt he could lie down on creek gravel and sleep soundly, so great was his fatigue. He could not remember how it felt to be truly rested. He thought about his Kentucky highlands and the coolness of the moss on the limestone boulders along Greasy Creek and the softness of the forest duff warmed by early October sun and the coolness of the dark green, laurel-shaded streams and the taste of spring water in a tin cup.

He dozed again, feeling curiously weightless. Rufus swayed beneath him; the sound of hoof beats drifted into the distance. He did not hear the first sharp, distant report of Bob's rifle — only the rolling echo. He assumed that Bob had shot an antelope. He reined Rufus to a stop and squinted eastward. Another shot. Romack and Mullins stopped the wagons two hundred yards away. Logan could see them looking anxiously about. He heard only the rising wind and swishing grass and the creak of his saddle. Then the Indian was upon him. He saw the black eyes and scruffy mane and vermilion paint on the neck of the little mustang coming up on Rufus's left flank; then the thick waist-length braids, sinewy arms and hideously swollen face peering over the scalp-festooned horse hide shield; and lastly the raised battle ax.

In an instant he realized there would be no fleeing. He would meet this wild man hand to hand. Fatigue dulled his fear. He simultaneously wheeled his horse and raised his rifle barrel to parry the Indian's blow. The ease with which the heavy octagonal barrel came up surprised him. The little mustang closed and Logan smelled sweat and tobacco and something sweetly putrid and felt the force of the ax handle against the rifle barrel and saw the grimace on the young Comanche's disfigured face and the heat in his good eye.

Pain shot through Logan's right wrist. He struggled to hold the barrel against the force of the blow. He pushed upward with his left arm and the horses screamed in protest and lurched apart then each wheeled to face the other. Logan lowered his rifle and fired from his waist. Batting flew from the edge of the Comanche's shield as he fell backward from his horse. Recoil drove the trigger guard painfully into Logan's knuckle.

Right handed as he was, with his rifle gripped in his right hand, there was no way to draw his pistol and no time to reload. The Comanche was on his knees now, the shield still strapped to his right arm as he nocked an arrow. Logan did not think. Instinctively he spurred Rufus and rode at the Indian.

Just before he lost sight of the Comanche beneath Rufus, he heard a twang and felt searing heat against his cheek and ear. He grabbed at his face and Rufus bucked. Logan fell clear and rolled, dropping his rifle and groping for his pistol. He got to his knees and awkwardly drew the heavy revolver. He searched frantically for his target then remembered to pull back the hammer.

He saw no one. He stood and looked about with a mixture of panic and relief. Perhaps the savage had fled. Or perhaps he was about to materialize from the shortgrass as he had moments before. Rufus pricked his ears. Logan wheeled and saw the young Comanche, forty yards away, catch and mount his horse in one smooth motion. Logan raised his pistol and tried to aim. Between his heavy breathing and the weight of the pistol, the front sight wobbled hopelessly. He squeezed off a shot; the pistol bucked and for all Logan could tell, the ball went twenty feet over the Indian's head. His legs trembled. He touched the wound on his face, and his fingers came away red. Yet he could tell that the wound was already clotting. Rufus eyed him with suspicion. Logan spoke softly to the horse who then refused to looked at him. Nevertheless, he allowed Logan to take the rein. The sun glinted on something in the grass. He dropped the rein and walked a few feet to pick up the Comanche's battle ax. He had fought hand to hand with a savage and had lived to tell about it. He offered a quick, fervent prayer of thanks, and slipped the ax into his saddlebag.

Another shot. He had forgotten about the others. He mounted and rode toward the wagons. In the distance he could see Mullins leveling Ezra's Henry across the kill wagon and Elizabeth standing in Romack's wagon, trying to cock the shotgun. Romack was on the ground obviously pleading with Elizabeth to get down and take cover.

Another Comanche materialized from a shallow swale, riding on the lee side of his horse with only a leg over his horse's back. The Indian fired arrows one after the other. Logan saw the puffs of smoke from the weapons then heard their reports and saw Elizabeth fall backward out of the wagon. His throat constricted.

He rode for the protected side of the wagons. He looked again for the Indian and, like the one he had fought moments before, this one had vanished on the open prairie.

He found Elizabeth sitting on the ground, legs spread, toes pointed upward. She was glaring insolently at Romack who was in the throes of a tantrum.

"Damn ye hard-headed girl. I oughta cut a switch and wear ye out right here! When I tell ye to get down outta the wagon, I mean get outta the wagon!" He spat angrily. "And I don't goddamn mean maybe!"

"I reckon I hit him."

"Oh ye reckon ye hit 'im. Well then. I oughta jerk a knot on ye bottom."

"Believe I did."

"You don't have no idee where ye shot. You was too busy fallin' outta the wagon."

"He might come back," Logan said, reloading his rifle.

Elizabeth and Romack stopped arguing and scrambled for the shotgun.

Mullins retched. "Boys, I'm hit," he croaked.

"Now look." Romack shouted, "Ye shot Louis."

"Oh lord."

"Oh lord nothin'. Don't go runnin' out there."

Logan ran toward Mullins who by now had leaned back against the wheel of the kill wagon. The mules stood placidly. An arrow had pinned Mullins's shand to the rifle stock. Logan took his arm. "Come on back here with us. Hold on to your gun."

"Hell, I can't do nothin' else," Mullins said weakly. "I'm stuck to it." He got unsteadily to his feet then hunkered behind Logan as they ran back to the cook wagon. He collapsed between Elizabeth and Romack.

"Oh no," Elizabeth said.

Romack looked at Mullins's hand. "Lord Louis." The arrow head had cut through his middle two fingers, just above the knuckle.

"I knowed I didn't shoot him," Elizabeth said indignantly.

Romack ignored her comment. "Best just lop that finger off, Louis. I don't see no other way."

"Welp," Mullins said. He sat with the rifle in his lap and his head hung between his knees. There was another shot in the distance. They looked up to see Bob three hundred yards distant sitting his horse and yelling against the wind, waving and motioning for them to follow.

"Oh lord, there's no tellin'," Romack said.

"What about my finger?"

"We'll hack it off first chance we get," Romack said. He helped Elizabeth into the wagon.

Logan rode after Bob's dust plume. The fatigue and sickening fear had left him. Only a hyper-alertness and metallic taste remained. He wanted a drink of water.

Bob disappeared over a low rise. Logan cleared it seconds later to find Bob leaning over Ezra whose buckskin shirt was soaked with blood. "Sweet Jesus. He alive?"

"About gone, I'm afraid. Ezree, can you hear me?" Ezra's eyelids fluttered. "Best do what you can do fast," Bob said. "He's leavin' us. Them heathens got a lance in him." There was a look of hopeful pleading on Bob's face.

Logan kneeled and placed his hand on the dark spot on Ezra's chest. He felt something then took his knife and cut open Ezra's shirt. "There's somethin' in his ribs; we gotta pull it out or ain't nothin' I can do."

Bob wiped away the blood with his bare hand to reveal part of a huge, dark stone spear point wedged between Ezra's two upper ribs. "I ain't never see such a lance head. It's almost buried."

Logan could just get his index finger and thumb on the blood-slick flint. He pulled until his fingers slipped. Bob untied his neckerchief and used it to improve his grip on the lance tip. With fingers twice as thick as Logan's he jerked the eight-inch fragment free with two hard tugs. Ezra gagged weakly; Bob sobbed, "I'm sorry Ezree. I wouldn't hurt you for nothin' in this world." He threw the tip angrily and wiped his eyes with his sleeve.

Logan put his hands on Ezra's face and prayed. He prayed for the Lord's tender mercy and healing power. He prayed on the Blood of the Lamb, and asked for the bleeding to halt. Bob bowed on one knee behind him and nodded at each exhortation. The others arrived in the cook wagon; there was a collective gasp and then Elizabeth whimpered.

Logan continued, ever louder. "And when I passed by thee, and saw thee polluted in thine own blood, I said unto thee *when thou wast* in thy blood, Live; yea, I said unto thee *when thou wast* in thy blood, Live."

"Amen," Bob said softly.

Logan put his bloody hands on his thighs. "Bob."

"Huh?"

"He's gone. The Lord called him home. I couldn't do it this time."

"Well." Bob sighed. "Lawd, Ezree." He took off his hat.

For the first time, Logan noticed the two Comanches lying in the grass ten yards away. He closed Ezra's eyes, stood up and looked at the others and shook his head slowly. Elizabeth cried softly; Romack wrung his hat in his hands and stared at the mules.

One of the Comanches, a young man lying on his back, groaned and tried to raise his head. He had taken a 500-grain bullet through his midsection. Logan grabbed for his pistol. Bob took casual note of the young warrior's struggle. "He ain't goin' nowhere. I best go ahead and finish him. Be the only Christian thing to do." His shoulders slumped as if he were exhausted and for the first time Logan thought he looked small and aged.

Elizabeth leapt from the wagon wielding Romack's butcher knife and ran for the dying Comanche. The men watched open-mouthed. The young warrior tried to roll away, but she hurdled him and then turned and kicked him in the ribs. Then with one stroke, she cut away his breechclout.

"Lizbeth! Lord!" Logan started toward her; Bob grabbed his arm.

"I believe Miss Lizbeth just now remembered somethin'. Best let her be."

The men turned their heads just before she emasculated the young Comanche and threw the gore into his face. Bob drew his pistol and finished him. Elizabeth threw down the knife and ran sobbing to the wagon. She leaned on the side of the wagon and buried her face in her arms. "Oh Lord! Oh Lord! What if my Daddy knowed what I done? What if he *does* know right now? Oh Lord," she wailed. "Logan, I'm sorry I done it. I know you could've saved him."

Romack and Mullins watched awkwardly. Bob pushed Logan toward the girl. "Say somethin' to that gal; she's hurtin' bad. Ain't no tellin' what's in her."

Logan went to her side. "Now Lizbeth, we all see why you done what you done."

She looked up. "What?"

"Won't nobody blame you for geldin' that Indian."

Elizabeth Keltner cocked her head and squinted to focus through her tears. "What'd you do to your face?"

CHAPTER 33

The broken lance tip was a bad omen. Cuts Something had never dealt with such a powerful man. But of course Black Durham would keep formidable company.

They had ridden out of a dry wash, he and two young warriors, Shouts From Hills and Three Fires, and had surprised the big white man, but before Cuts Something could get a lance in him, the big man leveled his rifle and blew the top of Three Fires's head off. Cuts Something rushed him and drove the lance head into his rib cage and was trying to run it clean through when the big man dropped his rifle and grabbed the lance shaft, jerked it from Cuts Something's hands and slammed the butt up into his chin causing him to bite the tip of his tongue nearly off — his throbbing mouth still tasted of blood. Cuts Something grabbed the lance and the big man again heaved, lifting Cuts Something from his horse and breaking off the lance tip. The man was mortally wounded, however. Cuts Something and Shouts From Hills rushed him, hoping to finish him and count coup and take his scalp. But a rifle bullet knocked Shouts From Hills off his horse. Black Durham was hidden in the distance and would have his rifle reloaded before Cuts Something could scalp the big man or drag the two downed warriors away for proper burial. Cuts Something caught his horse and fled southward to meet That's It and Otter Belt.

He rode on toward their meeting place, the head of a small creek in the brakes north of the river. The sun was high now, and his horse's rough gait jarred his sore mouth. He stopped for a drink, and the salty Canadian River water burned his split tongue. His lust for the big man's scalp increased with every painful swallow. He hoped That's It had the girl and Otter Belt had the boy's scalp. He dreaded telling Otter Belt and That's It about the death of Shouts From Hills and Three Fires. He hated leaving fallen warriors, yet had he gone back for them Black Durham would surely have cut him down. He would recover the bodies after nightfall.

He found the mouth of the dry creek then rode to the head where he found That's It applying another thistle poultice to Otter Belt's wounds. That's It looked up and nodded grimly. "They fought bitterly. The girl shot my horse, but he will live. I got an arrow into one of them." He pointed to Otter Belt's tattered shield. "The boy is still alive."

"I will take his balls when we meet again," Otter Belt gurgled. Cuts Something did not think Otter Belt would get another chance. That's It finished applying the poultice and raked the excess from his palm. "Where are Three Fires and Shouts From Hills?"

"Dead. The big man shot Three Fires's head off. Black Durham killed Shouts From Hills from far away. I killed the big man, I think. But my lance is broken now."

"Why are you talking like that?"

Cuts Something stuck out his bloody tongue. "It was a bad fight. The man was stronger than a bull. I got a lance in him and he lifted me from my horse before I could push it in deep."

"The bodies?"

"Black Durham was hidden in the sage. He would have killed me with his rifle. We will get the bodies tonight."

Again, That's It nodded grimly. "We should go home. We can fight them another time. The spirits are not with us now. We did not make medicine before we fought them."

"We can lose them in the brakes to the south. I do not want Black Durham riding on our camp with a herd of Texans."

"Do you think he is coming?"

"He is coming. He and that boy. They will try to kill us before we get home. Perhaps we can surprise them in the canyons."

"Black Durham is cunning and strong."

"Yes, but I killed the big man. We can kill Black Durham."

"Yes, and the boy."

Cuts Something nodded. "We need to kill that boy. We can give his scalp to Otter Belt's wife." Realizing his insensitivity, he glanced at Otter Belt. The young warrior regarded him calmly with his good eye. "Yes," he said.

They buried Ezra Higginbotham on a grassy knoll. The dry, hard earth and the dense prairie rootage made for hard digging. Logan, Bob and Romack took turns until they had a deep grave which they tamped down to discourage coyotes and wolves. They placed no marker, for they did not want to draw the attention of anyone who might rob or defile the grave.

Sweating profusely, Logan gave a short eulogy from I Corinthians Chapter 15. Bob stood with his head bowed and hands clasped before him. Romack and Elizabeth stood open-eyed and dazed. Mullins lay in the back of the wagon, drunk now, with his hand still pinned to the rifle stock.

"So when this corruptible shall have put on incorruption, and this mortal shall have put on immortality, then shall be brought to pass the saying that is written, Death is swallowed up in victory. O death, where *is* thy sting? O grave, where *is* thy victory? The sting of death *is* sin; and the strength of sin *is* the law. But thanks *be* to God, which giveth us victory through our Lord Jesus Christ. Amen."

"Amen," Bob said. He took a deep breath, put on his hat and walked to his horse.

"I never thought about Ezree gettin' killed," Elizabeth said.

Romack nodded. "Nope. Ye never think about somebody bein' dead." He turned toward his wagon. "Louis, I reckon we'd best go ahead and lop them fingers off." He spat then dug through the cook box in search of his knife. "We 'bout to get in bad shape for skinners," he said.

They camped in the open. At first light they headed eastward for Adobe Walls trading post. As before, Bob rode ahead, sometimes a mile or more, while Logan watched the rear and sides of the little convoy. Mullins, sans two fingers, lay passed out in the kill wagon which Elizabeth now drove. Romack sat listlessly in the seat of the cook wagon. Near midday, Bob rode back toward the wagons and motioned for Logan to come in as well.

"Soldiers up ahead. I never seen so many."

"Thank God," Romack said.

"I don't 'magine they're here to save us, Earl." Bob said.

"Hell. Maybe we can fall in with 'em."

"Well. They'll be goin' back to Fort Sill sometime. Maybe Miss Lizbeth can ride with 'em."

Elizabeth slapped her thighs. She had a look of pleading on her face. "I don't know them!"

"Be much safer, Miss Lizbeth," Bob said.

Elizabeth wiped her eyes. She did not answer.

Dust rose to the east. They rode on. They crested a low rise and before them stretched a column of black soldiers — mounted cavalry and infantry riding in wagons and thirty or so Indians, naked save for knee-length breechclouts. The Indians rode scruffy, speckled mustangs and wore their hair long and disheveled. Several wore rude tattoos of birds and horses and deer on their chests. All wore many brass bracelets on their wrists; feathers and shells dangled from their ears and hair. Each carried a Spencer carbine.

"Oh Lord!" Romack said.

Bob seemed unconcerned. "Tonkawa scouts," he said casually.

A big, dark-bearded white man rode out to meet them. He wore homespun pants and a filthy buckskin shirt and a badly drooping wide-brimmed hat. He nodded cordially then spat a long stream of amber. "Nigger Bob Durham," he said.

Bob smiled and shook his head. "Burl Doggett. I swear. I allowed you was still up in Kansas."

"Was. But they ain't nothin' left to shoot. Better livin' to be made lookin' for Comanches and Kiowas."

Bob surveyed the Indian scouts. "Bad lookin' bunch of Tonks you got there. I hear they're bad about stealin'."

"I'm tellin' you what. I imagine we'll end up hangin' every one in the bunch before we're through up here."

"Lazy too, I reckon."

"Doggett laughed. I'll take Tonks over Apaches. I'm afraid to go to sleep when we're usin' Apaches. Where's Ezree?"

"Buried him yesterday. Run up on a little bunch of Comanches."

"Goddamn. They're all stirred up since you boys come over here from Kansas and started shootin' their buffaloes. They burned half the farms on the Brazos this spring." He took a deep breath. "I'm truly sorry about Ezree. I know you boys go way back."

"Ain't gonna be the same no more. I 'magine I'll get out of hides. Go back to haulin' freight, maybe."

"What happened to that pup's face?"

Logan looked at Bob for permission to speak. Bob nodded. "I was tryin' to run one of them Comanches down and he grazed me with an arrow."

Doggett looked carefully at Logan, then laughed. "Tried to run him down, huh? How'd you ever get a Comanche afoot?"

"I blowed a hunk out of his shield, and it knocked him off his horse. He about got me though."

"Yeah, but he didn't. Get him did you?"

"No sir. Fell out of the saddle when he shot me with that arrow, and he run off before I could shoot him. Look here." He took the battle ax from his saddle bag.

Doggett took it and turned it over in his hands. "Be damn. Hammered the head out of a piece of barrel hoop." He looked again at Logan, then winked at Bob. "Right strappin' boy, ain't he? Now Bob, where'd you get that girl at?"

"Some Kiowas had her. She come from down on Ioni Creek."

"I heard they stole a girl from down there. I reckon that's her. She's right healthy."

"They been feedin' me good," Elizabeth said.

"We've growed very attached to Miss Lizbeth," Bob said.

"I ain't never seen so many niggers in one place in my life," Mullins said drunkenly. "How many you say Earl?"

"Three hunnerd head if there's a one."

"And all good boys," Doggett said, looking back. "They'd foller Rogers Samuel Maddox right into hell. Old Nuchols, the sergeant — he's done run all the sorry ones off."

Bob arched his brows. "Maddox? Colonel Maddox?"

189

"Yeah. Tenth Cavalry. We rode out of Fort Sill sixteen days ago."

Four Tonkawa scouts rode in from the south, and the procession halted while white officers and a black sergeant conferred with the returnees. "I best go see what's goin' on," Doggett said. "We sent six out." He rode toward the conference. The dust-covered troopers sat their horses and talked softly among themselves. They carried short carbines and no sabers. Most had holes in the knees of their breeches. Some lacked shirts and simply wore suspenders over sweat-stained long johns. Nearly all had beards. They cast curious glances at Bob.

After a few minutes, Doggett returned with one of the white officers, a strikingly handsome young man with a few days' growth of dark beard, a lightly muscled build and gray eyes. The young officer thrust out his hand to Bob. "Colonel Rogers Maddox," he said with an Eastern accent. "You'll be Bob Durham, the intrepid rescuer of women and children."

Bob took his hand and shrugged. "A man has got to live with hisself."

Maddox laughed. "Some manage more effortlessly than others, I'm afraid."

Logan was shocked by Maddox's youth. He had not supposed colonels could be so young. He guessed the man to be less than thirty years old.

"Our scouts cut Comanche sign south of here." Maddox said. "Two went ahead in pursuit. I suspect these are the same heathens you encountered yesterday. Very sorry about your partner, by the way."

"We knowed the risk when we come. Them we run into yesterday is from that bunch that used to live on the Pease. There was two old ones; I know both of 'em. I 'magine they'll head back to the Pease."

"That makes no sense at all Mr. Durham. The Pease River band was driven onto the reservation years ago." He hesitated. "Then again, Colonel Grierson said the bands are coming and going as they please. Still, I suspect they're part of Quanah's band."

"Yes suh, but they headin' south."

"Probably to lose us in the brakes."

"I don't mean to argue, suh, but they could lose us plenty easy on the Llano. And I seen that old boy. Me and him goes back a ways."

Maddox shook his head. "No offense taken, Durham. In any case, it's purely academic. What we know is that we have Comanches riding southward toward the Quitaques." He looked at Doggett who nodded, then back at Bob and Logan. "Gentlemen, I have a proposition. We are in serious need of long-range riflemen to protect our flanks. Without them, we're constantly harried by the enemy. They disrupt our bivouacs and shadow every maneuver. Sharpshooters could keep them at bay. As far as pay, I can make no promises, but you have my word as an officer that I'll do everything I can to see that you're fairly compensated."

"He will too," Doggett said.

"As a minimum, we can provide protection for the young lady."

"We was thinkin' of headin' in to the tradin' post," Bob said. He looked at Logan, then Romack.

"Mr. Durham, that trading post will likely be sacked very soon unless we run these heathens onto the reservation this summer. I'll offer further incentive. You can take a half dozen Tonkawas, and with Burl's help, take three days to pursue your friend's killers. Our scouts report that the savages are traveling slowly — they probably feel very secure."

"Or they're layin' for us."

Maddox smiled. "Ours is a business fraught with risk — as I'm sure you know, Mr. Durham. What do you say?"

"How long you need us for?"

"Two weeks, perhaps. We'll continue westward just above the river. Take your three days to pursue the killers, then you can rejoin us. We'll be sending patrols out daily in search of the enemy. The young lady and the rest of your party will be safe with us in the meantime."

"What you say, Logan?"

Logan had assumed he would remain with the soldiers. His stomach roiled. "You the boss, I reckon."

"I'd like to get me a pair of greasy scalps," Bob said.

"Excellent," Maddox said. "Sergeant Nuchols will see to your provisions. The Tonkawas will get you to the trail and the other two scouts. What about your horses? What kind of shape are they in?"

"They in fine shape. We been movin' easy."

"Good. There's one thing, however. I need your word that you'll carry out the mission without putting my men in unnecessary danger."

"Colonel, I'm near sixty year old. I never got that way bein' wild."

Maddox smiled again. "Very well. I see you have hides."

"They'll keep. We done 'em right."

"Of course. Good luck gentlemen."

Late afternoon, they rode southward leaving Elizabeth and Sergeant Nuchols in an animated discussion on the durability of parfleche boots. Logan did not think she noticed his departure. They watered their horses and filled their canteens at the river and continued toward the red scarp canyons. The four scouts were led by a tall, powerful Tonkawa named Abraham who spoke fair English and trader Spanish in addition to his native language. The other three Indians rarely spoke and then only among themselves and to their leader.

The Tonkawas set a brutal pace. They picked up the Comanche trail at twilight — unshod hoof prints in a dry wash — then, much to Logan's amazement, they continued in the dark for two hours.

They camped on a grassy shelf above a clear, gypy creek. They ate dried meat and hardtack and washed it down with water. Logan sat next to Bob who laboriously chewed his supper. "Old teef 'bout to quit on me," Bob said with a full mouth.

"How'd them Indians track in the dark?"

Bob swallowed with obvious effort. "They guessin' from what they seen in daylight. Guessin' right, I expect."

Logan fell asleep immediately. Bob shook him awake two hours before dawn. Doggett was already cinching his saddle. "Growin' boy needs his sleep, Bob. I figured we'd just let him lay and fetch him on our way back."

Bob laughed. "Uh-huh. But I'm afraid some heathen might need trompin' on."

Doggett reminded Logan of Ezra. He felt mildly perfidious for liking him.

About noon they began encountering cairns left by the other Tonkawa scouts — piles of rocks, strategically placed sticks, drawings in the sand. Logan would have missed them had Bob not pointed them out. After the first two cairns Abraham began stopping and pointing to make certain that Logan distinguished each marker from the natural clutter. Then, satisfied, he would nod like a white man and push on without speaking. After a dozen or so finds, Logan identified the cairns without help.

They entered the scarp canyons mid-afternoon on the second day and the trail seemed to point toward a huge gathering of circling turkey vultures. They followed a narrow game trail deeper into the canyons, climbing through mesquite, prickly pear and little bluestem, then juniper, shin oak and cholla. Logan glanced at the broken, eroded plains to the east and the sky swirled. He turned back to the winding trail.

Heat reflected off the red walls; no breeze stirred amid the junipers. "By god, it's blisterin' hot for May," Doggett said. He, Bob and Logan were drenched with sweat; the Tonkawas did not seem to sweat.

"I reckon them Tonks was born for this," Bob said. "I swear, I keep smellin' somethin'."

Abraham's pace quickened and the Tonkawas shot hard glances at one another. They descended another narrow trail and rode into a dry creek bed, and there in the glaring sun and reflected heat, lay the two forward scouts, scalped and bloating on the red, salt-splotched clay.

Abraham dismounted and commenced cursing in three languages. The other Tonkawas wept and moaned. Doggett looked impassively at the bloating corpses. "Well, Bob, I'd say they was layin' for 'em. Done this just to goad us. Havin' their selfs a good laugh about now, I imagine." Logan sat his horse and barely kept from vomiting.

The scouts hurriedly buried their dead beneath fist-sized rocks. The party pushed on. The Tonkawas worked the Comanches' trail while the others watched for any sign of ambush. At times, the Tonkawas argued among themselves, and Bob and Doggett would enter the conversation. There was no time now for lessons; Logan listened and watched to pick up whatever he could which was very little — a piece of hoof print, a faint scratch on rock, slightly bruised grass.

Twice the Tonkawas leapt from their saddles and took cover and the others followed, but, after a short wait, they remounted and continued. Logan listened, desperate and intent, but heard little above the pulse beating in his ears. He started to take a drink from his canteen then stopped when he realized that tilting his head back, no matter how quickly, would take his eyes from his surroundings and slow his reaction to ambuscade.

They stopped at the base of a talus-covered slope to look and listen. The disbanded flock of vultures, foiled by the dead Tonkawas' burial, now hunted gracefully in groups of two and three. A mockingbird buzzed at the riders from a plum motte. Mourning doves cooed from brush on the slopes above them.

Two doves flushed, wings whistling, from nearby shinnery oak. The Tonkawas rolled off their horses into the scrub. Logan followed their example and hit the ground so hard he lost his breath. He rolled painfully over a clump of prickly pear into a saltbush thicket and came face to face with a staring Tonkawa. A Comanche arrow protruded diagonally from both sides of the dead scout's head. Logan turned away and fought for his breath. It came in shallow, wheezing gulps.

There was no sound but the wind moaning in the canyons and his own ragged breathing. He wanted to close his eyes and cover his head with his arms. What if he were the only member of his party still alive? How would it feel the instant the knife edge cut into his sack?

From the grass to his left came the faint click of someone setting a rear trigger. Logan's pulse beats ran together forming a roar that nearly drowned the muzzle blast from Bob Durham's Sharps. There was a distinct thud and a sliding sound on the slope above them, then the clatter of unshod hooves.

"By god, Bob," Doggett whispered from a tangle of dead cedar, "I believe you hit somethin'."

"Believe I hit a horse; that's all I seen. We lose anybody?"

Logan's tried to speak and his larynx failed him. He swallowed and tried again. His voice came in short honks. "There's a dead scout over here."

Bob could be heard scratching his head. "A dead cow. Well."

Doggett grunted. "What in hell has a dead cow got to do with anything?"

Logan cleared his throat. "A dead *scout*; a Tonk."

"Aw — well — hell."

Bob got to his knees and brushed bits of dead grass and sand burrs from his hair. "I'd say they're gone." The Tonkawas were already kneeling over their fallen companion.

They found the bleeding mustang lying on its side on a narrow deer trail amid boulders near the head of the canyon. A brown leg and moccasined foot protruded from beneath the horse. A staring Comanche lay with his head turned to one side on a tuft of buffalo grass. Logan recognized the face. "Fall must've killed him," Bob said. "I shot the horse right through the lungs." He took out his knife and grabbed the dead man's hair then let go and recoiled. "Sweet Jesus almighty! Lawd have mercy!"

They stared at the grotesquely swollen face. "Hell, his face is movin'," Doggett said. He spat, then shook his head and spat again.

Bob took in a breath and held it. He stepped close to take a good look at the man's face. He backed away and exhaled. "Screw worms. God Almighty. Look there; he's tied to his horse."

Sweat ran down Logan's sides. "Where the worms dieth not and the fire is not quenched," he said.

Bob looked at him. "Huh?"

Logan wiped his eyes and shook his head. "Nothin'."

Below them, the Tonkawas were lifting their dead comrade onto a horse.

Bob sighed. "I'd say we're done. Looks like them Tonks is quittin'."

"You gonna take that scalp?" Doggett asked.

Bob put away his knife. "I don't believe I wanna touch the man, Burl."

Cuts Something had been so close. The arrow should have gone through the boy's chest. Instead the doves flushed and the wretched Tonkawa lurched for cover and took the arrow in the head. Could the boy's medicine be that strong? Nothing had gone well since he first saw the boy that day on the Canadian. Three more warriors dead. His band was dwindling. Except for That's It, he had no seasoned warriors to lead. He needed to summon the full power of his badger medicine.

He had grown to love and respect the once belligerent Otter Belt. Now he was returning home without the young man's body. Had he or That's It tried to recover it they would surely have been killed by one of Black Durham's bullets. Over most of his life, he had never been forced to leave a fallen Comanche, yet since they left the reservation, the white buffalo hunters, with their big rifles, had forced him to leave more than he could remember. Of course had Otter Belt been merely wounded, Cuts Something would have taken the risk — a Comanche would much rather die than desert a wounded warrior. But the young man had died the previous night.

Cuts Something and That's It rode south over the barest, rockiest country they could find. They filled their water bags only once — at a spring well above the layers of gypsum that tainted the creeks and river prongs. After a day's ride, they turned southeast toward the Middle Pease and home. Cuts Something had lost track of how many days they had been away. Some of the Wanderers undoubtedly had given them up for dead. He hoped camp was where he had left it. He dreaded the women's wailing, but looked forward to his lodge and wives and new son.

They camped at dusk a few miles upriver from the main encampment. They talked very little and then only of the hunting they needed to do to replenish their larder. Cuts Something had never been so tired. They drank the last of their water so that their full bladders would wake them before dawn.

There could only be one reason for the Tonkawa presence on the High Plains, he thought. The buffalo soldiers were hunting the People. "I think we should move soon," he told That's It. "We need to join Quanah out on the Llano. I am told he plans to winter in the Canadian Gorge. The *tahbay-boh* will never find us there. They will die of thirst."

That's It was already snoring.

At dawn they sat their horses in the cedar hills above the Wanderer encampment. They blackened their faces, and when the sun cleared the eastern horizon they rode slowly toward their lodges.

CHAPTER 35

"A man gets in sorry shape for water in three days," Burl Doggett said.

Bob took a drink from his canteen. "That sun beatin' down ain't doin' him no good neither."

Logan wondered if the hapless man, a Comanchero named Ybarra, would be able to talk if he ever decided that was what he wanted to do. Bob shook his head and walked away to sit in the meager shade of Romack's wagon. Maddox and Sergeant Nuchols continued to interrogate their prisoner in trader Spanish. Nuchols kept cocking his head to talk to the man. Logan wondered if Nuchols should stand on his head to better talk to the prisoner who was naked and tied upside down to the wheel of a gunnery wagon.

Doggett watched with interest. "I should've shot that sumbitch twenty years ago. Hell, I figured surely somebody had killed him by now. There ain't no tellin' how many guns that Meskin bastard has sold to the Comanches and Kiowas." He nodded emphatically. "He's in for it now though, by god. Look there; why even his peter's blistered."

Nuchols continued his soft-spoken interrogation, occasionally looking back at Maddox who stood watching with his hands clasped behind his back. After several minutes, Maddox shook his head in exasperation. "Let him think about it awhile, sergeant."

The graying, powerful Nuchols stood up stiffly. "Yes, suh. He's a strong one."

"Quite. Ugly business, this. I'll be damned glad when he breaks." He caught Nuchols' expression. "I know; I know; but it'll save suffering in the end. Doesn't make it any easier in the meantime, though — does it?"

"No, suh." Nuchols wiped his brow and the inside of his hat rim with his fingers. "Men ain't doin' too good with it neither, suh. I might oughta talk to 'em."

"Yes. Go ahead then." He watched Nuchols walk back among the bivouacked soldiers. He turned to Logan and Doggett. "For some reason, the Almighty has always seen fit to bless me with excellent sergeants. Some would call Nuchols ignorant, but he speaks two languages and gets on well with the Tonkawas."

The Comanchero moaned. Maddox stiffened and looked away. The man yelled something unintelligible in a hoarse voice. Maddox wheeled. "Sergeant Nuchols!" Nuchols came jogging back. "I think he might be ready," Maddox said.

Nuchols knelt again and spoke to Ybarra. They talked for perhaps a minute, then Nuchols stood. "Middle Pease, suh. Just west of the Tongue."

"Well done sergeant. See that the man's needs are met. We're not savages here. He can be properly hanged when we reach civilization. No need for him to suffer needlessly in the meantime. We'll move at first light."

"Yes, suh, Colonel."

Logan took a canteen to Ybarra. At first the Comanchero let the water pour from his mouth; then he gulped frantically.

"Maybe we oughta go ahead and cut him loose," Nuchols said. "I don't believe he's goin' nowhere."

In the council lodge, Cuts Something argued his case against stiff opposition. "The *tahbay-boh* will never find us out on the Llano," he said.

Hears the Sunset snorted. "Who is to say they will find us here? Was it not your vision that led us back to our home? And are we always to run and hide from the soldiers?"

"We can raid from the Llano. They will never follow us there. Quanah still raids south of the Del Norte. He engages the soldiers only when it is to his advantage."

"Who is this Quanah everyone speaks of? Why should the Wanderers care about his deeds?"

"He was one of us. Have you forgotten?"

"I am tired of fleeing. This is our home. If the *tahbay-boh* come, it will mean their death."

"Friend, we have few warriors now. We can move to the Llano and regain our numbers. Then our sons and grandsons can take back what is theirs."

"I would rather die a warrior."

Cuts Something sighed. "And you will. Very soon. I will live like a warrior and strike another blow yet. Who is with me?"

That's It and Sees How Far It Is nodded. As did Otter Belt's father and two uncles. None of the other elders or mature warriors spoke or nodded. For a moment Cuts Something sat rigidly. Then he began preparing a pipe.

Logan, Bob and Burl Doggett rode the flanks of the long cavalry procession. After three days they had encountered no threats, yet Maddox continued to order cold camps. Logan would have loved a pot of coffee. Whenever they stopped to rest or bivouac, the Tonkawas, the hunters, the black troopers and the white officers mostly kept to their respective groups, although Nuchols occasionally visited with the hunters. Maddox conferred frequently with his officers and occasionally with Bob and Doggett. Logan listened from the periphery but said nothing. They would reach the Pease in another two days, Bob said.

"Then what?"

"Depends."

"On what?"

"On how many there is and where they're camped."

"We aim to attack?"

"I'd say so. I reckon me and you and Burl be shootin' long from a good rest."

"Lord God."

"That's what we hired on for. That and keepin' them heathens back 'til we get to Sill."

"Keep 'em back?"

"We won't get 'em all and they'll be after our horses and scalps, I 'magine."

"What about Lizbeth?" He felt another pang.

"Too many soldiers here for them heathens to get her. There's more men in this outfit, I imagine, than there is Comanches in all of Texas. They might get a scout or two. Or me and you." He winked. Logan saw little humor in the comment. It seemed to him that he was simply drifting toward some destiny he had no choice in or control over.

The Tonkawa scouts came and went. Abraham had been gone for two days, and Logan despaired of ever seeing him again. Doggett seemed unconcerned. "Why that murderin' heathen sumbitch'll be all right," he said.

They rode on. On the fourth day of the march, a thunderhead formed to the west, and just before dark, lightning, hail and a torrential downpour halted their progress. Logan sat under Romack's wagon with Elizabeth, Bob and Romack. Mullins sat forlornly under the kill wagon. He had managed to stay drunk the first two days after Romack amputated his two arrow-damaged fingers. Romack had since hidden the remaining whisky and had kept Mullins in sight for the sake of both the dwindling whisky supply and Elizabeth. Now sober, the skinner obviously felt the extent of his loss.

"I wouldn't be a soldier for nothin'," Elizabeth said.

"You're right about that," Romack answered.

"I mean if I was a man."

"Huh?"

"He means he wouldn't be a soldier neither, Lizbeth," Logan said. He could just imagine how all of the hours of conversation between Elizabeth and the old cook went. He wondered how Elizabeth would manage after they reached Fort Sill. It had lately occurred to him that he had no idea what he would do. Bob seemed little inclined to continue hunting now that Ezra was dead. Perhaps Bob would employ him in the freight operation. Logan was beginning to think that spreading the true Gospel might have to wait until staying alive was no longer the major concern of the day. He could not go back to Kentucky; he had given his word to his father. But then the Shawnee and Iroquois had been subdued the better part of a hundred years before the his father came into his position as a healer and lay pastor. Still, a promise was a promise, he thought.

Elizabeth remained in his thoughts. According to Doggett, reports from the settlements left little doubt that her family had been slaughtered by the Kiowa raiders. Elizabeth's actions toward the dying Comanche led him to wonder if she had witnessed her family's murder and now was pushing the memory away. He could not imagine where she had stashed the memory — all the butchery he had seen was still quite fresh in his mind.

It seemed unlikely that Elizabeth would stay with him and Bob; an unmarried women simply did not live with two men. Nor could he imagine ever courting Elizabeth under the present or probable future circumstances. In any case, he was uncertain about wisdom of courting a girl who had gelded a savage. Then again, other than the Dodge City whores, Elizabeth was the only white female he had seen since he had left Independence. A sudden influx of attractive white women seemed unlikely.

"I ain't never seen rain like this," Elizabeth shouted above the roar.

Bob gave up on his pipe. "That's the way it is on these plains. Bad hot; bad cold; bad dry; bad wet. Ain't never just right."

"It was nice early this spring," Logan said, although the vernal pleasantness now seemed distant. "How much further we got?"

"Day or two. You in a hurry?"

"Ready to get it done."

"I reckon you'll grow out of it."

"I hope I live to."

Bob laughed. Romack obviously saw no humor in the conversation. "Y'all wear me out," he said. "I wish they'd let us build a fire. I'd make us a little bannock and coffee."

"Ain't gonna be no fires for a while," Bob said grimly.

The rain subsided. The troops huddled about. Guards were posted. Logan and Bob took their assigned positions on the perimeter of the encampment.

They pushed on at dawn then stopped around noon. Logan slept soundly in the shade of the wagon while Elizabeth repaired her boots and discussed her family with the nodding Romack. Mid-afternoon, Abraham returned from the east. The resulting clamor woke Logan. He lay under the wagon watching Maddox and his officers conferring with Doggett, Bob, Nuchols and Abraham. The heat was stifling; the air humid. Another thunderhead was forming.

Bob walked briskly back to the wagons. "We damn near on top of 'em." His eyes were wide. "We movin' near midnight. Best get some more sleep."

Logan snorted. "Get some sleep, huh?"

Bob shrugged. "Might as well. Whatever's gonna happen's gonna happen. Bein' wore out won't make it no better."

"Somebody's got to tell me what to do."

"You won't have to worry about that. Doggett'll be by after while. I best go see what else is goin' on."

"Don't you need no sleep?"

"I'll catch up after the fightin'." He laughed. "Old men don't need a whole bunch of sleep." He walked away toward Maddox and the officers. Logan propped himself up on his elbow and watched the preparations. Several sergeants, including Nuchols, stalked about barking orders at their charges.

At dusk, they supped again on hardtack and water. Elizabeth chewed in silence while Logan struggled in vain to think of something to say.

Bob returned. "Miss Lizbeth, you and Earl and Louis be stayin' with some soldiers. You be safer that way." Romack nodded. Elizabeth did not acknowledge Bob's announcement.

"Hallelujah!" Mullins shouted. "You boys'll do just fine without me."

"They surely will," Romack said. "I expect we would too." Mullins ignored the comment; he put his good hand behind his head and lay back, smiling.

Logan finished eating and walked a short distance from camp and sat on the wet grass. He tried to pray but his prayer deteriorated into simple pleading. The night was pitch black. He could hear the camp bustle behind him, the horses and murmur and movement of the troopers. He sensed a presence nearby. He stiffened and held his breath, listening.

"A God fearin' man." Nuchols said in the darkness. "I knowed you was."

"Yep. You?"

"Powerful fearin'. But come dawn we both have to forget all about it."

"What're you sayin'?"

"Mister Logan, at dawn, you gonna be up in them hills with Nigger Bob and Mister Burl lookin' out over them heathens' camp. When us soldiers go ridin' in there, you best shoot anything that ain't wearin' blue. If it moves and it ain't no soldier, it needs killin'."

"I ain't shootin' no women."

"Mister Logan, them heathen women up on the Little Red 'bout had all the hide peeled off my nephew, Quincy. There was flies all over him and he was beggin' me to shoot him in the head. We hauled him around for two days in the back of a wagon, him moanin' and squallin' 'til the Lord finally called him on home." He paused. "If it ain't black or white or a horse, it needs killin'. You ain't gonna have time to tell whether it's a man or a woman or youngun no way."

"I don't know what to tell you."

"You be doin' the right thing when the time comes, I reckon. We can't be leavin' nothin' standin'. I best get on back."

Logan felt rather than heard Sergeant Moses Nuchols' departure.

* * *

Lightning lit the western horizon and the low rumble of thunder followed; but the air was deathly still as the buffalo hunters, the Tonkawa scouts and Captain Shaw, Commander of Scouts, rode ahead of the main column. Logan shuddered at the thought of crawling around in the brakes above the Pease. He had no particular fear of rattlesnakes — only a healthy respect. But then he did not typically crawl around in rough terrain in the dark during warm weather. His cousin Nathaniel Lewis had lost a hand reaching blindly into a woodpile. Logan had seen the horrible swelling and finally the split flesh and oozing fluids before his father convinced the young man that the hand had to come off if he wanted to live.

Logan rode in the rear. He wanted the trip to take forever, yet he knew that sunup was less than three hours away. In the darkness he could not see Abraham or Captain Shaw or Doggett — he wondered how far ahead they were. Bob rode just ahead; Logan suspected the old plainsman did not want to leave him alone with the Tonkawas and he was grateful. He did not fear the Tonkawa scouts, and he had grown to like Abraham, but the others simply did not acknowledge him.

The riders slowed against steep terrain. At times Logan could not see where he was riding; he simply followed Bob and trusted Rufus and felt the odd falling sensation in his testicles. Another flash of lightening, and he saw the rough brakes and his companions strung out before him.

Bob stopped suddenly and dismounted. Logan did the same. They led their horses down a sandy wash then veered to the west and back into the hills. He and Bob tethered their horses to a big hackberry tree. Then, crouching, Logan followed Bob to a clump of mesquite. Bob cupped his hands to Logan's ears. "Move over a ways and take cover where you got a rest to shoot from. Make sure you're pointed north towards the river bottom," he whispered.

Logan crawled westward, cringing each time he put a hand down. A dog howled in the river bottom. he stiffened. Had the dogs smelled them? Surely the Tonkawas had considered the wind. The dog howled again. Logan would have thought it was a coyote howling had he not heard the half-wild yowling that day in the Kiowa encampment. After a few minutes of silence he crawled on until he came to a level, grassy bench. He lay on his stomach and positioned his rifle for firing and looked out over the black river bottom.

The faint scent of wood smoke came to his nostrils — the Tonkawas obviously had considered the wind, however slight. Lightning lit the river valley and a hundred and fifty yards out, buffalo hide lodges strung a quarter mile along the river shone pale white as if luminescent. His stomach rolled. His eyes readjusted to the darkness, and he made out the faint glow of small fires burning within the lodges. He tried to picture the sleeping inhabitants. He caught himself imagining only warriors asleep in the lodges. He felt he was looking at some large, unsuspecting wild thing.

At first light one company of cavalry would attack from the southern brakes; another from upriver; yet another from downriver, hopefully in time to keep the savages from escaping into the northern hills. So said Captain Shaw in his briefing. The sharpshooters were to kill as many hostiles as possible, especially those on the perimeter of the skirmish.

Logan accumulated detail with each lightning flash. He hoped the rain would hold off until after the attack. Gnats swarmed about his face. He wished for a breeze.

Despite Bob's proximity, he felt alone as he always felt alone in his fear. Alone within 150 yards of a Comanche camp. He wanted to make water, but dared not move. He imagined the trundling cavalry working its way toward the river and wondered if experienced fighters felt the same sickening fear that always seemed to overtake him. He had fought at close quarters with a Comanche warrior and had survived, yet the experience brought him little comfort. The Comanche attack in the canyons had nearly paralyzed him — perhaps because he had not seen the attackers. Silent, violent death frightened him the most, and the Comanches were masters of that kind of warfare. Even on the open plains they seemed to materialize on bare ground.

A faint glow formed on the eastern hills. His pulse quickened. He thought briefly of making water right where he lay, but decided instead that he would stay constantly prepared for battle. He hoped the troopers would wait for shooting light before attacking. Although he could just make out some of the nearer lodges, finding a target would be hopeless in such poor light and he had every intention of restricting his shooting to adult male targets despite Nuchols's urging.

He could see the savages' horses now, hundreds of them grazing in the river bottom beyond the encampment, and human movement at last. He could see the upright forms, little more than shadows moving among the lodges. More dogs barked. All about him, birds were beginning their morning chorus. He suddenly felt very exposed despite the dense grass cover. What if one of the Indians saw his rifle barrel?

His view of the camp inhabitants improved. There were women, their hair chopped shoulder length, and naked children, and a few long-braided figures who appeared to be warriors. He began to understand Nuchols's comment about the difficulty in resolving targets.

He watched in fascination as his pulse roared in his ears. His stomach fluttered. He watched cook fires come to life. He heard first the shrill chatter of the children then the liquid voices of the women. The women were all about camp now, squatting by fires, chattering, yelling at the children. Logan spied a broad-backed man, naked save for breechclout and moccasins; his braids hung nearly to his waist. The man stood briefly outside his lodge, looking eastward. He stretched then walked to a nearby cook fire as if to see what the women were preparing.

The first two shots came from downriver. The sound rolled and faded, and the birds went silent. The Comanches froze, looking eastward. Then came a volley and shouts and more shooting. The women ran screaming for their confused children, and warriors emerged from their lodges. Bob's rifle boomed and the three companies converged upon the encampment. Logan searched the melee for a target. He could no longer distinguish men from women.

The sudden appearance of the troopers shocked him. He had expected to see and hear them coming from a distance. He picked a running target and fired but lost the result in the churn of dust and humanity. The shooting became a continuous roar. A line of troopers swung northward to cut off all escape. The dead and dying lay about in the dust and blood-stained grass. He picked another target, this one with a bow, kneeling to shoot. He fired and the figure pitched forward and he saw the short hair of a Comanche woman. He heard the cries of the troopers; he picked targets as fast he could and fired. He did not look to see the results. He loaded and fired; loaded and fired. His fingers worked smoothly; the gun came up easily; the front sight settled quickly. He felt curiously detached, although Nuchols's words never left his ears.

The lodges were falling now; screams of panic were replaced by howls of lamentation. Smoke billowed from burning lodges, brush arbors and food caches. From north of the encampment came the sound of careful shooting as the troopers finished those fleeing toward the northern hills.

Logan searched for another target, but saw only the troopers running from lodge to lodge or pursuing Comanches in the distance. He waited. Neither Bob nor Doggett fired their rifles. Two dozen soldiers and several Tonkawas circled to contain the Comanche horse herd. Sporadic gunfire persisted in the distance but ceased around what remained of camp. Bob called out to Logan. "We best go on down."

They rode through the killing field among dead men, women and older children lying in the grass. Bodies moved and Doggett finished them with his pistol. "Can't abide even a heathen sufferin'," he said. "Might as well hurry 'em on to hell."

Logan numbly took in his surroundings. Now the soldiers were busy killing the camp dogs. Bob caught Logan's expression. "They'll dig up every grave if we don't shoot 'em," he said.

The few surviving Comanche women were wailing at the tops of their lungs; troopers were awkwardly trying to comfort crying infants still strapped to papoose boards. Captives were being gathered at the east end of camp. Logan led Rufus around a dead, scalped trooper who had an arrow through his neck. Ten feet away lay a dead Comanche no older than fifteen still clutching the dead trooper's scalp.

Bob cleared his throat. "Kinda hard on a God-fearin' man, I know."

"Lord."

"Ain't no other way I know of. Ain't a one of 'em wouldn't feed your balls to you and laugh while they was doin' it. Can't forget that."

"I reckon."

"Ain't gettin' sick on me are you?"

"Nope. Just kinda shaky."

"I heard you shootin'."

"I don't know what I done."

"Done some good, I imagine."

Stone-age weapons, shields, copper pots and all manner of guns from muskets to lever-action repeaters were strewn with the dead. Smoke burned Logan's eyes and nostrils; it carried a horrid stench. "Good lord," Doggett said. "They've managed to set fire to somebody."

Captain Shaw rode out of the smoke. "Well done gentlemen. We suffered few casualties."

Doggett nodded. "Thank you, Cap'm. Where to now?"

"We'll have to wait for the Colonel's order. Back to Fort Sill, I imagine."

Maddox couched with his officers near the center of camp; he nodded to Bob and Doggett then turned his attention to a large map spread on the ground.

"White woman here!" a trooper shouted. He was looking beneath a brush arbor he had been about to set ablaze.

Maddox stood. "Is she alive?"

"Yes, suh. But prob'ly not too happy 'bout it."

"Dear lord." He looked at one of the four white officers. "Captain, see to the matter."

"Yes sir." The captain wheeled smartly and strode toward the brush arbor. Troopers were already digging a mass grave. Bodies were being gathered for burial. A light drizzle began. Several Mexican captives and Comanche women and children that had been spared because they had not resisted, stood dazed, looking at the white officers. Some of the slaves had resisted, however. A gaunt middle-aged Mexican man lay dead near a new elm saddle frame.

A black corporal jogged up to Logan and Doggett. "Mr. Fletcher, Cap'm Reynolds is askin' to see you."

"Me?"

"Yes suh, if you don't mind suh. Just follow me please suh."

Logan looked at Doggett who shrugged. The two rode behind the black man who led them through the burning encampment to the crude arbor where the white woman lay. The young captain had a red mustache and sun-burned nose and was standing over the naked white woman. He averted his eyes. "For God's sake, boys, get something and cover this poor woman up," he barked, obviously shaken. Two black troopers ran to look for a blanket. "Mr. Fletcher, Sergeant Nuchols here seems to think you might be able to do something for this woman."

Logan nodded and dismounted. He went to the woman, taking care not to stare at her. Yet he could not help but notice the fragment of dirty cartilage where the woman's nose had been. She was tall with matted red hair and covered with welts and bruises. "Sweet Jesus," Logan whispered.

"It's beyond me what you're gonna do," Captain Reynolds said.

"I'm not sure I oughta do anything. Pray for the Lord to take her maybe."

"Nobody would fault you for it," Nuchols said gently.

The troopers returned with two horse blankets. They covered the woman and stepped back and stood awkwardly. Logan knelt and put his hand on the woman's forehead. He bowed and struggled to think of words. The Captain and Doggett and the troopers took off their hats and watched in silence. Logan prayed silently for an end to the woman's suffering, yet he felt nothing but fatigue. He felt he could simply lie in the dust and sleep. He prayed on. The woman stared, occasionally licking her lips or tucking her dusty hair behind her ears.

A shrill cry jolted Logan from his mechanical praying. Two troopers dragged a young Comanche woman and a third carried a hysterical toddler. Reynolds sighed. "What the hell is it now?"

"Suh, she's hit and bleedin'. We found her layin' out in the grass. She's got a youngun'."

"Why the hell didn't you finish her?" Doggett snapped. "Now who's gonna take care of it?"

The three troopers looked at their feet. Captain Reynolds looked coldly at Doggett. "Doggett, my men are soldiers, not executioners. It's one thing to kill in battle and another thing altogether to kill after their blood has cooled. Perhaps you'd like to finish the job."

"Goddamnit, I'm just a scout. I can't just up and shoot a woman."

The woman was suffering from a sucking chest wound. The trooper had let the little boy go to her and she clung to him and tried to turn her body to shield him from her captors. The child wailed. His mother's frothy blood now covered his face. The white woman furrowed her brow as if trying to locate the source of the cries.

"I'm afraid this poor white lady ain't gonna die," Nuchols said. "At least her body ain't gonna die. Her soul's long dead, I 'magine."

Captain Reynolds sighed and shook his head. The smell of the burning lodges lay thick in the air, and in the distance the thunder resumed and mingled with the roar of the wind-driven flames. The Comanche woman sobbed and gurgled for breath. She was tiny, less than five feet tall and bow-legged, and her cream-colored buckskin dress looked immaculate save for the growing pink blotch on her breast. Tears streamed down her face. She gently rocked and held her son.

Logan took his hand from the white woman's face, stepped across the arbor and reached for the forehead of the Comanche woman. Her black eyes rolled in terror, and she sobbed and tried to turn away. Logan was struck by the coarseness of her shoulder length hair. Like a horse's mane, he thought.

He kept his hand on the side of her head. He struggled to focus and felt the sobbing woman's trembling and then her death shudder. He lifted his hand and sat back in the dust. His eyes scraped in their dry sockets. He looked northward at the sere hills and tried in vain to simply pick a thought and stay with it for more than a second.

"I don't b'lieve He's here with us, Mister Logan," Nuchols said softly. "Not in this place. You done all you could."

The youngest trooper, a tall, lanky teen, sobbed. Tears and sweat cut furrows through the dust on his clenched jaws. He swallowed hard and wiped his running nose with a gloved hand.

Nuchols looked at the young trooper. He sighed. His eyes appeared unfocused. "I swear Douglas, get aholt of yoself. I'm sorry suh, he's still a youngun. He needs some mo' work."

Captain Reynolds looked over the carnage then at the two women. "Who can blame him sergeant? Son, step away and gather yourself," he said gently. "When you can comport yourself like a soldier again, you'll need to help with the dead."

"Yes, suh." The young man turned and walked twenty yards away and stood with his hands on his hips, looking away from the burning camp.

"Fletcher, we drew you into an impossible situation," Captain Reynolds said to Logan. I'm sorry; we didn't know what else to do."

"It's okay. Nobody would've knowed what to do." He walked to his horse and climbed into the saddle. The two troopers were struggling to pull the squirming, screaming child from his dead mother's arms.

"I swear, the po thing gotta a bear hug on this youngun," one trooper said.

Logan and Doggett rode back toward the center of camp. "Where's Bob?" Logan asked.

"Right in the middle of it, I expect. Well I want you to look."

Just north of camp, the Tonkawa scouts stood about a fire built from the Comanches' lodge poles. With a hand ax, one of the scouts hacked away at a naked corpse, then pulled an arm free and tossed it into the fire. Other stripped corpses lay about in the bloody grass. Abraham skewered a hunk of charred flesh — what appeared to be a foot-long strip of muscle — and held it up to cool. Two other scouts squatted, chewing.

"Havin' 'em a little breakfast, I reckon," Doggett said.

"My Lord."

"He ain't here son. Old Nuchols knowed what he was talkin' about."

C H A P T E R 3 6

Cuts Something was glad for the heavy rain, though it impeded his band's progress. He knew very well the aridity that lay before them on the Llano. They rode northwest through the brakes country, eleven warriors and their women and children. They stopped at every pool and seep to fill their water bags. They moved into the scarp canyons and visited the sweet water springs near the canyon heads where the water had not yet trickled through the layers of gypsum. They drank all they could hold to saturate themselves against the coming drought. In the driving rain the men and women rode with their faces upturned and mouths open to catch the drops. To conserve the contents of the water bags, the women squeezed water from rain-soaked strips of bartered cloth and buckskin into the mouths of their little ones.

The band proceeded with scouts fore and aft. The bedraggled dogs trotted alongside, tails adroop and tongues aloll even in the downpour, and Cuts Something regarded them grimly. He did not relish the thought of his dogs going without water on the Llano, yet every drop had to be saved for his band. At times he and That's It called their dogs and urged them to drink from puddles, but the soaking wet curs only rolled onto their backs and wagged their tails between their legs.

The tough, frowzy little mustangs seemed to sense the coming misery and drank at every opportunity. Cuts Something worried little for the plains-bred horses. They would survive long after the People had perished from thirst.

Although Cuts Something had lived his entire life on the South Plains, his few forays onto the Llano had been hunting and raiding trips just west of the escarpment. The Wanderers were people of the rough brakes and the eroded rolling plains. The flat, seemingly endless High Plains had always seemed foreign and mysterious to him, as did the Antelope, whose insolence in the face of the *tahbay-boh* incursion he greatly admired. Quanah would be delighted to see them and would welcome them into the band, for the young war chief had been a Wanderer before the skunks Ross and Goodnight killed most of the Wanderers on the Pease and stole Quanah's mother and sister. Afterward, the bereaved boy rode onto the Llano in search of a new life with the Antelope.

The easiest course to the Llano lay along the Canadian where water would have been constantly available, but the soldiers would surely look there first. They were coming, he knew. If they chose to follow, he would lead them into the waterless tracts where they would perish. Yet he knew the Llano only slightly better than the soldiers. There was a spring two sleeps east of the Canadian Gorge. The People had used it during their peregrinations since they first moved from the mountains, and it was said that the Old Ones had used it since the Beginning. He had never seen it himself, but like all Comanche warriors, he knew of it and its general location. If they could find it, they would reach the Antelope. But unless the playas held water, they might be near death when they reached the spring. If they did not find it — at least they would not die on the miserable reservation.

He hated leaving his home in the Pease River brakes. Yet he realized that the past autumn and spring were only a brief respite from the harassment and humiliation. Since returning from the Canadian he had felt penned, so much so that at night he found breathing difficult, as if someone were standing on his chest. His people who remained on the Pease would be dead shortly. He forced himself to think of the task at hand. He would deliver his band or kill them with the quest. He thought of his infant son. Should his entire band perish on this journey, had he lived his life in vain?

He looked ahead. The riding was easy now. Except for the dearth of water there was little danger immediately ahead. But to the rear, the soldiers and their Tonkawa minions were coming. And Black Durham. In all of his planning, he had not thought of his nemesis for several days. What if Durham was still coming? The soldiers he could lose on the Llano. But Durham and that cursed boy . . .

He decided that he should ride to the rear for a while.

CHAPTER 37

The thunderhead threatened, but rain did not come. Logan sat in the meager shade of a juniper that blocked the breeze as much as it blocked the sporadically appearing sun. The Tonkawas lay asleep in the grass, satiated after their morning meal.

Logan waved his hand absentmindedly at the swarming gnats and wondered if Elizabeth was thinking about him. He wondered, too, if his participation in the expedition would raise her estimation of him. After a moment he decided that it probably would not. He felt certain that if he were just two or three years older she would regard him with the same disinterest with which she regarded the skinners; or at best, with the avuncular affection she seemed to hold for Romack, Bob and Ezra. Yet there had been that night on the plains above the Canadian. He did not believe for an instant that Elizabeth would have gone to Mullins.

The trip to Fort Sill and the decisions as to what arrangements to make for Elizabeth were forthcoming as were decisions about his own life. His pledge to his father now seemed distant. Yet his extended family and church members back in Kentucky knew of his promise and would regard his return as a breach of faith. He thought again of Bob's freight-hauling business; perhaps Elizabeth *could* stay with them if she chose to — if she had no extended family or friends she could live with. Back in the settlements, he could use his gift and work toward fulfillment of his obligation, and he could bathe weekly. Perhaps he could think more clearly when circumstances were less urgent and did not force him into such intimate proximity to Elizabeth.

The worry tired him. He found it far more pleasant to contemplate Elizabeth's muscular thighs. He dozed.

Doggett's sudden arrival startled him. Logan squinted against the reappearing sun. Doggett looked smugly down from his horse. "I wouldn't get too settled if I was you," Doggett said. He spat and wiped his chin with his sleeve. "Bob just rode in from them hills to the north. Cut Comanche sign up there. About twenty headin' for the Llano, looks like. Colonel aims for us to run 'em down. Me and you and Bob and Shaw and them Tonks, and I 'magine Nuchols and his boys."

"What makes him think we can catch 'em?"

"Bob says they're movin' slow. Got women and little ones with 'em. You know we never did turn up that bad sumbitch that got Ezree. I'd say the murderin' heathen's gettin' away right now."

Logan wondered if he could stand up, let alone endure another extended jolt atop Rufus. "When we leavin'?"

"Water wagon oughta be here by now. Best get a bite to eat and fill up your canteen. Colonel told Shaw to take care of the matter. I believe we all know what he's talkin' about. We gotta catch 'em before they get too far out on the Llano."

"Why's that?"

"Them bastards knows where the water is and we don't."

The Wanderers cleared the escarpment via a canyon trail that had been cut by the feet of human hunters long before the People arrived on the Plains astraddle Spanish mustangs. The High Plains lay before them now, quivering beneath heat waves. They stopped and took long drinks from their water bags. Cuts Something and That's It conferred.

"Five sleeps to the spring, I think," Cuts Something said.

"Five sleeps for you and me riding alone. Longer with these women and young ones."

"We do not have enough water in our bags."

"There is other water. The Antelope know where it is."

Cuts Something took another drink. He wanted to drink the bag dry. "Perhaps the playas hold water."

"Perhaps. I am worried about Sees How Far It Is. He has not spoken since we left the river."

Cuts Something also was concerned. His old friend usually talked nonstop. Perhaps the old man had had a vision and knew what lay ahead and did not wish to alarm the others. "I think he is not talking because his mouth is so dry," Cuts Something lied.

That's It smiled. "Tell your thoughts to the women, Cousin. Maybe they will believe you." He fingered his medicine bag. "I cannot go back to the reservation. We are too old for that. Cousin, do you think dying of thirst will be bad?"

"We will make it to the spring."

"Sees How Far It Is told me of a Ute who had his horse shot from beneath him. The old man said this Ute ran out of water and was found with no skin on his fingers. He had been digging for water in a dry creek bed. Before he died, he said that vultures had followed him for miles. They walked along behind him while he crawled and whenever he stopped to rest in the shade, they stopped and watched him from an arm's length away. He said they spoke to him and said, 'We will have you, Brother, before the sun goes down tomorrow.' The Ute threw stones at them and they flapped away and puked a stream across his ankle. He said he heard the vultures murmuring among themselves, arguing over who would get his eyes. When Sees How Far It Is rode up on the wash, the vultures flushed from where the Ute lay. He looked so miserable that Sees How Far It Is could not bring himself to lift his scalp. He offered him water but the Ute could not drink much. Sees How Far It Is stayed until the Ute died and then buried him where the vultures could not get him."

"I have heard that story many times. Oftener as our old friend ages."

"We cannot allow ourselves to get that thirsty."

"We will make it."

"Perhaps we will. But, cousin . . . "

Cuts Something looked solemnly at his friend. "Do not worry. We will not die digging in the sand." He took another drink from his buffalo paunch and wiped his mouth with the back of his hand. He sighed. "But the vultures might get me in the end."

The meal of jerked meat, hardtack and water rejuvenated Logan. He realized just how hungry and thirsty he was when he smelled the food and watched the water being poured into his tin cup. As he ate and drank, he felt as if his strength were some quantity being poured into him, filling his body from his feet to the top of his head.

They rode into the red northern hills, he and the Tonkawas, Captain Shaw, Bob, Doggett, Nuchols and a company of troopers. The Comanches obviously had departed in a hurry; they had made no attempt to cover their tracks. Their travois marks were evident even on the rocks. They rode hard; Bob and the Tonkawas, Logan and Doggett rode to the front. Again, Abraham pointed out to Logan all important sign. Just before dusk they struck the first Comanche camp, small fire rings and feces and the surrounding prairie churned by unshod horses. They made a cold camp, and Logan lay awake thinking with discomfort that he was lying where a savage had lain only a few nights before. He fell asleep in ardent prayer. Bob woke him well before daylight and after a cold breakfast he climbed groggily into the saddle.

They emerged from the hills onto a gently rolling plain cut here and there by dry creeks and washes and dotted with heaps of bleached bison bones. They followed the wide Comanche trail, stopping at times to examine some piece of chattel: a broken horse hair bracelet, a child's moccasin, fragments of rawhide rope. Logan thought he could follow the Comanches by their dog and horse shit alone.

They found the second camp by noon on the second day and pushed on for the canyon country's sweet water springs. Logan saw the red brakes in the distance and the smell of the staked-out, flayed Tonkawas returned to his nostrils, and the flush of the doves and the hiss of the arrow that killed the Tonkawa scout came to his ears.

They rode into the mouth of a large, dry creek. Abraham stopped and turned to Logan as if to see his reaction.

"Be damn," Doggett said.

The remains of a Holy Bible lay on the white mineral deposits between travois drag marks. The brown leather cover and gilded pages flapped in the wind. Logan dismounted and pick up the tattered remains while the rest of the party sat their horses and watched. Two thirds of the pages were missing. Inside the front cover, written in uncertain, left-leaning cursive was, "With Love to Eunice Perry, Elkhorn, Kentucky, December 24, 1861." Logan thumbed the remaining pages. He wished for Nuchols's company, but the troopers were an hour's ride to the rear. He slipped the defaced Bible into his saddlebag.

Bob looked away toward the caprock. "Tore them pages out to stuff a horse hide shield, I imagine."

They traveled an ancient canyon trial. Road runners dashed about in the brush to either side, and Bob pointed out where the Comanches had difficulty getting their travois through narrow or washed-out sections of the trail. At times, they could look eastward over the tortured red brakes until buttes and prominences faded into the horizon.

Vultures circled languorously hundreds of feet above the canyon floor, but from his position on the high trail Logan could see the dark red eyes set against the lighter red heads of the adults and the dark gray heads of the juveniles. Doves cooed from the rimrock, and kestrels hovered with their larger kin, the darkly hooded and barred falcons that took wing and climbed and stooped out of sight toward airborne prey. Swallows of various kinds and colors swept the air for insects.

Higher still, skinks and other kinds of small lizards, striped and spotted, scuttled among the rocks, keeping the riders mindful of rattlesnakes. Late afternoon, the upper canyon in shadow, they found a recent Comanche camp beneath an overhang. Dripping, white-tipped stalactites hung from the rock ceiling, and huge ferns clung to walls darkly stained by mineral-laden water. The horses drank from two spring-fed pools.

Nuchols and the other troopers caught up just before dark. Captain Shaw posted guards and again ordered a cold camp. Shaw kept to himself and studied his maps, occasionally making notations.

"Goddamn, I don't like this place," Doggett said. He sullenly chewed his jerky. The troopers were spread all about beneath the overhang.

"Best enjoy the water," Bob said. "I don't imagine we'll see no more for a while."

"I aim to," Doggett answered with a full mouth. "I aim to drink all I can hold then piss all night long."

"Prob'ly won't oversleep that way," Logan offered.

"Sleep hell," Doggett said. "There ain't a level place to lay down nowhere. I'm afraid I'd wake up at the bottom of this canyon."

"Pot of coffee would go good about now," Logan said. "I'd almost be glad to see Earl Romack."

Bob laughed. "We need Miss Lizbeth here to think us up a big meal. She can make me think hardtack is baked hen."

Logan could have done without Bob's comment. He had finally cleansed his mind of everything but his surroundings. After he found the remains of Eunice

Perry's Bible, something in him retreated and he simply rode and there was nothing but wind and rock and sky, the creak of leather and the low murmur of his companions and whatever wild things they encountered. For nearly a day, he had not considered what might lay ahead; to have done so would have meant living every second under a suffocating layer of dread. He did not know if months on the prairie had hardened him or if fatigue had dulled him.

But the mention of Elizabeth chafed him. The remembrance of her mouth as she blew some fleck of debris from his eye and the strong scent of her hair stirred him. Suddenly he was anything but apathetic and living through his current predicament became everything.

"We closin' on them heathens," Bob said. He took off one boot and shook it as if trying to rid it of a small pebble. "We'll be runnin' into their rear guard tomorrow, I expect." He stared into his boot.

"By god, Bob, I figured a prosperous business man would own a pair of socks," Doggett said.

Bob laughed. "I imagine he would. Me now, I never owned a pair in my life." He pulled his boot back on.

Logan wondered how Doggett could think about socks in light of Bob's comment about engaging the Comanche rear guard. He hoped he lived long enough to become so casual about deadly combat.

"No goddamn wonder I can smell that boot from here," Doggett said.

Bob took off his other boot. "I hope you'll be puttin' that nose to good use tomorrow."

"Don't need much nose to smell a Comanche if you're downwind of him. All that grease and smoke from burnin' buffalo shit. And sweat — their sweat don't smell like ours does."

Bob scratched his head beneath his hat. "I believe their food makes their sweat smell that way."

"I reckon. It might just be different though. A Comanche buck don't seem like no regular man to me. No more than a panther or a wolf."

"You ain't never talked to one, have you?"

Doggett raised his eyebrows. "Hell no, and I don't aim to neither."

"When they ain't lookin' to scalp nobody, they laugh and carry on like regular folks. Seems like they like company. They'll feed you 'til you're about to pop."

"Fattenin' you up for slaughter, I imagine."

Bob dug in his pouch for his pipe. "I believe they're just bein' kindly."

"Know their tongue, do you?"

"Barely. Most of the bucks can speak Meskin. I can get on all right with 'em."

"What do they sound like?" Logan asked. He was relieved that the subject had changed from fighting to talking. "I never heard a Comanche. That one I tried to run over never made a sound."

Bob studied his empty pipe. "It don't sound like regular talk. Sounds kind of like they're singin' when they talk in their own tongue. Even sounds a little bit like singin' when they talk Meskin."

"I heard 'em squall a few times," Doggett said dryly. He was hidden by the darkness now.

Bob laughed softly. "I've had 'em sit off out of rifle range and give me a cussin'. I don't hardly get a word of it, but I know what they mean."

Doggett spat loudly. "I've spent my whole manhood chasin' Comanches or runnin' from Comanches or worrin' about the goddamn heathens, but I can count on both hands the times I seen one alive off of the reservation." He paused and the others waited in silence. "But I lost count of the butchered farmers I buried."

"I believe it's about done with though," Bob said thoughtfully. "I hope we live to see it."

Nuchols's voice came from the darkness above them. "There'll be more buryin' yet, I'm afraid."

"There's a man that's done his share of it," Doggett said. "Nuchols, by god, come down here and tell us somethin'."

Nuchols could be heard easing down the slope. He laughed. "I can always tell somebody somethin'. It's about the only thing I'm any count at. Mister Logan, you ain't payin' no attention to these two are you?"

"Never."

"A bright young gentleman." He sat down next to Logan.

Doggett leaned back against a flat rock. "What you think Nucks?"

"I believe if we don't get it done right in the next two days, it ain't gonna get done no time soon."

"I *would* like to get that bad heathen," Bob said.

They sat in the darkness. Down canyon, a horned owl issued its low, resonant notes. "Bad night to be a cottontail," Nuchols said.

Cuts Something sat his horse and looked westward. Beneath the morning sun, the brakes country appeared as a thin, pale blue line on the horizon. At his back, the Llano stretched unchanging to the western horizon and to the northern and southern horizons. Most of the playas they had encountered had been dry, some with cracked bottoms, others with bottoms covered by clumps of rough, brittle weeds. The first playa appeared damp. They dug through the heavy cracked mud and found water and strained it through a saddle blanket, but found it too heavy with caliche to drink. They pushed on and Cuts Something and That's It and the younger warriors rode fore and aft and the woman and children continued trustingly. The water bags were only half full now, yet no one had asked Cuts Something about the distance to the next water source.

Early in the journey, he had hoped they would reach their destination unimpeded; but as the days passed he became ever more convinced that Black Durham and the boy and Maddox's soldiers were coming.

They *were* coming. The only question that remained was when and where they would catch up with the People and what their condition would be. The further out on the Llano the encounter, the greater the Texans' concern for water, and the less their resolve toward extended fighting.

Those who had stayed behind at the Pease were dead now, he thought. He tried to think of other matters. He had done his best to convince his entire band that they must leave the brakes country and move out onto the Llano where even the Rangers did not venture. One could only do so much. His medicine was his own. He could take no responsibility for the decisions of others. Those who followed him were another matter. They trusted him completely. The women jabbered contentedly; his wives looked at him expectantly each time he rode by. Only That's It and Sees How Far It Is understood the severity of their situation.

Perhaps, he thought, they should have ridden along the Canadian. In his moments of greatest doubt and fatigue, the advantage of this route seemed painfully obvious. But in his morning freshness and hopefulness, he knew very well that such a route would lead the enemy to one of the Antelopes' most important winter sanctuaries.

At best, he would kill Durham and the boy and many of the soldiers and the People would ride safely on to the spring and ultimately to the Gorge. At worst, they would fight, suffer losses, and the surviving People would die horribly of thirst to feed the vultures. He hoped that at least he would fight hard and die well. Better for a Comanche — even a Comanche woman — to be cut down in battle than to die digging hysterically in the sand. He took another long drink of water and sat watching the eastern horizon.

CHAPTER 38

At first light the Tonkawas rode out along a faint westward trail. By late afternoon they had not rejoined the soldiers and partisans. Bob, Logan and Doggett rode in after reconnoitering the plains to the south. Captain Shaw stood atop a butte, watching the western horizon for movement. He lowered his field glasses, closed his eyes tightly and massaged his temples.

The men sat about camp. "Run off, I reckon," Doggett said. He blew out a worn-out chew of tobacco then worked his finger around the inside of his mouth to loosen any remaining flecks. He spat again. "Heathen bastards. I oughta knowed better than to ever trust 'em."

Logan could not imagine Abraham running from a fight. "Maybe they're just late gettin' in."

"They're late all right," Bob said. "I imagine the flies is crawlin' all over 'em by now. Run into that bad heathen." He had his flint and steel out and had fashioned a knot of grass for tinder. "I'm fixin' to have me pipe if it hairlips the general. Lawd, a fire would go good about now."

Captain Shaw left the butte and walked back to camp. "I'm out of light. Perhaps the scouts will come in shortly."

Bob had his pipe lit now. "Afraid not, Cap'm. They done run into that Comanche rear guard. I imagine that bad one and one or two more peeled off and laid for 'em."

"We should've warned them."

"Them Tonks knowed very well what they was doin'. They just thought they was too sharp to get killed."

Captain Shaw rubbed his eyes again. "Two more days. That's all."

"We ain't got no choice, Cap'm; 'less we run across a water hole."

"What are the chances, Burl?"

Doggett bit off another chew and moved it to a cheek. "This is farther than I've ever been, Cap'm. But we're headin' west. If we ain't findin' water here, don't seem like there's much chance of findin' it before we get to the mountains. What do your maps say?"

Shaw laughed humorlessly. "Why according to my map, we're truly in the middle of nowhere. It shows not a single land feature west of the escarpment. I'd say we're farther out on the plains than the United States Army has ever been."

"I thought Carson came across from Taos or thereabouts," Doggett said.

"He kept to the Canadian." Shaw looked westward again. "And we don't have his howitzer."

Logan sat halfway up a small butte. There was only a sliver of moon, but he did not want to risk exposure by sitting at the top. He looked to the west and tried to remember his last hot meal and cup of coffee, but his mind was sluggish from fatigue. The day had been brutal. Following a broad trail, he and Doggett and Bob had ridden miles ahead of the troopers. By late morning, it was clear that the Comanches knew they were being pursued. The progressively fainter trails led them over hard caliche; side trails and maddening loop-backs slowed tracking to a crawl. They found no more chattel. Raw nerves exhausted them.

Early afternoon, Bob decided that he should stay with the trail while Doggett and Logan rode back to warn Captain Shaw that they were very close. But Doggett refused to leave Bob alone on the trail. After a heated argument, the three rode back together. Seeing Bob and Doggett so jumpy made Logan's pulse race in his ears. He did not look for sign on the ground — he could not force himself to take his eyes off the horizons.

But tonight he thought mostly of sleep and food. Occasional images of Elizabeth came to him, but he was too exhausted to become aroused. The wind overpowered any sound from camp which was only sixty yards away. They had bivouacked later than usual. Bison had razed miles of prairie so that there had been no forage for the horses and mules. Just before dark, they rode out of the beasts' wake and found a suitable campsite. Bob and Doggett both supposed that the bison herd had come through only a few days prior. Now there were none to be seen.

He could not recall how many days had passed since they had left their hunting camp on the Canadian River. Sixteen? He could not be sure. He nodded, then jerked awake and forced himself to focus on a clump of sage eighty yards distant. He squinted and blinked until the edges became distinct. He was surprised at how well the waning moon lighted the prairie. Looking back toward camp, he saw the troopers' dark forms and the horses picketed close by. Somewhere on the far side of camp, Bob was watching the prairie to the north. Other guards were posted as well.

He looked back to the west and found another clump of sage to focus on. He dozed again despite his best efforts at alertness. He forced his eyes open and sat bolt upright. Had the clump of sage suddenly elongated or had he dreamt it? Or were his exhausted eyes fooling him? He strained to remember what he had seen. He squinted into the darkness and listened but heard only his pulse and the wind.

He eased his fingers off the trigger guard and onto the rear trigger. He glimpsed movement at the base of the butte. He had been looking too far out on the prairie. An upright figure walked steadily toward camp. Logan raised his gun and steadied his elbows on his knees. He knew immediately that the figure was not a white man or a trooper out to relieve himself. No sane person who would do such a thing camped in the middle of Comancheria within sight of a fresh trail cut by unshod horses. The figure was lithe, feral, and very close now.

The rear sight nearly covered the dark chest. Logan set the rear trigger, thankful now for the noisy wind. He silently pleaded, *God help me . . . God help me . . .* then another thought came to him: should he yell a warning? No. The gunshot would warn the camp. He drew in a breath and let it out. The front bead steadied on the man's chest. Logan felt the front trigger in his finger joint.

The figure fell from sight. Logan searched frantically. Now it was up again, moving forward. Logan drew another bead. The figure fell again, then stood and staggered. There was a wisp of voice on the wind; something in Spanish. Logan ran down the hill, yelling for help. The man was down again, but Logan caught his scent on the stiff wind and found him kneeling.

Troopers were running toward him from camp. Bob yelled, "Where in thunder are you boy?"

"Right here. It's Abraham. There's somethin' bad wrong with him."

"Still got his hair?"

"I can't hardly see nothin'."

Abraham moaned, then muttered something in Tonkawan. He tried to stand, then fell backward.

"Somethin's wrong with his feet," Doggett said.

Captain Shaw moved to the front of the small throng. "Perhaps they're sore from walking."

"Them feet is sore all right," Bob said. "We best get him back to camp and look him over. Cap'm, we might oughta spell Logan."

"Very well. Sergeant Nuchols, post another guard."

"Yes suh. Douglas, get on up there and keep your eyes open." The young private scrambled up the side of the butte and disappeared into the darkness. Four troopers carried Abraham back to camp and laid him on the first pallet they came to.

"Well hell!" Doggett said. "That's my damn bedroll."

Captain Shaw whirled to face Doggett. "Burl! For god's sake, man!"

Doggett waved his hands. "Well. I reckon you're right."

They built a small dung fire and erected a blanket lean-to to hide the flames which grew and lighted Abraham's feet. "Lord have mercy," Doggett said. "Them sumbitches sliced off the bottoms of his feet."

Bob stood and sighed. "I knowed it. Ezree said they done the same thing down on Plum Creek."

Doggett's face was pale in the meager fire light. "I never should've said what I did. There's no tellin' how bad he's been hurtin'. Hell, he can *have* the bedroll."

Logan wondered again if a heathen could be healed. He had never known of severed body parts being restored through prayer. Bleeding stopped, yes, or fevers broken or cholera defeated. This man was a cannibal who would gleefully torture any enemy he could catch. Nevertheless he was suffering.

Logan felt the men's eyes. Nuchols spoke in Spanish to Abraham. The big scout blinked and stared upward.

"About the best I can do is ask the Lord to ease his sufferin'," Logan said. "I never heard of nobody prayin' missin' parts back on."

"We could all stand to hear a word or two, son," Captain Shaw said softly.

Logan placed his hands upon the raptor tattoo on Abraham's chest. "Therefore being justified by faith, we have peace with God through our Lord Jesus

Christ. By whom also we have access by faith into this grace wherein we stand, and rejoice in hope of the glory of God. And not only *so*, but we glory in tribulations also; knowing that tribulation worketh patience; and patience, experience; and experience . . . "

Shouts came from the perimeter of the encampment. The men looked up with pupils contracted by the firelight. Hoof beats came out of the darkness and in an instant a horseman was among them. Something hard and heavy smashed into the side of Logan's face and then a dense and clammy mass fell on him. He saw a flash of red light then darkness, and all sound faded—then returned as a roar, and he struggled to crawl from beneath the suffocating dead weight. Sickening pain shot through his jaw and temples. There were shouts and curses and then the moan of the wind. He felt hot tears on his cheeks then chill as the wind dried them.

More shouting. Bob kneeled beside him. "Can you hear me son?" Logan nodded. Bob helped him to his feet. "That bad Comanche — he hit you with a dead Tonk he was draggin'. Just rode clean through camp and we never scratched him."

Captain Shaw was shouting at the troopers to gather the horses and form a perimeter defense. Nuchols ran by, crouching, holding his rifle. He dropped to one knee and looked westward. "That Douglas! That Indian musta rode right underneath of him!"

"I don't 'magine the young man was able to tell us, Nucks," Bob said gently.

"Lawd, I never shoulda sent that youngun up there. But he was the one that was handy."

"It should've been me up there," Logan slurred. He could not bear to close his mouth, so great was the pain in his jaw. "I never done no good here in camp."

"Just hush now," Bob said. "You can't hardly talk." He lay on his stomach with his rifle steadied on a bundled bedroll.

"What happened to Mister Logan?" Nuchols asked.

"That bad heathen whapped him with that dead Tonk he was draggin'."

"Lawd."

Shrill whoops came from the darkness, first from the west and then from all directions. Shots rang out on the eastern perimeter of camp; then silence followed by Captain Shaw's terse command against wild shots at fleeting sound.

Logan shivered and fought the urge to vomit, certain that retching would be poor form while fending off savages. He checked his teeth for looseness; the pain made him dizzy.

Someone crawled up beside him. Logan turned his head and saw Abraham's ashen face. The Tonkawa looked grimly westward and muttered something in Spanish.

"Wha . . .?" was all Logan could utter.

"He wants to borrow your pistol," Nuchols said.

"My lord, give him your pistol then," Bob said. "Did anybody ever give the heathen a sip of water?"

At times they heard hoof beats and glimpsed dark movement. Mostly there was blackness and the moan of the wind. Twice, nervous troopers shot at imagined enemies and were roundly cursed by Captain Shaw and Sergeant Nuchols. Logan saw movement on the low butte and then the faint outline of horse and feral rider. He wondered if his imagination and pain were getting the best of him; then came the hoarse cries, and his shivers and cold sweat returned. Once he felt Abraham's huge hand on his back.

He moved in and out of consciousness, jerking violently at times. After a period of wakefulness, he would doze and all pain and the wind would subside and queer images would play in his mind: a toothless Elizabeth sitting in his father's chair; Bob speaking in some sonorous, indecipherable tongue; Mullins's head falling off and into a camp fire.

He opened his eyes to a gray lightness on the plains to the west. His sleeve was soaking wet with drool. Bob sat cross-legged to his left. Abraham lay with his face on his arms. Bob looked at him with bloodshot eyes.

"Mornin'."

"Morn . . . Oh lord."

"Side of your face is as black as mine and twice as big. You'll make it, I expect." He nodded toward Abraham. "I don't have no idea what we're gonna do about his feet."

"Just wrap 'em up." Doggett said hoarsely. He was sitting cross-legged with a blanket wrapped about his shoulders. Nuchols was walking about camp rousing his troopers. "We can't spare the water to clean him up."

"We'll prob'ly have to tie him up to work on him," Bob said.

Doggett kept his eyes on the dim prairie. "I s'pect."

Logan sat up. The pain had dulled, but the nausea returned. He looked toward the remains of the fire and saw the naked, hacked body of the youngest Tonkawa scout. "Dear God." He heaved, but there was nothing on his stomach.

Bob ignored him. "I imagine they're gone. Just tryin' to buy time for their women and younguns. And tryin' to collect a few scalps. They always want scalps."

Indeed the prairie appeared empty. Bob and Doggett retrieved Douglas's body. They buried him beneath the hard caliche after much effort. They found enough rocks to make a cairn headstone. Captain Shaw issued a short eulogy. Just as he finished, Nuchols spoke quietly to him. "Certainly Sergeant," Shaw said. He looked at Logan. "Fletcher, the men would appreciate a few words."

Logan stepped forward to the shallow grave and looked at the pitiful pile of rocks. His ears rang. Already, the sun had raised sweat on his upper lip. He searched for a piece of Scripture and settled on I Corinthians, Chapter 15. He recited the verses in slurred monotone. He still could not close his mouth. He finished and put on his hat. The others did the same.

The troopers prepared to mount and ride. Logan stood looking at the grave. Again he felt Nuchols's presence. "Maybe He won't never drown His children again," the old sergeant said, "but I declare I believe we pain Him so He just turns a deaf ear sometimes."

Cuts Something, That's It and the eight young warriors rode in a southwesterly arc then circled to the north to rendezvous with the rest of their band. Ambushing the Tonkawas had been easy. So intent were the Tonkawas on their tracking that they had not considered the possibility of three small parties of Comanches attacking from the rear and sides. The Tonkawas fought bitterly — especially the tall, old one — but the fight was finished in a few heartbeats.

Allowing the tall, bloody-footed Tonkawa to stagger into the soldiers' encampment had been a perfect diversion for Cuts Something's quick attack. He had ridden among the soldiers knowing that if he were knocked from his horse his comrades would be unable to recover his body. But the risk had paid off; he had counted several coups, but again Black Durham and the boy had evaded him.

He had been nearly within arrow range when the boy ran down the hill to the Tonkawa. Then the black soldier had taken his place. The young black man was strong; even with two arrows in his chest, he had grabbed his throat as Cuts Something bent to take his scalp. Afterward, his throat hurt so that he was unable to scream curses at the encircled soldiers.

But the soldiers had not panicked as he had hoped they would. They remained alert; further attack would have been suicide. He hoped their sleepless night would erode their fighting spirit. In any case, he had bought his band some time. He had left Sees How Far It Is to lead the women and children northwest well into the night. They were not to erect lodges, but were to sleep in the open, then push on at first light.

Cuts Something felt better now. He still worried about finding the little High Plains spring, but the whites probably did not know of its existence. In another day or so the soldiers — and hopefully Black Durham and the boy — would be forced to return to their fort for lack of water.

He had not been at all pleased to see Black Durham kneeling by the fire looking at the Tonkawa's feet. Or that boy. Why did the boy worry him so? That's It rode up beside him and pointed to his own parched lips and held up an empty water bag. Cuts Something grimly acknowledged his friend's concern. They rode on. The country gradually became more broken with washes and buttes. Cuts Something formed a plan.

CHAPTER 39

Abraham climbed onto Douglas's horse. His feet were wrapped in strips of blanket. He looked as if he might pass out, but he stayed in the saddle and rode southwest, alone.

Doggett watched him go. "Tough old man-eatin' sumbitch, ain't he? Maybe you done him some good."

Logan eyed Bob's dented coffee pot. No steam yet. "He's prob'ly just hard to kill." He turned his attention to Captain Shaw who appeared to be discussing the water situation with Sergeant Nuchols. Both men were nodding grimly at the water barrels.

Bob sat smoking his pipe. "I hate to say it, but we ought to quit and ride for home. Them heathens is headin' out on the Llano to who knows where. We won't catch 'em unless they want to get caught."

Shaw finished his conversation with Nuchols and joined the scouts. "Gentlemen, we have water for another day's pursuit. The savages have probably faded into the wastes by now, but they may still be close by. We'll do whatever we can to punish them."

Bob shook his head. "Cap'm, I don't b'lieve their band is anywhere around here. That little bunch that deviled us last night was just holdin' us up so the rest can get away."

"Be that as it may, we have to pursue as long as our water holds out."

"Cap'm . . . "

"Durham, you *will* pursue the hostiles. You scouts proceed carefully and restrict your range to five miles. We've lost too many men already."

Bob tapped the ashes from his pipe. "You're the man with the mules carryin' the water."

They rode west, quartering. By late morning, they had found little sign and nothing they could trail with confidence.

An hour later, in the middle of a dry creek, Bob pointed to a cairn — dried bison flops stacked a foot high. A second cairn led them up a tributary rising to the north. At the head of the drainage, a V made of six-foot yucca stalks pointed west toward a series of minor buttes.

Two miles further on, Logan spotted Abraham sitting his horse, waiting, a dark speck a quarter mile away.

Doggett laughed. "Crazy bastard." He pushed his horse to a trot.

Abraham greeted them with a nod and turned his horse westward. Logan studied the Tonkawa's eyes. Mirth. Very slight, but unmistakable.

Abraham led them into a prairie dog town that stretched out of sight before them. The rodents barked from atop their mounds, and prairie rattlers buzzed then slithered into burrows. Hawks hovered and soared, always keeping their distance so that the riders drew no closer.

Bob glanced over his shoulder. "I ain't seein' it yet."

Logan shrugged. They'd see it soon enough.

The dog town finally gave way to gray-green buffalo grass. Abraham paused on a gentle rise, and Logan looked to the southeast. On the horizon the column of troopers appeared as if spilling over the edge of the world. Logan luxuriated in the breeze and the relief from gnats and biting flies it brought. His face throbbed.

A mile further, they struck a dry wash rife with sign. Bob said, "They spread out back there on that hard ground. Here's where they came back together." He held up eight fingers. Abraham nodded.

Doggett shrugged. "I'd have said more than two or three but not quite a dozen."

Westward, the country became more broken by gullies and hillocks. Bob slid his rifle into its scabbard and drew his Colt Walker. "Fightin' be close in this rough old country."

Logan put away the Ballard, drew the Dragoon and rested the barrel across his saddle. He remembered the last time he fired the huge pistol and how badly he missed the young Comanche.

They spread out and rode slowly, keeping to higher ground to avoid attack from above. They stopped often to listen or to stare at some clump of brush or perceived irregularity. Logan felt alone only thirty yards from his companions.

Bob raised an open palm and motioned for the group to come together. "We're gettin' real close," he whispered. Sweat dripped from his chin whiskers. "Closer all the time. They're layin' for us."

Abraham's eyes shone. He patted his horse's neck.

"We're just supposed to find 'em," Doggett said. "We fight 'em in here and we're dead for sure."

Bob said, "Them heathens will be long gone by the time Nucks and his boys get here."

"Hell Bob, the devils know we're comin', and there's eight of 'em."

"And we know they know it. We best get amongst 'em or find another line of work. That one that got Ezree is old as I am. He won't do no different than he's ever done. They'll be carryin' bows."

Doggett spat. "Hell. They ain't payin' me enough for this."

"Talk to the Colonel. Anyways, this bunch ain't itchin' to fight. I'd say it's just them two old ones and six younguns. But they ain't runnin' neither. Else they'd have lost us by now. "

Logan considered his outfit. Two old scouts, a lame Tonkawa and himself. He failed to see their advantage. He thought of the silent death in the canyons and the arrow protruding from the head of the staring scout. This was lunacy. Surely Bob's lust for revenge was clouding his judgment. But there was no way out. Even though Bob had no formal command, riding away would be treason — a hanging offense. What good would his life be then? He could not abandon Bob and face Elizabeth, even if she never learned of his cowardice. He could never live with himself or turn his eyes up to his Lord. There was the matter of riding alone through these savage-infested brakes. He tried to spit, but could not. His face tingled.

"It don't take too many Comanches to make a mess of a man's hair," Doggett said.

Bob wiped his eyes with his sleeve. "Let's not get in no hurry. Just work 'em out in the open where we can keep 'em back with our rifles. They ain't about to take us to their women and little ones — I don't care what the Cap'm says."

They rode out of the badland, following the spoor across another table-flat plain. "I thought sure they'd jump us back there in them brakes," Bob said. "Maybe they're just tryin' to outlast us. They're about to do it. I'm out of water."

The trail looped eastward and grew clearer. Logan enjoyed the wind on his sweaty back. They slowed their horses to a walk. Abraham stopped and pointed at fragments of tracks on bare caliche between tufts of shortgrass. Bob studied the sign. "Plain as day even in this wind. We're damn near on top of 'em." He looked nervously about. "But there ain't no place to hide out here."

Abraham muttered something Tonkawan and cocked his Spencer carbine. His eyes were riveted on something in the distance. The wind shifted, and Doggett's horse nickered.

Bob thumbed the hammer of his Walker. "Sweet Jesus. I want you to look."

Logan glimpsed movement along the edge of a dry playa sixty yards ahead. A flick of a horse's ear just above the knee-high bluestem. Then a mustang's head and withers as it gathered its forelegs to stand. The rough buckskin saddle came into view; but no rider.

Bob aimed, and Logan searched for a target. He saw nothing but mustang and grass. Then movement in the shadow beneath the horse; a warrior kneeling, bow drawn. Logan raised the Dragoon. Then came *twang* and hiss and pistol blast. Mustangs sprang up from the playa and surrounding bluestem. Warriors rose with their horses, mounted and shot arrows in smooth, continuous motion.

Rufus bucked, and Logan fought to stay in the saddle. Bob turned his horse to aim at another Comanche. An arrow protruded from his thigh. Abraham and Doggett fired their rifles but their jumpy horses flung the shots wide.

Rufus spun and skittered sideways. A horse ran broadside across Logan's path. The saddle was empty, save for the brown leg that held the warrior on the lee side of his mount. The painted face and drawn bow appeared beneath the horse's neck. Logan heard the hiss and *thuck* as the arrow struck flesh. He braced himself for the cutting pain, but none came. Shots and curses rang out behind him. Rufus gurgled and stumbled. Logan kicked out of his stirrups.

The horse's forelegs buckled, and Logan flew over his head and hit the ground rolling. His wrist buckled beneath him. Pain shot up his right arm, but he held the pistol. He would have screamed but could draw no breath. He got to his knees and looked back at his companions.

Doggett's horse struggled weakly on her side. The scout jerked his rifle from the scabbard, dropped to one knee and aimed at two warriors veering eastward three hundred yards beyond the playa. The big Sharps spoke, but the riders disappeared amid the heat waves and grassy contours. The others had disappeared as well.

Logan caught his breath and checked the Dragoon. It seemed fine. He struggled to his feet.

Bob sat his horse and reloaded his Walker. "Burl, come pull it out." The arrow had pinned his thigh to the saddle fender. Doggett propped his rifle against the belly of his dead horse and drew his knife. Bob holstered the pistol and stared beyond the playa. Sweat dripped onto his saddle horn. Doggett sawed through the arrow shaft between the inside of Bob's leg and the saddle. The arrowhead had not cut into the horse's side.

He tossed the barbed head over his shoulder. "About ready?"

"No. But go ahead."

He started to pull the arrow then hesitated. "I swear, Bob, you've lost some color." He jerked the shaft out.

Bob screamed and let go a wild backhand. Doggett sidestepped the blow and grinned. "Anything for an old friend."

Bob grimaced as he dismounted. He sat and began dressing the wound with his bandanna. "She ain't bleedin' too bad. If she don't blow up on me, I'll make it." He nodded to the north, then to the south. "Might not make no difference."

A half mile away in each direction, Comanches rode in broad circles forming living wheels that seemed to breathe, expanding, contracting, coming together as if to grind their prey into bone meal.

Bob cinched the bandanna. "We're fixin' to make a stand. There ain't no out-ridin' these heathens." Doggett pulled him to his feet.

Abraham sat his horse and excitedly checked his weapons. Logan thought the Tonkawa looked much improved. The prairie seemed morbidly calm; silent save for the wind.

Logan knelt, transfixed. Bob squinted in one direction, then the other. "Best be callin' on the Old Marster, Logan. Ain't many seen this sight and then been in a shape to tell about it. Just have to hold 'em off 'til Nucks and them boys gets here. I hope they heard us shootin'."

The circling riders moved closer. Logan could see their brown faces now. Their hoarse screams rose and fell on the gusting wind. He and Doggett took cover behind Rufus's corpse to defend against the northern wheel. Bob and Abraham sat cross-legged facing south and laid their rifle barrels on stick rests.

Logan shouldered the Ballard, but his wrist hurt so that he could not snug the stock to his cheek nor squeeze off a shot. He could only try to steady the fore-end and jerk the trigger. He dreaded the recoil's effect on his bruised face and loosened teeth.

Doggett said, "They're carryin' bows, son. Just keep 'em back. We can't get caught empty at the same time; they'll move on us for sure then." Dried blood from his nose striped his lips.

The Comanches closed. Eighty yards away, a warrior swung to the lee side of his mount and arced three arrows in as many seconds.

Doggett fired, and Logan felt the shock wave in the roots of his teeth. "Son of a bitch! Stopped my gun! I can't hit nothin' when it's movin' like that!" As Doggett pounded the ground with his fist, there came a whish like the sound of a falcon stooping for prey. An arrow fell two feet short; two others went well over their heads. Bob's rifle boomed behind them and Abraham laughed triumphantly.

While Doggett reloaded, another warrior rode into the field of fire. Logan covered him and jerked the trigger. He flinched at the recoil and for an instant saw nothing. Doggett rolled leftward. "Move goddamnit!" Logan rolled the opposite direction and two arrows stabbed the ground where his feet had been. Abraham fired his Spencer then followed with a booming oath.

"I ain't seen nobody ride like that," Logan said, breathless.

Doggett snugged his cheek to his stock. "Damn right you ain't."

The wheels continued to turn. Another warrior, closer by ten yards, crossed their firing lane. Doggett shot and missed again. The rider pulled away and revealed a second horseman. Logan shoved another cartridge into the breech. The second rider came directly at them. Doggett's screams were drowned by the report of Bob's rifle. Logan covered the Comanche's chest with the front sight and slapped the trigger. The horse went down, but the warrior lit on his feet and nocked an arrow. Logan ducked and grappled for another cartridge. An arrow cut just beneath the skin of the dead horse's flank. The iron head protruded inches to the left of Logan's face.

Still, the Comanche came, now with his battle ax raised. Logan saw the age in his face; the cords in his neck; the black eyes fixed upon *him*. The bowed legs churned; rifles boomed and Doggett cursed. No time to reload. He grabbed his pistol with his left hand, steadied it on Rufus's flank and fired. The Comanche went down rolling. Logan snapped off two more shots. Spumes of dust appeared five feet to the right of his target. The warrior crabbed into a slight swale and disappeared.

"Well I swear," Doggett muttered. "Damn!" Another Comanche horseman crested a low hump, and the old warrior leapt out of the swale, grabbed the rider's arm and swung himself smoothly onto the horse.

"Love of god!" Doggett yelled. "Four or five more of them bastards and we'd be cooked sure enough."

The circling riders scattered and disappeared.

The afternoon sun cast harsh light on the grass. Logan's eyes hurt from constant squinting. No one spoke. The wind had laid, and white smoke and powder stench hung thick about their heads. The prairie lay quiet except for the sound of ragged breathing and the buzzing of horseflies.

"Look at that," Doggett said. His voice carried no emotion. Just beyond rifle range, seven Comanche riders and a horse bearing a dead man moved single file along a slight rise. The warriors stopped and screamed hate-laced invective then turned and rode northwest, and Logan felt their cold defiance.

Abraham struggled to his blanketed feet, returned the curses and finished with an artistic flourish involving his knife and crotch.

A mile eastward, dust rose behind the approaching troopers.

CHAPTER 40

After two days without water, Cuts Something and That's It stalked and killed two nursing antelope and their fawns. The smaller children drank the curdled milk from the fawns' stomachs; the women drank from the does' severed teats while the men looked away. The band pushed on for the spring and ultimately the Canadian River Gorge. They encountered no bison, but they knew the gorge would be rife with the beasts.

Cuts Something thought often of the skirmish with Black Durham and the boy. He and his warriors had lain downwind, waiting, their horses lying with them. They had clamped their hands on their horses' muzzles to keep them from nickering at the approaching horses.

Black Durham was cunning, but he could be fooled. Another few steps, and Cuts Something would have put an arrow into his head, but the wind shifted and the white man's horse smelled the Comanche mustangs. That boy's medicine had caused many problems. He could have made good use of their water. The boy had confounded him again, ducking behind the dead horse, and he nearly killed Cuts Something with the pistol.

The People were edgy from lack of water. That's It, in a fit of rage, shot three vultures that were picking at the antelope remains. The normally sanguine warrior had lost all tolerance for vultures — the common sight of the soaring birds infuriated him.

Worse yet, the women and the younger warriors were beginning to cast nervous glances at Cuts Something whenever he rode by. By firelight, he would catch them searching his face for signs of uncertainty, which he felt constantly but tried to hide.

He knew the spring lay two days southeast of the gorge and a half-day immediately east of three large alkaline lakes. The warriors spread out and reconnoitered westward but found the plains pocked with hundreds of dry, white-crusted playas. Game trails meandered and played out among a seemingly infinite number of dry creeks and drainages. They saw no tracks of unshod horses. The now apparent folly of trying to find a mere seep on the trackless Llano gnawed at him and ground his resolve. Simply riding northward to the Canadian was no longer an option. They would die of thirst before they reached its salty pools.

Nursing mothers no longer produced milk for their babies. The dogs walked slowly, tongues dusty, tails adroop. Cuts Something knew they had to be very near the spring, and only that knowlege kept despair at bay.

In the heat of the afternoon, Sees How Far It Is fell from his horse. The old warrior lay on his side in the dust despite his friends' concerned prodding. At length he sat up and began his thick-tongued death song. Cuts Something and That's It begged to no avail until their begging gave way to tearless sobbing. But the old man, now voiceless, continued his raspy chant.

They rode on without looking back. Sees How Far It Is had outlived his wives and two daughters; some of the older women wailed until their voices failed them.

Mid-afternoon the next day they stopped to rest and hastily erected arbors against the brutal sun. Cuts Something's swollen tongue now made swallowing difficult, yet he quickly fell asleep amid the incessant crying of the infants. In his dreams the big buffalo soldier's hand squeezed his throat, and he could not break free. He slashed with his knife, but the man's long arm kept him away so that he cut only air. He fought for breath, but none came and the harsh light grew soft and there was the raven, wheeling over the canyons, and the bison. Then he was flying northwest above the plains, looking down on the playas, buttes and draws. His breath came easily again. From above he saw two long lines of the People facing east, one line behind the other. Each line stretched to the northern and southern horizon. In the center of the front line, a faceless shaman sat his horse and crossed two sticks, each tipped with an antelope hoof. These he passed to riders on his left and right who rode away, one northeast, the other southeast to begin a vast circle. At length, they passed one another beyond the eastern horizon then completed their circle by riding back to the two lines of People. The circle began anew; the lines followed the riders to form a vast human circle. The People sang antelope songs and closed the circle slowly. They closed the circle and crowded together; the human walls grew ever thicker until three bands of antelope were within sight inside the circle. The closure continued until the frightened animals, despairing of escape, stood watching their captors. The circle closed until the faceless shaman, still on his horse, pointed his hoof-tipped stick at the largest buck which fell stone dead.

He awoke to failing light and a loud buzzing. He wanted to swallow but could not bear the pain. Miles to the west, the low buttes were in shadow. He lay on his tanned bison skin and looked at the ground. Large black ants labored among tufts of blue grama. He moved his hand beneath his cheek and squirmed to find a comfortable position. He did not relish the thought of facing his band's doubtful glances. The buzzing annoyed him. He rubbed his temples. His eyes chafed in their dry sockets. What was that buzzing? Perhaps he was going mad, he thought. He started to push himself up then froze, still looking at the ground. Along the edge of his robe lay three thin slivers of chert. He picked up each one and placed them in his palm. He arose and walked northward out of camp. The buzzing grew louder. He struggled to keep his feet. Above him, the reddening clouds spun. At his feet lay many pieces of worked flint; discarded arrow heads, broken palm-sized ax heads and countless tiny flakes. He stopped. The horses grazed peacefully in the distance, picket ropes trailing.

He staggered back to camp and prodded That's It awake. His friend rolled to his back and squinted questioningly up at him. He rubbed his temples and touched his ears. "What is that sound?" he croaked. "I am going mad."

"No, cousin!" Cuts Something said, shaking now in silent laughter. "Not madness!" He pointed northward. "Frogs!"

Cuts Something luxuriated in the cool, dry night breeze. He thought he might need his robe before the night was through. Once the Wanderers had quenched their thirst at the spring, their appetites returned. He and the young men had spent the following day hunting antelope. His belly was full; his muscles deliciously tired. He enjoyed a pipe for the first time since he had left the canyon springs. He was nearly out of tobacco, but he did not worry. Soon the Mexican trader Ybarra would be visiting the People's canyon camps.

They would leave in a few days for the gorge. The garrulous Quanah would be delighted and surprised to see them. But for now they enjoyed a camp complete with lodges and good arbors. They had erected their lodges on teepee rings formed by People four generations removed. Cuts Something suspected that The Old Ones might have used this sweet spring. Tomorrow he would search among the flint relics for another huge point for his lance. The thought made him grieve for Sees How Far It Is. Arrow material would be plentiful at their new winter home; he would miss his old friend's advice and commentary.

A thunderstorm was building to the west. Everyone else had taken shelter. His wives slept in their lodges. He tossed another chip into his little fire. He would retire to his lodge if the storm moved much closer. Lightning lit the many buttes that rose from the plains to the west.

C H A P T E R   4 2

A week later, Logan rode alongside Romack's wagon, listening to Elizabeth's chatter. The old cook occasionally spat over the mules' backs, but said nothing. Bob ranged ahead with Doggett and Abraham. Logan felt left out; he had been issued a recalcitrant mule while the three older scouts rode excellent mounts. The Tenth Cavalry stretched a quarter mile fore and aft.

That morning they had ridden southeastward out of the Panhandle sand hills and now pushed on for Fort Sill. They rode out of a dry creek onto a table flat plain, and the stench of rotting flesh hit them full in the face. Hundreds of naked bison carcasses, swarming with turkey vultures, lay under the mid-afternoon sun. Here and there, wolves rushed the seething, brown hummocks, scattering the croaking buzzards. A wave of revulsion moved through the entire column.

Elizabeth wrinkled her red, peeling nose. "Lord that stinks!"

Logan nodded. "I know it."

She seemed to forget the smell. Her eyes widened. "That sure was bad about old Mullins. His hand just blowed up on us. And you gone. He was drunk the whole time, though. I don't know if it hurt him or not."

"Well."

They rode through the killing field.

Elizabeth said, "Boy my Mama and Daddy sure will be surprised about me, won't they?"

"I imagine so."

"They'll never believe what all has happened." She hummed "Rock of Ages."

A coyote chased a vulture onto a dead bull's hump thirty yards left of the wagon. The bird spread its wings and hissed at its antagonist.

Logan shook his head. "For Thy pleasure."

Elizabeth frowned. "Huh?"

"Nothin'."

"I heard you say somethin'."

He looked westward toward the High Plains, grateful for the hot, dry wind in his eyes. "Just talkin' to myself," he said. "Just talkin' to myself."

At dawn on June 27, 1874, some three hundred Comanche, Kiowa, and Southern Cheyenne warriors, led by Quahadi Comanche war chief Quanah Parker and the Comanche prophet Isatai, attacked the Adobe Walls trading post on the Canadian River in present Hutchinson County, Texas. Although the post held only twenty-seven men and one woman, the warriors' lances, carbines and courage were no match for .50-caliber Sharps rifles and the long-range marksmanship of the plains-hardened hide men. Quanah's horse was killed beneath him during the initial charge; he escaped only by crawling behind a rotting bison carcass. The raiders pulled back, dragging their dead and wounded.

After a sporadic five-day siege, the enraged warriors scattered and struck hunting camps all over the Panhandle. Commercial hide hunting came to a virtual halt.

The U.S. Army responded with a five-pronged campaign to trap the bands in their winter refuges in the caprock canyonlands where they could be annihilated or forced to surrender.

Eight companies of the Sixth Cavalry and four companies of the Fifth Infantry under Colonel Nelson A. Miles pressed southwestward out of Fort Dodge. Another column under Major William R. Price moved east from Fort

Bascom, New Mexico. The relentless Colonel Ranald S. Mackenzie, with eight companies of the Fourth Cavalry and five companies of the Tenth and Eleventh Infantry, rode out of his supply camp on the upper Brazos River west of Fort Griffin. The buffalo soldiers — the black Ninth and Tenth Cavalry — pushed northwest out of Fort Griffin and Fort Sill respectively.

From the beginning, the campaign, later known as the Red River War, was characterized by brief, deadly skirmishes. Quanah shadowed Mackenzie's column as it moved along the edge of the caprock. Mounted warriors materialized and vanished in the moonlight. Pickets and scouts worked under constant threat of silent arrows.

But the Army's dogged pursuit paid off. By early autumn, the harried bands had few refuges and little time for hunting. On September 27, Mackenzie's scouts peered over the rim of a giant crevice in the High Plains that would come to be known as Palo Duro Canyon. Comanche, Kiowa and Cheyenne lodges lined the canyon floor for miles; hundreds of horses grazed the curing grass. The Fourth Cavalry struck at dawn, stampeding the Indians' remuda. The surprised warriors put up ferocious resistance while their women and children escaped up the canyon walls and onto the plains.

Mackenzie's force killed only three warriors, but he now had over fourteen hundred horses, scores of lodges and the Indians' winter food cache. Rather than pursue, the ever pragmatic Mackenzie allowed his Tonkawa scouts to select a few of the captured horses, then ordered his men to shoot the remainder of the remuda. The Southern Plains' finest horsemen now faced winter afoot, without food and shelter.

The Buffalo Soldiers of the Ninth and Tenth Cavalry harried the scattered bands throughout fall and winter, skirmishing, burning lodges and food caches. The constant hunger and threat of attack weakened the bands' cohesion. Emaciated, broken Cheyenne and Kiowa warriors and their families drifted back to the reservations.

But the defiant Quahadi Comanches held out, hunting on foot, eating rodents and grubs. Finally, in June 1875, Quanah gathered his starving, demoralized people and surrendered at Fort Sill. The barrier that had blocked Spanish, Mexican and Anglo settlement of the Texas plains for nearly two centuries had been broken.

With the Comanche threat removed, the hide men renewed their assault on the southern bison herd. For the next four years, hunters' wagons carried millions of bison hides to Rath City, Fort Griffin and Fort Worth.

In autumn 1878, Indian agent P. B. Hunt arranged for the tribe to leave the reservation under military escort for a short buffalo hunt. The elated warriors made medicine and recounted their exploits to their young. Comanche scouts searched the bone fields in vain for days, but the old warriors grimly pressed on, and sympathetic Army officers let them be.

The snow came, and the men killed their ponies for meat. Hunt's emissaries found them starving in their lodges and pleaded with them to return to the reservation. Faced with certain death on the plains, the People broke their final hunting camp.